Starry
Eyes

Also by Jenn Bennett

Alex, Approximately
Starry Eyes

Coming Soon

Serious Moonlight

Praise for _Alex, Approximately_

★"A must for romance readers."

—_Booklist_, STARRED REVIEW

★"An irresistible tribute to classic screwball-comedy romances that captures the 'delicious whirling, twirling, buzzing' of falling in love."

—_Kirkus Reviews_, STARRED REVIEW

"A sexier, modern version of _You've Got Mail_ and _The Shop Around the Corner_, this will hit rom-com fans right in the sweet spot."

—_BCCB_

"A strong addition to romance collections."

—_School Library Journal_

"Sympathetic characters and plenty of drama."

—_Publishers Weekly_

Praise for _Starry Eyes_

★"A sweet and surprisingly substantial friends-to-more romance."

—_Kirkus Reviews_, STARRED REVIEW

"Vivid plots and endearing characters make this novel impossible to put down."

—_School Library Journal_

"A layered adventure–love story that's as much about the families we have and the families we make ourselves as it is about romance."

—_Booklist_

Jenn Bennett

Simon Pulse

NEW YORK   LONDON   TORONTO   SYDNEY   NEW DELHI

SIMON PULSE

An imprint of Simon & Schuster Children's Publishing Division
1230 Avenue of the Americas, New York, New York 10020
This Simon Pulse paperback edition January 2019
Text copyright © 2018 by Jenn Bennett
Black-and-white interior illustrations copyright © 2018 by Jenn Bennett
Cover photograph copyright © 2018 by plainpicture/Cavan Images/Nick Roush
Photograph of boy by the campfire copyright © 2018 by Jill Wachter
Photograph of starry sky copyright © 2018 by Thinkstock
Also available in a Simon Pulse hardcover edition.
All rights reserved, including the right of reproduction in whole or in part in any form.
SIMON PULSE and colophon are registered trademarks of Simon & Schuster, Inc.
For information about special discounts for bulk purchases, please contact
Simon & Schuster Special Sales at 1-866-506-1949 or business@simonandschuster.com.
The Simon & Schuster Speakers Bureau can bring authors to your live event. For more
information or to book an event contact the Simon & Schuster Speakers Bureau
at 1-866-248-3049 or visit our website at www.simonspeakers.com.
Cover designed by Sarah Creech
Interior designed by Tom Daly
The text of this book was set in Adobe Garamond Pro.
Manufactured in the United States of America
2 4 6 8 10 9 7 5 3 1
The Library of Congress has cataloged the hardcover edition as follows:
Names: Bennett, Jenn, author. Title: Starry eyes / by Jenn Bennett.
Description: First Simon Pulse edition. | New York : Simon Pulse, 2018. |
Summary: When teens Zorie and Lennon, a former couple, are stranded in the California
wilderness together, they must put aside their differences, and come to terms with lingering
romantic feelings, in order to survive. Identifiers: LCCN 2017025646 |
ISBN 9781481478809 (hardcover) | ISBN 9781481478823 (eBook)
Subjects: | CYAC: Survival—Fiction. | Friendship—Fiction. | Dating (Social customs)—
Fiction. | Camping—Fiction. | Family problems—Fiction. | California—Fiction.
Classification: LCC PZ7.1.B4538 St 2018 | DDC [Fic]—dc23
LC record available at https://lccn.loc.gov/2017025646
ISBN 9781481478816 (paperback)

To my brother and sister-in-law, who married
after getting lost in the wilderness on an overnight camping trip.
Nothing like a little fear of dying to spark a great romance.

Part 1

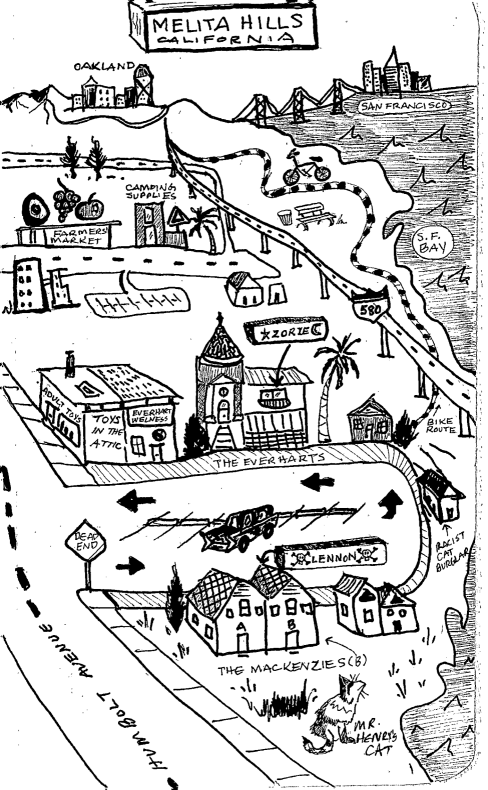

I

Spontaneity is overrated. Movies and television shows would like us to believe that life is better for partygoers who dare to jump into pools with their clothes on. But behind the scenes, it's all carefully scripted. The water is the right temperature. Lighting and angles are carefully considered. Dialogue is memorized. And that's why it looks so appealing—because someone carefully planned it all. Once you realize this, life gets a whole lot simpler. Mine did.

I am a hard-core planner, and I don't care who knows it.

I believe in schedules, routines, *washi*-tape-covered calendars, bulleted lists in graph-paper journals, and best-laid plans. The kind of plans that don't go awry, because they're made with careful consideration of all possibilities and outcomes. No winging it, no playing things by ear. That's how disasters happen.

But not for me. I make blueprints for my life and stick to them. Take, for instance, summer break. School starts back in three weeks, and before I turn eighteen and embark on my senior year, this is my blueprint for the rest of the summer:

Plan one: Two mornings each week, work at my parents' business, Everhart Wellness Clinic. I fill in at the front desk for their normal receptionist, who's taking a summer course at UC Cal in Berkeley. My mom's an acupuncturist and my father is a massage therapist, and they own the clinic together. This means that instead of flipping burgers and being yelled at by random strangers outside a drive-through window, I get to work in a Zen-like reception area, where I can keep everything perfectly organized and know exactly which clients are scheduled to walk through the door. No surprises, no drama. Predictable, just the way I like it.

Plan two: Take photos of the upcoming Perseid meteor shower with my astronomy club. Astronomy is my holy grail. Stars, planets, moons, and all things space. Future NASA astrophysicist, right here.

Plan three: Avoid any and all contact with our neighbors, the Mackenzie family.

These three things all seemed perfectly possible until five minutes ago. Now my summer plans are standing on shaky ground, because my mom is trying to talk me into going camping.

Camping. Me.

Look, I know nothing about the Great Outdoors. I'm not even sure I like being outside. Seems to me, society has progressed far enough that we should be able to avoid things like fresh air and sunlight. If I want to see wild animals, I'll watch a documentary on TV.

Mom knows this. But right now she's trying *really* hard to sell me on some sort of Henry David Thoreau nature-is-good idealism while I'm sitting behind our wellness clinic's front desk. And sure, she's always preaching about the benefits of natural health and vegetarianism, but now she's waxing poetic about the majestic beauty of the great state of California, and what a "singular opportunity" it would be for me to experience the wilderness before school starts.

"Be honest. Can you really picture me camping?" I ask her, tucking dark corkscrew curls behind my ears.

"Not camping, Zorie," she says. "Mrs. Reid is inviting you to go *glamping*." Dressed in gray tunic scrubs embroidered with the clinic's logo, she leans across the front desk and talks in an excited, hushed voice about the wealthy client who's currently relaxing on an acupuncture table in the back rooms, enjoying the dated yet healing sounds of Enya, patron saint of alternative health clinics around the world.

"Glamping," I repeat, skeptical.

"Mrs. Reid says they have reservations for these luxury tents in the High Sierras, somewhere between Yosemite and King's Forest National Park," Mom explains. "Glamorous camping. Get it? Glamping."

"You keep saying that, but I still don't know what it means," I tell her. "How can a tent be luxurious? Aren't you sleeping on rocks?"

Mom leans closer to explain. "Mrs. Reid and her husband got a last-minute invitation to a colleague's chalet in Switzerland, so they have to cancel their camping trip. They have a reservation for a fancy tent. This glamping compound—"

"This isn't some weird hippie cult, is it?"

Mom groans dramatically. "Listen. They have a chef who prepares gourmet meals, an outdoor fire pit, hot showers—the works."

"Hot showers," I say with no small amount of sarcasm. "Thrill me, baby."

She ignores this. "The point is, you aren't actually roughing it, but you feel like it. The compound is so popular that they do a lottery for the tents a year in advance. Everything's already paid for, meals and lodging. Mrs. Reid said it would be shame to let it go to waste, which is why they are letting Reagan take some of her friends there for the week—a last-hurrah trip with the girls before senior year starts."

Mrs. Reid is the mother of Reagan Reid, star athlete, queen bee of my class, and my kind of, sort of friend. Actually, Reagan and I used to be good friends when we were younger. Then her parents came into money, and she started hanging out with other people. Plus, she was training constantly for the Olympics. Before I knew it, we just . . . grew apart.

Until last fall, when we started talking again during lunchtime at school.

"Would be good for you to spend some time outside," Mom says, fiddling with her dark hair as she continues to persuade me to go on this crazy camping trip.

"The Perseid meteor shower is happening next week," I remind her.

She knows I am a strict planner. Unexpected twists and surprises throw me off my game, and everything about this camping—sorry, *glamping*—trip is making me very, *very* anxious.

Mom makes a thoughtful noise. "You could bring your telescope to the glamping compound. Stars at night, hiking trails in the day."

Hiking sounds like something Reagan could be into. She has rock-hard thighs and washboard abs. I practically get winded walking two blocks to the coffee shop, a fact of which I'd like to remind Mom, but she switches gears and plays the guilt card.

"Mrs. Reid says Reagan's been having a really tough time this summer," she says. "She's worried about her. I think she's hoping this trip will help cheer her up after what happened at the trials in June."

Reagan fell (I'm talking *splat*, face-plant) and didn't place in the Olympic track trials. It was her big shot for moving forward. She basically has no chance at the next summer Olympics and will have to wait four more years. Her family was heartbroken. Even so, it surprises me to hear that her mother is worried about her.

Another thought crosses my mind. "Did Mrs. Reid ask me to go on this trip, or did you hustle her into inviting me?"

A sheepish smile lifts my mom's lips. "A little from column A, little from column B."

I quietly drop my head against the front desk.

"Come on," she says, shaking my shoulder slowly until I lift my head again. "She was surprised Reagan hadn't asked you already, so clearly they've discussed you coming along. And maybe you and Reagan both need this. She's struggling to get her mojo back. And you're always saying you feel like an outsider in her pack of friends, so here's your chance to spend some time with them out of school. You should be falling down at my feet," Mom teases. "How about a little, *Thank you, coolest mom ever, for schmoozing me into the event of the summer. You're my hero, Joy Everhart?*" She clasps her hands to her heart dramatically.

"You're so weird," I mumble, pretending to be apathetic.

She grins. "Aren't you lucky I am?"

Actually, yes. I know that she genuinely wants me to be happy and would do just about anything for me. Joy is actually my stepmom. My birth mother died unexpectedly of an aneurysm when I was eight, back when we lived across the Bay in San Francisco. Then my dad suddenly decided he wanted to be a massage therapist and spent all the life insurance money on getting licensed. He's impulsive like that. Anyway, he met Joy at an alternative medicine convention. They got hitched a few months later, and we all moved here to Melita Hills, where they rented out space for this clinic and an apartment next door.

Sure, at the ripe age of thirty-eight, Joy is several years younger than my father, and because she's Korean-American, I've had to deal with genius observations from bigoted people, pointing out the obvious: that she's not my real mom. As if I weren't aware that she's Asian and I'm so Western and pale, I'm rocking an actual vitamin D deficiency. To be honest, in my mind, Joy *is* my mom now. My memories of Life Before Joy are slippery. Over the years, I've grown far closer to her than I am to my dad. She's supportive and encouraging. I just wish she were a touch less granola and chipper.

But this time, as much as I hate to admit it, her enthusiasm about the glamping trip might be warranted. Spending quality time outside of school with Reagan's inner circle would definitely strengthen my social standing, which always feels as if it's in danger of collapsing when I'm hanging around people who have more money or popularity. I'd like to feel more comfortable around them. Around Reagan, too. I just wish she'd asked me to go camping herself, instead of her mother.

The clinic's front door swings open and my father breezes into the waiting room, freshly shaved and dark hair neatly slicked back. "Zorie, did Mr. Wiley call?"

"He canceled today's massage appointment," I inform him. "But he rescheduled for a half session on Thursday."

A half session is half an hour, and half an hour equals half the money, but my father quickly masks his disappointment. You could tell him his best friend just died, and he'd pivot toward a meet-up at the racquetball club without breaking a sweat. Diamond Dan, people call him. All sparkle and glitz.

"Did Mr. Wiley say why he couldn't make it?" he asks.

"An emergency at one of his restaurants," I report. "A TV chef is stopping by to film a segment."

Mr. Wiley is one my dad's best clients. Like most of the

people who come here, he has money burning a hole in his wallet and can afford above-average prices for massage or acupuncture. Our wellness clinic is the best in Melita Hills, and my mom has even been written up in the *San Francisco Chronicle* as one of the Bay Area's top acupuncturists—"well worth a trip across the Bay Bridge." My parents charge clients accordingly.

It's just that the number of those clients has been slowly but surely dwindling over the last year. The primary cause of that dwindling, and the object of my dad's anger, is the business that set up shop in the adjoining space. To our shared mortification, we are now located next to a store that sells adult toys.

Yep, *those* kind of toys.

Kind of hard to ignore the giant vaginal-shaped sign out front. Our well-heeled customers sure haven't. Classy people usually don't want to park in front of a sex shop when they are heading to a massage therapy appointment. My parents found this out pretty quickly when longtime clients started canceling their weekly sessions. Those who haven't fled our desirable location near all the upscale boutique shops on Mission Street are too important to lose, as Dad reminds me every chance he gets.

And that's why I know he's upset by Mr. Wiley's cancellation—it was his only appointment today—but when he leaves the reception area and heads to his office so that he can stew about it in private, Mom remains calm.

"So," she says. "Should I tell Mrs. Reid you'll go glamping with Reagan?"

Like I'm going to give her a definitive answer on the spot without considering all the factors. At the same time, I hate to be the wet blanket on her sunny enthusiasm.

"Don't be cautious. Be careful," she reminds me. Cautious people are afraid of the unknown and avoid it. Careful people plan so that they're more confident when they face the unknown. She tells me this every time I'm resistant to a change in plans. "We'll research everything together."

"I'll consider it," I tell her diplomatically. "I guess you can tell Mrs. Reid that I'll text Reagan for the details and make up my mind later. But you did well, Dr. Pokenstein."

Her smile is victorious. "Speaking of, I better get back to her and take out the needles before she falls asleep on the slab. Oh, I almost forgot. Did FedEx come?"

"Nope. Just the regular mail."

She frowns. "I got an email notification that a package was delivered."

Crap on toast. I know what this means. We have a problem with misdelivered mail. Our mail carrier is constantly delivering our packages to the sex shop next door. And the sex shop next door is directly connected with item number three in my blueprint for a perfect summer: avoid any and all contact with the Mackenzies.

My mom sticks out her lower lip and makes her eyes big. "Pretty please," she pleads sweetly. "Can you run next door and ask them if they got my delivery?"

I groan.

"I would do it, but, you know. I've got Mrs. Reid full of needles," she argues, tugging her thumb toward the back rooms. "I'm balancing her life force, not torturing the woman. Can't leave her back there forever."

"Can't you go get it on your lunch break?" I've already made the trek into dildo land once this week, and that's my limit.

"I leave in an hour to meet your grandmother for lunch, remember?"

Right. Her mother, she means. Grandma Esther loathes tardiness, a sentiment I fully support. But that still doesn't change the fact that I'd rather have a tooth pulled than walk next door. "What's so important in this package anyway?"

"That's the thing," Mom says, winding her long, straight hair into a tight knot at the crown of her head. "The notification was sent by someone else. 'Catherine Beatty.' I don't know anyone by that name, and I haven't ordered anything. But the notification came to my work email, and our address is listed."

"A mystery package."

Her eyes twinkle. "Surprises are fun."

"Unless someone sent you a package full of spiders or a severed hand. Maybe you jabbed someone a little too hard."

"Or maybe I jabbed someone just right, and they are sending me chocolate." She steals a pen from the desk and stabs it into her hair to secure her new knot. "Please, Zorie. While your father is occupied."

She says this last bit in a hushed voice. My dad would throw a fit if he saw me next door.

"Fine. I'll go," I say, but I'm not happy.

Summer plans, how I knew and loved you.

Sticking a handmade AWAY FROM THE DESK. BE BACK IN A JIFF! sign on the counter, I drag myself through the front door into bright morning sunshine and brace for doom.

2

Sitting on the corner of Mission Street, Toys in the Attic, or T&A as my mom jokingly refers to it—until my dad gives her his *not funny, Joy* ultradry look—is a boutique sex shop that markets itself toward women. It's well lit and clean. Not skuzzy and filled with creepers, like Love Rocket across town, which has painted-over windows and is open twenty-four hours. You know, just in case you need fuzzy handcuffs at three a.m.

It also has a themed display window that the owners change every month. This month it's a forest, and like toadstools, a curated collection of bright rubber dildos rise from fake grass. One even has a squirrel molded into its side. This might be funny, except for the fact that plenty of people I know see this window regularly, and I have to endure lurid, snickering commentary about it from certain people at school.

Our dueling businesses—and nearby homes—sit together at the tail end of a tree-lined shopping promenade filled with local boutiques, organic restaurants, and art studios. Most of our cul-de-sac contains old Victorian houses like ours that have been sectioned up and converted into apartment units. Not exactly the place you'd expect to find sex for sale.

My dad says a place that sells "marital aids" is "no place for a young girl." The two women who own the sex shop darken his dazzling smile on a regular basis. They are the Hatfields to his McCoy. The Hamilton to his Burr. Our neighbors are the Enemy, and we do not fraternize with the Mackenzies. Oh *no*, we do not.

My mom used to be on friendly terms with the Mackenzies, so she only half agrees with my dad on this. And me? I'm caught in the middle. The whole situation just stresses me out. It's complicated. Very, *very* complicated.

Pink walls and the synthetic scent of silicone envelop me as I duck inside the sex shop. It's not quite noon, and only a couple of customers are browsing—a relief. I divert my eyes from a display of leather riding crops as I make a beeline toward a counter in the middle of the store, behind which two women in their early forties are chatting. I'm behind enemy lines now. Let's hope I don't get shot.

"It wasn't Alice Cooper," a woman with dark shoulder-length hair says as she lifts a small cardboard package on the counter. "It was the guy married to the redheaded talk show host. What's-her-name. Osbourne."

The woman standing next to her, green-eyed and fair-skinned, leans against the counter and scratches a heavily freckled nose.

"Ozzy?" she says in an accent that's a soft blend of American and Scottish. "I don't think so."

"I'll bet you a cupcake." Brown eyes dart over the counter to meet mine. Her oblong face lifts into a smile. "Zorie! Long time, no see."

"Hello, Sunny," I say, and then greet her freckled wife: "Mac."

"Sweet glasses," Sunny says, giving a thumbs-up to the retro blue cat-eye rims I'm wearing.

I have a dozen other pairs, all different styles and colors. I buy them dirt cheap from an online store, and I match them to my outfits. Along with crazy bright lipstick and a love for all things plaid, cool glasses are my thing. I may be a geek, but I am chic.

"Thanks," I tell her, meaning it. Not for the first time, I regret that my dad is fighting with these women. It wasn't that long ago that they felt like my second family.

The entire time I've known Sunny and Jane "Mac" Mackenzie, who have lived directly across the cul-de-sac since we moved into the neighborhood, they've insisted that I call them Sunny and Mac. Period. Not Mrs. or Ms., or any other titles. They don't like formalities, not in names or clothes. They are both quintessential Californians. You know, just your average former *riot grrrl* lesbian sex-shop owners.

"Help us out. We're playing Rock Star Urban Legend Game," Mac says to me, pushing fiery hair shot through with silver away from her face. "Which heavy metal star bit the head off a bat onstage? Back in the sixties."

"The seventies," Sunny corrects.

Mac rolls her eyes humorously. "Whatever. Listen, Zorie. We think it's either Ozzy Osbourne or Alice Cooper. Which one?"

"Um, I really don't know," I answer, hoping they'll give this up so I can get what I came for and leave. They're both acting like nothing has changed, that I still come over for Sunday dinner every week. Like my father didn't threaten to bust up their shop with a baseball bat for driving away his clients and they didn't tell him to go screw himself while dozens of people looked on from across the street with cell phones recording. The footage was uploaded to YouTube within the hour.

Yeah. Fun times. Dad has always disliked the Mackenzies, when they were just the "weirdo" neighbors across the street. But after their sex shop opened last fall and our clinic started tanking, that dislike turned into something stronger.

But okay, if Sunny and Mac want to pretend as though everything is still normal, fine. I'll play that game, as long as it gets me out of here faster. "Alice Cooper, maybe?" I answer.

"No way. It was Ozzy Osbourne," Sunny says confidently, slicing open the package on the counter with a box cutter. "Look it up, Mac."

"My phone's dead."

Sunny makes a clucking sound with her tongue. "Likely story. You just don't want to lose the bet."

"Lennon will know."

My stomach tightens. There are plenty of reasons for me not

to want to come over here. The dildo forest. The fear of being seen by someone I know. My dad's ongoing feud with the two women bantering behind the counter. But it's the seventeen-year-old boy casually strolling out of the stockroom who makes me wish I could turn invisible.

Lennon Mackenzie.

Monster T-shirt. Black jeans. Black boots laced to his knees. Black, fringed hair that's all swept to the side, somehow messy and perfectly spiked at the same time.

If an evil anime character sprang to life with a mission to lurk in dark corners while plotting world destruction, he would look a lot like Lennon. He's a poster boy for all things weird and macabre. He's also the main reason I don't want to eat lunch in the school cafeteria with the rest of the hoi polloi.

Carrying a zombie-splattered graphic novel in one hand and something small and unidentifiable tucked under his other arm, he glances at my blue plaid skirt, then his gaze skims upward to settle on my face. Any looseness in his posture immediately becomes tight and ridged. And when his dark eyes meet mine, they clearly reinforce what I already know: We are *not* friends.

Thing is, we used to be. Good friends. Okay, *best* friends. We had a lot of classes together, and because we live across the street from each other, we hung out after school. When we were younger, we'd ride bikes to a city park. In high school, that daily bike ride morphed into a daily walk down Mission Street to our local coffee shop—the Jitterbug—with my white husky, Andromeda, in tow.

And *that* turned into late-night walks around the Bay. He called me Medusa (because of my dark, unruly curls), and I called him Grim (because of the goth). We were always together. Inseparable friends.

Until everything changed last year.

Gathering my courage, I adjust my glasses, paste on a civil smile, and say, "Hi."

He tugs his chin upward in response. That's all I get. I used to be trusted with his secrets, and now I'm not even worthy of a spoken greeting. I thought at some point this would stop hurting me, but the pain is as sharp as it's ever been.

New plan: Don't say another word to him. Don't acknowledge his presence.

"Babe," Sunny says to Lennon, unpacking what appears to be some sort of sex lube. "Which rock star bit the head off a bat? Your other, less-hip mom thinks it's Alice Cooper."

Mac pretends to be affronted and points to me. "Hey, Zorie thinks so too!"

"She's wrong," Lennon says in a dismissive voice that's so scratchy and deep, it sounds as though he's speaking from inside a deep, dark well. That's the other thing about Lennon that drives me nuts. He doesn't just have a good voice; he has an *attractive* voice. It's big and confident and rich, and entirely too sexy for comfort. He sounds like a villainous voice-over actor or some kind of satanic radio announcer. It makes goose bumps race over my skin, and I resent that he still has that effect on me.

"It's Ozzy Osbourne," he informs us.

"Ha! Told you," Sunny says victoriously to Mac.

"I just picked one," I tell Lennon, a little angrier than I intend.

"Well, you picked wrong," he says, sounding bored.

I'm insulted. "Since when am I supposed to be an expert on the abuse of bats in rock music?"

That's more his speed.

"It's not arcane knowledge," he says, sweeping artfully mussed-up hair away from one eye with a knuckle. "It's pop culture."

"Right. Vital information I'll need to know in order to get into the university of my choice. I think I remember that question on the SAT exams."

"Life is more than SAT exams."

"At least I have friends," I say.

"If you think Reagan and the rest of her clique are real friends, you're sadly mistaken."

"Jeez, you two," Sunny mumbles. "Get a room."

Heat washes over my face.

Um, no. This is not an *I secretly like you* fight. This is *I secretly hate you*. Sure, he's all lips and hair and baritone voice, and I'm not blind: He's attractive. But the only time our former friendship dared to risk one pinky toe over the line—a period of time we referred to as the Great Experiment—I ended up sobbing my eyes out at homecoming, wondering what went wrong.

I never found out. But I have a pretty good guess.

He gives his mom a long-suffering look, as if to say, *You done now?* and then turns to address Mac. "Ozzy's bat story was exaggerated. Someone in the audience threw a dead bat onstage, and Ozzy thought it was plastic. When he bit the head off, he was completely shocked. Had to be taken to the hospital for a rabies shot after the show."

Sunny bumps her hip against Mac. "Doesn't matter. I'm still right, and you still owe me a cupcake. Coconut. Since we skipped breakfast this morning, I'll take it now. Brunch."

"That actually does sound good," Mac says. "Zorie, you want one?"

I shake my head.

Mac turns to Lennon. "Baby, my baby," she says in a coaxing, jovial voice. "Can you make a bakery run? Pretty please?"

"Mother, my mother. I have to be at work in thirty minutes," he argues, and I hate how he can be so cold to me one second and warm to his parents the next. When he sets the book he's carrying on the counter, I see what he's cradling in the crook of his elbow: a red bearded dragon lizard about the length of my forearm. It's on a leash connected to a black leather harness that wraps around its tiny front arms. "Got to put Ryuk back in his habitat before I go."

Lennon is obsessed with reptiles, because *of course*. He has an entire wall of them in his room—snakes, lizards, and his only nonreptile pet, a tarantula. He works part-time at a Mission Street reptile store, where he can be creepy with other likeminded snake lovers.

Mac reaches over the counter to scratch the lizard on top of its scaly head and coos in a childlike voice, "Fine. Guess you win, Ryuk. Oh dear, you're coming out of your harness."

Lennon sets the bearded dragon atop his manga book. Ryuk tries to get away, nearly falling off the counter. "That's an inefficient way to go," Lennon dourly informs the lizard. "If you're going to off yourself, better to overdose on reptile vitamins than jump."

"Lennon," Sunny scolds lightly.

A dark smile barely curls the corners of his full lips. "Sorry, Mama," he says.

When we were younger, people used to taunt him mercilessly at school—*How do you know which mom is which?* To him, Sunny is Mama, Mac is Mum. And even though Mac gave birth to him, neither woman is more or less in his eyes.

Sunny twists her mouth and then smiles back. He's forgiven. His parents forgive him for everything. He doesn't deserve them.

"So, Zorie. What brings you by, love?" Mac says to me as Lennon adjusts his lizard's tiny harness.

I'm forced to step to the side of Lennon in order to have a conversation that doesn't involve me speaking at his back. When did he get so freakishly tall? "My mom's looking for a FedEx package."

Mac's eyes shift toward Sunny's. A subtle but sharp reaction is communicated between the two women.

"Something wrong?" I ask, suspicious.

Sunny clears her throat. "Nothing, sweetie." She hesitates, indecisive for a moment. "We did get something, yes," she says,

reaching under the counter to pull out a manila mailing envelope, which she hands to me, apologetic. "I may have accidentally
opened it by mistake. I didn't read your mom's mail, though. I
noticed the address after I slit it open."

"That's fine," I say. It's happened before, which sends my dad's
blood pressure through the roof, but Mom won't care. It's just
that Mac is now looking extremely uncomfortable. Even Lennon
feels more distant than usual, his energy shifting from mildly
chilly to arctic. Warning bells ding inside my head.

"Okay, well, gotta get back," I say, pretending I don't notice
anything amiss.

"Give Joy our best," Mac says. "If your mum ever wants to get
coffee . . ." She trails off and gives me a tight smile. "Well, she
knows where to find us."

Sunny nods. "You too. Don't be a stranger."

Now *I'm* uncomfortable. I mean, more than usual, having to
endure the humiliation that is this shop.

"Sure. Thanks for this." I hold up the package in acknowl-
edgment as I'm turning to leave and nearly knock over a display
model of a giant blue vibrator sitting next to the register. I instinc-
tively reach out to steady the wobbling piece of plastic before I'm
fully aware of what I'm touching. *Dear God.*

Under a fan of black lashes, Lennon's eyes shift to the floor,
and he doesn't lift his face.

Must get out. Now.

Nearly tripping over my own feet, I stride out of the shop and exhale a long breath when I'm back in the sunshine. I can't get back into the clinic fast enough.

But when I'm settled behind the shield of the front desk, my eyes fix on the envelope the Mackenzies gave me. It's from a PO Box in San Francisco and is, indeed, clearly addressed to Joy Everhart. Not sure how they missed that, but whatever.

After checking the back hallway and finding it clear, I peek into the envelope.

It's a piece of paper with a handwritten note and a small book of personal photos. I recognize the photo book's brand from online ads: upload your photos, and they send you a printed book a few days later. This one says *Our Bahamas Trip* on the cover in a frilly font.

I open the book to find a million sunny vacation photos. The ocean. The beach. My dad snorkeling. My dad with his arm around some woman in a bikini.

Wait.

What?

Flipping faster, I stare at glossy pages printed with more of the same. Dinner and tropical drinks. My dad smiling that dazzling smile of his. Only he's not smiling at my mom but some stranger. A stranger with a gold ankle bracelet and long lash extensions. He's got his arms wrapped around her, and—in one photo—is even kissing her neck.

What is all this? Some fling after my mother died? Someone before Joy? I pull out the letter.

Joy,

You don't know me, but I thought you'd want

to see this, woman to woman. Photos from our

vacation last summer.

Good luck,

One of many

My fingers go numb. Last summer? He was here, working at the clinic, last summer. No, wait. There was a week he went to Los Angeles for a massage therapy conference. And came back with a shockingly dark tan . . . that he said he'd gotten after lying out by the hotel pool every afternoon.

"Oh, shit," I whisper to myself.

My dad is having an affair.

3

It's all I can think about. That evening, after Mom returns from seeing Grandma Esther in Oakland and lets me borrow her car, I'm sitting inside the Melita Hills Observatory's dark auditorium for my monthly astronomy club meeting. Sometimes we head up to the roof with our telescopes, but this month, it's an info-only gathering. And thanks to that Bahamas photo book, I'm paying zero attention to Dr. Viramontes, the retired Berkeley teacher who's president of our local chapter. He's addressing the group—a couple dozen people, mostly other retirees and a handful of students my age—while standing at a podium near the controls that turn the ceiling into a light show of the night sky. I lost what he was saying a quarter of an hour back, something about where we were going to be watching the Perseid meteor shower.

Instead, my mind is stuck on that photo of my dad kissing that woman.

He lied to my mom. He lied to me.

And he forced *me* to lie, telling my mom that the Mackenzies hadn't received any of our mail, because no way was I handing over that ticking-bomb package of agony over to my mom. Not right now, when she's full of cheer and sunshine, encouraging me to go on the camping trip with Reagan. Maybe not ever. I don't know. This will tear our family apart.

I've never been in this kind of position, being forced to decide where I should hide photos of my dad two-timing my mom. Or three-timing. Four-timing? What did that woman mean by "one of many"? The photos are from last summer, and I doubt this woman would want to call him out to his wife if she were still seeing him. So when did the affair end, and how many others were there? *Are* there?

Does he just pick up random acupuncturists from alternative health conventions?

Are they all locals?

Do I know any of them?

Ugh. Considering all the possibilities hurts my brain. And what's even weirder about the whole thing is that the strange woman in the photos looks a *lot* like my birth mother. I mean, clearly it's not her, and this stranger is younger than my mother was when she died, but there's an uncanny resemblance. And that just freaks me out.

My dad is having an affair with someone who looks like his dead first wife. That's not normal.

What am I saying? None of this normal, no matter what she looks like. I think of Mom smiling this morning, completely oblivious to the fact that Dad's cheated on her, and it makes my stomach hurt all over again.

Thank God the normal clinic receptionist came in to take over for me at lunch, because no way could I handle looking my dad in the eye.

My stomach is sick. My heart is sick. Everything about this is wrong, wrong, wrong.

And the cherry on top of this shit sundae is that *the Mackenzies know*. Sunny and Mac saw what was inside the envelope. They had to. I mean, judging from the awkward way they acted, and all that business about meeting for coffee if we ever needed to talk? It's hard for me to blame them for looking at the photo book. If they really did open it by accident, I'm sure curiosity got the better of them. It did for me.

Huge mistake.

Oh, God. Does Lennon know too?

"What's wrong?"

I snap out of my thoughts and realize the meeting has ended. The person speaking to me is a brown-haired girl sitting at my side. I've known Avani Desai as long as Lennon and Reagan, when we first bonded over astronomy in seventh-grade science class, both acing a quiz about the planets. Avani and I used to carpool to Reagan's house for sleepovers, staying up late to listen to music and gossip while her parents were asleep. But when I followed Reagan to the elite courtyard at school, Avani stayed behind, secure with her social status. I always envied her confidence. Now the only time I really talk with Avani is during astronomy club.

"Nothing's wrong," I tell her. No way am I bringing up the humiliation that is my father's affair. "I'm just thinking about something."

"Yeah, sort of figured," she says with a brief smile, crossing her arms over a T-shirt silk-screened with Neil deGrasse Tyson's face and the words NEIL BEFORE ME. "You've been 'thinking' all the way through Viramontes's meteor shower plans."

Most of the club members are filing out of the auditorium now, but a few hover around Dr. Viramontes's podium. Avani is waiting for me to explain my mood, so I say the first thing that comes to mind to placate her curiosity.

"I've been invited to go on a camping trip with Reagan," I tell her.

To my surprise, she brightens. "Oooh, I heard about that."

Wait, she knew, but I didn't? And since when had she started talking to Reagan again?

"I overheard Brett Seager talking about it," she explains excitedly, twisting sideways to face me in the auditorium chairs while she sits cross-legged. "He was at the drugstore with his older sister earlier today."

"What?" Now I'm interested. *Very* interested.

She nods quickly. "I was behind him in the checkout line. He was talking to someone on his phone, saying that he was going camping near King's Forest with some other people from school. I didn't catch any names but Reagan's. He was trying to convince whoever he was talking to on the phone to go with him."

Brett Seager is a minor celebrity in our school. His parents don't have a ton of money, but somehow he's always doing things like skydiving, or going backstage at cool concerts, or jumping off the roof of some rich friend's house into their million-dollar pool. But he's not just a party-boy daredevil. He reads Jack Kerouac and Allen Ginsberg . . . all the American Beat Poets. Most guys I know don't even know what a bookstore is.

So yes, he's pretty and popular, but he's more than that. And I've been nursing a crush on him since elementary school. A crush that turned into a small obsession ever since he kissed me at a party over spring break. Sure, he got back with his on-again, off-again girlfriend the next day, which was humiliating and upsetting for me at the time. Reagan tried to cheer me up by playing matchmaker, introducing me to a couple of boys. Guess it wasn't meant to be for any of us, because I never clicked with those boys, and then Brett and his girlfriend broke up over the summer.

The important thing here is that if what Avani overheard is true, it sounds like Brett could be going on Reagan's camping trip. And that makes the great outdoors a *lot* more enticing.

More panic-inducing, too, because Brett was not a factor in my mental plan for this trip. Reagan's mom had said it would be all girls. No way would my parents let me go on a weeklong unsupervised camping trip with boys. My father would flip the hell out.

Guess this information is under the table.

"Are you *sure* Brett said he was actually going?" I ask Avani.

"Yep." She hikes up her shoulders to make herself look muscular and pretends to be Brett. "'Bruh, you've to go with me. I *need* to jump off that wicked waterfall. We can Instagram the whole thing.'"

I snort at her bad imitation.

She shrugs. "I'm just telling you what I heard."

"Who was he talking to on the phone?" I ask.

"No idea. Probably his latest bromance. He's always changing friends, usually to whoever's parents are out of town and have a house big enough for one of his legendary blowouts."

"That's just an act," I argue. "He's not really that way."

Her face softens. "I'm sorry. I know you like him, especially after that party . . ."

I wish I'd never told her about the kiss. It feels like a weakness.

"Anyway, I guess he's been expanding his friend list this summer. Katy even said she thought she saw him in the passenger seat of Lennon's car a couple weeks ago."

Wait, what? Lennon and Brett, friends? Surely that's a sign of the apocalypse. "I seriously doubt it."

"Maybe not. Lennon seems way out of Brett's league, if you ask me."

"I think you have that turned around," I say with a snort.

"And *I* think whatever happened between you and Lennon is—"

"Avani," I protest. I don't like to talk about Lennon. Avani doesn't know about the Great Experiment. All Avani knows is that we were supposed to meet up with her for homecoming. She doesn't know why that never happened. No one does. Not even me, really. But I stopped trying to figure out Lennon's motivations a long time ago.

It's easier not to think about him at all.

"Never mind," she says. "I'm sorry I brought it up. It's none of my business."

After I'm quiet for a few seconds, she elbows me. "So . . . camping. Alone in the woods. Maybe this is your chance with Brett. When is this trip?"

I texted Reagan earlier, but she only confirmed that the trip was happening and said she'd get back to me later with details. Normally, that would drive me nuts, but I was busy freaking out about hiding the photo book of my dad's affair. Now I wish I had pressed Reagan for more information. All of these Unknowns and Possibilities are stressing me out.

"I think it's in a couple of days?" I say. "Pretty sure she's planning on staying a week."

Avani's face falls. "That's during the meteor shower. I was kind of hoping you were going on the weekend trip with the group."

"What group?"

"*Our* group. East Bay Planetary Society," she says, brow wrinkling. "Weren't you listening at all?"

I wasn't.

She fills me in. "Instead of gathering here at the observatory, Dr. Viramontes is taking the club on a road trip to the dark-sky area on Condor Peak to watch the meteor shower there."

Condor Peak State Park. They host the annual North California Star Party.

"All the other astronomy clubs in the area will be going," Avani adds.

Apart from Death Valley, Condor Peak is the closest dark-sky preserve. That means it's protected from artificial light pollution, which enables people to see more stars. Astronomers take amazing photos in dark-sky areas, especially during star parties—which are basically nighttime gatherings of amateur astronomers to watch celestial events. And though we've hosted a few minor star parties here at the observatory, I've never been to one this big with other astronomy clubs. That's kind of huge.

I weigh my options. On one hand, the geek in me really wants to attend this star party. I mean, hello. The Perseid meteor shower happens only once a year. But on the other hand, Brett Seager.

Rolling a two-wheeled laptop case behind him, Dr. Viramontes ascends the aisle and stops when he sees us. I like the way his eyes crinkle in the corner when he smiles. "Ladies, are you joining us on our pilgrimage to Condor Peak? We'll get some amazing photos. Great thing to add to your college applications, and there'll be other astrophysics professors there, along with many important members of the Night Sky Program. And I didn't want to say this to the group, because I'm not entirely certain, but I've got intel that Sandra Faber could make an appearance."

Sandra Faber teaches astrophysics at UC Santa Cruz. She won the National Medal of Science. She's a big deal. Meeting someone like her could help me get into Stanford, which is where I want to study astronomy after I graduate.

Avani draws in an excited breath and pokes my shoulder. "You have to come now."

"I'm supposed to be camping with a friend in the High Sierras," I tell the professor, suddenly filled with doubt. Why can't anything be easy?

Dr. Viramontes shifts the long silver braid that hangs over his shoulder, bound at the tail by a beaded clasp made by someone in his local Ohlone Indian tribe. "That's a shame. Where?"

I relay the details that my mom shared with me about the glamping compound.

Dr. Viramontes scratches his chin. "I think I know which one you're talking about, and it's not far from Condor Peak." He slips a piece of paper out of the front pocket of his rolling case and hands it to me. It's an information sheet on the trip. He points to the map and shows me the general area of the glamping compound in relation to King's Forest and Condor Peak. "Probably a couple hours' drive on the highway. Maybe you could stop by. We'll be there three nights."

"You can meet me there," Avani says encouragingly.

"I'm not sure what the transportation situation will be like, but I'll definitely check into it," I tell him, folding up the paper.

"We'd love to have you. Let me know what you decide." He raises two fingers to his forehead and gives me a loose salute before reminding us to be safe getting home tonight.

."You're going, right?" Avani whispers excitedly as he walks away.

My mind is aflutter. So is my stomach. "God, I *really* want to."

"Then come," she says. "Meet me at Condor Peak. Promise me, Zorie."

"I'll try," I say, not completely sure, but hopeful.

"Star party, here we come," she tells me, and for a moment, it feels like old times between us.

But after we leave the auditorium and she walks me to the parking lot, I remember what awaits me at home.

I push away the dread and concentrate on enjoying the drive as I leave the hilltop observatory and descend into town. It's a perfect summer night, and stars blanket the sky. My stars. Every winking point of white light belongs to me. They are wonderful, the town is quiet and dark, and I'm just fine.

Only I'm not.

Normally, I love driving my mom's car, even though it's several years old and smells faintly of patchouli. The stereo speakers are bass-heavy, and I relish taking the long way home, cruising the road between the freeway and the dark blue water, with San Francisco twinkling in the distance. Except for the occasional run to the grocery store, this is the only time I really drive. But, hey. At least my mom trusts me with her sedan, unlike my dad, who won't let me near his vintage sports car. It's worth too much.

But now I can't stop thinking about that whole "one of many" line in that letter, and I wonder if my dad has driven other women around in his stupid car. Just how many others have there been? I've always thought my dad was a decent person, if not a little plastic and fake when he's in full-on Diamond Dan mode, but now I'm picturing him dressed like Hugh Hefner with two curvy women on his arms.

It makes me want to vomit.

Dark silhouettes of skinny palm trees greet me as I turn into our cul-de-sac and park the car behind my dad's Corvette in the narrow driveway next to our building. The clinic is dark, so no one's working late. Hesitantly, I hike the steps of the connecting house and warily open the front door of our apartment.

A ball of white fur pads across the open living area to greet me. Andromeda is getting old, but she's still sweet and pretty. No one can resist her dual-colored brown and blue husky eyes. I stick my fingers under her collar and give her a good scratch while kissing the top of her head.

"Hey, sweet thing," my mom says. She's stretched out on the couch under a blanket, reading a magazine under a dim lamp while the mute TV flashes a commercial in background. "How was astronomy club?"

"Fine." I hand her the car keys. "Where's Dad?"

She nods toward the balcony off the kitchen, where I spot a dark shape. "On the phone."

My gut twists when I hear his voice, too low for me to make out what he's saying. He's always on the phone, and those phone calls usually are taken behind closed doors after he steps away. I assumed he was just being polite; my mom is old-school about people talking on cell phones in public.

Now I wonder who's on the other end of the line.

Hoping she doesn't notice my anxiety, I briefly tell Mom about Dr. Viramontes's invitation to the star party while she's flipping magazine pages. She's *mmm-hmm*-ing me, completely distracted. I see her glance toward the balcony door, and a little line appears in the middle of her forehead.

Or maybe that's my imagination.

All I know is that I can't fake a convincing smile around my father, so after feigning weariness, I kiss Joy good night and make an escape upstairs, Andromeda at my heels.

My bedroom is in a converted attic space. My parents' master bedroom is downstairs, so I have the entire upstairs to myself. Just me, an ancient bathroom without a shower, and a storage room filled with overflow supplies from the clinic.

Embarrassingly, my room hasn't changed a lot since I was a kid. The ceiling is still covered with glow-in-the-dark stars—the "glow" ran out years ago—painstakingly arranged to match constellations. Pegasus lost the stars that make up his leg during a minor earthquake. The only decorative room additions from the last couple of years are my oversize handmade wall calendars, or "blueprints"—I have one for each season of the year, and they are all systematically color-coded—and my galaxy photos. I've had my best ones printed and framed. My Orion Nebula is particularly beautiful. I took it at the observatory with a special equatorial mount borrowed from

Dr. Viramontes, and tweaked its purple luminance with stacking software.

After locking my door, I move past framed star charts and duck beneath a mobile of the solar system that hangs over my desk. I stashed the photo book in a deep desk drawer earlier, and when I double-check, it's still there, under a neat stack of graph-lined planning journals and a rainbow bin of highlighters, gel pens, and rolls of *washi* tape. My parents don't touch my stuff—it's all carefully organized—so I'm not sure why I'm so worried. I guess I just feel guilty.

Best not to think about it. "Until I can figure out what to do, it's our little secret," I tell Andromeda. She jumps up on my bed and curls into a ball. She's an excellent secret keeper.

The only window in my room has a Juliet balcony that overlooks the cul-de-sac. There's not room enough for me to stand outside, but it's wide enough for my telescope, Nancy Grace Roman—named after the first woman to hold an executive position at NASA. I open the balcony doors and take the telescope from its black carrying case to set it up. I actually have two telescopes—this one, and a smaller portable model. I haven't really used the portable one much, but now I'm daydreaming about taking it to that star party on Condor Peak.

I wonder if I can really do the camping *and* the meteor shower.

It would take a lot of planning.

I dash off a quick text to Reagan: So, about this glamping trip. Who's going? Are you driving? What day are you leaving?

She responds almost immediately: Slow your roll. I'm in bed. Super tired. Want to go pick up camping gear with me tomorrow afternoon? We can talk about it then.

I'm both relieved and disappointed. Relieved, because I guess it's cool with her that I tag along. And disappointed, because though I need to plan things well in advance, Reagan does everything by the seat of her pants. She's always telling me I need to lighten up and embrace spontaneity.

Spontaneity gives me hives.

Literally.

I have chronic urticaria. That's a fancy name for chronic hives. They're idiopathic, which means doctors can't pinpoint an exact cause for why, when, and how long they flare. Sometimes when I eat certain foods, touch an allergen, or—especially—get super anxious, itchy pale-red bumps appear on the inside of my elbows and on my stomach. If I don't calm down and take an antihistamine, they'll spread into huge welts off and on for days, or even weeks. It's been several months since I've had a breakout, but between Reagan and this thing with my dad, I can already feel the itch coming on.

I answer Reagan's text, asking for details about meeting her tomorrow. Then I assemble my telescope and set up the tripod in the middle of the balcony's open doors.

As I'm adjusting the mount, I look over the balcony railing to scan the cul-de-sac. Viewed from up here, our street looks like a fat raindrop, its center filled with a dozen public parking spaces. At night, they're mostly empty, so I have a pretty clear view of the other side of the street, where I spot Lennon's car. It's hard to miss. He drives this hulking black 1950s Chevy that looks like a hearse, with pointy tailfins cradling a hatchback door that lifts up to carry the coffins, or whatever dastardly thing he hauls back there. And right now, it's parked in front of a pale blue duplex house directly across the street from us: the Mackenzies' apartment unit.

I can't pinpoint the exact moment Lennon morphed from the boy-next-door comic geek to the boy-in-black horrorphile, but I guess he's always been a little odd. Some of that may be due to how he grew up. His biological dad—Adam Ahmed, who used to date Mac—is the former guitarist for a radical San Francisco punk band that was popular during the Bay Area's '90s punk revival explosion. His moms took three-year-old Lennon on tour when his dad's band opened for Green Day.

So yeah, he hasn't always led a so-called normal life, but he always *seemed* normal.

Until junior year, that is. After the night of the homecoming dance, we didn't speak for days. No more hiking down to the Jitterbug to get coffee after school. No more night walks. Weeks passed. I'd see him occasionally at school, but our brief interactions were tense. He started hanging around other people.

Golden light shines from a window on the corner of the Mackenzies' house. Lennon's room. I know it well. We used to signal each other from our windows before sneaking out late at night to meet up for walks around the neighborhood with Andromeda.

We made a game of creating and naming detailed routes.

Lennon would draw them all out, streets labeled with his neat handwriting and tiny sketches. He's drawn maps since we were kids. Some were fantasy maps based on books he read; he redrew Middle Earth about twenty times. And some were of Melita Hills. That's how our friendship started, actually. I'd just moved to Melita Hills and didn't know my way around, so he made me a neighborhood map of the Mission Street area. He gave me a larger, updated one for my birthday last year—one that included our favorite late-night walking route, which extended out along a bicycling path curving around the Bay. It had funny little drawings, all the points of interest we considered important, and a legend of symbols he'd made up.

It's currently upside down at the bottom of the same drawer where I've hidden my dad's stupid photo book. I wanted to throw it away after we stopped speaking, but I couldn't make myself do it, because that walking route he drew? It's where the Great Experiment started.

Who knew walking could lead to heartbreak?

Out of curiosity, I screw on a low-power eyepiece and hesitantly aim my assembled telescope toward the Mackenzies' duplex. Just for a quick look. It's not as if I usually spy on all the neighbors. I quickly focus on Lennon's room. It's empty. Thank God. After an adjustment, I can see an unmade bed and, right beyond it, his reptile terrariums. The last time I was in his room, there were only two, but now there are at least six sitting on shelves and one big floor model. It's a freaking jungle up in there.

I scan the rest of his room. He has a TV and a million DVDs stacked precariously, out of their cases. Probably all horror movies. An enormous map hangs over his desk. A map of what, I'm not sure, but it's professional, not one that's he's drawn himself—definitely not one of our late-night walking routes. Silly even to think it could be.

A shadow catches my eye as the door to his room swings open and closes. Lennon walks into view. One by one, I watch him turn off lights and heat lamps inside the terrariums. Then he sits on the edge of his bed and begins unlacing his boots.

That's my cue to bail.

Only, I don't.

I watch him take off both boots and chuck them in the middle of his floor. Then he tugs up his shirt and pulls it off. Now he's bare-chested, wearing only black jeans. I should definitely look away before this turns X-rated. But holy mother of God, when did he get all . . . *built?* I mean, it's no soccer-player physique, or anything. He's too lean to be buff. But he flops on his bed, lying on his back with his arms spread, and stares at the ceiling while I keep staring at him.

And staring . . .

There are now muscles where there weren't before, and his chest is a lot bigger. Is he lifting weights? No way. That is not him *at all.* He hates sports. He'd rather hole up with a comic book in the dark.

At least, I think he would. I suddenly feel like I don't know him anymore.

"Of course you don't," I whisper to myself. He's changed.

I've changed. Only, I haven't, or I wouldn't still be looking at something that should be off-limits.

When I sharpen the focus, I home in on a stack of muscles rippling down his stomach as he sits up again. And—

I pan to his face. He's staring this way.

Not in my general location, but RIGHT AT ME.

Heart racing, I jerk back from the telescope and lurch to the floor. Smooth move. Like he didn't see me do that. If I had just kept a level head and shifted the telescope to the sky, I could have played it cool and pretended I wasn't really spying on him. But now? My humiliation is total and complete.

Good job, Zorie.

I lie on the floor, dying. Wishing I could take back the last few minutes.

Guess I can add that to the list of everything that's gone wrong today. Andromeda jumps off the bed and licks my nose in concern.

New plan: I *am* going on that glamping trip—and to the star party on Condor Peak—if it kills me. I have to get away from this place. Away from my cheating dad. Away from the daily mortification of living next door to a sex shop. And far, *far* away from Lennon.

4

"Oh, check out this one. It will look great on you," Reagan says in a loud, raspy voice as she pulls a Barbie-pink backpack off a hook. We've been inside this specialty outdoor gear store for all of ten minutes, and she's already filled up a shopping cart with enough hiking gear to outfit the Donner Party. The store's owner is probably counting up the total in his head and putting a down payment on a new house. Reagan's mom gave her a credit card and told her to go wild.

Must be nice.

"Jesus! Look at the price tag. It's too expensive," I tell her. It's one of those structured backpacks that covers your entire back from head to butt and holds whatever it is that backpackers need when they're hiking—sleeping bags and tent poles, things like that.

"Mom said we could buy anything, as long as it's in this store," Reagan argues, giving me a mischievous look as she swings a light brown ponytail over one shoulder. "She will regret that. Besides, my dad just made a shitload of money on the stock market. Why do you think my parents suddenly decided to fly to Switzerland? They can afford a couple of backpacks."

"There're four in the cart already," I point out.

Four backpacks. Three tents. Hiking sticks. Sleeping bags. Headlamps. And a set of enamel cookware, because it was "cute."

"We'll be needing it," she says casually.

"I thought this was glamping," I argue. "Your mom told my mom that the tents are already set up and that all the meals were provided."

Reagan pushes the shopping cart into an outdoor clothing area. "Yeah, I stayed there last year for my sixteenth birthday. The compound has really nice yurts."

"Yogurt?"

"Yurt," she enunciates, pretending to snap at my nose with her teeth. "They're giant round tents. You could host a huge party inside one. Anyway, the tents we're buying today are for the back-country trip we're taking."

I don't like the sound of that. "No one mentioned this."

"It's just walking, Zorie. Anyone can do it."

I snort. "Says the athlete who gets up every morning at the butt crack of dawn to exercise."

A tortured look clouds her eyes. Is she thinking about her Olympic failure? I think of what Mom said about Reagan struggling, and I immediately regret teasing her.

"I suppose you're right," I say quickly. "It's just walking."

Reagan glances down at my plaid skirt and surveys my bare legs. "Hiking will do you good."

I'm not sure what she means by this, but I choose to ignore it, and instead route the conversation in a different direction. "You're planning on pitching tents in the wilderness? Like, with wild animals and stuff?"

Reagan smacks her gum and wheels up to a display of hiking boots. On the nearby wall is a giant poster of pretty models dressed in flannel, grinning with perfect teeth as they brave the wilds of their photo shoot, pretending to be roughing it. "There are a zillion campgrounds in King's Forest. I'm sure we'll be sleeping in one of them," she assures me. "At least, I think so. I don't know. All I've been told is that the place we're going is a couple hours' walk from the main compound. Your average Silicon Valley wannabe hikers don't know about it. We're talking totally *off trail*, baby."

Off trail sounds awful. Unlike Reagan, I don't have boundless natural energy and calves of steel. I need to be where there's caffeine in walking distance, not fighting off bears and mosquitoes. I make a face at Reagan.

"We can be as loud as we want and no ranger will be there to shush us," Reagan says in her big, raspy voice. "The people who run the glamping compound are nice, but they know my parents. We can't really let loose around them, you know? I don't need them giving my mom a report card on our activities."

Now I'm wondering what kinds of activities she has in mind.

Reagan points to the poster of the hiking models. "In the

backcountry . . . that's where things will get good. There's a hidden waterfall inside King's Forest to die for, and it's not far from the glamping compound. I'm talking bucket list. Do you know how many people get internet famous just for having the guts to travel to cool locations and take photos?"

Avani's story about overhearing Brett talking on the phone pops into my mind. My pulse quickens. "You still haven't told me who's going."

"I thought I did," she says absently. "Summer."

One of Reagan's troop. Summer sometimes eats lunch with us in the courtyard at school.

"And?" I coax. "Who else?"

"Kendrick Taylor." Goes to the private school across town, Alameda Academy. Which is where Reagan would be going if they had a decent athletics department; they don't, and that's why a lot of rich kids who play sports go to public school with the rest of us riffraff.

"Summer started seeing Kendrick a few weeks ago," she explains before I can ask, and then mutters, "Why are hiking boots so ugly?"

"Because no one cares what you look like when you're sweating your way up a mountain?"

"Look, if you don't think you can handle a little hiking, don't come."

Her words feel like a slap to the face. And could she have said that any louder? Her booming voice carries through the store, and another customer has turned to look quizzically at us. Public shame is the best.

"I'm sorry," she says, mouth pulling tight to one side. "I didn't mean it to come out that way."

I pretend I'm not upset. Ever since the Olympic trials, Reagan has had the shitty tendency to lash out at people to make herself feel better, so whatever is bothering her probably has nothing to do with me. But now I'm wondering whether I *can* handle this trip.

"Quit scratching your arm," Reagan chastises.

I hadn't realized I was doing that. Stupid hives. I'm going to need to take medication.

Exhaling a long sigh, I calm myself and try to focus on what's important. "Who else is going?" I press. "It can't be just Summer and Kendrick."

She shrugs. "Brett Seager and some dude he's bringing."

Bingo. "Oh, really?"

"Yes, really. Don't faint on me."

"I won't," I say.

"I just know how you are about him," she says. "You get obsessed and freaky, and I don't want things getting weird."

"Why would they get weird? You think I'm going to attack him in the woods?"

She chuckles. "You never know. What happens in the woods stays in the woods."

I clear my throat and try to sound breezy. "I did hear he's single again."

Reagan makes a noncommittal noise. "I thought you were over him?"

"I am." Mostly.

"Okay, good. But seriously. This is supposed to be a drama-free trip. I don't want it to be awkward."

"It won't be awkward."

"Excellent." After a nod, she wheels the cart toward a wall of paddles. Colorful kayaks are suspended alongside them, greens and reds and purples.

"So this waterfall we're hiking to is only a couple hours away from the glamping compound?" I ask.

"That's what Brett says. He's trying to convince the guy who told him about it to lead us there. Oh, that reminds me. Bikinis. We'll be swimming. Do they sell those here?" She cranes her neck to peer around the store.

No way am I getting in a bikini in front of Brett. Forget it. My stress meter goes up, but I mentally push it back down and try to focus on what I was going to say. "I'm just wondering exactly where the waterfall is, because there are some people I know doing a meet-up on Condor Peak, and I thought about trying to find a ride out there one night."

Reagan's nose wrinkles. "Who do *you* know who'd be meeting on Condor Peak? Oh, hold on. Is this an astronomy club thing?"

"Meteor shower," I confirm. "There's a big star party."

She considers this. "That's not far from where we'll be, and you can definitely find a ride out there. The High Sierra bus line has a stop near the compound. I'll bet even Uber picks up there, if you throw enough cash at them."

That sounds promising, but I need firmer details. I don't want to scramble at the last minute. "I guess I could email the compound and ask for advice."

"Is Avani going to be there?" she asks. "At Condor Peak?"

I nod. Sometimes I think Reagan might be jealous of the astronomy connection Avani and I share. This is ridiculous, because I only spend time with Avani during our club meetings. Before summer started, I saw Reagan every day.

Trying not to scratch my itchy arm, I pretend to browse a display of wide-mouthed water bottles. An idea suddenly hits me. "You could come with me to the star party. I know Avani would like to see you."

Reagan's quiet. Just for a second. Then she shakes her head. "I can't invite people camping and then abandon them."

I chuckle, slightly embarrassed. "Of course not. Duh."

A heavy awkwardness fills the space between us, and I don't know why. Maybe she's remembering how we used to all be better friends. Maybe she actually wants to go with me to Condor Peak but needs a little push. Sometimes if I prod her, she'll let down her guard and show me the other Reagan—the girl she used to be when we were younger. Before all of the pressure of the Olympic training. Before her parents got rich.

She slaps my shoulder, startling me. Sometimes Reagan doesn't know her own strength. "Don't be such a worrywart. It's all good," she says, voice bouncing with positivity. "I think everything will work out for both us. You can spend a little time glamping with my group and then head to your astronomy thing with Avani."

"Might take some coordinating," I say, still unsure.

"Nah, it'll work out fine," she insists, bugging her eyes out at me comically and then sticking her tongue out briefly. "Just roll with it, Zorie. Let life happen."

I'm not sure if she realizes, but that's Brett's motto. He says it all the time.

Maybe it's time I take this advice.

The next morning, I'm letting life happen in the only way I know how, which is me going over my extremely detailed fifty-five-bullet-point list for the camping trip while sitting behind the clinic's front desk. We leave tomorrow, which doesn't give me a lot of time to ensure that I have everything I'll need. I'm a little worried I might forget something.

What that is, I'm not sure. I've never been camping. But I'm poking around the glamping compound's website, and it's mostly magazine-worthy photographs of the surrounding landscape. The only information I find is a glowing write-up of their chef and wine collection. That and a list of their prices, which are insane. You'd think we were staying at a four-star hotel instead of in a tent.

Avani and I talked on the phone for almost an hour last night. We firmed up plans to meet up at the star party, and she helped me research the bus lines that run out there in the Sierras—which are not frequent. Seems as though I have two chances each day to catch a bus heading toward Condor Peak. At least I now have a plan, which is all I ever wanted.

The clinic's door opens, and I look up from the front desk's computer, expecting to see my mom's next acupuncture appointment. My dad doesn't have anything booked until after lunch, so he left a few minutes ago to run errands around town. Fine by me. I've still barely spoken two words to him. I'm not sure what to say. *How's it going? Any new mistresses this week?* Or perhaps, *What's there to do in the Bahamas besides betraying your marriage vows and destroying our family?*

I shove all of that into the back of my mind and slip on my polite dealing-with-the-public face. But the smile I'm conjuring quickly fades when I see who's walking toward the desk.

The Lord of Darkness himself, Lennon Mackenzie.

My first thought: *What the hell is he doing in here?*

He never comes in the clinic. Ever, ever, ever. It's probably been a year since he's stepped foot inside this waiting room.

My second thought: *OH SWEET LORD, HE SAW ME SPYING ON HIM IN HIS BEDROOM.*

If there's a God above, please let him or her grant me the power of time travel, so that I can rewind the clock and completely avoid this nightmare of a situation. I blink slowly, hoping Lennon will disappear when I reopen my eyes, but no. He and his too-tall body—*don't you dare think about his bare chest*—are still taking up too much room on the other side of the clinic's desk.

"Hello," he says. It almost sounds like a question.

I think about lifting my chin without saying anything, like he did to me the other day, but quickly decide I'm classier than that. "Good morning," I say formally. No smile. He's not worth the effort.

His eyes drop. He balls his hand into a fist and slowly, gently taps it on top of the desk a couple of times while sucking in a long breath between gritted teeth . . . as though he doesn't know what to say. Or he does, but he *really* doesn't want to say it.

"So . . . ," he finally says.

"So," I agree. Is he avoiding my eyes? It feels as if he might throw dynamite over the desk and race out the door. Now I understand why people say you can cut tension with a knife.

Is he not going to say anything else?

Is he here to confront me?

What do I do?

"I wasn't spying on you," I blurt out defensively. "I was just making adjustments to my telescope. It was repaired. Recently. Recently repaired. I was checking it."

Oh, *now* he's looking at me. Something akin to horror is dawning over his face. Or shock. Or he thinks I'm an idiot. *Why can't I read him?* And why is he not saying anything?

"I didn't even see much," I insist.

He nods slowly.

"Anything, really," I amend. "I was testing my telescope."

"You mentioned that," he says, squinting at me through tight eyes.

"Sorry. I mean, I don't have anything to be sorry about, because I didn't do anything."

"Right."

"It was an accident."

"Got it."

My eyes flick to his arms. He's wearing short sleeves, so now I'm staring at muscle. *Look away! Look away!* Too late. He caught me. Again.

WHAT IS WRONG WITH ME?

"So anyway," he says, setting down a pile of envelopes on the desk, as if nothing is amiss. "I was told to come here and drop off your mail. It got delivered to our shop this morning."

Oh.

I can barely control the low groan of misery that's burring from the back of my throat. If I'd just kept my mouth shut . . .

"Uh, thanks." I shift the letters toward me with one finger and try to recover what little of my pride is left. "These seemed to be sealed, so I guess you guys didn't open them by mistake this time."

He tugs his ear. Chipped black fingernail polish glints under the light. "She really didn't mean to open it. I was there when it happened."

Crap on toast. *He knows.* Of course he does. It's not as if I didn't wonder or consider that possibility. But this doesn't stop embarrassment from washing over me now. I busy myself neatly stacking the letters and avoiding his judgmental eyes.

"Hey," he says in an unexpectedly gentle voice.

I look up and he has a strange expression on his face. I can't tell if it's pity or tenderness, or maybe something else entirely. But it *feels* like he knows something I don't know, and that only increases my panic-fueled pulse.

The door to the clinic swings open. My dad rushes inside. "Forgot my . . ." He spots Lennon and halts. His brows narrow to a dark point. "What the hell are you doing in here?"

Lennon raises both hands in surrender, but the look on his face is baldly defiant. "Just delivering mail, man."

"I'm not your 'man,'" my dad says, voice thick with displeasure.

"Thank God for small favors."

"Show some respect."

"I'll show you mine when you show me yours," Lennon quips, and then adds, "Sir." But he sounds anything but polite.

I'm not sure what to do. Why did Lennon come over here in the first place? He knows how my dad is. To stop things from escalating, I pipe up and say, "Lennon was bringing over mis-delivered mail."

It's as if my dad doesn't even hear me. He just points to the floor and says, "You aren't supposed to step foot on my property."

Lennon shrugs. "*Your* property? Last I checked, you rent this place like the rest of us."

"Don't be a smart-ass."

"Better a smart-ass than a dumb-ass."

Oh, that was a bad thing to say. My dad's expression goes from angry to furious. "Get out."

Lennon gives him a dark smile. "On my way."

"Damn right, you are," my dad mumbles.

Footsteps pound in the hallway behind the desk, and my mom emerges, breathless, head swiveling in every direction as she surveys the scene. "What is going on?" she whispers loudly. "I've got a client on the table!"

"Mrs. Everhart." Lennon nods politely. "Your husband was just throwing me out."

"Dan!" my mom chastises.

My dad ignores her. "Don't come back," he tells Lennon.

"See you, Zorie," Lennon tells me as he pushes the front door open.

"You talk to my daughter again, I'll call the cops," my dad calls out.

Oh, for the love of Pete.

Lennon turns in the doorway and stares at my dad for several long seconds before shaking his head. "Always a pleasure, Mr. Everhart. You're a beacon of civility and chivalry. An absolute *gem*."

Now my dad is livid, and for a second, I'm worried he might punch Lennon. Worse, I'm concerned that Lennon will bring up the Bahamas photo book.

But Lennon's gaze flicks to my mom's, then mine. Without another word, he leaves. The door shuts behind him, and I watch his dark form disappear down the sidewalk.

"Dan," my mother says again, this time in quiet exasperation. In defeat.

Silence fills the waiting room. My father reins in his anger, and just like that, all of his tumultuous energy dissipates into a slant of sunlight that beams through the front windows. He turns to me and calmly says, "Why was he in here? I thought you weren't speaking."

I wave the envelopes Lennon brought. "We aren't. He was telling the truth."

Does he understand how humiliated I am by what just happened? Whatever issues Lennon and I have are ours alone, and I'm sick of being stuck in the middle of my dad's squabbles. All of it: his beef with the Mackenzies, and what he's done to my mom. If he only knew what I was hiding in my bedroom desk . . .

Maybe I should show him the photo book privately and see what he says.

Would he try to talk his way out of it? Or would he come clean? I don't think I have the guts to find out.

Dad stares at me, seemingly expressionless, but I can tell that gears are turning inside his head. Does he have some inkling about what I'm thinking? I relax my features to match his.

After a moment, he sniffles softly and jingles the car keys in his hand. "If that boy bothers you again, Zorie, please tell me. Immediately."

He can hold his breath, but I don't think I'll be confiding anything to him any time soon.

Maybe ever.

5

That was all my dad and I said to each other before he apologized to Mom for making a scene at work. Then he made a pit stop in his office and jogged out the door again. Like nothing had happened. A couple hours later, he's still gone, phoning to tell us to eat lunch without him. He claims he's playing racquetball with a client. Only, I'm not sure I believe that's what he's really doing.

I may not believe *anything* he says anymore.

Mom closed the clinic for lunch, and after nibbling on farm-to-table veggie tacos at her favorite vegetarian restaurant, we are strolling back home through the main Mission Street shopping district.

Apart from food and coffee, the sycamore-lined promenade has nothing anyone really needs, but everything you want. Specialty shops selling Swedish toothbrushes, craft sake, exotic hand puppets, and toys made from recycled wood are tucked between a handful of national chain stores. And all along the sidewalks in front of these shops, moms and tattooed street punks share benches as they listen to a student jazz ensemble that plays for donations outside the Jitterbug coffee shop.

"You barely said anything in the restaurant," Mom points out, carting the leftovers from our meal in a white plastic bag. "I know it was busy and loud in there, but you usually get in at least *one* joke about vegetarians."

It's easy to do. Tacos should have meat. That place goes against nature. Half of the people who eat there are in need of a good iron supplement.

"Just thinking about the trip," I lie.

"The trip . . . or your dad making an idiot of himself in front of Lennon?"

"Maybe both," I admit, slanting my eyes toward hers. "Diamond Dan went a little nuts."

"Diamond Dan can get carried away by his emotions sometimes." She sighs deeply, tugging on the diagonal seam of her tunic scrub top. "I've never agreed with how he's treated Lennon. If the Mackenzies ever treated you that way—"

"But they don't."

She nods. "I know. And it's not much of an excuse, but your father is really stressed out right now about the business. He's lost so many massage clients. We're bleeding fairly profusely now, and I'm not sure how to stanch the wound until the business bounces back."

I consider this for a moment. "You could call Grandpa Sam. He'd loan you money."

Grandpa Sam is my mom's dad. He's the nicest guy in the world. Her parents came to the US when she was a baby, and they own a shipping company, Moon Imports and Exports—Moon is their Korean family name—that ships machinery from South Korea. The Moons aren't wealthy, but they're doing all right. Grandpa Sam's the one who bought me Nancy Grace Roman and all my other astronomy gear. I text him my best constellation photos every month, and he texts me back in nothing but repeated, enthusiastic emojis. He used to send only smiley faces, but lately he's been branching out to thumbs-up signs and stars.

"No, we're not asking my parents for any more money," Mom says firmly. "They've already done enough."

We walk in silence for a few steps, and then I think about something she said. "Why aren't you losing acupuncture clients?"

"Hmm?"

"If the Mackenzies' sex shop is pushing away Dad's massage clients, then why are most of your clients still around?"

She shrugs. "Who knows? Maybe because there are more massage therapists in Melita Hills than acupuncturists. I'm a rare commodity."

"Maybe Dad should take up acupuncture too."

"Believe me, your father and I have considered a dozen options. We've analyzed the business to pieces over the last few months."

When we get to the end of the block, a woman dripping with beaded jewelry wants to tell us about the benefits of psychoneuroimmunology while a man in a shabby suit across the sidewalk tries to hand us a pamphlet about salvation. I wave both of them away. "Can I ask you a question?" I say after we cross the street. "Are you happy with Dad?"

Mom's head turns toward me. "Why would you ask that?"

"I don't know." But now I wish that I hadn't.

"Of course I am," she assures me.

I don't know how to feel about this. How can she be happy while my dad is gallivanting around the globe with other women? Shouldn't she realize that something is wrong? I think I'd know something was awry if my partner was cheating on me. At least, I'd hope so. My only personal experience with relationships is Andre Smith. I started seeing him after homecoming, but right before our second date, his mom got a job in Chicago, and they moved. Our third date was at his farewell party, and because we were never going to see each other again, we got a little . . . carried away with the goodbyes. Bad choices were made. Apart from my taking three pregnancy tests after he left—just to be triple certain—and then confessing what we did to my mom for health advice to be *quadruple* certain, the whole experience was a letdown. For me, anyway. Andre emailed for weeks, trying to keep things going, until I was left with no choice but to flag his email address as spam.

This is what happens when I don't stick to a plan. Complete and utter disaster. Never again.

Mom runs a hand over the top of my head. "Money problems are a strain on any couple. But we'll get through it. Bad times don't last. You just have to hang on until they pass."

But she doesn't know how bad they really are. And the thing that's bothering me, other than Dad's unhinged fit of anger this morning, is the worry that I'm not the only one keeping secrets about Dad's extracurricular activities. The Mackenzies know. Lennon knows. How long before that knowledge leaks and my mom finds out?

I can't let that happen.

"Are those hives?" my mom asks, stopping to look at my arm. "Jesus, Zorie. You're covered in them. Have you had shrimp?"

"No." Sometimes shellfish causes them, but mostly it's stress and the occasional random allergen. It's unpredictable. My body is a mystery.

She frowns at me, worry tightening her face. "You have to get back on daily antihistamines. And we need to get some more of that homeopathic cream from Angela's shop."

The cream gives me a headache, but I don't say this. Mom is telling me that we can stop and pick it up on our way back if we hurry, but something across the street catches my attention. Lennon's big, black satanic hearse is parked at the curb. We're half a block or so away from his place of employment, so he must be working. And thinking about his fight with my dad this morning makes me realize something: I will be gone for a week, while Lennon will be here. All it would take is one more standoff with my dad and Lennon might say something about the photo book.

I need to make him promise that he'll keep his mouth shut.

"Look, you don't need to be late for your next appointment," I tell Mom. "I can walk down to Angela's and pick up the hive cream."

She hesitates before digging inside her scrubs pocket and handing me some money. "All right. Ask her if she'll give it to you for a free cupping session in exchange. Sometimes she'll barter."

"Honor among healers?"

"Something like that. Take an antihistamine when you get home, and let me check on you later, okay?"

"Will do."

"I mean it. Don't make me have to take you to Sacred Heart."

"Not *those* monsters," I say dramatically. "Conventional medicine is for chumps."

She pokes a tickling finger into my side, making me laugh. "Watch your hives, young lady."

I assure her that I will.

After we part ways, I backtrack down the sidewalk to cross the street, passing Lennon's car. Then I head toward the business on the corner.

Reptile Isle is one of the oldest reptile shops in California. The brick shop front is covered in an enormous rainforest mural, complete with lizards and turtles and snakes, oh my. I walk past giant pieces of driftwood and tropical plants flanking its recessed entrance and push open the door.

Inside, my eyes adjust to diffuse light as the thick, musky scent of substrate and snake fills my nostrils. Hundreds of tanks and terrariums line the walls, their UV lights and heat lamps creating a warm atmosphere. Most of the reptiles here are for sale, but the people who own the shop also have a breeding program in the back, and they do a lot of educational outreach.

A large checkout counter sits near the entrance, but Lennon's not running the register, so I glance around the expansive shop and try to spot him. Under wooden beams that crisscross a large, open ceiling, I wind around aisles stacked with plastic caves, plant replicas, and endless reptilian supplies: tank thermostats, feeding dishes, lizard hammocks. In the center of the store, inside a massive habitat cage, the skeleton of an old tree stands, its bare branches decked with tiny wooden platforms. Tropical plants hang from the cage's ceiling and flowering vines creep up its screened walls.

This is where I spot Lennon.

He's standing inside the cage with a giant green iguana draped around his shoulders.

"Her name is Maria," Lennon is telling a child standing on the outside of the cage with her nose pressed to the screen. "She's from Costa Rica."

"How old is she?" the girl asks.

"She's five years old," Lennon says.

"That's how old you are," the mother reminds her.

The girl seems suitably impressed. "This is where she lives?"

"She has the entire cage to herself," Lennon confirms. "She's almost four feet long, so she needs a lot of space to roam around. Want to see her tail?"

He ducks low on the other side of the screen to give her a peek.

Eyes wide, the little girl is both fascinated and wary. "Will she bite?"

"If she's scared," Lennon says, coaxing the big lizard from his shoulders to a platform above, where it crawls beneath a potted tropical plant. "She only likes to be handled by a few special friends. It takes her a long time to trust people enough to let them get close to her. But she doesn't mind if you admire her from out there."

"Can I have her for a pet?"

Lennon pretends to think about this. "She needs a lot of space, and we'd be sad if we couldn't see her every day. If you like lizards, a better pet would a green anole or a leopard gecko. They are pretty easy to take care of, if your mom is willing to buy live insects. . . ." He glances at the mother, who shakes her head firmly. Lennon quickly says, "*Or*, you could just come here to visit Maria."

The girl considers this thoughtfully while the mother gives Lennon an enthusiastic thumbs-up. His face relaxes into a warm smile. I haven't seen him smile like that in a long time. It's sweet and boyish. Unexpectedly, a hollow ache wells up inside my chest.

Stop being ridiculous, I tell myself.

I wrestle unwanted emotions down, packing them away as the mother thanks him and leads her daughter toward the turtle area of the store. When Lennon is alone, I approach the cage with trepidation.

"Hey," I say.

He swings around and spots me. His head jerks back in surprise, and he glances around, as if hidden cameras might appear, more wary than the little girl was about the possibility of an iguana bite. "What's up?"

"I was on my way back from lunch and saw your car," I say, as if this is a totally normal thing, me stopping by. As though I haven't refused to walk on this side of the street for months to avoid accidentally bumping into him.

He shifts into a defensive stance, arms crossing chest. "Sure you aren't here to serve me with an arrest warrant for trespassing?"

I wince inwardly. "My dad is—"

"A dick?"

"Anxious."

Lennon snorts. "So *that's* what we're calling it."

"Look, you'd be stressed too, if the business you built was going to hell because all your clients were scurrying away faster than rats on a sinking ship."

He makes a low, thoughtful noise, and the sound rumbles through the screen, scattering my thoughts and doing strange, unwanted things to the inside of my chest. It's the feeling you get when a large truck trundles down the road. You can't see it, but you can feel it, and that makes you leery for no logical reason.

"That's wrong, actually," he points out. "The original phrase was, 'When a building is about to fall down, all the mice desert it.'"

"Yeah? Well, you better *actually* hope that doesn't happen, seeing how we're all stuck in the same building," I say, suddenly irritated with his know-it-all factoids. "If we fall down, the rubble might bury your shop. And then where would all the neighborhood perverts buy their butt plugs?"

"Gee, I don't know." He braces his hands on the wooden frame of the habitat and leans down until his face is at my level, pressing his forehead against the screen between us. A clean, sunny scent wafts from his clothes, one that's painfully familiar. The scent of Lennon. "Maybe they'll go to the same store where your dad buys the sticks that are stuck up his ass. I think it's next to Adulterers Are Us."

Fury bubble ups. "You . . . ," I start, and then realize how loud I'm being. I lean closer to the screen and lower my voice. "You cannot tell anyone about that photo book."

"I think anyone with a working bullshit meter already knows he's a scumbag."

"My mom doesn't!" I shout-whisper at his stupid face.

Sharp eyes lock with mine. He makes a small noise. "You didn't give her the package."

"Because it will break up their marriage," I whisper. "I can't do that to my mom. It would kill her."

Lennon doesn't respond. Just studies my eyes.

"You cannot say anything to my mom," I plead. "And until I figure out what to do, you need to tell your moms to keep quiet about it too."

"I can't control what they say to your mom. If you recall, they were once all friends. Come to think of it, so were the two of us, before you decided moving up the social ladder was more important."

"What?" That's not how things went down. *He* ditched me.

"Frankly, I'm surprised you'd risk being seen in public talking to me," he says. "Every second you're near me, your hit points drop. Better watch it, or your life meter's going to drop to zero."

"I don't even know what that means."

"That's because you've been hanging around with Reagan effing Reid for too long."

"Says the boy who sits home alone with a bunch of snakes."

"Hey, you would know, spymaster general."

I press my forehead again the screen. "I already told you, that was a mistake."

His dark eyes are centimeters from mine. "Was it?"

"Huge."

"If you say so."

"Enormous."

"I'm flattered."

"I . . ." *Wait. What are we talking about?*

His smile is slow and cocky.

I pull back from the screen. My ears suddenly feel like someone's holding a blowtorch up to my head. Tugging the curling ends of my bob, I try to cover the telltale redness, wishing it away before the blush spreads down my neck.

"Screw this," I say. "I was going to apologize for my dad's behavior, but now I might be glad he bit your head off. I hope you have to get a rabies shot."

"Am I the bat or Ozzy? Because if your dad was doing the biting, technically he'd have to get the rabies shot."

"I hate you so much."

"You know," he says after huffing out a single, sarcastic chuckle, "I genuinely felt bad for you. I really did, for all of two seconds. Guess I was an idiot, because I can see now that nothing's changed. You're still the same cold-as-ice girl. You're just like him. You know that, right? More concerned with appearances than anything real. Maybe lying runs in your blood."

Chaotic emotions bubble up. Embarrassment. Pain. And something else I can't identify. Anger. That must be what it is, because without warning, my eyes sting with unshed tears.

Don't you dare cry in front of him, I tell myself.

"Zorie," he says, voice low and rough. "I . . ."

He doesn't finish, and it doesn't matter. I don't care what Lennon Mackenzie thinks. Not now, and not ever.

"I thought I could come in here and talk reasonably with you," I say, using the calmest, most professional voice I can muster as I step farther away from the cage. "But I guess I was wrong. All I ask is that if you and your parents have any respect for my mother—"

"Zorie—"

I raise my voice to talk over him. "—that you'll stay out of her business and let me handle it. If anyone's going to destroy her life, it should be me, not some stranger who doesn't care about her."

And with that, I walk out of the store.

Tomorrow can't come soon enough.

6

"You have everything?" Mom asks, testing the weight of my backpack. It's almost ten in the morning, and Reagan's supposed to
pick me up in a few minutes. I stopped by the clinic to tell my
parents goodbye. "Good lord, this is heavy."

"That's my portable telescope and camera." Who knew ten
pounds could be so heavy? It takes up a lot of space in the pack,
so I've got one of the tents Reagan bought stuffed in the bottom,
a compressed sleeping bag, clothes neatly rolled to save space, a
couple of energy bars, peanut butter cups, and some chocolate-
covered espresso beans—you know, all the major food groups.

I also *may* have brought a grid-lined journal. Just a small one.
And a few gel pens.

"You have the emergency cash I gave you?"

I pat the pocket of my purple plaid shorts. They match my
purple Converse, which match my purple eyeglass frames. Did
I mention the glittery purple nail polish? I'm killing it. Someone

should pay me to look this sharp. One modeling contract, pronto.

"Portable cell phone charger?"

"In my pack," I lie. It's an older model that weighs a ton, and in the battle of heavy versus heavy, my telescope and camera won. Besides, they'll have electricity at the glamping compound. I can just plug my phone in.

Mom inspects my arms. "Hive cream?"

"Yes, I've got the stinky homeopathic cream. Where's Dad? I need to leave soon."

"Dan!" she calls out to the back rooms, cupping her hands around her mouth. Then she turns back to me. "He's rushing to head out to the bank. I tried to get an increase on the clinic's credit card, and they say our credit score is too low because we're over-extended. Which is crazy, because that's our only credit account, and I paid off your father's car loan last year. There must be some mistake. He'll get it sorted out. Oh, there you are," she says as he jogs into the reception area, keys in hand.

And toward the front door.

"I'll be back in a jiff," he says, keys in hand.

"Dan, Zorie's leaving for her camping trip," Mom says, sounding as exasperated as I feel.

He turns around and blinks at me, and apparently is just now noticing my backpack. "Of course," he says, smoothly covering up his faux pas with a charming smile. "Excited to spend time with the Reid daughter?"

"Reagan," I say.

"Reagan," he repeats. More smiling. He turns to my mom and says, "Everything checked out at the campsite, right? The girls will be safe there?"

"They have security and everything," Mom says. "I told you, remember? Mrs. Reid talked to the owner, and they're going to pay special attention to their group."

"Right, right," Dad murmurs, nodding enthusiastically. Then he smiles at me, starts to extend his arms as if he might hug me—which is weird, because we don't normally do that anymore—and then changes his mind and pats me on the head. "Have a great time, kiddo. Stay in touch with Joy and take your pepper spray in case there are any boys with roaming hands."

There will be boys, and I certainly *hope* there will be roaming hands. But no way am I telling him that, so I just laugh, and it sounds as hollow as his smile looks.

He nods stiffly, and it's awkward. "Gotta get to the bank. See you when you get back," he says, and before I can answer, he's jogging out the front door.

When he's gone, I vent at Mom. "Hello! I'm leaving for an entire week. Does he realize this?"

She holds up a hand in shared exasperation. "He knows. I told him I could take care of the bank on my lunch break, but he insisted it had to be now. He's just—"

"Stressed," I say, resigned. "Yeah."

And what's up with this credit thing at the bank? That sounds fishy. Or maybe I'm just suspicious of everything my dad touches.

"Hey, forget him. I'm right here," she says, holding my face in her hands. "And I'm going to miss you like crazy. I will also worry every day, so please call or text to check in when you can."

"Spotty cell service," I remind her. We read warnings about it on the glamping compound's website.

She nods. "If I don't hear from you, I won't alert state troopers. Not unless you aren't standing here in front of me at noon next Friday. In one piece, I might add."

"Don't know about one piece, but I'll be here. Reagan's got to be back for some presemester orientation thing for her cross-country team," I remind her. "Speaking of, I'd better get outside. Need to stay on schedule."

She grasps my arm to peer at my watch and winces at the time. "Crap. I need to get the room ready for my first appointment."

Good, because I really want to get out there alone before Joy decides to walk me outside and greet Reagan. Like my father, she's still under the illusion that this is a girls-only trip, and I'd like to keep it that way.

"I changed my mind. Don't go." She hugs me extra hard and then clings dramatically.

"Mom," I say, laughing. "You're unbalancing my life force."

"Have I told you how much I love you?"

"Not today. But you *did* buy me turkey jerky, and if that's not a token of affection, I don't know what is."

"I love you, sweet thing."

"Love you back," I tell her.

When she finally lets me go, I lift my heavy backpack onto one arm and salute her goodbye.

"Don't forget to feed Andromeda at dinner," I remind her. That's usually my job; Mom feeds her in the morning.

"I won't," she assures me as I'm opening the door. "You don't pee on your shoes and try not to provoke any bears."

"If I see a bear, I'll pass out from fear, so he'll just think I'm dead."

"That seems reasonable. And, Zorie?"

"Yes?"

"Don't be cautious, be careful. Have a good time, okay?"

I give her a confident nod and head outside.

It's a perfect summer day. Not too hot, not too cool. Pretty blue sky. I'm feeling a weird mix of anxiety and anticipation as I lug my backpack toward a striped no-parking space in front of the curb.

No sign of Reagan yet, so I decide to do one last practice run on my backpack. I tried it on when it was empty, but now that it's full, I'm forced to squat in order to lift it and am struggling to get it on both shoulders. When I finally manage it, I wobble clumsily and nearly topple over backward. How am I supposed to hike a dirt trail with this thing? Feels like an overweight sloth is clinging to my neck. Maybe if I secure the strap that buckles around my waist . . .

"You've got it packed wrong," someone calls out.

I turn around slowly, in case I actually *do* fall over—which is a real possibility, not kidding—and it takes me exactly one second to spot the voice's owner: black Converse high-tops, black jeans with artfully ripped holes in both knees, and a T-shirt with a heart inside an X-ray skeletal chest.

Lennon is sitting on the hood of his hearse, which is parked a few yards away in one of the public spaces in the middle of our cul-de-sac. "You're supposed to pack the heavy stuff in the center, near your back. Let your hips carry the weight, not your shoulders. When it's packed right, you won't be the Leaning Tower of Pisa."

"I'm not . . ." I shift my feet and lean forward slightly, barely preventing a bodily avalanche. *Dammit.*

Lennon's smile is slow and annoying. He's wearing jet-black sunglasses, so I can't see his eyes. Double annoying. Why is he even talking to me? Didn't I tell him I hated him yesterday?

"What do you have in there?" he asks. "Gold bricks?"

"My telescope."

"You fit Nancy Grace Roman inside that pack?"

I'm shocked he remembers. "No, the portable one."

"Ah. Well, it's packed wrong."

"And I should trust you because you're *such* an expert on back-packing," I say irritably.

He leans back on both hands and lifts his face to the sun. "Actually, I kind of am."

"Since when?"

"Since forever. I backpacked with my moms in Europe when I was thirteen—"

Oh, yeah. I forgot about that. "But that was in hostels."

"And campgrounds."

Right.

"And three times this year. Three? Wait, maybe four," he says, more to himself than me. He shrugs a shoulder lightly. "One of them doesn't count, but anyway."

"You went to Europe this year?" I say, surprised.

"No, I backpacked here in California. My parents gave me a national park pass for Christmas and took me camping in Death Valley over spring break. I even took a wilderness survival course."

Does not compute. This isn't Lennon at all. The boy I knew didn't spend time outdoors. I mean, sure, we technically spent most of our time together outside on all those walks, but that was here in the city. Before I can make sense of this new development in Lennon, Man of Mystery, he speaks up again.

"I can help you repack if you want," he says, still looking up at the sky, where misty trails of morning fog are drifting back out to the Bay, silver streaks against bright blue.

Lennon Mackenzie with his hands on my private stuff? *I don't think so, buddy.*

"No, thanks." I let the pack's straps slide down my arms until it's back on the ground. And then, in an attempt to shut him up, I add, "My ride should be here any second."

"Yeah, I just got a text."

Huh? Wait just one stinking second.

Backpack advice. Camping in Death Valley. Spotted hanging out with Brett . . .

Oh, no. Oh *no, no, no.*

This is not Brett's new bromance. This is not the "guy" who's leading us to a secret off-trail waterfall in the Sierras. It can't be! Reagan knows I avoid him. She doesn't know *why*, exactly, but she should have told me. Why didn't she tell me? There must be some mistake.

Panic fires through my limbs as a dark blue SUV whips into the parking lot. Lennon casually jumps from the hood of his car, landing lightly on his feet. He bends to pick up something out of sight, near the front wheel. When he stands back up, he's pulling a red backpack onto one shoulder. The top outer pocket is covered with vintage punk-rock buttons and retro national parks patches. A foam bedroll is neatly secured to its bottom.

Holy hell.

Blaring electronic dance music, the blue SUV skids as it brakes between us, and then Reagan's light brown head pops up from the driver's door. "Glamping time, bitches!" she shouts merrily over the stereo. "Packs go up top in the cargo container. Let's hustle."

My mind can't form a coherent thought. I know I'm staring stupidly as Brett lurches out of the SUV to clap Lennon soundly on the shoulder. "Lennon, my boy," he says, voice full of joy. "That shirt is sick! I love it. Come on, I'll help you get the cargo box open. The latch is screwed up." Brett notices me for the first time.

My stomach flips over.

You know how people say they are blinded by love? That's what happens to me when I see Brett. He looks like a celebrity, all tanned legs and sandy brown curls, a face too perfect for a mortal high school boy. And don't get me started on his teeth. They are insanely perfect. I never knew teeth could be so attractive.

He flashes me those million-dollar teeth in a dazzling grin. "Zorie. Still rocking that sexy scientist vibe," he says, pointing finger guns at my glasses while making a zinging noise. Then he waves me closer for a hug. "Bring it on in, girl. Haven't seen you in forever."

Oh, wow. I'm overwhelmed by the spicy scent of aftershave. He smells a little like my dad, which is a weird thing to think. *Shut up, brain!* This is all Lennon's fault for surprising me. His presence is throwing me off my game. And now Brett lets me go, so I wasted the entire two-second hug with the boy of my dreams thinking about (A) my dad and (B) the boy of my nightmares. Terrific.

"What you been up to this summer?" Brett asks lightly.

Say something. Do not blow this. "You know, working."

Working? That's the best I could come up with? I work twice a week at the clinic for a few hours, so why am I making it sound like I'm slaving over a paycheck at a real job? I want a do-over, but Brett's attention has shifted to the task of opening the big plastic cargo carrier attached to the SUV's roof rack. Meanwhile, Lennon is looking back at me—nay, full-on staring—and I can't tell what he's thinking because of those stupid sunglasses, but it *feels* judgmental.

Is this really happening? Lennon is coming with us?

Brett pops open the cargo carrier and helps Lennon lift his pack inside, nestling it in among several others. Lennon gestures silently with one hand and a tilt of his head, offering to help me lift my pack. I try to do it myself, and end up having to let Lennon and Brett boost it up. Which is humiliating.

"Hey," I say in greeting to Kendrick Taylor, closing the door as I get settled in my seat.

Kendrick's family owns a successful winery that's lauded in the press for being one of the best vineyards in Sonoma County. Since he goes to private school in Melita, I've only met him once, when Reagan hauled me to a party.

"Zorie, right?" he says, squinting one eye closed. In a chambray button-down and khaki shorts that contrast pleasantly with his dark brown skin, he's better-looking than I remembered, and has a friendly, confident demeanor.

A tall girl with long, sun-streaked hair leans around the front passenger seat. Summer Valentino. If you crave gossip about anyone in school, she knows it. And even though her grades were so bad that technically she should have had to repeat eleventh grade, she's on the yearbook committee *and* the online school newspaper— which apparently saved her.

"Zorie's into astrology," Summer tells Kendrick.

"Astronomy," I correct.

"D'oh!" she says, smiling. "I always get those mixed up. Which one is the horoscopes?"

"*Astrology*," Kendrick enunciates, pretending to give her a slap on the head, which she ducks with a silly grin.

Brett speaks up from behind me and introduces Kendrick to Lennon.

"This is my boy," Brett tells Kendrick, roughly shaking Lennon's shoulder. "This kid is *wild*. Right, John Lennon?"

Lennon's sitting behind Kendrick, so I can see him better than Brett. "If you say so," Lennon deadpans.

"Is that really your name?" Kendrick asks.

"Minus the John," Lennon says. "But Brett never lets that stop him."

If I didn't know better, I might wonder if this is a jab. But Brett just laughs as if it's the funniest joke in the world.

Um, okay. What is going on here?

"Lennon's father is Adam Ahmed from Orphans of the State," Summer supplies. "They opened for Green Day a million years ago. His dad was that Egyptian-American drummer dude."

"Guitarist," Lennon corrects quietly, but I don't think anyone hears him except me.

"Didn't one of your moms crash at Billie Joe Armstrong's house for a few weeks?" Reagan asks, programming a route into the SUV's navigation system. "Doesn't she know his wife, or something?"

Before he can answer, Summer pipes in with: "Is it true that your moms were, like, together with your dad all at the same time?" She pauses, and says in a lower voice, "I mean, the three of them?"

"I got your meaning," Lennon says.

"That's just what I heard around school," Summer tells him apologetically. But not so apologetic that she's shutting the question down.

"I've heard that around school myself," Lennon says.

"Well?" Summer prompts.

"My parents did a lot of things," Lennon says enigmatically.

The intrigue inside the car is high. Scandal! Gasp! Thing is, Sunny and Mac are one of the most in-love, devoted couples I've ever known. Whatever they've done or haven't done is none of anyone's business. I start to say this, then wonder why the hell I should defend Lennon if he's not even bothering to defend himself. I know it used to bother him, all the rumors people at school spread behind his back. Everyone loves to discuss his family life. Even my dad has accused Sunny and Mac of being heathens.

Maybe Lennon doesn't care anymore. Maybe he's just embracing it.

"One hundred percent rock-and-roll," Brett says. "Kerouac would have *so* approved of that. Did you know he and his best friend Neal Cassady both slept with Carolyn Cassady, Neal's wife? Wild, huh? I bet you have crazy stories growing up in a punk-rock household."

"So crazy," Lennon says flatly.

Brett claps his hands together and tells us all, "This dude right here has legendary blood in his veins. San Francisco punks were the Beat Poets of the eighties and nineties."

Huh. Now I'm connecting the dots. Brett thinks Lennon has pedigree. That's why he's decided Lennon is a "wild man."

Lennon looks wild, all right. About as wild as a depressed corpse.

"Okay, we're all here and everyone's acquainted," Reagan says. "Are we ready to roll?"

"We're gonna have some crazy-ass fun this week," Brett says, throwing his arm over Lennon's shoulder so that he can snap a quick selfie. Lennon's expression remains dour while Brett sticks out his tongue toward the screen. "Right?"

Lennon leans back in his seat and echoes his previous words. "If you say so."

"Right, Reagan?" Brett calls out to the front.

"Let's do this," she confirms, shifting the SUV into drive. "Sierras, here we come."

As Reagan drives down Mission Street, she informs us that the drive to the glamping compound is more than four hours. And for the first few minutes, the car is loud and chaotic, everyone trying to talk at once. Reagan is telling Kendrick about the camp's amenities while Summer adds her own commentary about a glamping site in Colorado that her parents visited for their anniversary. Brett is trying to tell Reagan about nearby places mentioned in Jack Kerouac's *On the Road*. And surprisingly, Reagan seems interested. This is news to me, because she usually tunes out whenever Brett goes all rhapsodic about the Beat Poets at school. He's always trying to get people to drive across the Bay Bridge into San Francisco for afternoon excursions to Beat-friendly City Lights Bookstore—"It's a historic landmark." And Reagan is always complaining that poetry is boring.

And throughout all of this, Lennon stays quiet.

Maybe it will be easy to ignore him.

I glance around the car, and it really hits me that, minus Lennon, I'm going on a weeklong trip with some of the most popular people at school. Mom was right. I needed to do this to feel less like an outsider. I'm going to have fun. Everything's going to be fine.

Lennon's unwanted presence can't ruin this.

And I am *definitely* not scratching my arm. If anything was going to make my hives worse, it would be Lennon. So I can't let him. Deep breaths. I'm okay. I'm totally okay.

After we head out of the East Bay, conversation becomes as monotonous as the valley scenery. Outside my window, I spy flat farmland, fruit trees, wide blue skies, and the occasional small town. Long stretches of highway are punctuated with truck stops and roadside fruit stands, and people turn to their phones for entertainment. A little over halfway through the trip, Kendrick points out Bullion's Bluff, a tiny historical mining town just off the highway. "They've got a fairly big winery," he says. "My parents brought me once. The downtown is totally nineteenth-century Gold Rush era. I'm talking Old West saloon and general store. Gold Rush museum. The works. It's schlocky, but it's fun."

Since Summer complains that she needs to use a public restroom after drinking an enormous soda, Reagan decides to pull off the highway. After passing a run-down gas station, we spot the downtown area easily enough. Kendrick was right: It looks like a set from an old Western movie. A sign even brags that one was filmed here in the 1980s.

The Gold Rush museum looks pretty shabby and has an entrance fee. We agree to forgo that and head to the Bullion General Store instead, parking alongside a line of travel trailers in front of a wooden hitching post—no horses, alas—and a water trough filled with planted cacti.

Inside, the spacious store is bustling with tourists, jammed from floor to ceiling with goods for sale—everything from old-fashioned candy and brown bottles of sarsaparilla, to gold-nugget jewelry and a mining cart filled with polished stones. It also smells like peanut butter fudge, which makes me hungry. Peanut butter is my weakness.

The candy counter has a line, so while Summer looks for a restroom with Reagan, and the boys are magnetically drawn to a display of mining pickaxes—complete with a cardboard standee of a cartoon old-timey prospector—I meander around the aisles until I'm in an outdoor gear section. A sign advertising "bear vaults" catches my attention. Or maybe it's the gigantic stuffed bear that's standing on two legs with its arms raised. A sign hanging around its neck reads KINGSLY THE BEAR.

"Gross," I whisper, seeing that part of its dusty fur is ripped. It also smells funky. But honestly, I'd take all the motley smells in this place 100 percent over the SUV, where Brett's aftershave was starting to give me a headache.

"You have one, right?" a deep voice says.

Lennon steps next to me like a ghost from the shadows.

"Jesus, sneak up on people much?" I complain under my breath. "Have one what?"

He points to the canisters lining a wooden cubby on the wall. A pleasant scent wafts from his clothes. "Bear vault."

"Not planning on capturing any bears, so no."

"They're for storing food, foolish human."

I give him a sidelong glance. He's holding a square of candy inside wax paper. When he takes a bite, I realize why he smells so nice. Peanut butter fudge.

"So good," he mumbles. He knows I'm a PB addict. At least, he used to know. Maybe he forgot and is completely oblivious that me watching him eat this is total food porn.

I ignore his little moan of ecstasy. "I still don't know what you're talking about."

Juggling his fudge, he grabs a black barrel-shaped canister off the shelf and flips open a hinged lid. "Bear vault, to store your food. Bears can smell food from a couple miles away. Not even kidding. They will tear down cabin doors and break car windows to get their grub on. You have to keep everything inside one of these babies. Food. Toiletries. Anything with a strong scent, like Brett's cologne."

I give Lennon a dirty look. Brett's wearing aftershave, not cologne. At least, I think. Who wears cologne? I mean, other than my cranky grandpa John. That's my dad's homophobic and slightly racist father, who thinks everyone should "speak English." My grandpa Sam doesn't speak English, but he sure as hell doesn't wear cologne.

"I'm sure the glamping compound knows how to keep bears out of food," I tell Lennon.

"They do, which is why no food is allowed in the tents, unless it's in a bear vault," he says, crinkling the wax paper as he peels it back for another bite of candy.

I hold up an invisible phone and pretend to talk into it. "Hey, Siri, is Lennon full of shit? What's that? Oh, he is. Great. Thank you."

"Hey, Siri? Is everything I just said true?" he says, playing along. He pretends to wait for a response and then talks into the bear canister. "Why, yes, Lennon. It most certainly is. You're in a Bear Zone. It's against federal law to store unprotected food."

"That law sounds completely made-up," I tell him.

"Didn't you read the rules?"

What rules?

Lennon rolls his eyes toward the ceiling. "I also emailed Brett a list of things we'll need on the trail. He said he was going to share it with the group."

What list? I'm suddenly worried that I was left out of the loop. Forgotten. And this just reignites my anxieties about whether my presence is wanted on this trip. But I'm not telling Lennon this.

"Reagan bought a lot of stuff for this week," I report. "But I don't remember any bear containers. She's been camping here before, so maybe she knows something you don't. Maybe we don't need them."

Lennon mumbles an unintelligible curse under his breath. "We'll definitely need them when we go backpacking." He holds the canister behind his neck to demonstrate. It's about the same size as his head—too big. "You can strap it to the top of your pack like this, or down at the bottom, which might be better for people prone to balance problems." He smirks at me with his eyes.

I fantasize about bashing his big head with the stupid bear vault. "Why are you here?"

"Why are any of us here, Zorie? Life is a mystery."

I groan. "On this trip."

"Oh," he says innocently. He's not smiling, but there's a fraction of humor behind his eyes. "The cologne bandit invited me. I'm 'the coolest,' apparently," he says making air quotes with one hand while he takes another bite of fudge.

Again with the snark. Why is he hanging out with Brett if he hates him so much?

"But you knew I was coming?" I probe.

"I did."

"Why didn't you say something?"

He shrugs. "I only recently decided to go."

Is that true? I remember back to when Reagan first told me about off-trail backpacking and her not being sure if Brett's "friend" who told him about this bucket-list hidden waterfall was committed to coming.

"Why?" I ask.

"I have my reasons."

"Which are . . . ?"

Lennon stares at his fudge for a long moment. Then he seems to change his mind about what he was going to say and hands me the open canister. "Get this. And maybe a bear bell," he says, pointing to a display of big silver bells designed to be clipped to a backpack. "It gives bears a gentle warning that you're in the area, so that you don't surprise them. A surprised bear is a defensive bear, and a defensive bear kills."

Is he serious? I *think* he is, but I'm not totally sure. And before I can ask for clarification or point out that he's avoiding my question, he retrieves something from his pocket and dumps it inside the open canister. Then he walks away.

I look inside the canister. Sitting at the bottom is a square of peanut butter fudge wrapped in wax paper.

What am I supposed to think about this?

I retrieve the fudge and return the canister to the display shelf, abandoning Kingsly the Bear to catch up with the others. Just because Lennon cries bear vault, doesn't mean I really need it. It's insanely expensive. Besides, Lennon has a penchant for being super technical and obsessive about details. I think he's exaggerating the urgency of bear protection.

Probably.

At the last second, I double back and grab a silver bear bell off the rack.

Better safe than sorry.

Part II

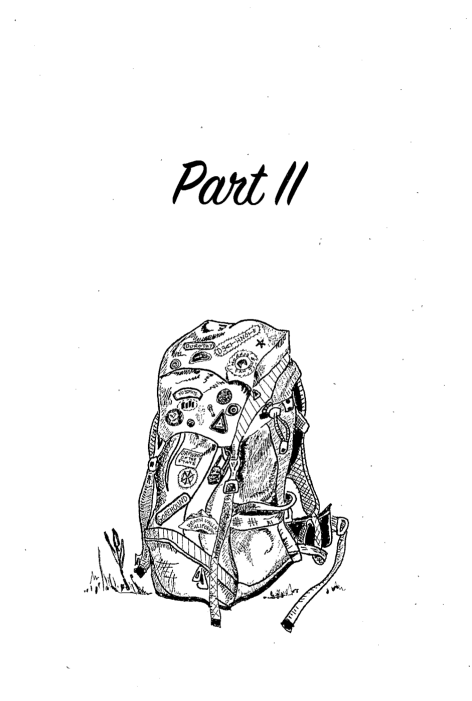

7

The monotonous fruit fields change to rugged foothills covered in lodgepole pine trees as we head west. When we turn off the highway, gray granite cliffs flank the twisting uphill road toward the national forest. Carved wooden signs with painted white lettering point the way to a variety of sights, each marked with distance and pertinent details:

CANYON WALK, 6KM. 3.5 HOUR RETURN.

SCEPTER PASS, 4KM. WEAPONS PROHIBITED.

BLACKWOOD LAKE, 10K. NO PETS. NO FIRES. OVERNIGHT STAY REQUIRES WILDERNESS PERMIT.

And then finally, our destination:

MUIR CAMPING COMPOUND: 2K. 1 HOUR RETURN. WHEELED VEHICLES PROHIBITED PAST PARKING AREA.

Wait, what?

"This is us," Reagan reports, turning. I make a mental note of a High Sierra bus stop here and wonder if this is the route I'll need to use to get to the star party on Condor Peak.

A small, paved parking area sits at the end of a rocky driveway. A dozen or so cars are parked here, most of them luxury vehicles. We find an open space near some wooden steps that lead into thick forest. Another sign sits near the steps, stating that the trail is private property and only for guests of the compound. People using the trail must fill out a form and deposit it inside a locked box.

There is no road past the parking lot.

"Get everything you'll need," Reagan reports. "Unless you want to spend all your time hiking back and forth to the car. The walk back is fine, but it's all uphill to the compound."

"We're hiking to the compound?" I say, staring at the sign. "Two kilometers?"

Reagan gives me a labored look. "Don't start, Everhart. I warned you about hiking."

I'm not even that upset about the hike. It's just unexpected, is all. "I didn't—"

"How long is two kilometers?" Brett asks.

"It's nothing," Reagan tells him brightly.

"A little over a mile," I elaborate.

"Oh, cool," he answers, but he's smiling at Reagan.

And Reagan is smiling back at him. "Easy-peasy, lemon squeezy."

Why are they smiling so big? Did I miss a joke? And now they're high-fiving each other—hard enough to hear the *smack* of palm-on-palm. It's so . . . goofy. Lennon's head turns toward mine, and even though a fringe of black hair obscures one eye, a single dark brow rises in shared judgment of the stupid high five.

Or maybe he's judging *me*.

We all fill out the trail registration cards at the information sign—in case anyone goes missing or gets murdered along the way, they'll know your name and next of kin. And after Brett and Lennon haul down everyone's stuff from the rooftop travel carrier, I'm soon reminded that I'm a human Weeble toy, barely able to stand under the misaligned weight of my backpack. But it's not as if I can repack everything in the middle of the parking lot. So I do my best to strap it on and adjust my stance.

"Saddle up, team," Reagan says loudly to the group. "Luxury awaits us at the end of the trail."

It's just two kilometers, I tell myself. And the woods are pretty amazing, all shady and smelling of pine needles. Birds are chirping, and it's not too warm. I can do this. About five minutes up the first steep hill, I begin to have doubts. Ten minutes up an even steeper incline, I'm picturing Reagan with one of those prospector axes from the general store lodged in her skull. By the time we reach the final stretch toward the compound, I'm just wishing I could drop into a fetal position.

The sign for Muir Camping Compound appears, and I nearly weep when I spot a big building inside a break in the trees. My head is sweating, and I've been walking uphill in a hunched-up position for so long, I'm a hundred-year-old woman with osteoporosis.

But it doesn't matter. The promised land is in front of me, and by God, it may have been worth all that misery, because the compound is *gorgeous*. A modern cedar lodge sits at the forefront: walls of enormous windows, fat timber beams, stacked-stone fireplaces jutting from the roof. Lush forest surrounds it. Jagged mountains in the distance. The whole scene looks like something out of a dream. We head inside.

Warm sunlight streams through double-high windows as we tread across floors of polished river rock and stop at the registration desk. It smells so nice in here, like cedar and fresh-cut flowers. And they have expensive candy sitting in a bowl for the guests. I resist the urge to fill my pockets; Brett does not. He holds a finger up to his mouth and winks at me, stealthily emptying imported chocolate into a pocket on his backpack, while Reagan informs the middle-aged woman working the desk who her mother is.

The woman's name tag reads CANDY. For a second, my oxygen-starved brain reads this as some sort of sign that Brett's been busted, then I realize it's actually her name. "You're Belinda's daughter?" she says to Reagan. "I barely recognize you. Didn't you stay with us last year?"

"I did," Reagan reports cheerfully. "Mom called you about the change in guests, right?"

Candy looks us over. "I was under the impression that your group would be girls. . . ."

You and me both, Candy. I sense a kindred planner spirit in her as she's double-checking her computer screen and an old-fashioned paper registry. Reagan assures Candy that nothing is amiss with our guest list and begins providing her with everyone's names. I meander around the room, and Brett joins me while I examine a wall of framed scenic photos. "Lennon said you take crazy-good photos of stars. I thought you just looked at them."

The jittery feeling I get whenever Brett is nearby returns. Why can't I just feel normal around him? "I . . . do both. Look and take pictures. Of stars. With my camera."

Ugh. Zorie sound like cavewoman.

Brett just laughs, easy and warmly. "Not with your mind?"

"No," I say, hoping my cheeks aren't red.

"Do you just stick a camera on a telescope and zoom in?"

"Sort of. Not exactly? It's . . . There are a lot of fiddly, techy parts. Hard to explain."

His smile is gentle. "Maybe you can teach me how? Because I'd love to take photos of the night sky. Especially the moon. That would be *so* badass."

Is he serious? He's interested in astrophotography? I want to scream, *I WILL TEACH YOU! I WILL TEACH YOU SO HARD.* But Kendrick calls his name, and Brett ducks around me to answer. Before I can open my mouth, he's gone, laughing with Kendrick about a carved wooden statue that looks like two squirrels having sex.

Dammit.

I can't shake the feeling that I'm being watched. It's the same prickly feeling I had in the car, and it makes me anxious. I glance around, and my eyes immediately meet Lennon's. The intensity of his stare is startling.

For the love of Pete, what do you want? It's as if he's accusing me of something. I haven't said a word to him since the Gold Rush store, so I'm not sure what his problem is. I used to be able to read his expressions, but now he's like the mediocre mime who performs outside the Jitterbug on Mission Street, and I can't tell if he's trying to get out of a glass box or signal a taxi. Does Lennon expect a thank-you for the peanut butter fudge? Or is he just trying to unsettle me?

If so, it's working.

But I'll never let him know that. I quickly turn away and head toward Brett and Kendrick and the mating squirrels.

After we're registered, Candy leads us to our cabin tents, giving us an abbreviated tour and answering questions along the way. The main lodge has several lounge areas and connects to a screened-in dining pavilion where dinner will be served later. Outside, winding paths lead to dozens of canvas cabin tents nestled in the woods. Some are rectangular, some round—the yurts—but all are the color of unbleached muslin. They're grouped into areas named after birds, each area a short walk from the next. It takes us about ten minutes to get to our area, Camp Owl, where two of the rectangular tents sitting near a dense forest are reserved for us.

Reagan isn't happy about this. "We're supposed to have a yurt," she argues, "with a view of the valley."

"Sorry, but Camp Falcon was accidentally overbooked. I put a family of six in my last one earlier this morning."

"Not cool," Reagan says grumpily. "We've had the reservation since last summer. My mom isn't going to be happy."

"If you'd like, I'll call her and explain," Candy says. "But this might work out better for you. Girls can take one tent, and the boys can take another."

The implication is obvious. Candy will call Mrs. Reid and inform her that her daughter has brought along three boys. Reagan fumes quietly, but acquiesces. We really don't have a choice.

"Just let life happen," I tell Reagan.

"Yeah," Brett says cheerfully. "That's right, Zorie. You're preaching my word, and I dig it."

The look Reagan gives me could slice through steel.

The tents are both exactly alike: sealed cement floors, canvas walls fixed to a wooden frame, a screen door, slatted windows that can be opened to take advantage of the breeze during the day and closed at night to keep the cabin warm, along with a glass-front tent stove. A small seating area surrounds the stove, with a real sofa and brightly patterned Navajo rugs. Two sets of bunk beds stretch across the back of the tent, all with feather-top mattresses, luxury linens, and down pillows.

Behind the bunks, past a canvas divider, is an en suite toilet and sink. No showers. Those are in the bathhouse down the hill, shared with six other cabins in Camp Owl, Candy reports.

Candy reports a few other things, as well. "You're in bear country, and yes, they've gotten through the national park fence and come into the compound. For everyone's safety, all food must be stored in the food locker when it's not in the process of being served or eaten," she says, pointing outside the tent's door to a green metal box that sits beneath a canopy with two rocking chairs. "Either there, or inside a portable food locker, meaning a bear-resistant food container that's approved by Yosemite and King's Forest."

Lennon's head slowly turns toward mine.

Why, oh, *why* does he have to be right? That peanut butter fudge is not sitting well in my stomach right now.

Candy ticks off a list on her fingers of what we need to store in the locker. "Unopened food, even in cans. Snacks, drink mixes, vacuum-sealed pouches. Every bit of it. All toiletries with a scent. Lotion, makeup, deodorant."

"Cologne, too?" Lennon asks.

"Yes," she says.

"I'm talking *strong* cologne. Like, some kind of extreme body spray."

"Most definitely," the woman answers, perplexed.

Lennon flicks his eyes toward Brett. But Brett is completely oblivious, as he's currently trying to restack water bottles into a pyramid on a console table behind the sofa.

Candy points to the bathroom. "If you need extras of anything—water, razor, towels—just ask at the front desk. You can call, of course, but cell phone service is hit-and-miss up here. If you ever need to make an emergency call, we'll let you use the landline. If it's after ten p.m., Bundy and I stay in the log cabin to the right of the lodge."

"What about backcountry permits for King's Forest?" Lennon asks. "Your website said you can arrange it and have one delivered to our tent."

"For a fee," she says. "We have to drive to a park station to pick them up."

"Put it on my credit card," Reagan says breezily.

Candy gives Reagan a withering look. "You can stop by the desk at your convenience and fill out the form."

Yikes.

"No music is allowed in the tent cabins," Candy says to all of us. "No loud talking after sunset when you're inside your camp. Other guests may be trying to sleep, and these walls aren't sound-proof. Quiet hours start at ten p.m. and last until seven a.m."

"Geez," Summer mumbles under her breath near my ear. "This place is a dictatorship."

Candy points in the general direction of the lodge. "We have a small store that sells sweatshirts and rain gear. You can also rent bear canisters and camp stoves. It's run on the honor system, so you'll need to put cash in the bin or write your tent number and name on the sheet to have it added to your final bill. Also—"

Brett's water-bottle pyramid crashes. Bottles roll across the floor. "Oops, sorry," he says.

Candy pauses, and her inner struggle with patience is showing in the slant of her brows, but, clearing her throat, she finishes her speech. "Evening social time starts at six. We serve drinks, then a four-course dinner. We encourage you to mingle with other guests at the nightly bonfire afterward. The pavilion closes at nine. Any questions, come see us at the registration desk."

What if I have questions now? No one else is paying attention to Candy, but I wish they'd listed all of this stuff on the website or given us a printout so I could review it and memorize everything. I'm itching to ask her to repeat everything so that I can write it all down. Actually, I'm literally itching and resist the urge to scratch. Lennon's gaze flicks to my arms, and I feel as if he knows, which only makes the itch worsen.

If I make it through this week without having a nervous breakdown, I'll consider it a win.

8

Since it's already late in the afternoon, there's no time to do anything before dinner. So the boys retreat to their tent, and we all unpack. I stash all my food and toiletries in the food locker outside and check my telescope for visual damage; it seems to have survived the bumpy trip on top of the SUV and arrived intact. Then I try to call Mom to let her know *I* arrived intact. But there's no service in the tent cabin. There's Wi-Fi at the lodge, so I go ahead and text—both to her and to Avani—and trust that my messages will go through when I get a signal.

Reagan disappears, so Summer and I set out and explore the Camp Owl section of the compound on our own. There's a picnic table between our tent and the boys', and a small trailhead behind us, with a sign warning that the trail feeds into the national forest; Muir Camping Compound absolves itself of responsibility should hikers choose to leave their property. A group of wild, unsupervised kids is running into the woods here, so it can't be all that scary.

We avoid the screaming kids and follow a fastidiously land-scaped trail: cream-colored rocks banded by the occasional flowering shrub and a steady line of path lights. The trail leads to a cedar-shingled bathhouse.

"Whoa," Summer whispers appreciatively when we peek inside, and I'm feeling the same way. It's practically a spa, one that's themed to match our beautiful surroundings, and even nicer in person than it was in the online photos: stained wood countertops, stone benches, pretty lanterns hanging from iron hooks near the mirrors. Unlike our tents, there's electricity here, and a woman is charging her cell phone while she blow-dries her hair. There's even a small sauna in the back.

"I'm getting naked with Kendrick in that sauna later," Summer tells me as we step back outside.

"Too much information," I say.

She laughs. "If you want to get naked with someone, I wouldn't care. Are you still hung up on Brett?"

"Umm . . ."

"He told me you guys hooked up."

What? "We didn't—not like *that*." It was just a kiss, for the love of Pete.

"You're so easy to embarrass," she says, grinning. "Did you know your ears turn red? That's so cute."

Jesus.

"Hey, I was just teasing," she says, slapping my arm playfully. "Brett's sweet. And I like how he's so cool with everyone. Like,

I never would have hung out with Lennon in a million years because I didn't know how cool he was."

I'm not sure how to take this. I think I understand what she's trying to say, and maybe there's a core of earnestness in there somewhere. But I think she's also implying that Lennon wasn't okay until Brett decided he was.

"You and Lennon used to be a thing, huh?"

My body stills. "Who told you that?"

"I just remember seeing you together at school all the time."

"We were just friends," I insist. "Nothing else."

Lie.

One that Summer seems to buy. With a shrug, she says, "I think you guys would make a good couple."

"No," I say, and it sounds like a dog barking. "Absolutely not. We aren't even friends anymore."

She holds up both hands in surrender. "Hey, I only call 'em like I see 'em. Think about it, Miss Astrology."

I won't. And I don't bother to correct her again—not about her word mix-up or Lennon. It's true that people at school used to tease us about being best friends—which was often said with a wink and air quotations—and rumors were spread that we were more. That's precisely one of the reasons we decided to conduct the Great Experiment privately. To avoid gossip at school. Mainly, though, to avoid my dad finding out. Because no way in *hell* would Diamond Dan allow his daughter to date the son of two heathen women.

Anyway, I don't know why I care that Summer assumed something was going on between Lennon and me. I think I should be more concerned that Brett told Summer we hooked up. Maybe Summer heard it wrong or made assumptions. She's making it sound like he was bragging, but I shouldn't assume the worst. He could have been telling her that he liked me, for all I know.

Anything's possible. But now I'm self-conscious about my ears flaming up, which makes me want to avoid the entire topic. I discreetly make sure my bob covers the telltale redness and don't say anything further.

By the time we've finished walking the path around our area of the camp, we spot Reagan and the boys lounging at the picnic table between our tents. I'm a little worried Summer might try to tease me about Brett in front of the group, but she just runs to Kendrick, throwing her arms around him and begging for a piggy-back ride. As though the whole conversation about Brett and Lennon is forgotten.

Good.

It's nearly time for dinner service, so we all decide to trek back up to the lodge. We aren't the only ones. Small groups of campers are headed in the same direction, and once the pavilion is in sight, we join dozens of other guests. Wineglasses in hand, they mingle on rattan-and-carved wood outdoor furniture overflowing with plush pillows on a massive wraparound deck that overlooks a beautiful rocky valley. Everything is suffused with golden light from the setting sun. It's photographic. Literally. Brett is breaking out his phone to take pictures as a waiter circulates with a tray of hors d'oeuvres.

Brett whistles. "They must make a killing here."

"Maybe not," Kendrick says, eyeing a bar that's been set up outside the dining area on a side deck, away from the stunning views. "That wine they're serving isn't cheap."

"Think they'll serve us?" Brett asks with a devious smile.

"That's the same bartender from last year," Reagan says, shaking her head. "He's a dick. I think he's Candy's cousin, or something. He'll probably remember me."

"I'll try," Summer says. "He won't know me, and I look legal."

She casually strides to the bar and flashes the bartender a smile. After several seconds of small talk, she turns around and returns empty-handed.

"No way," Brett says, disappointed. "He wouldn't do it?"

"You were right, Reagan. He's a dick," Summer reports. "Says he was warned by Candy that a group of underage teens had just checked in, and we're not to be served alcohol."

"We'll see about that," Brett says, and turns to Lennon. "We need a plan to get that wine."

"I'll get right on that," Lennon deadpans.

Brett laughs, either unbothered by Lennon's sarcasm or not noticing it. Nothing ever seems to bother Brett. He's always so happy-go-lucky and at ease with his life. I wish I could be more like that.

We trail a group of retirees and investment bankers in

catalog-perfect outdoor clothes. Reagan spots a place for us to sit inside the pavilion, and we follow her lead to a large, round table. It's set with modern-rustic china, and the confusing number of glasses and utensils intimidates me. I'm also sitting between Brett and Lennon, which makes me nervous. It's exciting to have Brett so close, and he's pretending to stab my hand with a fork, his mood fun and playful. But I'm self-conscious and trying to play it cool.

And then there's Lennon. I wish I could just block him out. While Brett's presence feels light and capricious—he's moved on to fake-stabbing Reagan, and she's laughing in that husky voice of hers—Lennon's feels . . . solid. Weighty. Like I can't forget that his leg is a few inches from mine. If Brett is Sirius, brighter than anything else in the night sky, Lennon is the moon: often dark and hidden, but closer than any star. Always there.

One after the other, each table is served the first of four courses, which is some sort of zucchini-and-basil soup. Once it's on the table, I realize how sorry I am that I've only had Lennon's gifted fudge to eat today, and forget all about the silly tableware and practically inhale the soup. I don't even care if I'm using the correct spoon. The second course is grilled scallops with some sort of fancy sauce and a tiny salad. The scallops smell amazing. I'm all in.

"Someone's feeling plucky," Lennon notes, gesturing toward my plate with his knife. "Hive-wise."

"Scallops are a shellfish with which I'm compatible," I tell him stoically. Shrimp and crab are iffy, but anything in the mollusk family is low-risk.

"Oh yeah, that's right," he says, nodding slowly.

We both eat in silence for several seconds.

Then he asks, "Remember when we had that shrimp scampi?"

"You never forget a trip to the ER."

I was fifteen, and at the time, Sunday dinner with the Mackenzies was a regular event. It was just takeout, typically, and a movie in the living room. Sunny is the chef of the Mackenzie family; Mac, not so much. So it was a big deal when Mac decided she'd make something from scratch. It turned out pretty good, but for some reason, I had a major allergic reaction. Face swelling up, throat closing, trouble breathing—the works. Mac freaked out and took all the blame. My parents were out to dinner, so Sunny rushed me to the hospital emergency room in her car.

"Bad shrimp! Bad shrimp!" Lennon says, mocking Sunny in a high-pitched voice.

Sunny had yelled that at the nurse in front of the entire ER waiting room. Loudly. We repeated it for months out of context. It was our inside joke. Anything that went wrong, we blamed it on "bad shrimp." It never got old.

It's still funny. I chuckle softly with a mouthful of scallop and nearly choke.

Lennon's eyes slide toward mine. The corners of his mouth turn up as he struggles with a smile.

Okay, hell has officially frozen over. Pigs flying. Lightning strikes. It's all happening. Because we are both smiling at each other. Actual smiles!

What's going on here? First peanut butter fudge, now this?

Just stay calm, I tell myself. It doesn't mean anything. Enemies share a laugh now and then. I keep my eyes on my plate and try to act normal. But when the third course comes, some kind of braised meat—leg of lamb, I think—and Brett has the rest of the group focused on tracking the location of the bartender, I pick up the next fork in my place setting and accidentally bump his hand. He's left-handed, so his right hand is propped on the edge of the table. And it stays there, even when I snatch my own hand back.

"Sorry," I mumble.

He shakes his head dismissively. "So many forks. And why do we need two spoons? I already used one for the soup. Are they backup spoons?"

"One pair of fancy chopsticks would have saved them some major dishwashing," I say.

"Amen to that."

My mom taught him how use chopsticks. The Korean kind, made of stainless steel.

"What's that quote from that martial arts movie *Once Upon a Time in China*?" I ask. "Jet Li says it when he sees the Western place setting."

"'Why so many swords and daggers on the table?'" Lennon quotes.

"That's it. God, you were obsessed with martial arts movies."

"Jet Li is the king," he says before taking a sip of water from his glass.

"I thought it was Bruce Lee."

"Bruce Lee was a god."

"Oh, that's right," I say. "You made me watch so many of those movies."

"And you liked most of them."

I did.

Lennon picks at his braised lamb. "I also seem to remember watching an awful lot of old. *Star Trek* episodes, and not even the good ones. All because someone had a crush on a certain Klingon."

It's true. Worf was my everything. I still follow the actor who played him, Michael Dorn, online. And I've probably seen every Worf meme on the internet. "I'm not ashamed."

Before I can say anything else, Brett's arm shoots out in front of me. I'm forced to lean back while he taps Lennon's shoulder.

"Dude, are you seeing this?" Brett says.

"You know she's sitting here, right?" Lennon says, slipping back into glum-and-dour mode.

Brett glances at me. "Oh sorry, Zorie." He chuckles and flashes me a sheepish smile before focusing on Lennon again. "But check it out. The bartender leaves the bar unattended. All of those bottles are just sitting there."

Lennon's disinterested stare doesn't seem to have any effect on Brett.

"For the taking," Brett elaborates.

"There are a hundred people sitting here," Lennon says.

Brett groans and lets his head loll backward for a moment. "Not now. Later. After dinner. People can't sit here forever."

"Everyone heads to the bonfire below the Sunset Deck," Reagan confirms.

"The bartender's walking back to the bar," Lennon points out.

"So we find a way to divert him," Brett says. "We just need people's attention on the bonfire while we figure out a way to get him to leave the bar. Then, boom! We plunder his stash."

I don't like this plan. We're surrounded by people. This isn't like playing pranks on teachers, like that time Mr. Soniak exited English class to go to the restroom and left his phone unlocked on his desk, and Brett jumped out of his chair and used it to take photos of his ass before Mr. Soniak returned . . . which Brett later claimed was worth the detention he got.

Kendrick gives Brett a distrustful look. "Call me crazy, but isn't that stealing?"

"It's the very definition," Lennon mumbles.

"You would know," Brett says, waggling his brows.

I glance at Lennon, and he looks . . . embarrassed. I wonder what that's all about.

"Look, people. They aren't selling the wine," Brett argues. "It's free to all the guests. If I asked for a second helping of this braised sheep—"

"Lamb," Lennon corrects in a weary voice.

"—they would bring it to me. It's all built into the cost. We're just getting our money's worth."

"My *mom's* money, you mean," Reagan says.

Brett grins. "Your mom is hot."

"Gross," Reagan says, smacking his shoulder with the backs of her fingers. And it *is* gross, but she doesn't seem all that upset about it. Not about that, and not about Brett's dicey proposal. Even Kendrick, who I would consider sensible, is convinced by Brett's arguments. So maybe my bad feelings about it are unwarranted.

After Reagan informs us that we're all going horseback riding tomorrow, Brett continues to hatch a wine-thieving plan throughout the rest of dinner. Dessert is served—some sort of weird strawberry sorbet with balsamic vinegar that I skip, because strawberries are on the "no" list when I'm having hive issues. And when guests begin filing outside to the Sunset Deck, lured by the scent of wood smoke and the sounds of acoustic guitar, opportunities to divert the bartender dwindle.

"I'll figure something out," Brett assures us. "The night is young."

Reagan tugs him by the arm. "Come on. Let's walk around."

He flashes his dazzling grin at her and allows himself to be dragged from the table, briefly linking elbows with her as he makes some joke that I can't hear. They're so easy together, so touchy and lighthearted. I wish I could be as bold as Reagan. I wish he were linking arms with me.

But more than anything, I wish I didn't feel Lennon's gaze on my face. All that memory dredging we did over dinner is overlapping in my brain with Summer's earlier assumptions about my relationship with Lennon. And a troublesome thought suddenly balloons.

Bogus gossip about my so-called hookup with Brett reached Summer's ears.

Did it reach Lennon's, too?

It bothers me that it might have, and it bothers me that I care. Then again, my caring about Lennon was never the problem. It was his caring about me. And a little peanut butter fudge and fond memories of bad shrimp aren't enough to convince me that anything has changed.

9

Following Brett and Reagan, we all head outside to a deck studded with tin lanterns. It's beautiful out here, actually. The sun still hasn't completely fallen, but it's getting close, and the mountains are limned in orange and pink behind darkening silhouettes of pine trees. Everything's in that middle stage between day and night, which somehow seems more exciting out here in the wilderness than it does in the city. As though something's on the verge of happening.

The deck quickly swells with people, some of them standing against the railing to watch the sunset, others claiming seats on the sprawling patio furniture to listen to folksy guitar music. Waiters begin circulating after-dinner coffee and tea. We stroll past Candy, who is chatting with some of her guests, and when she spots us, she calls Reagan over to meet them. The rest of us jog down the wide deck steps to a clearing and head toward the compound's fire pit.

It's a gorgeous bonfire, with rustic split-log benches circling it. A few guests are toasting marshmallows over the flames, and there's some sort of make-your-own-s'mores station on a table. Nearby, white lights are strung on a cedar pergola, beneath which three lanes of horseshoes are set up on sandy ground.

"Want to play?" Kendrick asks Lennon. "I have to warn you, I'm pretty much a horseshoes genius, so I'll probably beat you."

"Is that right?"

"Legendary," Kendrick confirms. "At least, I was when I was ten, which is the last—and, well, *only* time I've ever played."

Lennon chuckles. "If it's like ring toss at the fair, I kill at that. Let's do this." He glances at me. "You in?"

"Hand-eye coordination is not my strong suit," I tell him. Every time I've ever played games where you have to get up in front of others and do something in a spotlight—like bowling or charades—I generally am too concerned about onlookers watching me and end up looking awkward. "Maybe I'll watch a game and see how it's played first."

"Throw a horseshoe, try to hit the stake," Lennon says.

"You make it sound easy."

"No, I think *you're* making it harder than it really is," he says, one side of his mouth tilting. "Sometimes you just have to say screw it and go for it."

Summer chimes in that she wants to play, and it's only now I notice that Brett is missing. Maybe he hung back with Reagan to talk to Candy. Or maybe he's staking out the bartender. Who knows. But I wish he were here so that we could revisit his earlier interest in taking photos of the moon—and maybe so that he could be a natural buffer between me and Lennon.

While we've been talking, all the horseshoe lanes have filled with teams. So we stand at the edge of the pergola and wait for a free stake, watching the games in progress. That's when I feel a gentle tap on my shoulder.

I look up to see a woman about my mom's age, with pale brown skin and her hair pulled tightly back in a smooth ponytail. "Aren't you Dan Everhart's daughter?"

"Yes." My shoulders tighten. Then I recognize the woman. Razan Abdullah. I've seen her in the clinic. She runs a video production company. She used to be one of my dad's patients.

"I thought I recognized you," she says with a smile. "Is your family here?"

"No, I'm just vacationing with some friends." I glance toward Lennon and Kendrick. Lennon nods in greeting.

"Ah," she says. "Beautiful place, isn't it? I've been here the last few days filming a promo video with a small crew."

"That's really cool."

She nods. "It's been a great shoot. We leave tomorrow morning. How's your dad doing? I haven't seen him since he worked on my back this spring."

"He's okay." I feel like I should say something more positive than that, but honestly, it's hard for me to muster the words.

"Oh, I'm sorry." She makes a face, gritting her teeth. "Is your mom still with your dad?"

I'm baffled. "Of course. Why wouldn't she be?"

"I must be . . . confusing them with another couple." Rapidly blinking eyes dart sideways as she seems to be thinking about something, hesitating. "You know how it is. I meet so many people for work. . . . They all blur together sometimes."

"Right," I say. But now a strange, quiet panic is rising inside me. Did she really confuse my dad with someone else, or has she heard a rumor? Please, please, *please* don't let her be someone my dad's had an affair with. I think she's married, but I'm not sure.

Before I can press her for more information, her phone lights up and she excuses herself.

I watch her walk away, head muddled, and realize that if she's getting phone service, we should be in Wi-Fi range. I check my phone, and sure enough, I've got a signal. I also have several texts. Two are from my mom, and as I meander away to answer them, I can't help but think about Razan's question. It doesn't take long for thinking to become obsessing, and now I'm picturing my parents splitting up.

But not for long. Pulling me out of my thoughts, Brett jogs toward me, Reagan in tow. "It's happening," he says excitedly, urging me to follow them while Reagan gets the rest of the group's attention. "We have to go—now."

"I don't understand," I say.

Lennon dusts his hands off. "What's happening?"

"The bar," Brett says. "I convinced one of the guests to order three mixed drinks."

"Okay . . . ?"

"*Which means*," he says, "the bartender will head back to the kitchen to fetch them. The bar will be unguarded. Now is our chance. Are you going to sit around throwing scraps of iron with old geezers, or do you want to have fun?"

"Fun!" Summer says.

"Come on, then," Brett says, grinning wildly. He winks at me. "Let's go, Everhart."

He takes off, and I follow, slipping around the backside of the pavilion. Summer and Reagan are racing ahead across the darkening lawn, and when they make it to a short set of stairs that lead up to the smaller side deck, they pause for several seconds until Summer flashes us a thumbs-up sign.

We all climb three steps cautiously onto the narrow strip of deck circling the pavilion, staying hidden. The bar is only a few yards away, bathed in a strong cone of light. Like Brett predicted, the bartender seems to be headed toward the kitchen, and stops to talk to a pair of the serving crew, who are sweeping the floor and turning chairs upside down on top of the tables.

"That guest you convinced to order the drinks went to the Sunset Deck with her friends," Summer reports in a loud whisper. "I think she was telling the bartender to bring the drinks out there."

"Excellent," Brett says with a grin, waving Reagan and Summer behind him. "Where's my wingman?"

I realize he's talking about Lennon, and glance around. He's nowhere to be found.

"No time to wait," Brett says. "Zorie, you're taking his place. Stay here at the steps and keep a lookout in the shadows.

Everyone else, follow me when Zorie gives the word."

Keep a lookout? Why me? I frantically glance around while the others clamor onto the side deck. What am I supposed to be looking for? I check the lawn. I don't have a decent view of the bonfire from here. And the people mingling on the Sunset Deck don't seem to be paying attention to us. The only person who has a sightline on the bar is the acoustic guitar player. Can he see us? I can't tell.

"Is it clear?" Brett whispers.

This is too much pressure. I do one last survey of the inner pavilion and wait until a server turns his back. "Okay, now!"

Brett crests over the top step and takes three strides toward the bar, slipping behind it. He punches the air with a victory fist and then ducks out of view. When he pops back up, he has two wine bottles. He hands them to Summer. She tries to pass them to Kendrick, and he waves them away—at least, at first. She says something to him that I can't hear and shoves one of the bottles against his stomach. He caves and accepts it.

More bottles emerge. The clink of heavy glass echoes across the bar. It's taking them forever. Why are they giggling? Someone's going to hear. And just how many bottles of wine do they need? Summer's already holding three.

I suddenly smell roasted marshmallow.

"Stuck on lookout duty?" a deep voice rumbles at my ear.

A small yelp escapes my mouth. I punch Lennon in the arm.

"Ow," he complains, rubbing his sleeve.

"Stop creeping up on me like that," I whisper. "You'll give me a heart attack."

His white teeth flash in the dusk. "Sounds like a challenge."

"Glad you're so gung ho for my early demise."

"You used to like when I sneaked up in the dark."

Memories from last fall flitter through my head. Tiptoeing out of the house to find him waiting behind the palm tree at the bottom of the steps. His hand over my mouth to stop me from laughing. Feeling like my heart would burst out my chest with wanting his arms around me.

Don't think about it. Don't answer him. Just pretend he didn't say anything. Act casual.

"Where were you just now, anyway?" I manage.

"Not doing this stupid shit. And I also"—he holds up a flat-tened s'more—"found this. Never turn down toasted marshmallow. That's a sin."

"Oh, is it really?" I whisper, irritated that my heart is still racing. Because he startled me. Not because of what he said. Or that he's standing so close that I can smell wood smoke on his shirt. But why *is* he standing so close?

"Pretty sure that's what the preacher said last Sunday at church."

"You still go to church with Mac?" The New Walden Chapel. They have service outside in a small amphitheater, and people from different faiths go there. I think they mainly exist to feed the homeless and do other charity-work-type things around the Bay Area; Mac used to be homeless when she was our age, and she often got her meals from their soup kitchen. My dad says it's not a real church, but what would he know about divinity?

"I don't have a choice. She claims I wear too much black."

I snort. "Okay, so let me get this straight. Mac believes that God forgives her for selling things like . . ."

"Cock rings?" he provides.

That wasn't my first choice. His nonchalance frazzles me, and I get a little defensive. "Yet God doesn't forgive you reading all that gruesome horror manga? All those gory zombie movies?"

"Personally, I'd like to think so. Being prepared for the zombie apocalypse is just common sense."

"Yeah, pretty sure I remember that being mentioned in the Bible," I say sarcastically.

"It's an amendment to the commandments," he says. "Amendment number thirteen. Thou shall arm yourself with machete and shotgun, and remember to aim for the head."

I turn away to keep my eye on Brett.

Lennon reaches around my shoulder, holding up half of a marshmallow. "Want some?"

His voice is dark and velvety, so close to my ear that a thousand goose bumps race down my neck. An unwanted shiver chases them, and I pray he doesn't see it. "No."

"Are you sure?" he asks, voice even lower. Deeper. Seductive.

No. Not seductive. What I'm hearing is the equivalent of a mirage. See, this is where I went wrong before. Just because one person's feeling something doesn't mean the other person intended it. Just because my body wants to slowly turn around, to find him gazing down at me, and our eyes would lock, and—

What's the matter with me? I have to stop. *For the love of God, have some pride, Everhart.*

"No, thank you," I say more resolutely.

"Your loss," he says, sounding bored. His arm disappears.

And now I do turn to look at him. Slowly. But not because I expect anything. I just want to see if he really *is* bored, or if . . .

His eyes aren't on mine. Of course not. He's gazing off in the distance.

"Oh, look," he says casually. "Jack Kerouac is about to get busted."

What?

I swing around and spot the bartender in the pavilion, headed straight toward them. Crap, crap, crap.

"Brett!" I whisper loudly.

He doesn't hear me.

"Guys!" I say louder, panicked.

Summer glances around as if she possibly heard me, but isn't *quite* sure. What do I do? If I take a step into the light, the bartender will see me. But if I can't get Brett's attention—

Lennon whistles.

Brett looks up.

I wave frantically and point toward the pavilion.

He understands now. There's a short scuffle with the wine bottles, and then they're racing toward us. Problem is, when they get to the steps, the bartender can—

Son of a sea cook!

They've been spotted.

"Run!" Brett tells us.

He tears across the lawn, juggling four bottles of wine. Instinct for self-preservation has me running after him. The scent of damp grass and pine needles rise from my feet as my shoes slap the ground. We're all racing as if our lives depend upon it, a panic-fueled herd of buffaloes driven into shadow. I'm completely turned around. Where are the campgrounds? I don't remember all these trees and bushes.

Brett veers left just as I spot the main walkway. It's lit up by tiny gold path lights. Brett and Reagan leap over some flowering shrubs to get to the path. Something crashes.

"Oh, God!" Summer yells.

Glass crushes under my shoes. The scent of wine floods my nose.

"Keep going," Brett says, chest heaving. "Don't stop."

I glance back at the pavilion. It doesn't look like anyone's running after us. We leave the broken bottle behind and continue along the main path until we crest the top of a steep hill. The first camp of tents comes into view. Brett slows to a stop, and we all catch our breath and look down into the valley.

This camp is nothing but yurts, all of them the shape of circus tents. They're eerily lovely, glowing with warm, marigold light— sanctuaries in the darkening forest, one that parts to reveal a black sky. And everywhere—*everywhere*—in that sky, there are stars.

My stars.

It's as if they appeared from nowhere. As if this is a completely different night sky than the one back home. We have a pretty clear view at the Melita Hills observatory, but the cities clustered in the Bay Area collectively produce a lot of light pollution.

No cities out here.

Oh, the photos I could take with my telescope!

"Zorie!" Lennon calls.

Crap. The group is on the move again, and everyone but the two of us has already made it halfway down the hill.

"Sorry," I say. I get my butt in motion and explain, "I spaced out." I chuckle and catch my breath. "Literally."

What a dorky joke. All this physical activity is rotting my brain.

"The stars, you mean?" he says, glancing up briefly. "It's amazing, right? I knew you would love them out here."

He jogs faster to catch up with the group, and I race to follow, his surprising confession tumbling around inside my head. But not for long, because when we're a few yards from the camp, Reagan comes to a stop.

"What's going on?" Kendrick asks.

"On the path, near the third yurt," she says.

I scan ahead and spot the problem. A large man in a dark jacket stands with his back to us, chatting with a couple of campers. On the back of the jacket, the word MUIR is printed in white.

"Mr. Randall," Reagan says. "The compound's security ranger. If you think the bartender was a jerk, he's Santa Claus compared to Mr. Randall. We can't be seen with all this wine. He'll probably have us arrested."

Summer glances around. "What do we do? Should we go back?"

"To the place that's filled with people who saw us run?" Lennon says. "Yes, let's return to the scene of the crime."

"I don't know!" Summer says, eyes bright with panic. "Maybe we can hide until this Mr. Randall dude passes us?"

I gesture toward the yurts. "He's not the only roadblock. Look at all the tents. People are walking around."

"Guests are returning from the bonfire too," Lennon says, glancing behind us, where laugher and chatter carry from a short distance.

"We're trapped," Summer moans. "This sucks so hard. My legs are covered in wine splatter, and now we're going to jail."

"Or we could stash the bottles somewhere," Lennon says calmly. "And, you know, maybe not go to jail. But your plan works too."

Kendrick points to a waste disposal box. It's a metal bear-resistant one, cemented to the ground, with a funny latch. "I doubt they'd clean these out tonight. We can stash the wine inside now and come back later, when people are sleeping."

"My boys!" Brett praises, helping Kendrick unlatch the garbage bin. "Pure genius. Lennon, I was thinking you failed me back at the bar when you weren't there to watch my back, but your position as wingman is now restored."

"All my dreams are realized," Lennon says, voice thick with sarcasm.

While Reagan fusses about stashing the bottles near food scraps, they manage to clear out a space inside the bin for a dozen bottles. The last one doesn't fit, so Brett sticks it inside his pants. Crude jokes are made. I ignore them, mainly because I'm watching the ranger.

"Guys," I say. "Shut the bin. He's coming this way."

I don't think he can see us all that well, but then again, I can see him. And when Lennon points out that we look obvious, hanging out by the garbage bin, we leave it and begin walking down the path. Calmly. Slowly. No getting around the ranger. I steel myself as we approach him.

"Evenin'," Mr. Randall says, giving us all a once-over. "You kids lost?"

"No, sir," Brett assures him. "Just heading back to our camp."

"Which is . . . ?"

"Camp Owl," Reagan says.

He squints at her. "You look familiar."

"My parents stay here a lot," she says.

"If that's true, then I don't need to remind you that quiet hours will be starting soon. Plan accordingly."

"Thank you," Reagan says.

Mr. Randall nods, stepping aside to let us pass. I'm not sure if it's my imagination, but he seems to sniff the air. So now I'm paranoid that he smells wine on us. I mean, we *did* trample a broken bottle into the ground.

But if he suspects anything, he doesn't stop us. And after I sneak a glance back at him, I breathe out a sigh of relief when he passes the garbage bin and continues up the hill toward the lodge.

"I think we're in the clear," I tell the group as we make our way down the dark path through the yurt camp.

"Lucky us," Lennon says without conviction.

For once, I don't disagree with him.

IO

Turns out that "quiet hours" really do mean quiet. Even though the tent cabins in Camp Owl are spread apart, when it's pitch-black outside and the usual white noise of city life—traffic, air conditioners, TV—is replaced by crickets, you can hear everything.

And I do mean *e-v-e-r-y-t-h-i-n-g*.

The flush of toilets. Distant laughter. The crunch of gravel as a stranger walks. Even the smallest noise is amplified. So when all six of us converge in the girls' tent cabin to talk about how we are going to retrieve the hidden wine, it isn't long before we decide that Brett and Lennon will get up early and cart the wine back in their packs. Actually, Brett *volunteers* Lennon, and Lennon just says drily, "I've always dreamed of being a rumrunner."

The boys retreat to their tent, and we get ready for bed. It's been a while since I've slept in a bunk bed—and *never* since I slept in a tent. But after logging the events of the day in my mini-journal and a couple of hours spent lying wide-awake in bed, cataloging all the nocturnal noises in camp, I manage to fall into a restless and unsettled sleep, waking periodically.

When dawn pushes away the darkness, I give up on sleep and climb out of my bunk.

It feels strange to be up so early. But Reagan is a morning person, and when I shimmy to the floor, I find her facedown, sprawled on top of a still-made bed. She never got under the covers? It's insanely chilly in here. I'm a little worried something is wrong, so I shake her shoulder.

"Go away," she says in rough, muffled voice into her pillow. She sounds awful. And pissed off. So I leave her alone and gather my clothes as quietly as possible. Summer is still asleep, and I fear I'll wake both of them up if I use the en suite bathroom, so I head out to the camp bathhouse.

It's far brisker outside the tent than inside, but I see lights in some of the other tents and silhouettes moving around, so I'm not the only person up this early. But I'm able to snag a free shower stall in the bathhouse, and I don't hurry shaving and washing my hair so that my phone has time to charge. When I'm finished drying my hair, I hike back through the camp, feeling a lot more civilized. The boys' tent is dark and both of the girls in my tent are *still* asleep. Unless I want to sit here and listen to Reagan snoring, my best bet is to head up to the lodge for early breakfast.

Blue-gray light filters through pine trees as I hike up the main path. The compound looks different out here in this light, so I have trouble spotting the garbage bin where we left the wine. Maybe Brett and Lennon have already retrieved all the bottles. I mentally cross my fingers and continue along the path toward the lodge.

When I enter the pavilion where we ate dinner, I find an expansive breakfast bar set up on a couple of tables. Eggs, bacon, pastries. Also, an oatmeal station with a dozen topping choices, which one guest is browsing. Why anyone would want that over sausage is a mystery to me. Grabbing a plate, I lift up the lid of a silver chafing dish, and through the warm sausage steam, I get a hazy look at the person hovering over the oatmeal station. He's tall, dark, and hot, and—

OH MY GOD, I'm ogling Lennon.

It's like the telescope spying, only worse, because he's three feet away from me, and I can't duck to the floor and hide. At least he's not half-naked.

"Must be the end-times if you're up before dawn," he says, lips curling at the corners.

"I couldn't sleep. Roosters were crowing."

He laughs. "You're thinking of a farm."

"Look, all I know is it sounded like a bird, and it was irritatingly loud." I slide a quick smile in his direction. "So it was whatever you call mountain roosters."

"I think they probably call them hawks," he says, amused.

"Same difference." I load up my plate with sausage and bacon. "So, oatmeal. Really? Can't you eat that at home?"

"I love oatmeal. Oatmeal is life." He sprinkles a spoonful of almonds on his oatmeal. "You know, I believe Samuel Johnson in his infamous eighteenth-century dictionary described oats as something that the English feed to horses but the Scots feed to people."

I shake my head, smiling to myself. "You and the crazy factoids."

"And you're just desperate for meat because you live with Joy," he says, gesturing toward my plate.

True. It's not as if she cares that I'm a carnivore, but if she's cooking, it's a vegan freezer meal. "Last night was the first meat I've had this week," I admit. "So I'm going full-on cavewoman here. Just meat and coffee. Maybe some sugar," I say, adding a giant cinnamon roll to the top of my sausage stack. I spot some brown sugar among the oatmeal toppings and briefly consider sprinkling some on my bacon.

"Ah, the ol' Paleo Diabetes diet."

"I'm the picture of modern nutrition," I say.

"It gives your cheeks a healthy glow." Eyes merry, he looks me in the face for the first time this morning, *really* looks at me, and I feel my ears warming.

"That's just good old-fashioned fear," I tell him as I focus on the breakfast table, reopening a chafing dish I've already inspected once. "I had trouble sleeping last night. Too many things going bump in the night."

"It's different, isn't it? Even sleeping inside tent cabins. It's still . . . wild."

Indeed, it is.

Lennon hands me some silverware wrapped in a cloth napkin. "Want to eat on the deck and watch the sunrise? They've got patio heaters set up, and it looks like they're bringing around coffee."

"Say no more," I answer, hoping I sound casual and not as though I'm inexplicably happy to be eating breakfast with him.

We carry our plates outside and find a place away from the other early risers, near a patio heater. The juxtaposition of gently billowing heat and nippy morning breeze mirrors my feelings about being alone with him. He's both familiar and foreign, and I'm in a constant state of being on edge when we're together.

"Your plaid game is strong today," he comments, sliding a fleeting glance in my direction.

I smooth a hand over red-and-black plaid pants. They're tight, and a little punk rock—pretty daring, at least for me. I don't *think* he's teasing. It's hard to tell sometimes. "Thanks?"

He nods, and I relax.

"So," I say, digging into my mountain of food. "Did you and Brett retrieve the wine?"

"*I* didn't," he says. "He wanted Kendrick and me to go with him last night after we got back to our tent cabin. We both refused. Brett said he'd go himself, but I'm not sure how he planned to carry a dozen bottles, because he left without his pack. But he reeked like a French restaurant when I got up this morning—which is, frankly, better than that disgusting ax-murderer body spray he's been wearing."

"He got drunk by himself?"

"Or maybe he pulled a Summer and dropped another bottle," Lennon says, shrugging lightly. "But when I came up here this morning, I checked the garbage bin and the bottles were gone, so I assume he managed to rescue them."

We eat in silence for a while. I'm not sure I want to discuss Brett any further with him, and he doesn't offer any other information. He finally pats his pocket and says, "I picked up the backcountry permit at the front desk from Candy's husband, so we're good to go with that. I also checked out the store in the lodge. They've got bear canisters for rent. If you're caught with food and you don't have one, you get fined. It's on the King's Forest information sheet that comes with the permit, if you want to see it."

He starts to dig it out from his pocket, but I wave it away. "I believe you."

"But . . . ?"

"It's just . . . I don't know," I say, snapping off a piece of crisp bacon. "I joked with my mom about seeing wild animals on hikes, but it never truly struck me that they'd pose that much of a threat."

Lennon chuckles. "There's danger lurking everywhere. I'm talking deadly."

"Terrific," I mumble.

"Not just wild animals, either. Out in the Sierras, people have been killed by rock slides, drowning, falling off cliffs, heart attacks from hiking tough trails, being crushed by falling trees—"

"Jesus."

"—heat stroke, hypothermia, boiled to death in hot springs, killed by crazy serial killers, poisoned by plants, contracting hantavirus."

"Hanta what?"

"Transmitted through deer mouse droppings."

"Um, hello. Trying to eat, here," I complain.

"I'm just saying, there's a lot of lethal stuff out there. But that's half the fun."

"Not surprised you'd think that."

"I don't mean in a thrill-seeking way. I mean learning how to spot danger and avoid it in a responsible, careful way. You have to understand your environment. Respect it. Do you think my parents would let me go backpacking if they didn't believe I knew how to handle myself out there? They trust me because I treat it seriously. And that's why they wanted me to come. I mean, you know they wouldn't just agree to take care of my reptiles for a week unless it was important."

True.

"Wait," I say. "Your moms *wanted* you to come?"

One shoulder lifts briefly and falls. "I was worried Brett would go derping off to look for the hidden waterfall himself if I didn't help. And we both know what a moron he is. No offense. I know you used to be into him. Or maybe you still are. . . ." Eyes down, his gaze briefly flicks to mine.

I don't know what to say. I'm not even sure how I feel. The last twenty-four hours have been strange. I guess I thought it would be more thrilling to be around Brett outside of school, but we're barely ever alone together. Maybe if we spent any time away from the group, he'd let the whole super-bro personality drop. I know he does it for attention and that there's a different side to him. But then, we just got here.

There's also been Lennon. I hadn't planned on him. And when I wasn't getting spooked about animal noises in the woods last night, I spent my tossing-and-turning moments replaying all of our conversations in my head, trying to figure out if we're friends again, or if he wants to be—if *I* want to be. I haven't come to any conclusion.

Something clicks inside my head now, though.

"Your parents encouraged you to come on this trip," I say, "because of Brett? They know he's here?"

Lennon shrugs. "Yeah."

"Do Sunny and Mac know that *I'm* here?"

A brisk wind blows as he scrapes his spoon on the inside of his bowl, gathering a last bite of oatmeal. "That's why they wanted me to come. To . . . make sure you're safe."

A hundred emotions pummel me at once. I can't even begin to sort through them, so I lash out with the first thing I can wrap my mind around. "I'm not an idiot, you know. I can take care of myself. I may not be in Olympic shape like Reagan, but I can handle a stupid hike."

"Of course you can."

"I can identify thousands of stars, so I'm pretty sure I can read a map."

"Never said you couldn't. You're the smartest person here by a long shot."

"Then why are you making it sound like I'm incompetent?"

He groans. "You're competent. More than competent. I trust you a million times more than anyone else in this compound."

He does? After months of not talking? This does something funny to my heart.

"Think of it this way," he says. "If I needed to know whether Pluto was a real planet—"

"It's not."

"—then I would ask you. But if I needed to know how to build a bong, I would ask Brett. We all have our areas of expertise. Mine is wilderness backpacking."

"But I never knew that!" I say, exasperated. "Your expertise is supposed to be how to survive a night in a haunted house."

"In a way, they aren't that different."

I'm frustrated, and he's cracking jokes. I can't figure him out. "Is this about that photo book?" I ask, suddenly self-conscious.

"What?"

"Is that why you came? Why your parents forced you to come? If you and your moms are just feeling sorry for me about my dad cheating, you can keep your sympathy. I don't need it. I'm fine."

"I don't feel sorry for you. I'm *angry* for you. I want to cut off your dad's arms with rusty hedge clippers. I want to chainsaw his feet off. I want to—"

"Okay! I get it, I get it." Jeez. It's my dad, after all. Though, admittedly, I'm secretly pleased he's indignant. "If anyone's going to *Texas Chainsaw Massacre* him, it will be Joy." And I think she'd be going for something other than his feet.

He's quiet for a moment. "No one forced me to come on this trip. I wanted to. I was hoping . . ." He stops suddenly, groans, and shakes his head.

"What?" I say. "You were hoping what?"

He hesitates. "Don't you ever miss us?"

His words are a jab to my ribs. I'm surprised I don't fall out of my chair.

I want to scream, *YES*. I also just want to scream. How many nights did I lie awake in tears over Lennon? I wasn't the one who caused our downfall. The Zorie and Lennon show was going strong until the stupid homecoming dance, and its ending can be easily outlined in four steps. Trust me. I've literally outlined it hundreds of times in my planner.

(1) On the final week of summer vacation, Lennon and I accidentally kissed on one of our late-night walks. And before you ask how a kiss can be accidental, let me just confirm that it can. Laughter plus wrestling over a book can lead to unexpected results. (2) We decide to conduct the Great Experiment, in which we tried to incorporate intense make-out sessions into our normal relationship without telling anyone, in case it didn't work out,

so that we could still salvage our friendship and save ourselves from gossip and meddling parents. Mainly one parent: my dad, who has always hated the Mackenzies. (3) A few weeks later, the experiment seemingly going great, we agreed to come out of the nonplatonic friendship closet and make our first public appearance as an actual boyfriend-girlfriend couple at homecoming. (4) He never showed. Never gave a reason. Didn't answer my texts. Didn't show up at school for several days. And that's where we ended. Years of friendship. Weeks of *more* than friendship. Gone.

He ended us.

And next to my birth mother's death, losing him was the hardest thing I've ever had to endure. Now he wants . . . what? What exactly does he want from me?

I stumble over my answer several times, starting and stopping, unsure of what to say, and end up sounding like a fool. "I—"

A cheerful server walks up to us holding a tray filled with coffee in insulated cups. Lennon and I each accept one while the server makes small talk. I'm grateful for the intrusion, but it doesn't allow me enough time to formulate a response to Lennon's question.

Of course I miss us. You don't care about someone for years and then just decide to quit. Those feelings don't disappear on command. Believe me, I've tried. But other intense emotions are tangled up with our old friendship. At least, on my end. And that makes it complicated and confusing.

I like things that make sense. Things that follow identifiable patterns. Problems with solutions. Nothing I feel about Lennon fits any of that. But how do I tell him this without a repeat of the homecoming dance happening? I don't. That's how. I already had my heart broken once. Never again.

And yet . . .

Hope is a terrible thing.

"No worries," he says and stands. "I shouldn't have said anything."

"Wait!" I tell him, jumping up to stop him as he's walking away.

He swings around, and suddenly we're closer than I intended.

I blow out a hard breath and stare between us. "Do you . . . um, maybe want to walk with me to the lodge store so I can get a bear-proof food storage thingy?"

A long moment stretches, and my pulse is going crazy. I scratch my arm through the sleeve of my jacket.

"All right," he finally says, and I let out a sigh of relief.

All right, I repeat inside my head.

If I can't have what I want, then maybe we can find a way back to when things were simpler. When we were just friends.

I end up getting a few things from the store: a bear canister, a pocket water filter, and a multitool gadget that has a tiny shovel. Lennon says I'll need it for digging fire pits and cat holes. I'm not exactly sure what a cat hole is, though I have a bad feeling about it.

The walk back to the camp is mostly quiet but not entirely awkward. It's still nippy, but the sun is burning away the fog, and according to Lennon, it should be a nice a day. I was too fixated on our breakfast conversation to utilize the Wi-Fi.

When we round a curve and enter our camp, Lennon says, "Hold up."

My eyes follow his and spot the problem. Candy and the ranger we ran into last night are heading down the steps that lead into the girls' tent. They turn and walk north, headed in the opposite direction. We wait for them to disappear into the trees before continuing.

"What do you think that's about?" I ask.

"Don't know, but it doesn't sound good. Listen."

That's when I hear Reagan. Her raspy voice carries, and she's angry. We jog toward the tent cabin and rush into the middle of an argument.

"No, I won't calm down," Reagan's telling Summer. "Do you understand how much trouble I'm going to be in when my mom finds out?"

Kendrick and Brett aren't doing anything, so Lennon gets between the two girls. "What the hell is going on?"

"Everything's ruined," Reagan says, backing away from Summer to drop onto the sofa, head in her hands. "That's what's going on."

"They found the wine," Kendrick elaborates while Brett paces behind the sofa. "We're being kicked out."

"I thought you were going to go back for the wine last night," I tell Brett.

A look of distress passes over Brett's face. Instead of answering me, he groans and pounds a fist on the console table. "This is so ridiculous. They have their wine back. No harm, no foul. I don't understand why they're being such hard-asses."

"Because you pissed on a yurt," Reagan yells at him.

Umm . . . what?

"For the love of Christ," Lennon mumbles, shaking his head slowly.

"I was drunk, okay?" Brett says before pleading to Reagan, "We both were."

"You were out together last night?" I say, alarmed.

Reagan rubs her head roughly. "We drank the bottle Brett smuggled back."

The one he stuck in his pants, I suppose.

"And we were going to go back together and get the other bottles, but . . ."

"But we were buzzed," Brett says defensively to the group. "We forgot to take an empty backpack with us to carry the bottles. So we just took two and—"

"We planned to come back for the rest," Reagan says. "We just . . . got distracted."

This is not like Reagan. She's not a big drinker. I've been to parties with her, including *the* party—when Brett kissed me—and she never drank. It affected her cross-country running times, and she was always training for the Olympics.

Guess things are different now.

"Were all of you out drinking?" I ask, wondering now if this could explain some of the noises last night that kept me up. I'm also irritated and hurt that I was left out. But I guess Lennon was, too.

"Don't look at me," Summer says. "Kendrick and I went to the sauna, and then I came back here and fell asleep."

"Same," Kendrick says.

"Does it matter?" Brett gripes, throwing his hands in the air. "We're on vacation, and Reagan and I were just unwinding. It's not like we're criminals."

"Technically, since you're both underage . . . ," Lennon says.

"And the destruction of property," Kendrick adds, not bothering to hide his disgust. "You know, with the pissing on the tent."

Brett sighs heavily. "Not my proudest moment, for sure. But what's done is done." He plops next to Reagan on the sofa and rubs his head. "This is all so stupid."

"*Oh*, I'll agree with that," Lennon says, voice dripping with contempt. He turns to Kendrick. "What exactly did Candy say?"

"That the compound could lose its license to serve alcohol if they knowingly let this kind of thing happen and didn't take action. She said if it had just been the janitorial crew who found the bottles stashed in the garbage, they might have let it slide. But another camper reported it—I suppose it was the family inside the yurt."

Oh. My. God. There was a family inside the yurt when Brett . . . ?

"It could have been the other campers that complained about noise in the woods at two in the morning," Summer adds.

Reagan groans and rubs her temples.

"So, yeah. It looks bad for the compound," Kendrick finishes. "And we have until noon to vacate the tents, or they're calling the police."

"My mom is going to murder me," Reagan says.

"Maybe Candy won't tell her," Summer says, putting on an encouraging face.

"Don't you get it?" Reagan says. "My parents don't leave for Switzerland until tomorrow. That means if I come home tonight with my tail between my legs, I'm going to have to tell them why I'm back so early."

No one says anything. A sense of doom falls over the tent. At least I wasn't involved, so my mom won't be mad. But I'm honestly devastated that all of this is suddenly over. I revised my summer blueprint to accommodate this trip. I don't want to go home and face my dad and his cheating. And what about the star party? It's not for four more days, so I can't just take a bus to Condor Peak this afternoon. No one will be there.

If that weren't enough, I'm also freaking that Reagan was out with Brett last night. Isn't it kind of weird? They aren't saying that anything happened between them, and maybe it didn't. I try to remind myself that they've always been friends—just friends. And Reagan knows how I feel about him.

So why I am filled with unease?

Maybe it's because Lennon and I were "just friends" once too, until we started sneaking out at night together.

"So it's over?" Summer says. "We have to leave? No horseback riding or hiking?"

"You and I could pick up my car and drive out to my family's cabin in Napa Valley," Kendrick tells Summer quietly. "No one's using it right now. At least we can salvage some of this vacation." When he sees Reagan's head turn, he says to her in apology, "I'd invite everyone, but it's just a one-room cabin. It's my parents' getaway house. There's not even room for people to sleep on the floor, sorry."

"You guys! We're being stupid," Brett says, suddenly reinvigorated. "Why should we go home? Our plan was to hike to that hidden waterfall in King's Forest, so let's just do that. We'll spend the rest of the week there."

"Our *plan* was to spend a couple of nights at the waterfall," Lennon points out. "That's a lot different from six nights. We'd need more supplies if we were staying that long. Triple the food. And there aren't showers and flush toilets out there. Do any of you even have the most basic of things, like toilet paper? I gave you a list of stuff we'd need, and you ignored it."

"I didn't!" Brett insists. "I passed it along to Reagan."

"Then why don't any of you have bear canisters or water filters? You think there's a sink out there? You have to filter water from the river to drink."

"I have a water filter," Reagan says. "I didn't think we'd need a million of them. And I bought those campers' freeze-dried meal packets." She looks at me for confirmation. I have four of them in my pack. "And Brett said we could just hang our food in the trees."

"That's ineffective," Lennon says.

"Dude, it's worked for centuries," Brett argues. "You're being paranoid."

"Park rules clearly say no bear canister, no backcountry camping."

"Whatever," Brett says. "Stop sweating the details. It will be *stupid* fun!"

"You're half right about that," Lennon says.

Brett's forehead wrinkles. "Huh?"

"There are canisters for rent in the lodge store," I say quickly, before Brett and Lennon get in a fight. "And more freeze-dried food."

"Are we even allowed up there now?" Summer asks. "Are we banned from the lodge?"

Reagan pushes up from the sofa. "Screw it. They gave us until noon. Let's load up on supplies. Brett's right. So our plans changed. Big deal. We'll adapt. It will be way cooler out on our own anyway."

"So we're doing this?" Lennon says. "You want to spend a week in the backcountry?"

"Why not?" she says. "Better than going home. If Candy tells my parents, I'm grounded anyway. Might as well have fun while I can. I say let's go for it. Who's with me?"

One by one, everyone agrees. Even Lennon, though I don't think he's happy about it.

New plan: Don't panic. Everything will be fine. It's the same as it was, just a few extra days at the waterfall. I can just hike back here and catch my bus to Condor Peak when it's time to leave. Right?

Reagan looks at me. "Zorie? You're in, right? Because I don't need you going home early to tattle, and for all of this to get back to my mom."

I sort of want to punch her in the boobs.

Anxious thoughts bloom. Of camping in the woods. Of Reagan and Brett spending last night drinking together. Of my conversation with Lennon this morning. All of these things are giant question marks bouncing around in my head.

But when it comes down to it, I'm still left with one indisputable factor.

Luckily for Reagan, I don't want to my face my parents right now either.

"I'm in," I confirm.

Reagan smiles for the first time since we walked in here. "All right. We're going camping in the backcountry. But first I'm going to take a shower and get breakfast. I need grease and yeast. I've got a wicked hangover."

11

"Which way, my man?" Brett says to Lennon, adjusting his backpack at a crossroad. "There's no sign."

"That's the literal definition of an unmarked trail," Lennon says.

Brett laughs. "Oh, yeah. I guess you're right. How did you even find this hidden waterfall, if the trail isn't marked?"

"I read about it. The waterfall isn't officially listed on park publications because there are bigger falls that are easier for the public to access from the main trails," Lennon explains. "This one is inconvenient for the casual day-tripper. And when I originally found it, I was hiking from the opposite direction, so give me a second to find the southbound trail."

It's midafternoon. We waited until the last possible moment to leave, all of us loading up on sandwiches at the pavilion for lunch and filling up sport bottles with water. Then we had to hike back to Reagan's car and drive a couple hours on scary, twisting mountain roads to get to a national park parking lot. From there, we began hiking marked trails toward the waterfall.

And hiking . . .

We've spent three hours on the trail now. I've never walked so much in my life. But that's not my biggest worry. I'm starting to wonder how I'll manage to hike back on my own to catch a bus for the star party later this week.

"This trail isn't supposed to fork east," Lennon mutters to himself, examining a GPS map on his phone.

"How are you even getting a signal?" I ask. I've checked my phone several times along the way to make sure my mom got my last text explaining not to worry if she didn't hear from me for a few days. But nope. I might as well be holding a brick for all the good it's doing me.

"GPS runs independently of cell service," Lennon explains. "All my digital maps are saved on my phone. But this one is glitchy. Sometimes you can't trust technology. Luckily, I have a backup." He puts away his phone and digs out a small leather journal, its black cover bulging. Where my journals are neat and slim, meticulously kept, his is . . . not. Removing an elastic band that keeps the pages closed, he opens it, and I spy a collection of things: folded paper maps, park brochures, and pages filled with Lennon's distinctive block-letter handwriting and the occasional drawing—trees, wildflowers, trail signs, squirrels. I even catch a glimpse of what appears to be a rough anime-style sketch of Sunny and Mac.

I think of all the maps he drew when we were kids. And the map he made for me, sitting in the bottom of my drawer at home. And I feel a hard pang of nostalgia.

He's changed in so many ways. But not in this.

This is the Lennon I used to know.

Lennon catches me looking at his journal and quickly removes a folded-up paper map before shutting the cover with a forceful *slap*.

Silly to feel insulted. What's in there is none of my business. Not anymore.

He spreads the map over a large rock. Deciphering a tangle of topographic lines, he traces invisible paths with one finger. "Oh, wait. I understand now. Left. We go left."

"How can you even make heads or tails of that?" Brett says. "Are you sure?"

"As sure as you were that a yurt was a urinal, Mr. I. P. Freely," Lennon says, folding up the map and refiling it inside his journal.

"Low blow, man," Brett says.

"I'm just saying, if you piss on my tent, there will be disembowelment."

Brett grins. "I love how gruesome you are."

"Turn left," Lennon tells him in a calm voice, but his gaze is hard as steel. "We'll be there in an hour."

"We're headed left, team," Brett calls out cheerfully to the group, hands cupped around his mouth. He takes the lead with Reagan. Summer and Kendrick follow, and I lag behind with Lennon.

Even with the weight correctly distributed, my pack is heavy and keeps slipping farther down my back. It's a killer on legs, a killer on feet. I'm so glad I didn't get hiking boots like Reagan, because she's already complaining about new-shoe blisters. Besides, I notice that Lennon is still wearing his black high-tops beneath ripped black jeans, so I'm thinking hiking boots are overkill.

"You need to tighten the hip belt," Lennon says when I try to shrug my pack higher.

"I thought I already had." I halt and struggle with the straps. Somehow, I think one of them is stuck.

"May I?" he says, offering a hand.

"Um, okay."

He steps closer. I inhale his sunny, freshly laundered scent. Long, graceful fingers tinker with the fastener around my waist. His hands are more sinewy than I remember. They used to be friend hands, and now they're boy hands. It's strange to have him touching me again. Not bad strange. And it's not as if his hands are all over me—not that I'd want them to be. It's just not every day that a guy is touching me, busy concentrating on a task that falls right below my breasts. He's not even looking at them—not that I'd want him to. At least, I shouldn't. Damn these overactive ovaries!

Calm down, Everhart, I tell myself. I can't afford to let my imagination run wild around him. The last time that happened, I ended up in his lap on a park bench with his hands up my shirt.

The strap loosens. "Got it," he says. "How did you manage to get it knotted like that?"

"I've got all kinds of talents," I say.

He makes an amused noise. "You can be in charge of tying all the tent knots, then."

"No need. The tents Reagan bought are knot-free. They practically pitch themselves. Or so the guy at the outdoor store said. I think he may have been hitting on Reagan, though. Maybe he was just excited because she was spending so much money."

"I believe that. Some of your gear is primo. I'd almost be impressed, if I thought for a second that Reagan knew what she was doing."

With a sharp tug, he tightens the strap on my hip belt, and I gasp.

"Too tight?" he asks.

"Just unexpected. I think it's okay."

"It should be snug, but not uncomfortable." He inspects my shoulder harness. "Okay, now these need tightening. Shouldn't be a gap here, see?" Warm fingers slip between my shoulder blade and the strap. He wiggles them around to demonstrate, and a wave of shivers rushes down my arm.

"Tighten away," I tell him. In a weird way, all this methodical touching feels like getting a haircut at the salon. It's almost sensual, but not quite. Or at least you don't want it to be. The Norwegian man who cuts my hair is older than my dad and wears a lot of rings that clink together in a disconcerting, yet strangely pleasing way when he's using scissors. I really don't want to enjoy sexy feelings around Einar, and I *definitely* don't want to enjoy them around Lennon. Best to stop thinking about it.

"So, hey," I say, forcing my mind to concentrate on other things. "Now that I know some of the crazy noises I heard last night were probably Reagan and Brett trampling through the campground, I feel a little better about our earlier talk. You know, about all the wild animals. I mean, I know it will be different out here, but—"

"Oh, it will be completely different," he says, moving on to my other shoulder strap.

"But it can't be that bad if you're not worried."

"Actually, I was scared out of my ever-loving mind the first night I camped alone in the backcountry. I was so convinced wolves were coming after me, I nearly wet my sleeping bag."

I huff out a surprised laugh. "And how did you get over that fear, pray tell?"

"Knowledge is a beautiful thing. I found out that there aren't wolves in California."

"There aren't?"

"Apart from a few stray gray wolves that occasionally pass through, there's only one known pack—the Shasta pack. They're near the Oregon border." He tests both shoulders. "How's that feel now? Better?"

Yes, it actually does. Way better. The backpack feels more like an extension of me rather than a punishment. It's still heavy, but I can handle it.

"Anyway," he says. "We're completely safe here, wolf-wise. Better chance of spotting a werewolf."

"Oh, you'd like that, wouldn't you, Bram Stoker?"

"He wrote about vampires."

"Same difference."

"Do you enjoy being wrong?" he asks.

"I enjoy your sanctimonious defense of fictional creatures."

He chuckles. "I will gladly defend all woodland-bound fictional creatures. Werewolves, bigfoots, and definitely any wendigos. But, hey. You'll be happy to know that wendigos aren't native to California either. So you don't have to worry about a cannibalistic monster eating you for dinner in the middle of the night."

"This has been a great talk," I say. "Thanks so much for alleviating my fears."

He smiles down at me—the warm, boyish smile I used to know and love so well—and my stomach flutters wildly. "I live to give you nightmares, Zorie."

"Hey," I complain good-naturedly. "Not nice."

"Not at all," he says, still smiling.

And I can still feel the warmth of that smile long after he turns around to catch up with the group.

A few minutes into the next leg of our hike, the unmarked trail bends upward, and we're now battling an uphill climb. One that's rocky and dry and uncomfortably warm as the temperature rises with the elevation. But halfway up, we enter a forest of red firs. Their branches are heavy with pinecones, and they help with shade . . . just not with the incline. Hiking on flat ground isn't so bad; hiking on an incline with rocks poking the bottoms of your shoes is torment of the damned. I concentrate on Lennon's bear bell. Its jingle, along with my own bell's answering jangle, is strangely soothing, and this reassuring rhythm helps me put one foot in front of the other.

It could be worse. At least I'm not hungover like Reagan, who is complaining about her head and already had to stop and lie down for fear of being sick. She's also irritated at Brett, who claims to be feeling fine and won't stop teasing her. I watch them chatting from a distance and try to judge whether they appear to be any different after partying together last night. It's hard to tell.

I check the time on my phone. Lennon's "it's only three hours" hike is now becoming closer to four. The trail has leveled off, which is good. No more climbing uphill. But my upper thighs are on fire, and I'm going to have to pee soon. Just when I don't think I can hike another step, Lennon's head lifts.

"Stop," he says to the group. "Listen."

We listen.

"Do you hear that?" he asks.

We all look at each other. And then I *do* hear it. "Water," I say.

"Water*fall*," he corrects, a victorious smile breaking over his face.

We follow him through a grove of trees that seems to be getting thicker—so thick that I'd have trouble believing there's water here somewhere if it weren't so loud. But then the grove parts, and we step onto the green bank of a river. And there it is.

Lennon's waterfall.

Misty white water drops from gray, rocky tiers and collects in a blue-green pool. Enormous round rocks frame the pool and dot the small river that flows away from it, creating a natural stepping-stone bridge that leads to the other bank. Sturdy ferns gather around tree trunks and bright green moss creeps up the sides of stones.

It's not a big waterfall, but it's private and lush and lovely.

"Whoa," Brett says, looking around appreciatively. "It's even better than I hoped."

"It's beautiful," Summer says. "Look at the water. It's so clear."

"Our own private piece of paradise," Reagan agrees. "Screw you, Muir Camping Compound."

Kendrick points to a narrow path that leads up the left side of the falls. "Looks like you can go to the top and dive off. That's so cool."

"What do you think?" Lennon asks near my shoulder.

"I think it's like a dream," I tell him honestly.

"Yeah," he says, sounding satisfied. "That's exactly what I thought."

We're all exhausted and relieved to shuck off our packs while Lennon explains the lay of the land. Since he's camped here before, he's scoped out all the nooks and crannies. Across the stepping-stone bridge on the northern side of the river is the best place to gather firewood. Where we're standing is a good area to set up our tents, and the campfire can be built inside a granite shelter, where massive boulders form a natural barrier.

"Look," Lennon says, almost excited—almost. He pretty much operates on one even frequency. He kicks away debris on the floor of the granite shelter to reveal ashes. "No digging a pit. It's already here. We just load it up with kindling and wood, and voilà. Instant kitchen."

"Sweet," Brett says.

And the grove of trees behind us that we just passed through is our designated toilet area. It's downhill from the water supply, semiprivate, and has plenty of soft ground for digging cat holes, which are exactly what I suspected. You dig, do your business, bury it. This is part of a backcountry agreement among hikers called Leave No Trace. You're supposed to leave a campsite in the same condition it was when you arrived. This means not destroying anything, no cutting down trees, always putting out fires, and no trash. As in zero. Technically, we're supposed to carry around used toilet paper in a zip-top bag until we leave the park or find a designated trash bin. This is referred to as "packing it out." When Reagan balks at this, Lennon points out that it's illegal to leave trash out here. But I'm with Reagan. I'm not carrying around dirty toilet paper in a bag, and I'm certainly not going to go *au naturel* and wipe with leaves. I'm not a barbarian. Lennon admits that, though it's not strictly legal, the alternative is to use biodegradable paper, bury it deep, and cover it well. Good enough for me.

Brett is walking around with his phone, recording video of the waterfall as he narrates. When Brett finishes, Lennon suggests we get busy setting up the base camp. But no one is interested in doing this. Reagan just wants to rest, Brett wants to swim, while Summer and Kendrick are dying to explore the top of the waterfall. It's like herding cats, and when Lennon gives up trying and heads off on his own to claim a spot for his tent, I feel as if I'm stuck in the middle. I know he's probably right, that it's already past five, and we only have a few hours of sunlight to get everything done. But at the same time, I'm exhausted and ache all over. And it's hot. So hot, Brett is already stripping down to his shorts and wading into the edge of the river.

"It feels amazing, guys," he reports, pushing wavy brown hair away from his forehead.

I watch him splash through water that covers his ankles. It's not as though I'm staring. I've seen it before. Despite getting kicked off the soccer team, he still has a beautiful soccer body— one that he's comfortable displaying to the world. Literally. His Instagram is 75 percent Shirtless Brett Seager selfies. But he's now informing us that he's ditching the shorts to swim in his boxers.

"We're all friends here, right?" he says, grinning at me as he hops around on one leg and tries to remove his shorts without getting them wet. "You coming in, Zorie?"

"I don't know," I say. I brought a bathing suit, but where am I going to change into it—the woods?

"I am," Reagan calls out, sitting down to unlace her boots. Then she says to me, "I saw you getting close and comfortable with Lennon on the hike. Maybe you should go keep him company."

Her tone is playful. Confusingly so. She knows Lennon and I don't talk. She *doesn't* know about the Great Experiment. And Lennon and I were only talking on the hike. Not flirting. All he did was adjust my pack! So why is Reagan's comment making me feel so guilty? I double-check that Lennon is out of hearing range. I think he is. He's already found a flat piece of land for his tent and is unloading his pack.

"Don't you agree, Brett?" Reagan says louder.

He cups his ear. "About what?"

"That Zorie should help Lennon," she says louder.

Oh. My. God. Please shut up!

"If Lennon wants to play good little Boy Scout, let him. There's plenty of time for that later. Right now, I'm thinking about a line Kerouac wrote in *The Dharma Bums:* 'Happy. Just in my swim shorts, barefooted, wild-haired, in the red fire dark, singing, swigging wine, spitting, jumping, running—that's the way to live.'" Brett wads up his shorts and gestures toward me. "Catch!"

I lunge awkwardly to snag them midair. Brett cheers, and then swivels around and wades into the waterfall pool.

"For the love of God, put your eyes back in your head," Reagan tells me.

My attention snaps to her. "I'm not—"

"You are." She takes off her hiking boots, and then says in a lower voice, "I told you before we came on this trip that I didn't want it getting awkward. You promised it wouldn't."

"I didn't ask him to throw his shorts at me!" I whisper back.

"Just watch yourself."

I'm irritated now. And suspicious. What exactly did the two of them do last night when they were gallivanting around the campsite like teenage winos? I want to ask this, but I settle on, "Why do you care?"

She pulls off her T-shirt. She's wearing a bikini top beneath it. Her sigh is long and weary. I think she's still hungover. "You're taking this the wrong way. I've had a shitty morning, and an even shittier summer."

I blow out a hard breath. "I know you have, Reagan. And I'm sorry about the Olympic trials."

Her cheeks darken. "I don't want your pity." Almost immediately, she seems to realize that she's snapped at me and closes her eyes briefly before speaking in a lighter tone. "I just want everyone to enjoy this, okay?"

"Me too," I say, confused. "What does that have to do with Brett?"

"Look, you aren't the only person to take a bite out of him. Summer's been with Brett too."

"What?" This is . . . news to me. My awkward conversation with Summer about Brett and Lennon pops into my head, and now I'm wondering why she didn't mention this.

"I just don't want you to be territorial and get your feelings crushed like you did this spring after that party."

Is she trying to save my feelings or hurt them? Because she's doing a pretty good job at the latter. And how was I being territorial, for the love of Pete?

Reagan is already jogging toward the waterfall. And I'm left confused and stinging, guilty about something I didn't even do . . . and irrationally jealous over that Summer tidbit.

I glance back at Lennon, who is busy clearing away rocks to make a place for his tent, while Brett is whooping loudly beneath the mist of the waterfall, begging for Reagan to take his picture.

All this time, I've been freaking out about wild animals. Maybe I should have been concentrating on the bigger threat: trying to figure out where I fit into civilization.

12

"Tell us a ghost story," Summer says to Lennon from across the campfire.

The sun's been falling for a half hour or more, and we're gathered around the fire inside the granite shelter, watching Lennon carefully feed another stick of wood to the flames. He was right about the boulders: They make good benches. We've all been sitting here for the last hour, drying out from swimming in the waterfall pool, eating our rehydrated pouches of food. I'm still hungry and could eat another one. But then we'd have to boil more water, and it's so dark, I can barely make out the edge of the river. Definitely not worth the trouble.

"Why do you think I know a ghost story?" Lennon says.

A chorus of noises echo around the rocks as everyone encourages him.

"You *totally* know one, dude," Brett says. "Stop playing."

Lennon looks up from the fire. "Maybe I do."

"Ha!" Summer says. "I knew it. Tell us one about killer hillbillies in the woods."

"Please don't," I say.

"Not any about a boogeyman with a hooked hand who attacks people making out in parked cars either," Kendrick says. "I don't like hooks."

Summer laughs and tries to tickle him.

Everyone's in a good mood, relatively speaking. Reagan, in her own way, has sort of tried to make up for what she said to me earlier. She brought along a small hammer—one of her many purchases from the outdoor gear store—so she helped me stake down the poles for a tarp at my tent's entrance. She asked me if I was okay, and I lied and said that I was. Then she gave me one of her extrahard back pats, and that was that. We're good. I guess. She's been sitting on the same rock with me, and Brett just slid between us. Which should be exciting—his side pressing against mine—but I can't enjoy it. I'm too busy thinking about her earlier "territorial" speech and how it seems like she's trying to steer me away from Brett.

Why?

"Come on," Reagan begs Lennon. "You and your freaky goth fetish . . . We know you've got a good ghost story."

"You have the perfect voice for spooky tales," Summer adds. "You sound like one of those old horror movie actors from black-and-white movies. The Wolfman. Dracula. All of that."

"Vincent Price," Kendrick guesses.

"No, the other one. Dracula. He was in *Lord of the Rings*."

"Christopher Lee," Lennon supplies.

"Yes!" Summer says. "Thrill us, Christopher Lee."

Lennon pushes up from a squat and brushes off his hands. "All right," he says. "I heard something a few months ago. But it's not fiction. It's what someone actually told me. You sure you want to hear it?"

No, I do not want to hear, thank you. I don't like being scared. And now that it's getting dark, I'm starting to worry again about sleeping on the ground. The tents I picked out with Reagan are actually pretty cool, I suppose, as far as tents go. They're small, but made for two people, which means that there's some wiggle room inside with just one person occupying. But they're still not tall enough to stand inside, and knowing that I'll be stuck in that tiny space later with little more than a thin scrap of nylon between me and all the nocturnal animals that use the waterfall for a watering hole is starting to freak me out.

But everyone else is apparently a million times braver, and they all want Lennon to frighten them.

"I'm so ready," Summer says.

"Don't say I didn't warn you." Long legs bent, Lennon sits on the edge of a boulder and leans forward, settling his forearms on his thighs. "Okay, so back before school ended, I was taking weekend wilderness survival classes on the other side of Mount Diablo. It's run by ex-military people along with this retired search-and-rescue ranger who used to work in Yellowstone. His name was Varg."

"Varg?" Summer repeats.

"It's Swedish," Lennon says. "And this guy was no one to fuck around with. Six five, big as a barn, scars everywhere. He's rescued people from landslides and cave-ins. Fires. And he's found a lot of dead bodies. People go missing in the wilderness all the time, and if they're lost, they sometimes run out of food and starve to death, or they are attacked by animals or crushed by falling rocks. Fall into hot geysers."

"Jesus," Reagan complains.

"In winter, they freeze. Varg said he found an entire family frozen in the mountains. Amateur mountain climbers. They'd been there a week, trapped on a ledge. An animal had eaten the husband's leg."

"Ew!" Summer says.

I make a mental note to never, *ever* go camping in winter.

Lennon twines his fingers together loosely. "But Varg said even though he'd found dozens of corpses throughout his career—which is a lot of dead bodies—he never once believed in the possibility of ghosts. Not until he traveled to Venezuela."

"What's in Venezuela?" Brett asks, holding his phone up.

"Are you videoing this?" Lennon asks.

"Of course. Now I'll have to edit that part out."

As the waterfall cascades steadily behind him, Lennon gives Brett a long, unnerving look.

Brett shuts off his phone and pockets it.

Then Lennon continues.

"When Varg was outside Caracas, doing some kind of search-and-rescue seminar with local rangers, they spent the night in the mountains during a full moon. Nothing extraordinary happened. They built a fire. Ate. Talked. A lot like this, I suppose," Lennon says. "But when it got late and everyone had turned in for the night, he stayed at the campfire, making sure the embers were out. And as he was sitting there, the hairs on the back of his neck rose. He had the distinct feeling someone was watching him."

"Uh-oh," Kendrick murmurs.

Lennon points to the tree branch hanging above the granite shelter. "Varg looked up at a nearby tree and saw a boy about our age sitting on a branch. He was high up, and the trunk of the tree didn't have any low-hanging branches, so Varg couldn't figure how he'd gotten up there. He called up to the boy, but the boy didn't answer. And because it was dark, Varg couldn't see him well, but his mind tried to rationalize his presence, and—I guess because of the nature of his job—he was worried that the boy was stuck. In trouble, you know. Needed help."

"I don't like where this is going," Summer says, curling up against Kendrick's side.

Lennon continues. "When he got closer and stood beneath the branch, the light from the moon gave him a better view of the boy. He was wearing strange clothes. It took Varg a few moments to realize that they were a soldier's uniform . . . from, like, the eighteen hundreds."

"Oh, shit," Reagan murmurs.

Brett slings his arm around her shoulders. She leans into him. When Brett notices I'm watching, he says, "Come on, girl. I got enough for everyone." And he puts his arm around my shoulders too, and pulls me closer.

I'm not sure how I feel about this. Uncomfortable. I think that's how I feel. Really, *really* uncomfortable. Especially when Reagan's judgmental eyes slide toward mine. And Lennon has paused his story, so I glance in his direction. Murder. That's what his face looks like. Not toward me, but Brett. Flickering shadows cast by the campfire's flames deepen the hollows of his cheeks and outline the sharp planes of his face.

Don't you ever miss us?

Oh, God. Before I can think about it, I pretend to cough and pull out of Brett's arm, slapping a hand against my chest for added effect.

"You okay?" Brett asks, genuinely concerned.

I nod vigorously and cough once more before stealthily scooting an inch away. He doesn't try to put his arm around me again, and I've never been so relieved. My brain is telling me how backward this is—didn't I come out here for this exact reason? For a chance to spend time with him? But my body is telling me to move a little farther away.

What's wrong with me, anyway? Is what Reagan said earlier messing with my head?

"Is that the end of the story?" Summer asks Lennon.

He flicks an unreadable glance toward me before answering her. "Do you really want to hear the rest?"

"Yes!" Summer and Kendrick say.

Lennon complies. "So, Varg was alarmed to find a boy dressed in this manner, but he tried to be rational about it. He called out to him again, but the boy still wouldn't answer. Varg wondered if he couldn't understand English, so he ran a couple of yards away to the tents and woke one of the local men to help translate. When they returned to the tree, the boy was gone."

"Oooh," Summer says.

Goose bumps dimple my arms. I pull down the sleeves of my hoodie and cross my arms over my stomach.

"Varg was badly shaken up by this, naturally," Lennon says. "He didn't know if it was a ghost, or his imagination. Maybe he'd fallen asleep at the fire and dreamed it. He told himself all kinds of things. But that was his last night in the mountains there, so the next day, they drove to the city, and he got on a flight back to the States. When he returned to Wyoming, it was night before he made it into Yellowstone. He lived inside the park, in dormitory-style housing with other rangers. And when he got up to his room, which was on the second story, he opened his window to let in some air, and just outside, on an impossibly high branch, was the silent soldier boy. *He'd followed him home.*"

My eyes water. Not gonna lie: I am 100 percent scared.

"Wicked," Brett whispers.

"No way," Summer says. "Oh my God. What did he do?"

Lennon hunches lower over his legs, leaning closer to the fire. "Well, he—"

"He what? He what?" Summer says.

Lennon's head tilts. "Did you hear that?"

"Shut the hell up," Reagan whispers, visibly frightened. "Stop it, Lennon."

"Are you scared?" Brett asks Reagan, hugging her closer. "Oh my God. You totally are!"

"Hey!" Lennon shouts. "I'm serious. Listen."

The campfire is quiet. All I can hear is the steady cascade of the waterfall. And—

Oh.

"What the hell?" Brett whispers.

It's coming from the tents, and it sounds like—

Like someone's going through our stuff.

Lennon signals for everyone to stay where they are, and then he straps a small headlamp onto his head, flipping on the light as he jumps off the rock and heads out of the granite shelter.

A dozen scenarios race through my mind, and none of them are good. I'm terrified, but I not staying here while Lennon marches away to his death. I jump up and chase him into darkness, tracking the bouncing light of his headlamp until I catch up to him.

"Stay behind me," he whispers.

I can hear the rest of the group debating whether to follow, and they are soon behind us, making as much noise as the mystery interloper.

The sound of our footsteps creeping toward the tents is overloud in my ears. Twigs break. Leaves crunch. We head around a tree that marks the outer edge of the campsite. Our tents are all spread apart, some of them closer to the river, some closer to the woods. The first one is Lennon's. Mine is just to the left, near a big boulder. We creep between the two tents, watching each step. I hear noise, but the dull roar of the waterfall is confusing my brain. I frantically look around, trying to spot danger, when Lennon blindly reaches back a hand to halt me.

My heart slams against my rib cage. Then I spot it near the river.

Several yards ahead, the navy-blue silhouettes of Reagan and Brett's tents stand in the moonlight, their dome shapes like igloos rising from the dark riverbank. One of those tents doesn't look right. It's misshapen. A giant, half-deflated soccer ball. And when Lennon's headlamp shines over it, an enormous dark shape turns around to face the light.

13

Black bear.

Big black bear.

Big black bear tearing up Brett's tent.

The group catches up to us as shock winds through me. Reagan runs into my back, and I nearly topple over. Summer makes a terrified sound.

"Oh, Jesus," Brett whispers, spotting the bear. "Oh Jesus, oh Jesus!"

My mind empties. Every nerve in my body sings.

As if he can hear my panicked thoughts, the bear lifts his head to sniff the air. His small eyes glow chartreuse in Lennon's headlamp, reflecting the light.

"Don't move," Lennon says over his shoulder. "Don't run. He might chase you."

What the hell are we supposed to do, then? The wind blows the bear's musky scent in our direction, and my feet want to flee, despite Lennon's warning.

We all stand silently. Staring. The bear stares back. He sniffs the air again, and a huge pink tongue licks the side of his muzzle. He's curious about us, and completely unafraid. In fact, whatever he smells in the air has made him brave. He steps out of Brett's tent, paw ripping the fabric as his leg swings around.

He's going to charge us.

We're going to die. If I was scared during Lennon's story, I'm petrified now. I inhale a shaky breath. I *really* wish Andromeda were here. She would bark this bear into submission.

Or she'd tuck tail and run, which is exactly what I want to do.

"Hey!" Lennon shouts in a booming voice that makes me jump. "Get the hell out of here! Get out!" He's waving his hands over his head as if he's dressed up like a vampire on Halloween and trying to scare little kids. Only, he sounds absolutely furious. And because his big voice is so deep, it carries over the river and bounces back in a thundering echo.

The bear is now paying attention. He pauses midstep, one enormous paw in the air, and his head stills.

Lennon lunges forward—just one long stride. But he bellows once more as he does it, and images of him stupidly throwing himself at the bear flash behind my eyes. Blood. Screaming. Horror. I see it all unfolding, and I'm too terrified to do anything to stop it.

"I said, get out!" Lennon shouts, clapping his hands loudly several times. He quickly scoops something off the ground and throws it at the bear. A rock? I can't tell. But it hits the bear on the nose.

WHY WOULD YOU DO THAT?

The bear shakes off the projectile. My body prepares to flee. And then—

His big, furry body slowly turns around. The bear shambles away, crushing the tent beneath him in two steps.

Lennon claps again and starts walking toward it, slowly, casually. Shouting as if he's trying to get a horse to gallop. And then the bear picks up speed and runs into the dark woods.

Gone.

I stare at the edge of the forest until my eyes sting. Is it really gone? Or is he faking us out, only to turn around and race toward us on his hind legs? Wait, do black bears stand on their hind legs? Or is it just grizzly bears? I don't know. *Why don't I know?*

"It's okay now," Lennon is saying. His hand is shockingly warm and firm on my neck. "Hey, it's okay. He's gone."

I glance at him, dazed. It takes me several moments to find my voice, and when I do, my tongue is thick in my mouth. "Are you sure?"

"Pretty sure," Lennon says, glancing over his shoulder at the woods. "Listen. You can hear it retreating. Those are pinecones making all the noise under his feet."

I barely hear anything. Which is good. I don't want to hear bear feet making noise.

"Holy shit, that was intense," Kendrick says. "He's really gone?"

"For now," Lennon says.

"What do you mean?" Reagan asks. "Will he come back?"

Lennon shines his headlamp on the destroyed tent. "If he's after something, maybe. Whose tent is that?"

"Pretty sure it's Brett's," Summer says, flicking on a handheld flashlight.

She's right. Reagan and Brett both chose tent spots that were next to the river.

Lennon grumbles under his breath and cautiously walks toward the fallen tent as we follow to inspect the damage. I suspect it's pretty bad, but when Lennon picks up one side of the nylon, I now see that it's irreparable. This is no tear. A gaping hole extends down the length of the one-man tent. Lennon crouches and peers beneath the flap of fabric. "Are you kidding me?"

"What's wrong?" I say.

Lennon holds up the remains of a package of store-bought chocolate chip cookies. Crumbs fall. The whole thing's ripped wide open. It's not the only thing. When Summer shines her flashlight on the tent's floor, she illuminates pouches of tuna. Candy. Pretzels.

Brett's entire food stash.

It's spilling out from an open bear canister—one that Lennon forced him to get. The lid is several feet away, buried under the food rubble.

"The canisters aren't even supposed to be inside our tents," Lennon says. "At the campfire—that's where they need to be stored. And why is this open?"

"Maybe the bear opened it?" Summer says.

"They can't be opened by a bear," Lennon says. "That's the whole point!"

I look around. "Um, where is Brett?"

"I'm here," a voice says. Brett's curly head peeks out from behind a tree, and he puts up a hand to shield his eyes from the dueling lights of Lennon's headlamp and Summer's flashlight.

"Did you not put the lid on your food?" Lennon says, suddenly livid.

"Of course I did," Brett says, surveying the damage with his phone. He's videoing everything. "Holy crap. That bear really went to town, didn't he?"

"This isn't funny," Lennon says. "And you didn't put the lid on, or the bear wouldn't have smelled the food."

Brett's eyes tighten. "I said I put it on, dude. The canister was defective."

"Hmm," Kendrick says, squinting at the tent. "I don't know. I mean, it's a lid and it screws on. How could it be defective?"

"It's not. He forgot to put it on," Lennon says.

Brett bristles. "Are you calling me a liar?"

"I don't know," Lennon replies. "Are you?"

"Whoa," Reagan says. "Everyone calm down. Lennon, if Brett says it was defective, it was."

Lennon stands and gets in Brett's face. "Where were you?"

"Hey, stop shining that damn headlamp in my eyes," Brett complains.

"Just now. You weren't with the group. Where were you? Did you run from the bear?"

"Um, no."

Lennon gestures dramatically. "I told you not to run. They see you as prey, and they'll chase you. Black bears can run faster than humans."

"Not Reagan," Brett says, attempting to lighten the mood.

"Yes, even Reagan," Lennon insists. "Even freaking Usain Bolt, if the bear was angry and charging at full speed. That one there was easily three hundred pounds. It could have killed any one of us."

"Dude, you need to chill," Brett says, getting annoyed. "Your holier-than-thou shit is starting to stink."

"Yeah, well, I'll stop preaching when you pay attention and quit treating this like a game."

"I haven't done anything."

"*You* neglected to put the lid on your canister," Lennon says, stabbing a finger in the air accusingly. "Then *you* ran from the bear after I said not to."

Brett roughly pushes Lennon. "Guess what? You aren't in charge, dude."

Lennon shoves Brett's shoulder. "*You* put us all in danger, *dude*."

"Whoa, whoa, whoa," Kendrick says, getting between the two boys and forcing them apart. "We're not gonna do this. Let's all relax and figure it out."

"There's nothing to figure out," Lennon says.

Reagan steps into the circle. "Hey! Maybe you need to consider that Brett's telling the truth."

"Thank you, Reagan," Brett says, still angry. "I'm glad someone here trusts me."

Everyone tries to talk at once. Kendrick wants people to settle down. Lennon wants Brett to admit that he's wrong. Reagan wants Lennon to leave Brett alone. Summer wants to know if the bear is going to come back—which is something I think we all need to consider. So with her help, I start packing Brett's food remnants inside the now-empty bear canister, sweeping up cookie crumbs into my palm. My eyes fall on the canister lid, poking out from the rubble.

It crosses my mind that all I'd need to do is pick it up and test it out on the canister to see if Brett was lying about it being faulty. Do I *want* to know? If Brett was lying, he'll look like an idiot. Or Lennon might kill him. Conflicting emotions swirl inside my chest, so I continue cleaning up, avoiding the lid.

"This is a wreck," Summer says when the arguing dies down, lifting up a piece of shredded tent. "I know we talked about wild animals, but I swear, in a million years, I never really believed we'd see one. Like, maybe some squirrels or rabbits. But not this."

That makes two of us.

Sullen, Lennon kneels at my side and picks up a dented can.

"Did you see any bears when you were out here before?" Summer asks Lennon. "Is that how you knew what to do?"

He shakes his head. "I've seen them alongside bigger trails in other parts of the park, but they always kept their distance. This one is way too comfortable around people. I think I need to report it, so that the rangers can keep an eye on this area. But right now, we need to make sure the food is contained so that it doesn't come back."

"And figure out what to do about this tent," I say, glancing at Brett. "I don't think you can sleep here."

Summer shrugs at Brett. "You can just sleep in Reagan's tent. I mean, you'd end up there, anyway, right? No biggie."

My body goes rigid.

"Uh-oh," Summer murmurs. "Sorry, guys. I know I wasn't supposed to say anything."

I glance from Summer to Reagan and Brett. "Are you two . . . together?"

Brett turns around and mumbles something to Reagan that I can't hear as he takes a couple of steps toward the river.

"Reagan?" I say. "Is it true?"

"Zorie . . ." She squeezes her eyes shut.

Oh, God. It *is* true.

"You two are together? Why didn't you tell me?"

She lifts a hand to gesture and then lets it fall back down to her side and shakes her head. "I don't know. Because."

"Because why?"

"I knew you'd flip out, okay?" she says, suddenly defensive.

"I'm not—"

"You are doing it right now. Don't you see? You always get freaked out when things don't go exactly the way you've planned, with all your stupid blueprints and checklists, and maybe I just didn't want to deal with that."

I'm humiliated. And confused. If she was seeing Brett, why did she encourage me to go after him back after the kiss at that party? "How long have . . . ? I mean, since when?"

"Does it matter?"

"Yeah, maybe."

"Why?" she says, exasperated. "Don't you get it? I was trying to spare your feelings. That's why I made Brett invite Lennon along."

"What are you taking about?"

"I know you guys dated last fall. One of Summer's friends saw you guys mauling each other's faces near the skate park. Everyone knows!"

Oh, God. I want to die. I can't even look at Lennon. I'm utterly humiliated.

"And the thing is," she continues, "you insisted that the two of you were just friends, even when I asked you point-blank if you were seeing each other. I even asked Avani—because God knows you tell her more secrets than you've ever told me—but she covered for you and said nothing was going on."

This is impossible. Avani never knew, so there was no reason for her to "cover" for anything.

Reagan crosses her arms. "Apparently, I'm not part of the inner circle anymore. I'm just someone you use when it's convenient, like when you need a place to sit at lunch."

"That's not true!" Right? I'm not using Reagan—at least not more than she uses me. *She* cheats off my tests in class. *She* calls to ask for help with homework. Do I not help her?

"Clearly you don't trust me with your secrets," she says. "So why should I trust you with mine?"

I want to respond, but I'm stuck in place, dumbly staring.

"Reagan . . . ," Summer says in a tentative voice.

"You just couldn't keep quiet, could you?" Reagan says, turning on Summer. "A couple more days, and she would be gone on her stupid astronomy club meet-up. All I asked was that you not say anything about Brett and me until after she'd left, but you couldn't help yourself, could you?"

"I—"

"I just wanted one nice thing this summer. Just one!" Reagan's eyes gloss over with tears. "None of you has any idea what I'm going through. You have no idea what's it like to train every single day for years—years! Then my foot slips for a fraction of a second and I have to give up on my dreams."

"You aren't the only person here with dreams," I tell her.

"But I'm the only person here with the talent to back them up."

"Christ," Kendrick says. "Listen to yourself, Reagan."

"I don't care what you think of me," Reagan says, giving him a defiant shrug as she swipes away tears. "Your family has money—big deal. So does mine. But I don't see you trying to do something big with your life. I was headed to the Olympics, okay? The goddamn Olympics!"

"We know you were," Summer says, sympathetic. "And we're sorry."

"I don't need your pity," Reagan tells her. "The only reason Kendrick is interested in you is because you piss off his parents."

"Hey!" Kendrick says, agitated.

"This is *my* trip," she says, thumping her chest. "I paid for all this stuff and I arranged everything. This was supposed to make me feel better. It wasn't about any of you."

"You're being a huge asshole, you know that?" Lennon tells Reagan.

"I'm being real," she says. "And while we're getting everything out in the open, let me just say what a complete and utter dick you've been to Brett on this trip. He wanted you to come."

"Did he? Because he wants to glom onto my dad's fame? Or to distract Zorie from the fact you and Brett are seeing each other because you knew she'd be hurt by this? Either reason is shitty."

"Really uncool, man," Brett says. "I was just trying to help Reagan play Cupid. Everyone knows you're carrying a massive torch for Zorie, so why are you complaining?"

What? No way is that true.

Reagan points at Lennon. "See? Brett likes you, and you've been nothing but a prick to him since we left Melita Hills. You should be grateful he's impressed by your has-been punk-rock father."

Lennon's lips thin into a straight line. "Keep my father's name out of your mouth."

"No one cares! No one even remembers him."

I've seen Lennon angry plenty of times. But right now, he's

furious. He never used to be so defensive about his father. His moms, yes, but every time someone has brought up his dad, a storm cloud drops over his head.

"Everyone, please calm down," Summer begs.

Brett steps forward. "Look, we're all saying things we don't really mean. Zorie, I'm sorry we didn't tell you about us. But that doesn't mean we can't all enjoy each other's company. Reagan and I both want the same thing—for everyone to have a good time. Is that so wrong?"

"A good time?" Lennon repeats. "You could have gotten us killed tonight."

"You'd like to make everyone believe that, wouldn't you? Maybe the problem is that *you* led us out into bear country. Maybe you're a shitty wilderness guide."

This is the tipping point for me. All the revelations that have surfaced in the last few minutes line up in my head like coordinates on a map:

Reagan not only failed to tell me about her relationship with Brett, but she also tried to con me into starting something up with Lennon—just so that she could have Brett for herself.

She's been holding a grudge against me because I'm friends with Avani.

Summer has spread gossip all around school about me and Lennon.

Brett is definitely not interested in me.

I'm definitely not interested in Brett. Not anymore. The thrill is *so* gone.

All of these things stack on top of each other, incremental scraps of trash, piling up on the heap of garbage that is my life right now. Because back at home, I still have to face my cheating father. My unaware mother. The embarrassment of the Mackenzies knowing about our sordid family problems.

And Lennon. Being around him has awakened a dormant hope inside me, and to know that my interactions with him were manipulated is the worst kind of betrayal. I thought I was starting to enjoy his company again, but was I? Or were we both just being scripted to talk to each other inside Reagan's puppet show? Looking back now, I can't tell what was real and what's been forced.

Something snaps inside my head.

I pick up the lid and slam it onto the canister, twirling it into place until the safety mechanism double clicks. Then I walk the container over to Brett, shoving it into his hands. "Not faulty."

Brett blinks at the canister, then at me. No one says anything for a long moment. It's Reagan's voice that breaks the silence.

"You want to be petty?" she says. "Fine. You can forget about sitting with me when school starts back next week. We're done. Go back to Avani."

I turn around and face her, angry tears welling. "Avani never abandoned you. Avani still likes you, for some stupid reason! *You're* the one who started hanging out with private school kids after your parents got rich. *You're* the one who thought training for the Olympics was more important than hanging out with your friends. And what did that get you? A bunch of friends who only hang with you out of pity or social obligation. Wake up, Reagan. No one even cares that you failed the stupid Olympic trials. Running isn't even a talent—it's just moving your legs!"

"Zorie," Lennon says quietly.

I look around and everyone is staring at me as though I've just insulted them. It takes me a second to realize that maybe I did. And you know what? I don't think I care. Maybe it was unfair to drag Kendrick into this, but the rest of them can go to hell. Right now, I hate Brett for ever kissing me, filling me with hope. I hate Summer for trying to manipulate me. And I *definitely* hate Reagan for ruining my summer.

Until I look at her.

For one glimmering moment, she looks as though she might cry. And that makes me feel . . . horrible. I'm not this person. I don't get in nasty fights with people. Arguing gives me hives.

I want to tell her I'm sorry.

I want her to tell me *she's* sorry.

I want to rewind back to the morning my mom told me about this awful trip and tell her no.

Just when I open my mouth to apologize, Reagan says, "Thanks for destroying this trip." She gestures toward Lennon. "You can both go and screw yourselves." She pivots, about to turn around, but then stops. "Oh, and by the way, your skeevy dad tried to sleep with Michelle Johnson's mom after the Olympic fund-raiser in Berkeley this spring. I never told my mom, because she'd stop patronizing your parents' stupid clinic, but you can bet I'm telling her now."

Time stops. I don't move, don't breathe, don't even blink. It's not until I feel hot tears sliding down my cheeks that I realize I'm crying. And for a second, I'm still frozen in place, trying to summon a response. But I can't.

My head is empty. I just want it all to go away. Reagan. Brett. Lennon. This disaster of a camping trip.

My father.

All of it sticks painfully in my throat, unable to escape. I feel as if I'm drowning while tiny piranhas nip at my skin, eating off chunks of my pride. And because we're out here in the middle of nowhere, in the dead of night, with a hungry bear and God only knows what else nearby, I do the only thing I can do, which is to retreat to my tent.

I barely can find my way in the moonlight. It seems far darker out here than it does in the city. And after I nearly break my neck, stumbling over dead wood and rocks, I somehow manage to get inside and zip myself away from the rest of the group. It's an ineffective substitute for a door slamming, *take that!* moment, especially when I realize that I can still hear voices in the distance. I can't make out what they're saying, but it really kills the illusion of privacy.

If my hives were bad before, they're going to rage now. I forage around in my pack for antihistamines and take two, swallowing them dry with no water. Exhaling a ragged breath, I lie back on my sleeping bag and stare into nothing. The ground is hard and cold beneath me, and I can feel a sharp rock poking into my hip.

The fight tumbles around in my mind, and I'm wounded all over again by everything that just happened. And then there's my dad. Does everyone in Melita Hills know about him? Are Mom and I the only ones who've been in the dark? Jesus. How stupid are we? An empty pang stabs my chest, and I wish Mom were here now, so I could talk to her. Or maybe so she could talk to me.

Wind rustles the side of my tent as I take off my glasses and wiggle into my sleeping bag. Everything inside here smells strongly synthetic, like nylon and plastic. Maybe I have it zipped up too tightly. Should I open a vent flap? What if the bear comes back and smells me in here, like he smelled Brett's cookies?

I decide that it doesn't matter. I'm suddenly overwhelmingly tired. No sleep last night. Getting up early. All that hiking. The antihistamines. I feel myself teetering on the edge of sleep, and after a while, I stop fighting. I just let it take me under.

When I wake, the inside of the tent is pale gray and chilly. My fingers and nose are Popsicles, and when I try to move, I realize I fell asleep in my clothes. I also never did anything about that rock beneath the tent, and now my hip feels as if I've broken something.

On top of all that, I had weird dreams about Lennon. Very screwed up, very erotic dreams. He was killing that bear, and *dear God*, why is my brain so messed up? It must have something to do with Brett's comment last night about Lennon carrying a torch for me. Which is stupid, because Lennon's not carrying any sort of torch for me. And how could he be, really, because I'm the one with the unrequited feelings. I'm the torch carrier. Lennon left me.

I'd like nothing more than to stay cocooned in my sleeping bag and go back to sleep so that I can maybe redo those dreams in a different, nonerotic direction. But I sit up to check my hives—present, but under control—and soon realize I have to pee. Badly. There's room enough for me to get into a crouching position, but I can't really stand in here, so after rummaging through my pack for supplies and a pair of glasses, I crawl my way across the sleeping bag and unzip my way to freedom.

All is quiet. It's gray outside, but a marigold light shines through the eastern trees. Everything is damp, and the subtle scent of pine fills my nostrils when I walk. I've never been more awake in my life. I'm on edge, thinking of the bear, eyes flicking to every bird call, every rustling leaf. I don't see anyone. No bear, no people. Just the flattened husk of Brett's destroyed tent next to Reagan's.

After a trek into the forest to relieve my aching bladder, I trudge back to the base camp and spot movement across the river. Anxiety over last night's fight seizes me, and I dread seeing Reagan or Brett. It takes me several panicked heartbeats to clear away the antihistamine fog and recognize Lennon in a black hoodie. He's crossing the rocks from the opposite bank, a hatchet holstered to his hip and an armful of firewood. When he spots me, he lifts his head briefly, and I'm surprised how relieved I feel to see him.

Don't think about the erotic bear dreams.

He's headed for the granite shelter area, and I catch up with him there. He dumps the pile of gathered firewood near the pit. When his back is to me, my eyes roam the denim vest he's wearing over his hoodie. It's studded with horror-movie patches and enamel pins shaped like tombstones and severed body parts. Some things never change.

"Hey," I say. "Guess we're the only people up, huh?"

"Yes and no." He squats near the pit to arrange tinder in the center, bark and dead leaves.

"What do you mean, yes and no?"

"Are you hungover?" he asks, squinting. "You sound slow."

"Antihistamines."

"Ah. Hard drugs. Are your hives acting up?"

"Sort of. What do you mean, yes and no?" I repeat, looking around the camp.

He sighs. "Over there, on the bear canisters."

They're stacked in a row near the boulders we were using for seats, along with some camp cookware. Then I spot a strip of toilet paper sitting under a rock. Something's been written on it, a message in what appears to be eyeliner. It's Reagan's handwriting. I remove the rock and read the note:

> *Find your own way home.*

14

I reread Reagan's note again and again, but it's still not making sense. Did they . . . ? I mean, are we . . . ?

"They left us," Lennon finally says.

"All of them?"

"All of them."

"I don't understand," I say. "Where did they go?"

He carefully arranges sticks in the shape of a teepee around the pile of tinder. "Back to the glamping compound."

"They told you that?"

"Reagan and Brett had a fight after you went to your tent last night." Lennon keeps his eyes glued to his task, but his body posture looks . . . uncomfortable. "Long story short, he said this trip was too much drama for him. Reagan agreed. They decided to go back home."

Is this a joke? It must be. Right?

Gingerly, he props up larger branches over the sticks. "Reagan was going to leave last night, which was nuts. Kendrick and I had to convince her to stay until there was light to hike, and that we'd go back together. Earlier this morning, I thought I heard noise, but it wasn't loud, so I fell back asleep. By the time I'd woken up again and gotten dressed, they were gone."

He's serious. This isn't a joke.

I feel dizzy, so I sit on a boulder. "They left us? Summer and Kendrick too?"

"The last thing Kendrick and I talked about last night before I turned in was trying to estimate how much it would cost to hire a car at the glamping compound to drive him and Summer to his parents' vacation home in Napa Valley." He brushes off his hands and digs a lighter out of his jeans pocket. "But I didn't think they'd just take off like that."

"Without us?"

"Brett left me a note on the inside of that pack of cookies the bear ate. He basically said it was best we all parted ways to avoid further drama, and that he knew I could find my way back. Then I found the other note Reagan wrote outside your tent."

Find your own way home.

He gestures toward the riverbank. "They left Brett's destroyed tent and a bunch of the supplies. Guess Reagan is officially over camping. Nice of her to just leave a huge mess behind for us to clean up."

"How long have they been gone? Can we catch up to them?" Why is he just calmly building a fire?

"Zorie," he says, "if what I heard the first time I woke was the sound of them leaving, then they've been gone a couple hours. We'll never catch up."

"You could have woken me! We could have hustled!"

"I've only been awake for fifteen or twenty minutes. Don't you get it? It was too late an hour ago. By the time we hike to the parking lot . . ."

They'll have driven away already.

Okay. No need to panic. Just think. Make a new plan. What do we do now? It took us four hours to hike here from the parking lot. Another hour or so to drive back to the glamping compound, where we could catch a taxi or bus home. But we don't have a car. "How long a hike on foot is it from the parking lot back to the glamping compound?"

"There aren't shoulders on some of those mountain roads we drove. They aren't made for hiking. Christ, they're barely made for vehicles. You remember the drive here on that twisty main road."

We nearly hit a couple of other vehicles coming in the opposite direction when rounding switchbacks. It was sort of scary, and I definitely wouldn't want to be on that road in the rain or fog. Especially not on foot.

He shakes his head. "We'd be better off taking an actual walking trail the other way around the mountains, but that could take . . . a lot longer."

"How much longer?"

"A day."

"All day?"

"And night. We'd have to camp along the way. There's no straight shot back to the compound from the parking lot out here."

Holy crap. Is he serious?

"This can't be happening," I tell him as I pace across the shelter, trying to figure out what to do next. I'm absolutely panicking now and not even bothering to hide it. "They abandoned us in the middle of nowhere? It was just an argument!"

"Reagan was pretty upset."

"Reagan? *I'm* the one who was humiliated."

"There was a lot of humiliation handed out last night in all directions. Everyone was upset. After you left, Reagan cried . . . a lot. And yelled a lot. I think her Olympic failure is affecting her more than she lets on."

I stare at him. "You're taking her side?"

He holds up his hands. "Not taking her side. I don't even like Reagan and, frankly, don't understand why you and Avani were ever friends with her in the first place. You know how I've felt about her. That hasn't improved over time, especially seeing how she's given Avani the cold shoulder. I'm just saying that Reagan only pretends to be okay, but clearly she's not. As stupid as Brett can be, even he knew it. Reagan's been reaching out for anything to make her feel better, including him. After things calmed down last night, he told me that they'd been talking since spring break, while he was getting back together with his old girlfriend. But I guess they started officially hooking up after the Olympic trials fiasco."

Jesus. Wait. Since spring break . . . ? That party—where Brett and I kissed—was during spring break.

"Did you know they were a couple before last night?" I ask. "Brett and Reagan?"

He shakes his head. "They kept it from me, too. If you haven't noticed, Reagan has control issues. I guess when you and Brett got together at that party—"

OH, GOD. HE KNOWS.

"We weren't *together*," I say. "Not like that."

"It's none of my business."

How does Lennon know about the kiss? Did Brett tell him? Of course he did. I don't know why this upsets me so much, but I feel . . . exposed. "What exactly did Brett tell you?"

He averts his eyes and doesn't respond.

"Oh, terrific," I mutter. "Could this get any worse? It was just one kiss! And believe me when I say that I'm regretting it now."

"I didn't put a lot of stock in most things he told me," Lennon says. "I know his mouth is bigger than his brain. And it's not as if I didn't know you were dating people over the last year. Life goes on, right? I dated someone too."

He did? I had no idea. I want to ask who it was—when it was. Are they still dating? He said "dated," right? Past tense?

"Not that one thing has to do with the other," he says quickly. "Apples and oranges."

"Right," I say quietly. "Apples and oranges."

He shakes his head. "My point is, Reagan has issues. She's wounded and embarrassed, and she's not thinking straight. People do stupid things when they're acting on emotions."

"But I didn't do anything wrong!"

One brow lifts.

"Not wrong enough to get abandoned," I amend.

"Neither of us did. Well, I knew better than to agree to this trip, but I came anyway. So in a way, I was wrong. But, hey, all the agitators are gone, and I'm right where I want to be, so maybe it all worked out."

"Are you insane? This is a complete disaster. What are we going to do? Maybe there's another way to get back that doesn't involve hiking all day. A bus that stops near the parking lot? The Sierras public transportation here has to connect to other nearby towns. Surely, there's somewhere we can catch a Greyhound or something back to Melita Hills."

"Already thought of that. I have a map of the bus routes. The closest one is a grueling eight-hour hike back through the mountains. That's without breaks. And for someone who's not accustomed to hiking—"

He means me.

"—count on it taking ten, eleven hours. Up and down extraordinarily steep inclines. A hike for experienced hikers who want to challenge their bodies. It's labeled on the map as 'difficult.'"

Are you kidding me?

"I don't think they realized what they were doing by leaving us here," Lennon continues. "Reagan's an asshole, but she's not inhumane. Brett just operates on the belief that everything will turn out fine, and he probably convinced Kendrick and Summer of this. At least, that's what I hope."

I hold Reagan's note in my hands, staring at it blankly while Lennon gets the fire going, blowing the tinder and rearranging sticks. I think I'm in shock. Maybe I should put my head between my knees or blow into a paper bag.

"I'm going to miss the star party," I say, more to myself than to him. I know it's the last thing I should be worried about, but I'm having trouble focusing. My brain is moving too quickly, flashing through minor details as it searches for a solution to our predicament.

Lennon looks up from the fire. "Is that the meet-up Reagan mentioned last night?"

"Yeah," I say. "I was supposed to catch a bus to Condor Peak in a couple of days. My astronomy club—Dr. Viramontes, you know?" Lennon's moms occasionally used to drive me to the observatory for my meetings, so of course he knows. When he nods, I briefly explain the star party. "I was supposed to meet Avani there."

And now I know why Reagan was so eager for me to go. I would be out of her hair, and she could enjoy Brett's company in the open. God, what an idiot I've been.

"Suppose I can just text Avani when we get to a place where there's service," I say absently. There's definitely no service out here. "Avani needs to know not to expect me."

"Or you could just go to the star party like you originally planned," Lennon says, something devilish sparking behind his eyes.

A bird trills loudly on a distant branch. "It's too early to catch a bus," I explain. "No one will be at Condor Peak yet. I can't just sit around there twiddling my thumbs for a couple of days and wait for people to show up."

"I'm not talking about taking a bus. Condor Peak isn't all that far from here."

"It's not?"

He reaches into his jacket vest and pulls out his notebook. After a few moments of shuffling things around, he finds a map and unfolds it. "See," he says, laying the map down on a boulder and pointing. "This is where we are. And this is Condor Peak." He measures something and does a quick calculation, mumbling numbers under his breath as he counts them out. "A couple of days' hike through King's Forest. Maybe three."

I snort. "Okay, that's insanely far."

"Not really. The trails would be a hell of a lot easier than the one leading to the nearest bus stop, and we wouldn't hike the entire time, you know. We'd take breaks. Camp at night."

"We?"

"You and me, yes," he says matter-of-factly. "I'd take you there."

"The two of us hiking to Condor Peak? Alone?"

"I wasn't planning on inviting the bear along, but if you think we need a chaperone . . ."

I chuckle nervously and look at the map. "Are you serious?"

"Completely."

"Why would you do this?"

He shrugs. "I don't want to go back home yet. If you do, then I can walk you back to the bus stop. Maybe you'd be able to catch a bus tomorrow. Maybe there would be service and you could call your mom to come get you. Maybe you can hitchhike."

That's a whole lot of maybes. Definitely do not like.

"On the other hand," he says, "if you want to go to Condor Peak, I can plan a less dangerous and much easier hiking route into the national park."

"I don't know," I say, trying to think of a way to turn him down without sounding like a jerk. I mean, I can't do this. It's Lennon. My enemy. My former enemy. And also my former best friend. I have no idea what we are to each other now. We just started talking again, and my body is so stupid that it's already having erotic dreams about him, which is what got me into trouble with him in the first place. I don't want to get my hopes up. I don't even want to have hopes!

"How were you planning on getting home once you got to Condor Peak?" he asks.

"Avani," I say. "She's driving—following Dr. Viramontes and a few other people up there. The star party is for three nights, I think? So she's heading back when it's over. We were supposed to leave Friday morning to be back home by noon."

"Then I can catch a ride back to Melita Hills with you guys," he says, as if it's the most logical thing in the world. "Avani's cool. I'm sure she wouldn't mind."

No, she wouldn't. She likes Lennon. My brain flips back to the stuff she said about Brett not being in Lennon's league. God, she'd love to know what a total screwup Brett was during this trip. She'd probably gloat and say she told me so.

Or she wouldn't, because she's too nice.

This is not what I planned. Then again, none of it is. Nothing has gone the way it was supposed to go. At all.

How did it all go so wrong?

"Look," he says. "The way I see it, if you go back home, Reagan wins. Because now that she's humiliated herself and lost control of her perfect vacation, she wants everyone to be miserable along with her. When school starts, she'll tell her tribe in the courtyard a version of the story that makes her look the best. Like it or not, you will be the antagonist of that story. Don't you think she'd just *love* it if she could tell everyone that you had to take a bunch of connecting rural buses to get back home? Or pay a gazillion dollars to hire a car—or worse, call your mom to come get you?"

"Your knack for making me feel like a failure is extraordinary."

"*Or*," he says, holding up a finger, "*you* could tell everyone that *she* ran home like a spoiled brat who didn't get her way while you had a great time hiking with the coolest guy in school."

I push my glasses up.

"And you can tell them that you went to a star party," he continues. "People will say, *Ooh, what's that?* And you'll be able to say,

No big deal, I just hiked across a national park and met up with some of my fellow astronomers to view— Wait, what is it again?"

"The Perseid meteor shower."

"The Perseid meteor shower, which probably doesn't happen that often."

"Every year."

"Once every three hundred sixty-five days," Lennon says in a mystical voice, wiping his hand through the air dramatically.

"Shut up," I say, smiling a little, despite the dire situation.

"Hey, I know you didn't lug that telescope up here for your health."

I glance in the direction of my tent. I haven't even had a chance to use it.

"Do what you love. Don't let Reagan stop you. Screw her. Screw Brett, too, and his pretentious Kerouac worship. Kerouac drank himself to death. Neal Cassady screwed anything that moved and was a total misogynist—like most of the Beats, who were a bunch of immature dicks. Then he died of barbiturate abuse. So yeah, neither one of them lived past their forties. National treasures, my ass."

Yikes. Someone has strong feelings. "Didn't know you were so knowledgeable about literature," I say.

"I might surprise you yet, Zora May Everhart."

He already has.

"I'm sorry about Brett," he says in a gentler tone. "I really am. Especially if you liked him."

"Funny thing is, I'm not sure that I did. I mean, I thought I did, until . . ."

"You actually got to spend time with him?"

"Maybe."

"Me too. When he first started wanting to hang with me, I was like—I don't know. He's Brett Seager. Everyone loves him. But, Jesus Christ on a pogo stick, I couldn't spend an hour alone with him without praying for a nuclear bomb to hit, because at least I wouldn't have to endure another second of him quoting lines from 'Howl' or *On the Road*."

I think about Brett telling me he'd like to learn how to take photos of stars, and now I wonder if he really meant it, or if he was just preemptively placating my feelings.

"But," he says, "despite everything that's happened between us, believe it or not, I just . . . really want you to be happy. And if Brett is the guy to do that for you—"

"He's not," I say quickly.

"I'm glad," he says in a quiet voice. "I'm so, *so* glad to hear that."

I meet Lennon's eyes with my own. His gaze is unwavering. Too serious. I'm having trouble holding it, so I look at the fire instead.

A long silence stretches between us. Lennon uses a stick to poke the new flames, adjusting his kindling. Last night, I watched him construct this same pyramid-shaped campfire, and eventually the surrounding sticks burn and collapse into the middle. It's amazing, actually. I had no idea there was an art to building a fire.

I had no idea about a lot of things.

"I dare you," he murmurs.

I stop rubbing the cold out of my thighs and glance up at him. "You what?"

"I dare you to go to Condor Peak. Let me take you there. I can do it. I know I can. You used to trust me."

"You used to give me reasons to."

"I never stopped. You just quit paying attention."

Are we fighting? I don't *think* so, but the energy between us feels fierce. As flammable as his artful pile of sticks.

What do I want to do? Maybe he's right, and returning home would be a quiet sort of surrender. And really, didn't I come out here to get away from my family problems? Do I want to walk straight back into them, sitting behind the clinic's front desk, pretending to be okay while my father walks around in a cloud of lies?

But what's the alternative? Hiking in the boonies with my greatest enemy?

Former enemy?

God, I'm so confused.

Lennon squats by the fire and assembles a portable grill. Like everything else we're carrying, it's lightweight and compact, all the pieces fitting inside a single metal tube. When he's finished clicking all the pieces together, it stands on four legs. He gingerly settles it over the campfire, and then sets a pan of filtered stream water atop it. Flames lick the sides of the pan.

We both watch the water heating as if it's the most interesting thing in the world.

"Let's think this through logically, okay?" he says.

"Yes, please." Logical is good. Logical is safe. And I can tell by the look on his face that he's about to use logic against me, because he knows me oh-too-well. But I'm so stressed right now, I don't even care. I just need for things to line up in my brain.

He pushes dark hair out of his eyes and counts off a list of things on his fingers. "One, the group left us. Whether they thought through that clearly and realized what they were doing is inconsequential now. We're stranded. Two, we can hike all day on brutal trails and hope either a bus or a nonmurderous Good Samaritan willing to pick up two hitchhiking teens can take us out of the Sierras—"

"Oh, God."

"—*or* we can hike all day on easy trails and be halfway toward Condor Peak tomorrow. Three, you shouldn't cancel your plans with Avani, because she's a *way* better friend than Reagan ever was. Four, you have a perfectly capable guide who can take you where you want to go, and enough time to get there. Five, what do you have to lose?"

"Plenty."

"Like what? You afraid Joy will forget to feed Andromeda?"

Smart-ass.

"*No*," I say.

"Need to get back and press all your plaid skirts before school starts? Or maybe you're expecting a big order of imported *washi* tape to be delivered and need to spend all day organizing it by color and pattern?"

"Oh, ha-ha. You're a regular Bill Murray."

"What, then?"

"I don't know, that my dad would kill us both if he knew you were part of Reagan's group. I can't imagine what he'd do if he knew I was contemplating spending several days alone with you."

"Good point. Alone." He whistles softly and opens a bear canister. "We'll have trouble keeping our hands to ourselves."

"I didn't mean *that*." I sound like a Victorian schoolteacher, shocked by the very idea of impropriety—all *Heavens to Betsy!* and *How dare you, sir!*

"No?" he says, feigning disappointment.

Is he flirting with me? That can't be right. I think I'm losing my mind. "N-no," I stutter, and then say more firmly, "No."

"Let me take you to Condor Peak. Give your dad a big middle finger. Zorie and Lennon exploring the world. Like old times."

"Like old times," I mumble. "Hey, Lennon?"

"Yeah?"

"We don't really have a choice, do we? I mean, hiking to the bus stop . . . it was never an option."

He gives me a tight smile, and then shakes his head. "It will be okay. I promise. I'll get you to Avani in one piece. And if you

change your mind, at the very least I can get you to a ranger station inside the park by tomorrow."

The water is boiling. He carefully tilts the pan's contents into
his steel carafe before settling a mesh plunger on top. Then he sets
a timer on his phone.

"What's that?" I ask.

"French press."

"For coffee?"

"Yep."

"Real coffee? Not instant?"

"We're camping, Zorie, not living in a dystopian nightmare."

"I'll try to remember that when I'm digging cat holes."

He holds up two blue enamel coffee cups. "It could be worse.
It could be winter."

Or I could be stuck in the wilderness, miles away from civilization, with the boy who crushed my heart in the palm of his hand.

Oh, wait.

I am.

Part III

15

Over coffee and a couple of rehydrated gourmet breakfast pouches that Reagan left behind, Lennon breaks out his big topographic map of the area and a black metal compass that unfolds to reveal several dials, a clock, and a ruler. He makes several measurements and jots down numbers with a mechanical pencil, and it all looks complicated.

"How are you?" Lennon says, nodding toward my arm, which I'm scratching.

"A little itchy," I confess. Last night's bear attack and fight sent me back into Hive Overload. "I've got some stuff to put on it, but—"

"But what?"

"It's that stuff from Miss Angela."

He makes a face. "Oh, *God.* The miracle weed lotion that smells like a scented candle factory got hit by a bomb?"

I point at him. "That's the stuff. And not only does it make my eyes water, I'm sort of afraid to use it out here after last night. I don't want to attract bears."

"Hmm," he says. "Your worry is valid. I'll try to think of a solution. In the meantime, here's the route I have in mind."

He turns his map around to show me and opens up his journal, laying it on top. Across two of the journal's pages, he's drawn a not-to-scale map of our planned route, complete with a few tiny symbols sketched at various stopping points. I spot a notation for a waterfall near the bottom and point.

"This is us?"

"This is us," he confirms.

"And these tents are—"

"Camping spots. We have to pass over two chains of mountains to get to Condor Peak."

"Rock climbing?" I say, suddenly freaked out.

"No. Patience, grasshopper. If we go this way," he says, tracing a dotted line with his finger, "we can hike through a network of caves that passes under the mountains. The caves have four exits, and one of them is on the south side of the mountain. Once we make it through, there's an excellent valley where we can camp tonight."

"Hold on. Back up. Spelunking?"

"Walking through a cave is not spelunking. It's walking."

"In the dark."

"We'll have headlamps." He holds up his phone. "I saved a PDF of a hiking book that covers backcountry trails. It says there are several big caves along these foothills, but this one is the longest. And once we get to the other side of the mountain, we'll be able to pick up a bigger trail."

I look at where he's pointing on his homemade map. "I see three sets of tent symbols. Three nights?"

He nods. "To make it to Condor Peak without killing ourselves. And if you change your mind, this is the nearest ranger station. It's on the way, and we'll be passing by it tomorrow. Whatever happens, I won't leave you stranded. If you're thinking that I've abandoned you before—"

"I wasn't." I totally was.

He presses his lips together, then adds, "We can do this, I promise. As long as we follow the rules, we shouldn't have any more bear problems. This will be safer than spending three days in civilization. You're more likely to die in a car accident than in a national park."

"There you go, bringing up the possibility of death," I say drily. "I had forgotten about it, but now it's fresh in my mind, thanks."

"You're welcome," he says, grinning. "Now, let's pack up and hit the trail. Miles to go before we sleep."

Okay, I can do this. It's not the plan I wanted, but it is a plan. One that's been calculated and drawn on paper. I like that. It makes me feel less panicky. I just wish it were my plan and not Lennon's.

Getting ready to leave takes longer than I imagined. The group didn't leave just the corpse of Brett's mutilated tent behind. They left Reagan's and Summer's tents too, along with a bunch of camping supplies Reagan purchased for this trip. Guess she doesn't intend to use them again, but holy moly, what a frivolous waste of money. Lennon is mad, because all of this mess completely violates the leave-no-trace policy of the backcountry. And we can't physically take it with us: That would be impossible. All we can do is pack some of the food inside our bear canisters and scavenge a few items we may need. A single-burner camp stove. An additional Nalgene bottle. A backup lighter. Eco-friendly wet wipes. Reagan's water filter. Because of my telescope, I can't hold much of anything else in my pack, so Lennon carries most of it, attaching things to the outside of his pack with carabiner clips. What we don't need, he stacks in a single pile inside Reagan's tent.

"We can report this stuff when we get to the ranger station," he tells me. "They'll send a ranger to pick it up."

"If the bear doesn't come back and destroy it all first."

"Or that," he says with a sigh.

After all of this is finished, it's late morning. I change into fresh clothes, brush my teeth, and try to tame my frizzy curls. When I'm finished getting ready, I take down my dome tent. It's harder to pack than it was to unpack. And after watching from the sidelines, saying, "Nope," and "Wrong way," Lennon finally takes pity on me and helps. Then it's just a matter of getting it inside my backpack, and I'm ready to go.

As ready as I'll ever be, anyway.

We climb to the top of the waterfall, where Kendrick and Brett took turns diving the day before. I still can't believe they're gone. Or that I'm alone with Lennon. This is crazy. And it's also physically demanding. Climbing a hilly trail, as we did yesterday, is far different from pulling yourself up tiers of rocks with a giant backpack. It takes me longer than Lennon, but halfway up, I begin to get the hang of it. There's a sort of rhythm to climbing, one that's careful and patient. Looking for the right handhold, taking time to push up with my legs, leaning into it. By the time we get to the top, I'm breathing heavy but feeling exhilarated.

"Goodbye, Mackenzie Falls," I say, peering down into the waterfall's pool below.

Lennon laughs. "The book I found it in called it 'Unnamed Waterfall #2,' otherwise known as 'Greaves River Falls.'"

"Those are terrible names."

"Mackenzie Falls sounds way better," he agrees. "When I write my backpacking book, that's what I'll name it."

"Oh, you're a writer now? And when can we expect to see *Grim's Super-Gothy Guide to the Dark Wilderness* on the shelves?"

"You remembered my code name," he says, smiling.

"Of course I do. I'm the one who came up with it."

He makes a satisfied noise, and we smile at each other for what I'm now realizing is a little too long, so I break the connection and look away. You know, before things get weird.

Weird*er*.

"Come on," he says. "The trail I originally used to find this place is just beyond that boulder."

We make our way through the brush and spy Lennon's trail. Much like the one we used to get here, it's narrow and barely there. It could even be confused as a deer trail, or some sort of animal path. That makes me a little nervous, but Lennon assures me that it's a real trail for real people. And at least it's mostly under the trees, because the closer it gets to noon, the hotter it gets. I was prepared for this; I strip off my long-sleeved T-shirt to reveal a short-sleeved one beneath. It's all about layers.

After a half hour or so of hiking in silence, I feel more comfortable with both the trail and being alone with Lennon. He's intense and quiet, walking steadily alongside me with his eyes constantly scanning the distance. And despite the zombies, chainsaws, and anarchy signs covering his denim jacket, he looks . . . not out of place, oddly enough.

"When did your zeal for camping start?" I ask.

He pushes a dark slash of hair away from one eye. "Last year, I guess. I was . . . going through some stuff, and Mac suggested the family trip to Death Valley. It just clicked for me. I loved everything about it."

"Sleeping on rocks?" My hip still hurts from the rock poking into it last night.

"No, but that's better with a bedroll beneath your bag," he says, reaching back to pat the rolled-up pad attached to the bottom of his pack.

Wish I had known that.

"I just thought wilderness camping was exhilarating," he explains. "You're alone out here with your thoughts. No stress or pressure. No timetable. You could read all day, if you wanted to. Just set up your camp and do whatever. And I liked doing it all myself. At home, everything is provided for you. School is scheduled, dinner is served. You turn on the TV and everything's programmed. But out here, nothing happens unless I do it myself. And that may sound weird, but I feel like I'm doing something real when I build a fire and cook over it. Like, yeah, if the end of the world came, I could actually survive. Most of the people at school would die in the wilderness after a week or two, struggling to stay warm or forage for edible food, or getting attacked by wild animals."

"You were pretty impressive with the bear last night," I admit. "If you hadn't told me, I would've run and probably ended up as bear dinner."

"Bear attacks aren't common, but if you follow a few basic rules, you're fine. If you were aggressive to a mama bear around her babies, then the chances of you being mauled are higher. It's basically just common sense."

"Still. You knew what to do."

"The trick is avoiding them altogether," he says. "But when you can't, and the people you're camping with are blockheads—"

"Not all of us," I say.

"No," he agrees, a hint of a smile in the corners of his mouth. "But when you can't avoid animals, you just have to treat them as a real threat and respect that they have the upper hand."

That makes sense. "So you got into camping because you like making fires and outwitting bears?"

"I feel like I've accomplished something that's measurable. I can feed myself—"

He figured out how to make coffee out here, which is pretty much the pinnacle of cooking in my eyes.

"—and find my way without a computerized voice telling me which way to turn. I know first aid basics. I know how to collect water if there's no river in sight. I know how to build a lean-to in the woods. And that's . . ."

"Not nothing."

"Yeah," he says. "It's being a capable human being, which is something I think a lot of people have forgotten how to do."

"So you come out here to feel like a manly man," I say.

"Right," he says sarcastically. "Big, burly lumberjack. That's me."

Well, he has the big part down. When I walk by his side, his tall frame keeps the sun out of my face.

"I come out here because of all that, and because look at this place," he says, gesturing toward the trees. "It's serene. When Ansel Adams said, 'I believe in beauty,' he was here, in the Sierras. Maybe even walking this same path."

I have a weird sense of déjà vu, because this sounds like the Lennon I know, rattling off obscure quotes and talking about the city lights over San Francisco Bay as if they were magic. So maybe I *do* understand why he'd be attracted to hiking.

He becomes self-conscious now, and laughs a little. "Besides all that, you never know what can happen out here. And that's the thrilling part. A million things can go wrong."

I groan. "No, that's what I don't want to hear. I like all my things to go right."

"That's not how the world works."

"It's how it should work," I say. "I like plans that go smoothly. That's the beauty I believe in. Nothing is better than when things go exactly how I expect."

"I know that's what you like," he says, eyes squinting out the sun to peer down at me. "And there's comfort in that, sure. But there's comfort in knowing that when your plans fall apart, you can survive. That the worst thing imaginable can happen, but you can get through it. That's why I like to read horror fiction. It's not about the monsters. It's about the hero surviving them and living to tell the tale."

"It's nice that you feel that way," I tell him. "But I'm not sure I have that same level of comfort. Some of us weren't meant to survive."

"You survived the group abandoning us."

"For the time being. It's only been a few hours. I'm weak. I may not make it through the night."

He chuckles. "That's why I'm here. If you can't survive on your own, hire help."

"I hope you know that the Everharts are broke as a joke and you will get no reward for bringing me back alive."

"Alive *or* dead, then. Excellent. That actually takes a lot of pressure off me," he says with a devilish smile. "Oh, look. Here's the trail that leads to the caves. Am I good or what?"

A wooden post with several vertical symbols carved into it sits where our trail crosses with a wider one. It appears that the caves are a mere five-hour walk. In the midday sun. Uphill. Fantastic. It all looked so much simpler and kinder on Lennon's homemade map.

We walk until early afternoon, chatting occasionally about landmarks in the surrounding area and the places Lennon's hiked previously. But when I fail to answer a question because I'm staring too hard at the rocky path, worried I might be close to passing out, Lennon makes us stop for lunch.

We take off our jackets and sit on them, and after draining half my water supply, I break out my mom's gifted turkey jerky while he pulls out roasted peanuts and dried fruit. We decide to share. He informs me that high-calorie, high-salt foods are the best things to eat when you're hiking. These are pretty much my favorite foods, so maybe hiking and me will work out, after all.

After lunch, we fill up our Nalgene bottles with filtered water from a nearby creek and hit the trail again. The land here is rockier, which sucks, because an hour into the hike, I'm getting tired already, and my feet keep stumbling over loose pebbles that slide over the sandy ground. It's like trying to avoid thousands of land mines. I'm thinking the hiking boots might be better in this situation.

"Not much longer now," Lennon tells me after I slide and nearly fall.

I don't think I can make it. I really don't. The sun is low in the sky, and we've easily been hiking for hours. I'm one slippery pebble away from casting aside my pride and begging him to stop again, when we crest a hill and find a small trail breaking away from the main one. I look up, breathing heavy, and am surprised to see a massive granite mountain across a field. One second it was in the distance, and now it's right here.

"This is it," Lennon says excitedly, pointing toward the smaller path. "One of the cave entrances should be at the end of this trail."

"Oh sweet God, I thought we'd never get here," I say, finding a renewed burst of energy to head down the new path. It doesn't hurt that it's level ground. "I can't feel my feet. Should I be worried?"

"No. You should enjoy the numbness," Lennon says. "Later, when they hurt so badly and you're begging me to cut them off, then you'll look back on these moments with nostalgia. Oh, look. Do you see it?"

I do. It's a black mouth leading inside the gray mountain. And as we cross the field and approach it, I'm startled by how big it is. The path just ends. No warning. No posted sign.

"I thought you said this cavern has been explored," I say. "Shouldn't there be a park sign announcing it, or something?"

"That's only on the commercialized caves. A few around here have lights strung through them for tourists. This one gets a lot of cavers."

"Cavers."

"People who explore caves."

"I thought that was a spelunker."

"Spelunkers are the idiots who get lost in caves and have to be rescued by the cavers." Lennon slides a glance down at my face. "Brett would make a great spelunker."

I roll my eyes, but secretly I'm thinking he's probably right.

"So what's the plan?" I ask as we pause in front of the cavern's entrance to unhook our packs and retrieve our headlamps. I decided to snag the one Reagan left behind, since Lennon pointed out that it cost several hundred dollars more than my basic model and would be a shame to waste.

"It's only about two miles from here to the exit on the other side," he tells me as he straps on his headlamp. "It's completely safe, so don't worry. Thousands of people have been here before us."

"Okay," I say, feeling cool air emanating from the darkness inside. It's like natural air-conditioning. Feels nice. "What's the catch? Is there a cave troll we have to conquer?"

"This isn't Moria, Zorie. We aren't crossing the Misty Mountains."

"Evil armies of miner dwarves?"

"You mean orcs. The dwarves weren't evil. Did we not do an annual Christmas viewing of *The Lord of the Rings* trilogy during Sunday dinners every December?"

"Unfortunately, yes."

"You loved them."

I did. "Okay, Gandalf. What's the catch about this cave?"

"No Balrog to fight. No catch. That I know of. I mean, I've never been inside this cave."

"But you've been in others, right?"

"Just the Melita Hills Caverns and Zip Lines," he says, the corners of his mouth lifting.

"On that school field trip?"

"When Barry Smith vomited on the bus after the zip lines."

"Those are the only caves I've been inside too," I say, alarmed. And it was basically just an excuse for them to build a gift shop and charge everyone a million dollars for Cokes. "Maybe we shouldn't do this."

"We'll be fine," he assures me. "The book says the tricky part is that the tunnels are all connected. It's one big maze. There are supposed to be a pair of ropes that lead up to a higher level of tunnels, and that's what we're looking for."

"We're climbing ropes?" This is gym-class horror all over again. "No."

"Oh, thank God," I mumble.

"The ropes are just our visual landmark. There are several exits, and the one we need to find is near the ropes. It will take us out to the northern side, where there's a big trail that leads to that valley I told you about." He slips on his hoodie. "You might want to put a jacket on. It's going to be chilly inside. And it should take us about an hour to make our way through. Then there's an easy path down into the valley on the other side, where we can make camp by a creek and have dinner."

An hour. I can do that. Better than climbing up that rocky path behind us. And at least it's out of the sun. I should have brought a hat like my mom suggested. I think the part in my hair is sunburned. Pretty sure my cheeks are too. But who's got a vitamin D deficiency now, huh?

I flick on Reagan's headlamp as we step into the mouth of the cave. The entrance is a big, round room. Scattered rocks lay in heaps, as well as a couple of empty water bottles and what looks to be a pile of toilet paper. So much for "leave no trace."

A fat tunnel at the back of the room leads farther into the mountain, and that's where we head. Once we are inside, sunlight wanes at our backs, and our headlamps become our new sun. It's much chillier here, and the air smells damp and musty—like rock, I suppose. I never thought about rock having a strong scent. It's not an unpleasant one, though, and the cool air feels good in my lungs. Clean. Uncomplicated. Much like our path. The tunnel is wide enough for the two of us to walk side by side, and the ceiling is several feet over our heads. Veins of color thread through the rock walls—marble, Lennon guesses—and though the floor is rock, it's better than walking outside.

"This isn't so bad," I say, letting my headlamp bounce around the walls.

"I told you."

We soon come to another tunnel. Two, actually: one to our left, one to our right. They're both about the same width as the one in which we walk.

"What now?" I ask.

"You don't need to whisper, Zorie."

"Everything echoes in here."

"Echo, echo, echo," Lennon says in his deep voice, cupping his hand around his mouth. "If an echo bounces off the walls of a deserted cave in the middle of the woods, does anyone hear it?"

"Are you finished?"

"For now." Lennon unhooks his black compass from the belt loop of his jeans and flips it open. "We need to head south. Seems like this is the maze part I was telling you about."

"This isn't going to be like the hedge maze in *The Shining*, is it?" I ask.

"God, I hope so. I love that movie," Lennon says. "Did you know that in the book, there's an army of topiary animals that come to life?"

"Please don't talk about that while we're in the middle of a dark cavern in the middle of the wilderness where no one can come to our rescue," I say. "And no ghost stories, for the love of Pete. Did your survivalist teacher really tell you that story? Wait. Never mind. I don't want to know."

"I should tell ghost stories for a living," he says. "That was fun. Until the bear. Well, that was fun too. Until the fight." The bright beam from his headlight shines in my face. "Too soon?"

I hold up a hand to block the light. "Can you not do that?"

He turns his head away to beam light in front of us. "Sorry."

"I'm not sad about Brett, if that's what you're thinking," I tell him.

"Good. He's not worth your tears. Though, for the record, you have terrible taste in guys," Lennon says, shining his light back to the compass in his hands.

"Pardon me?" I say, lightly shoving his compass hand with mine.

He chuckles. "You're pardoned. And forgiven. And absolved

for all your sins. So let's focus and get through here, because I'm starving." He steadies his compass again. "Okay, so as I was saying, all of these tunnels eventually lead into a huge cavern room. If we hit that, we've gone too far west. So I think we can just choose a tunnel and try to walk in a northern direction."

"We go to the right, then?" I say.

"Wrong north. Otherwise known as south. Take a left."

He's awfully merry for someone who has only a vague idea about where we're going. We head left and continue into the cave, walking in silence for several minutes. A noise echoes in distant tunnels, and this raises my pulse. I probably should have asked about bats. Or maybe I'm better off not knowing.

As he navigates a sharp turn in the tunnel, I stew over his words.

"Sins?" I say.

"What?"

"You said I was absolved of all my sins. What did you mean by that?"

"I was just teasing."

I don't think he was.

After a short silence, he says, "I mean, you know how I feel about Brett. But Andre Smith, too? Are you into jocks, or something? What was up with that?"

This conversation is moving into territory that I don't care to relive. "Andre was nice to me when I needed a friend."

"Yeah, I saw him. Being nice to you." He pauses and then says,

"But I didn't know you were seriously seeing each other. Brett caught me up and told me . . . well, more than I needed to know."

I stop walking. "What did Brett tell you?"

"Can we talk about something else?" Lennon says.

"No, we can't. Because if Brett was gossiping about me, I think I have a right to know."

Lennon considers this and continues walking, until I have no choice but to either catch up with him or be left behind in the maze.

"Tell me," I insist.

"All right," he finally agrees. "Brett said you and Andre were, you know . . . exchanging body heat."

That's a funny way to put it. In a way, it makes it seem worse. Like Lennon—someone who sees all kinds of crazy sex toys on a daily basis—can't even bring himself to say what Andre and I did out loud.

"Andre and Brett talk," Lennon adds. "Multiplayer."

"What?"

"Online gaming. One of the sports games, *FIFA* or *Madden*, or something. I don't know. I only play survival horror games. Maybe a little *Minecraft*. Okay, and some *Final Fantasy*, but don't tell anyone about that."

"I don't care."

"Hey, I didn't ask for it," he says. "Brett volunteered it."

"I only saw Andre for a couple of weeks."

"I saw you guys out at Thai Palace once."

"You were spying on us?"

"The restaurant is across the street from my place of employment," he says irritably. "So no, I wasn't spying. I don't own a telescope."

Ugh. I was hoping we could avoid bringing up that mishap. Like, forever.

"And if you want to know the truth," he continues in a crabby voice, "I thought it was sort of shitty of you to flaunt that in my face."

"I didn't even know you saw us! How could I be flaunting?"

"A million restaurants on Mission Street, and you pick *that* one?"

He's actually 100 percent right. I did pick that restaurant on purpose. I was still mourning Lennon at the time, so yeah. I wanted him to see me with someone else. I know it was shallow, but I was in pain.

What's puzzling me now is his complaining about it. Because if I didn't know better, I'd think he sounds as if he's mad about me dating Andre, and why would that be? Could there be some truth in Brett's torch-carrying remark?

Is he having second thoughts about us? Why? What changed?

The path splits again, but this time one of the side tunnels only heads east. Lennon hesitates, checking his compass and glancing down our current tunnel. It looks to curve ahead, and that's back where we came from, so he points us down the eastern tunnel.

It's even wider here, and the walls begin changing. Gone is the smooth rock. Now it's craggy like the fabric of a curtain, and the ceiling is much higher. It also feels as if we're ascending.

"Funny that you heard all about me," I say after several minutes of walking. "Because I didn't even know you were dating someone."

I hear my own voice, and it sounds petty. What is wrong with me? Maybe I'm grumpy because of the dropping temperatures in here. My fingers feel like ice, and I really wish I weren't wearing shorts.

"Maybe you weren't paying attention." He's said this before, and I don't understand why. Am I missing something? Before I can ask, he throws me off guard and says, "I dated Jovana Ramirez."

Oh.

Jovana. She's one of the nouveau-emo girls who hang out at the skate park with the stoner kids. I don't really know much about her. I certainly had no idea she and Lennon were a thing. "When?"

"We started seeing each other a few months ago. We like a lot of the same bands."

Suddenly, all the defenses I've built up over the last year come crashing down like a poorly played Jenga move, and a horrible warmth floods my chest.

What is this strange feeling? Jealousy?

"Are you still dating?" I ask, and immediately regret it. *Take it back, take it back, take it back!* I don't want to know.

And when he doesn't respond immediately, I fear the worst.

That's when it hits me like a kick to the ribs.

I'm not over Lennon.

I tried so hard. I ignored him. I got rid of all the stuff that made me think of him. I stopped going places we used to go. I cried until there were no more tears to stop me from getting angry. And then I moved on.

Only, I didn't.

How did I not realize this before?

Something hits my shoulder. I swing my headlamp up to see Lennon's arm blocking my path. He's staring intently down a branching tunnel. I follow his gaze and squint into the darkness beyond my headlamp's reach. A shadow shifts.

"Someone's in here with us," Lennon whispers.

My pulse picks up speed, though I'm not sure why. This cave is open to the public. It's probably just another hiker. No cause for alarm.

"Hello," Lennon calls out. His big voice reverberates off the rocky walls.

No answer.

Okay, this is starting to worry me. The dark was fine when it was just the two of us. Sort of calming. Peaceful. But now that peace feels threatened.

Lennon gestures for me to move back a step, and then he leans down and whispers in my ear, "I thought I saw a man. But maybe I was imagining it."

"Why are we whispering, then?" Something drips on my arm,

startling me. It's just water from a stalagmite. Or stalactite. I could never get those right. Whichever one grows from the ceiling.

Lennon shakes his head and his chuckle sounds forced. "It just freaked me out a little."

Yup, me too. We listen for a minute. I don't hear anything. It's eerily quiet in here. Images of ax-murdering miners flood my anxious brain.

"Shouldn't we be out of here by now?" I say.

"We've got to be close to the exit."

"Is that the way we're supposed to go?" I ask. "Where you didn't see a creepy shadow troll?"

Lennon studies his compass and looks around. If I squint, I think I can make out two more branching tunnels ahead of us. Possibly a third. This maze is getting complicated.

He sees the tunnels too. "Stay here. I'll go check those out."

I watch his back disappear past my headlamp. I don't like this. At all. I'm beginning to feel a little claustrophobic and have to force myself to calm down when water drops on my shoulder again. I shift positions to get away from the cave drip and accidentally kick a big, loose rock. It clatters against the wall.

I wince and look down. Something's moving. It's a black-and-white striped ball. Only, one end of the ball is unraveling, like yarn. Shiny yarn.

It's a motherfucking snake.

16

I freeze.

The snake is unraveling faster. I've disturbed its hidey-hole, and now it's lifting up its head, looking around for the person who dared to wake it up.

I have no idea what to do. I quickly flick a glance at the tunnel ahead, but I don't see Lennon's headlamp right away, and I'm too scared to take my eyes off the snake.

Maybe I should stay still, as Lennon instructed during the bear incident. Do snakes have good eyesight? It can't smell me, right? Maybe I'm blinding him, and if I stay super still—

My headlamp flickers. This catches the snake's attention.

WHERE IS LENNON?

"Bad shrimp," I call out softly as the snake's head lifts. Its tail shakes, slapping against the rocky floor. That seems . . . not good. "Bad shrimp!"

The snake's head strikes.

I jump away.

My headlamp flickers out.

Panicking, I scramble backward and bump into the wall behind me. My foot feels caught on something. I jerk it, and it doesn't help. It's heavy and . . .

Oh sweet God, I'm dragging the snake! It's wrapped around my ankle, and I can't tell what's going on. I shake my foot around and that's when I realize that the snake is biting me. Its mouth is clamped onto my leg, just above my sock. I can barely feel anything—why can't I feel it? Is that poison, numbing me?

I scream.

Lennon's light bobs into view. He's running toward me, and now I can see the banded snake wrapped around my ankle. It's huge. I'm going to die.

"Whoa, whoa, whoa!" Lennon says, holding up his hands. "It's okay. Calm down. Stop kicking."

I take in a sobbing breath and nearly fall down.

"It's only a kingsnake," he tells me in a calm but firm voice, dropping in front of me. "Only a California kingsnake. Let me get it off. It's okay. He's just scared. I want you to stay still while I get him to release you."

I don't know what any of those words mean. He might as well be speaking in tongues. And maybe he realizes this, because he softly shushes me—or maybe the snake, I'm not sure. But his fingers are digging inside the snake's tightly wrapped coils, searching for the head, which is firmly attached to my leg.

"Shit," Lennon mumbles.

"What?"

"Hold on," he says. "Are you in pain?"

"Maybe. Yes. I don't know," I say. It's sort of pinching me. Smashing me. Like my ankle is being slowly crushed. "Get it off of me. Please, Lennon."

"I'm trying. It won't let go. I'm going to need to—"

"Kill it!"

"I'm not killing it," he says, unbuckling his pack and shrugging it off his shoulders with a grunt. "I can get it off. Just hang on. I need something."

He quickly unstraps the bear canister from the top of his pack and opens it, dumping out some of the contents until he spots a tiny plastic bottle of blue liquid. It isn't until he's got the cap unscrewed that I recognize the bottle's contents. Mouthwash.

Angling the bottle against my leg, Lennon pours a small amount in the side of the snake's mouth. The sharp scent of mint and alcohol fills the air. Nothing happens. Is he trying to freshen its breath? What the hell is going on?

He pours another few drops out. And suddenly, I feel the snake's mouth release me. Its black-and-white stripes shift, and it stiffly uncoils from around my ankle as Lennon holds it behind its head and forcibly helps to unwind it.

I gasp and start breathing faster. A *lot* faster. It sounds like I'm about to give birth, but I don't even care. I'm just so relieved. The second Lennon lifts it away from me, a terrible animal-like sound comes out of my mouth.

"It's okay," he tells me. "I've got it."

I smell blood. I *see* blood. It's dripping down my ankle onto my sock and staining it bright red.

I'm going to pass out.

"You're not," Lennon says.

Did I say that aloud?

"You're just hyperventilating," he says. "Sit down and slow your breathing. I need to take this somewhere and put it down, or I can't help you."

Take it far, far away. Better yet, take me and leave the snake.

"Breathe slower," he says again.

I close my eyes for a moment and try to calm down. I hold my breath until my lungs feel like they're about to burst. Then, after a few unsteady inhalations, I get myself under control.

"Okay?" he says.

I nod.

"What happened to your headlamp?" he asks.

"I don't know. It went out."

"Try to turn it off and back on again," he says.

My fingers fumble for the switch. "It doesn't work," I tell him.

"It's fine. You have a backup."

"It's in my pack," I say. But I really don't care about that. I just want the snake he's holding to stop moving.

"Okay. I'll get it for you as soon as I get back." He adjusts his arm as the snake's tail tries to wind around it. "I'll be gone just a second. Right where that first tunnel veers off to the left. See it?"

I do. But as much as I want that snake out of my sight, I really don't want Lennon to leave again. A fresh wave of panic rushes over me as darkness envelops my section of the tunnel. I can't think about it. Or wonder if that snake was a mama and there's a possibility that other tiny baby snakes are going to swarm in the dark. So I just slowly slide down the wall until my butt hits the cold, rocky floor. And I lean against my pack, watching the moving white light of his headlamp. When he ducks down the branching tunnel, the light disappears.

Total darkness.

Thoughts stutter inside my head, and I'm suddenly remembering being a kid, waking up in a dark house and not knowing where I was. For several seconds, I was panicked, trying to figure out where the door was and how I'd gotten there. But what was worse was the moment I *did* remember. My birth mother had died two days before, and my father had shipped me off to his parents—people I barely knew. Strangers. And I didn't know when my father was coming back to get me, or if he ever would, and in that moment, I'd never felt more alone.

It's okay. You're okay, I tell myself. *You're in a cave, and he's coming back.*

When Lennon turns around and jogs back to me, the light is like the sun, and I couldn't be any more grateful.

"Don't leave me again," I say.

"I'm not going to leave."

"That's what you do, you leave! Without any explanation, you abandon people." I'm crying, and possibly a little delirious. I feel stupid for being such a coward, and mad at him for dragging me into this stupid cave.

"I'm here," he says, holding on to both of my arms. "It's okay. You're just panicking. That's normal, but you're going to be okay. I promise."

"You don't know that."

"I do. Can I look at the bite? Does it hurt?"

"Yes," I say, angry. "I think."

His hand is warm on my leg. How are his fingers not cold like mine are in this icebox of a cave? Why are boys always so warm? My dad always tries to freeze me and Mom out of the apartment, cranking down the air-conditioning to subzero temperatures.

He's pulling up the edge of my sock to wipe away the blood. "Does this hurt?"

A lot less than I would have expected after being mauled by that devil serpent. "It's a little sting-y," I tell him.

"He got you pretty good."

"Am I going to need antivenin?"

Lennon chuckles. "California kingsnakes aren't venomous."

Right. I know this. I think. "Are you sure?"

"It's one of the most popular snakes we sell at Reptile Isle. I've handled a couple hundred of these. Been bitten by several too."

"You have?"

"And much worse. I know exactly what you're feeling now, and I promise it will go away. We need to get it disinfected, but you aren't going to die. I have a first aid kit in my pack." He glances down the tunnel as if he's wary of something. And that's when I remember the shadow troll Lennon thought he spotted in the cavern.

Lennon is clearly thinking the same thing.

"Get me out of here," I say in a shaky voice.

His headlamp shifts back to my face. His stoic features are chiseled and stark under the light shining down from his forehead. "Can you stand?"

I can. And after testing out my foot, I find that I can walk, too. I guess he was right: I'm not dying. But I'm in an intensive state of anxiety, forced to rely on Lennon's light to see. My muscles are so rigid, I'm in physical pain. And I can't see directly in front of my feet, which slows me down.

"I found the way out," he says. "It's just down this tunnel."

"You saw the ropes?" Our landmark near the northern exit.

"No, but there's sunlight. See it?"

I do. Even better than some stupid ropes. A literal light at the end of the tunnel. It quickens my awkward steps. I can do this. We're getting out of this hellhole, with its attacking snakes and lurking, nonexistent shadow trolls.

The exit is a lot smaller than the entrance we used to get in here. Only one person can fit through at a time, and Lennon has to clear away an old spiderweb before we can pass. But when we emerge into late-afternoon sunlight—so warm, so golden—I'm so happy, I could kiss the ground.

However, there isn't a lot to kiss.

"Oh, wow," I say, squinting.

We are standing on a narrow cliff bathed in afternoon light. Only a few meters of land stretch between the wall of mountain we just exited and a fall that would kill any living creature. We are far, far above a sprawling, tree-lined valley. Mountains rise all around us. Some of them are granite; some are green and covered in trees.

It's the most beautiful thing I've ever seen.

I'm awed. Completely and utterly awed.

And then I glance around the cliff, and that awe shifts into wariness. The ground we're standing on is little more than a balcony that stretches around the side of the mountain. A few trees and shrubs are growing, but nothing substantial. No creek. Certainly no easy path down into the valley below that Lennon promised. A giant bird soars above the trees, circling until it disappears into the canopy.

"How do we get down from here?" I ask.

Lennon is silent. That's not good. He walks around the cliff, heading past a lonely pine tree, and scopes out our landscape. Maybe the path into the valley is hidden. But even so, we are really far up.

"Shit," Lennon mumbles.

"What?" I ask.

When his eyes meet mine, I know it's bad. "I think we went the wrong way."

17

There are few worse words to hear right now. All I want to know is (A) How "wrong way" are we, and (B) how do we get back on track?

Lennon whips out his phone to study the book he's saved. His eyes flick over the screen, and then he whimpers softly. "I knew it. This isn't the right exit. We got turned around somehow. I knew it felt like we were going up. I just . . ."

"Where are we?"

"We're at the eastern exit. We need to be south, which is lower in elevation. A lot lower."

Do not panic.

"Is there a map of the cave?" I ask.

"If there were a map of the cave, we wouldn't be standing here, would we?"

Jeez. No need to get snippy. I'm the one with the snake bite. And speaking of snakes, I glance back at the dark, spiderwebbed exit. "I'm not going back in there. Forget it."

"I don't think we have to," he says, flipping to another screen to reread a passage. "This cliff goes all the way around to the exit we should have used. It's just . . ."

"Just what?"

He takes his compass out of his pocket. "It's roundabout. The other exit was a straight shot to the path in the valley. It's about a mile down from here to the northern exit, as a crow flies. But that's more like two or three miles, hiking around this cliff. Then another mile down into the valley."

"So, we're talking, what?"

"Two hours. A little longer. It won't be an easy descent. It's not an actual trail." Lennon looks down at my bloody ankle. It's starting to swell.

I glance around the cliff. How could a place that's so beautiful make me miserable?

"Hey, look," I say, spotting something dark on the mountain wall, several meters away from where we exited. Maybe Lennon's wrong. Maybe we are in the right place. That could be the southern exit there.

But as I hobble toward it, and Lennon shines his headlamp inside, I lose hope. It's another cave entrance, yes, but not to the network of tunnels we were just hiking. It's just a big, wide single cave. As though nature used a melon baller and scooped out a hole in the side of the mountain.

"This isn't an animal cave, is it?" I say, imagining us waking up some hibernating family of bears.

"It looks clear," Lennon reports.

We have to duck to enter the mouth of the cave, but once we're in, the ceiling is high, so we can stand and walk around. It's maybe a dozen feet wide and twice as deep. There are no hibernating animals. No stream. Not much of anything at all, except a dip in the rocky floor near the mouth that cradles the remnants of burned firewood.

"People have camped here," Lennon says, bending down to inspect it. "Not recently, I don't think. But look." He kicks a discarded, empty can of food in the corner. It's covered in dirt and bone-dry, so it's been here a while. "Bastards. What about 'leave no trace' don't people understand?"

I'm having trouble caring about that right now. I turn toward the half-moon mouth of the tiny cave and look toward the valley of trees. It's like gazing into a framed painting.

"Look, it's not what I'd planned, but I think we should camp here," Lennon says. "It's flat and protected. Seems reasonably safe—it's obviously been used as a site by other hikers. There's room enough for us to erect both of our tents inside this cave and build a fire."

"What about water?" I say.

"I've only taken a swig out of my bottle. How much do you have left?"

The entire bottle. I haven't touched it since we filled up at lunch.

"It's enough," he assures me. "I mean, we won't be washing

our hair or anything, but if we're careful, we can make it until we can hike down to the creek. Or, if you feel up to it, we can hike down there now." He checks the time on one of the compass dials. "It's almost six. It will get dark at nine. That should be enough time, but we'll be cutting it close. And this isn't a big trail, so it might be a little rough walking it during dusk. We also need to take care of your ankle."

I debate this. I'd like fresh water. It worries me that all we have is the precious little in our bottles. But I look at my ankle, and suddenly the weight of my backpack seems to double.

I'm tired and hungry and injured.

I want to stop.

"Let's just stay here," Lennon says encouragingly.

"What about your map? This wasn't the plan."

"No, but it's workable. The map was just a general guideline. Things happen out here, and you adapt."

I'm not good at adapting.

"This little cave is pretty sweet," he says. "And I'll bet you can see a thousand stars from this cliff."

He's probably right. I look at the clear sky above the mountains.

"Come on, take off your pack," he tells me. "Let's get you fixed up, okay? One thing at a time."

Maybe he's right.

Following his suggestion, I unbuckle my backpack and plop down on a boulder near the entrance of our little clifftop cave while he digs out the first aid kit. I spy my blue Nalgene bottle, and it makes me realize that I'm dying of thirst, but I resist the urge to drink. *Must save it.* Now I'm wondering if we need to spare water for cleaning my wounds, but Lennon has broken out alcohol swabs, and he squats at my feet to use one.

"Cold," I say, flinching. "Oww!"

"Hold still and let me clean it," he says.

"It stings."

"That's how you know it's working." He cradles my heel in one hand and cleans off the bite. "I once got bitten by an emerald tree boa. Beautiful snakes, but boy, do they have a mean bite." He holds up his hand and twists it around to show me. A U-shaped line of scars arches around his wrist and the heel of his palm.

"Holy crap. When did that happen?"

"About six months ago. She was eight feet long and this big around." He shows me with his hands. "I had to go the emergency room and get a couple stiches. The snake was upset about being moved into a new habitat. She was old and set in her ways. I get a lot of little bites at work, but they usually don't hurt. This one scared me. I was so shaken up by the whole thing, I was scared to pick up another snake for a couple of days."

"I don't ever want to see one again, much less pick one up. If I'd known to expect snakes in those caves, I wouldn't have agreed to go inside."

"Nobody expects the Spanish Inquisition."

"Don't quote Monty Python to me right now. I'm mad at you."

He snorts a laugh. "No, you're not. You're just grouchy because you're in pain."

"I'm grouchy because you led me into an evil serpent's nest!"

"Snakes get a bad rap," he says. "They only attack when they're scared or hungry. We're monsters in their eyes. And that snake that bit you shouldn't have been in that cave. The temperature is too low for a kingsnake. I'm thinking it must have gotten lost in there somehow. I hope it finds its way out."

"As long as it's not through some tiny crack in the walls here. This is our cave, you hear me, snake?" I call out. "I wonder how this cave formed. You know, thousands of years ago, or whatever."

"I don't know, but it reminds me of *The Enigma of Amigara Fault.*"

"What's that?"

"Well, Miss Everhart, I'm glad you asked," he says, jolly. "See, it's this Japanese horror manga story—"

"Oh, lord," I grumble.

"—in which thousands of human-shaped holes appear in the side of a mountain after an earthquake. People soon discover that there's a perfect hole for each person, made just for them, and when they find their own hole, they become crazed, trying to climb inside of it."

"That sounds . . . weird. What happens when they get inside?"

"Are you sure you want to know?"

I shake my head. "I really, *really* don't. No more creepy stories. Especially if we have to sleep here tonight."

He chuckles. "My work here is done. And yes, I think we should definitely stay here tonight. So I'm declaring that the official new plan. Agreed?"

"All right." I lean back on my palms as he finishes cleaning my wound. It's pretty swollen, I think. He says it will be fine by tomorrow. He finds a couple of Band-Aids to keep the puncture marks covered, so they won't get infected.

"We're not, by the way," he says quietly, pulling the paper backing off a bandage.

"Excuse me?"

"Jovana and I aren't dating. We broke up before summer break. Well, she broke up with me."

Oh.

This is unexpected, his bringing this back up now. I'm also a little embarrassed about how relieved I am to know it. "I'm sorry," I tell him. "I mean, if you were upset."

What a stupid thing to say. Of course he—

"I wasn't," he says, surprising me. His eyes are on my ankle as he adheres the bandage. "It was cool at first, me and Jovana. But we never really . . . clicked. I tried. I really did. It just felt like something was missing. She said I was distant and distracted, and that I was hung up on someone else."

My heart thumps rapidly inside my chest. "Were you?"

"Yes."

I hold my breath, unsure of what this means. Part of me would like to pass him a note that reads *Do you like me? Check YES or NO.* But I'm too much of a coward to say it aloud. Too afraid that he'll laugh. And then it will be awkward between us for the rest of the trip.

"Were you and Andre serious?" he asks.

It takes me a long time to answer. "I was hung up on someone else."

It takes him an even longer time to say, "Are you still?"

Does he know it's him? Or does he think it's Brett? I can't tell if he's just curious about my personal life, trying to make idle conversation. Being polite. I can't tell anything from his blank expression and monotone rumble. Whether he's talking to me strictly friend to friend, like when he had a crush on Yolanda Harris when we were fourteen, and I had to endure his ramblings about how cool she was, and would I help him talk to her?

But there's that hope again, poking its head up when I don't want it to.

Say something.

But I don't. And he doesn't. He just packs up the remnants of the bandage paper and stands up. "Don't know about you, but I'm starving. Let's make camp."

He spends the next half hour assembling both of our tents inside the cave while I find a place for our bear canisters outside, and farther around the cliff, find a few hidden places behind shrubs appropriate for an outdoor toilet. The cliff is narrow, but it's long—miles long—and now that I see the distance with my own eyes, I'm thankful we're not hiking it, because my ankle is starting to complain.

I find a few pieces of dry wood and carry them back to the

cave. Lennon has set up our tents side by side, and he's pulling out these twist-top LED lights that fit in the palm of his hand. He shows me how to use the light's handle on top to hook it to a loop on the ceiling of my tent. The tiny lanterns thoroughly illuminate the insides of our tents, which makes me feel better about the encroaching darkness as twilight falls.

While I unroll my sleeping bag and dig through my pack, Lennon gathers more wood and kindling. He finds some small rocks and uses them to ring the old fire pit, to ensure that the fire stays contained. Then he teaches me how to set up his pyramid-shaped fire, which seems complex, because he has a million little rules about the tinder and how thick the wood should be. But I like that he's so detailed and precise. I do the honors of lighting the tinder, and after a couple false starts—it needs more oxygen—I finally get the campfire going. Which feels . . . satisfying.

Once the wood settles into place, Lennon sets up his little portable grill and pan over the flames and we carefully measure out the exact amount of water we'll need to rehydrate a couple freeze-dried meals. I've never been so excited about beef Stroganoff. Scratch that, I've never been excited whatsoever about beef Stroganoff, but when we pour the boiling water into the pouches, it smells amazing.

We don't have any big boulders to sit on like we did back at the waterfall, so we spread out the rainflies from our tents on the ground near the fire and utilize our bear barrels as tables. And when we're done eating, we use a wet wipe to clean our sporks in order to conserve water. Lennon adds more wood to the fire and we sit and watch the sunset. Stars are already visible, and I'm so glad Lennon suggested we stay here.

"How does it feel now?" he asks, glancing at my leg, which is stretched out in front of me. It's hard to get comfortable on the ground.

"Still swollen. And sore," I say.

He waves my foot toward his lap. "Put it up here and let me look at it."

Hesitant, I prop the heel of my shoe on his thigh, and he inspects the bandages on my ankle. "I think it's going to be fine. Just leave it here," he says, stopping me from moving away with a gentle hand on my knee. "Keeping it elevated will help with the swelling."

"Or force germy snake saliva to make its way up into my bloodstream."

"That's already happened."

"Oh, good."

"Actually, that's the biggest worry with nonvenomous bites. Bad bacteria. You don't know when his last meal was, and he could have chowed down on something rotten or diseased."

"Are you *trying* to freak me out?"

He smiles. "Sort of. I like watching your face twist into horrified expressions. Everything shows on your face. You know that, right?"

"That's not true."

"It is. I can read you like a book."

This embarrasses me a little, and why is his hand still on my knee? Not that I'm complaining. It feels . . . nice. "Well, I can't read you at all, because you're expressionless."

"That's my poker face."

This makes me laugh. "You're a terrible poker player. Remember when your dad taught us to play? You lost so many Oreos to me that night." I haven't spent a lot of time with Lennon's dad, Adam, because Lennon mostly went to visit him in San Francisco instead of Adam coming to Melita Hills. But every once in a while, his father would come into town to visit, and last summer he brought playing cards and a supersize pack of Oreos to use for bets. We sat around Mac and Sunny's dining room table playing Texas Hold'em until past midnight. My mom had to cross the street and come get me because I'd turned my phone's ringer off and hadn't realized it was so late. Then she'd ended up playing a few poker hands—until my dad called at two a.m., and Mom and I both got in trouble.

Lennon smiles. "That was so fun. I remember laughing so hard, I sprained my side."

"It made us laugh even harder."

"Your mom cleaned up, didn't she? She took the entire pot. Who knew she was such a vicious poker player."

That surprised me, too. She was so loud when she won. Probably woke half the neighborhood with her victory shouts. "Your dad was hilarious, showing up in that casino poker dealer outfit with the green visor. When he does something, he goes all out, doesn't he?"

A wrinkle appears in his forehead. "Yeah," he says softly.

Sunny and Mac have framed photos in their hallway of Lennon and Adam dressed up for Halloween in superdetailed complementary costumes. Milk carton and cookie. Batman and Robin. Mario and Luigi. Surfer and shark. Luke Skywalker and Yoda. This went on from the time Lennon was a baby until the year I moved to Mission Street, actually. Lennon was too old to go trick-or-treating, and Adam went on some punk reunion tour.

"I never figured out where he got that giant package of Oreos. There were hundreds."

"I think he stole it from work. Or 'borrowed,' according to him," Lennon says, one side of his mouth turning up. "Mac gave him hell for it later when she found out. You know how she feels about stealing."

She has zero tolerance for it. I think it has something to do with her being homeless when she was a teen. May God have mercy on anyone who tries to shoplift vibrators from Toys in the Attic, because they will end up getting a tough-love speech from her while she calls the cops.

Now Lennon seems bluesy. I'm not sure what I said that made his mood go downhill, but before I can ask, he shoos away a moth that's flying around our fire, attracted to the light, and grabs my knee harder, shaking my leg to get my attention. "Hey.

I just remembered. I have cards in my backpack. For Solitaire. You want to play poker?"

"With what? We have no cookies. And Joy would kill me if I bet the emergency money she gave me for the trip."

Lennon thinks for a moment. "We could use the M&M's in your trail mix."

We could.

"Just a couple of games before it's black out here," he says. "Then you can break out your telescope and do some stargazing."

I chuckle. "All right. You're on, buddy. Prepare to lose!"

It's getting too dark to see all that well by the fire, and the bear canisters aren't big enough to play on. So we decide to shove both of our packs in Lennon's tent and play cards inside mine—it's the bigger of the two—where we can spread out the cards. The palm-size LED light Lennon loaned me provides illumination, and we open the outer door flap and zip up the mesh screen to allow airflow while keeping away the bugs. It takes a while to pick out all the M&M's from the trail mix, and then takes a couple of hands to remember how to play. I keep getting a straight flush confused with a full house, and Lennon forgets half of the rules. We're probably still playing wrong, but neither of us cares. We're too busy laughing.

And it feels natural and good. Easy.

We play until the moon rises outside and stars dot the black sky. The campfire nearly burns out. I even forget about my snake bite until he accidentally bumps into my ankle, apologizing profusely when I cry out. Then he rubs my leg, asking about my hives. I took a mild antihistamine at dinner, so they aren't bothering me *too badly* at the moment, or maybe it's just that his warm palm gliding over my bare skin is distracting me from the itching. It's *definitely* making me forget about the snake bite all over again. I forget about everything, actually, including my current hand of poker. He wins the entire pot of M&M's.

Despite the leg rub ending, I'm still happy. I smile to myself as I gather up the cards and stack them neatly in a single deck. "This is so not fair, you know." I was distracted.

"Totally fair," he says, carefully bagging all the M&M's to put them back in the bear canister. "Tomorrow you're going to be eating boring nuts-and-fruit trail mix, and you'll think, *Self, why did I go crazy with all those ridiculous bets? Sure wish I had some chocolate.* And I will just laugh like an evil overlord." He demonstrates said laugh in his deep voice.

"Okay, okay," I say, pushing his shoulder. "Your dad will be proud that you lived up to your poker potential. You'll have to tell him that you finally won next time you see him."

Lennon sniffles and rubs his nose, dark eyelashes fluttering. He keeps his eyes on the deck of cards as I'm sliding it over to him. "Yeah, that will be difficult."

"Why is that?"

His eyes lift to meet mine. "Because he's dead."

18

I freeze. "What are you talking about?"

"My father died."

"When?"

"Last fall."

How could this be? Last fall? "But . . ." I can't even talk right. "What do you mean? How?"

"He killed himself."

Without warning, tears flood my eyes. "No. That's impossible."

Lennon slips the cards into their cardboard sleeve. "He attempted once and failed. His girlfriend found him and got him to the hospital in time for doctors to pump his stomach. He said it was just an overdose of pain pills, and that he didn't mean to, but his girlfriend didn't believe him. And she was right. Because a few days later, he did it again. Successfully."

I'm crying now, not making any noise, but stinging tears are tickling my cheeks, plopping onto the nylon floor of the tent. "I didn't know."

Lennon's expression is somber. "I know you didn't. Almost no one at school noticed. I mean, I thought *you* might hear. . . . It was in the paper. It trended online for a few hours." He shakes his head softly.

"I didn't hear," I whisper, lifting my glasses to swipe away tears. "I'm so sorry. I just don't understand why I didn't hear. And I don't understand. . . . Your dad was happy. He was so funny, always laughing. How . . . ?"

"He'd been on antidepressants for years and didn't tell anyone he'd stopped taking them. He started obsessing about his music career being over. He was depressed that no one cared or remembered."

"That's not true! People still buy their records."

"Barely. And he had a skewed idea of his success. I mean, how many people can say they had their songs played on the radio? But he didn't see it that way. He wasn't making much off royalties anymore, and the band was never huge—not like others. I don't know. I guess being forced to work a nine-to-five job was failure to him. He couldn't handle being normal."

"Oh, Lennon."

He nods, eyes downcast.

Did no one in our group know? The way Brett and Summer were talking about his dad when Reagan drove us to the glamping compound—and what was said about him during the big fight last night—I'm almost positive they didn't realize.

I know Lennon didn't see his father every day—or even every month—but Lennon was closer to Adam than I am to my dad.

And now I'm thinking about Sunny and Mac, and how they must have been grieving too. And I never acknowledged it. What kind of monster do they think I am?

"When was the funeral?" I ask.

"Last October."

When everything fell apart between us. The homecoming dance. The sex shop opening. My dad fighting with Sunny and Mac.

Is this the reason why?

It makes no sense. Why would he shut me out? "I should have been at the funeral."

Pained eyes flick to mine. "Yeah."

"Why didn't you tell me?"

His face turns rigid, and he grabs the bag of trail mix. "I don't want to talk about it."

"Well, I do! I should have been there. Didn't you want me there?"

"Yes, I wanted you there!" he shouts, startling me. "My dad died. It was the worst time of my life. Of course I wanted you there, but . . ." He squeezes his eyes shut and lowers his voice. "Look, it's getting late, and we're both tired. I don't want to talk about it."

"Lennon!"

"I *said* I don't want to talk about it right now. Goddammit, Zorie. What don't you understand about that?"

This smarts. I'm shaking now, still fighting tears. And I'm

utterly confused. But Lennon is unzipping the mesh door, and he ducks out of my tent before I can think of the right words to stop him.

Dazed, I try to sort out the events that transpired last year. Try to make sense of them. To understand Lennon's anger. On the final week of summer vacation, Lennon and I kissed. We conducted the Great Experiment in secret. We decided make our first public appearance as a couple at homecoming. Lennon stood me up and stopped talking to me. The Mackenzies' sex shop opened. My dad started fighting with them.

New information: Lennon's dad died. He didn't tell anyone.

Where does this fit into our friends-to-enemies road map?

All this time, I thought he'd freaked before the homecoming dance and decided that he didn't want to go public with our relationship. That our experiment had failed, and he was too much of a coward to tell me to my face.

And yet he just blew up at me about not being there at his dad's funeral. Now I feel like he's bitter about our breakup—that somehow this is my fault.

What am I missing?

I crawl outside my tent, but Lennon isn't around. The light inside his tent shows the dark silhouette of his backpack. He's dumped my pack in front of my tent, as if to signal that we're done talking for the night.

Well, I have news for him. We're not.

I'm too chicken to trample after him in the dark and definitely don't want to catch him heeding the call of nature behind the bushes. So I wait by the fire's glowing embers, hugging myself to keep the chill away. He was right. The stars are amazing out here. I find the constellation Cygnus, and then Lyra right next to it, but I'm too upset to appreciate what normally brings me joy.

Several minutes pass, and Lennon doesn't come back. Now I'm worried, and a little angry. We need some kind of system. He should tell me where he's going so I don't sit around wondering if I should go look for him. What if he's attacked by a bear or falls off the cliff?

Anxious and irritated, I retreat into my tent and roll out my sleeping bag. Take off my shoes. Put them back on. Take them off again, because my ankle feels better with them off, and then decide to change quickly into my loungewear for sleeping. Halfway through, I remember that the light in the tent shows everything, so I turn it off and dress in the dark.

Guess he's getting the last word after all.

I don't hear Lennon until I'm zipped up inside my sleeping bag, wishing that we were sleeping on softer ground instead of the unforgiving rock of the cave floor. I listen to his movements, and hear him doing something to the campfire's embers—putting them out, I suppose—before he enters his tent.

The cave amplifies every sound. Zippers zipping. Plastic crinkling. Rummaging. He clears his throat, and it makes me jump. Then his light goes out, and after some rustling, all the noise stops.

And the silence is oppressive.

This is crazy. I can't sleep while I'm upset. And what's worse, my mind begins pulling up other anxieties. My swollen ankle. Snakes. Shadows moving inside the caves. Lennon's stupid manga story about people-shaped holes in the side of the mountain. And then I can't take it anymore.

"Lennon?" I say quietly.

No answer.

I try again, this time louder. "Lennon?"

"I heard you the first time." His voice is muffled yet close. I imagine where he is in relation to me and wonder if I could stretch my arm out and touch him if the tents weren't there.

"Remember when you thought you saw a shadow move in the caves? What if there really *was* someone creeping around and that someone comes out here?"

"They probably already would have if they were going to."

"Or they could be waiting to murder us in our sleep."

"Or that."

"I'm serious," I tell him.

"What do you want me to do about it, Zorie?"

He doesn't have to be so grumpy. "I'm not sure."

"Well, when you think of something, let me know."

I blow out a long breath.

"Hey, Lennon?"

"Still hearing you," he says.

"Are you sure there aren't any tiny holes in this cave?"

"What are you talking about?"

"Holes snakes can slither through."

I hear him cursing under his breath. "I'm sure. No holes. Go to sleep, Zorie."

Yeah, that's not happening.

"Hey, Lennon?" I whisper.

"Oh my God!"

I wince and grit my teeth in the dark. "So, I was just thinking. Since there's a possibility that shadowy cave trolls may sneak out here to murder us, you should probably keep your hatchet handy. Just in case."

"I sleep with it next to me."

"You do?"

"Just in case."

"That doesn't make me feel better," I argue. "That makes me feel like there really *are* threats out here at night."

"Of course there are. Do you see any door you can lock? We're completely unprotected out here. Anything could happen."

I sit up in my sleeping bag. "Hey, listen."

"I didn't know I had a choice," he mumbles.

I ignore that. "I think you should sleep in here."

Silence. For several seconds. Then he says, "Um, what?"

"This tent is for two people," I tell him. "I'm not trying to exchange body heat, as you so eloquently put it earlier. It's just that I would feel better if you were in here when I get murdered by the cave troll."

He doesn't say anything.

"Lennon?"

"I heard you."

"Well?"

"I'm thinking."

I wait, heart hammering. After some rustling, I hear a zipper, and then a silhouette appears outside my tent door. It zips open, and Lennon's dark head pops inside. "Give me your pack."

I pull it across the tent floor and shove it toward the door. It disappears and *thud*s nearby. I think he stashed it in his tent. Another zipping sound. Then my mesh door parts and something unrolls next to me. Some sort of foam sleeping pad. The one that stays rolled up, strapped to the bottom of his pack. It's followed by a sleeping bag, which he throws on top.

Lennon crawls into the tent and zips the door to close it. And before I know it, he's slipping into his bag, a flash of black boxer shorts below his T-shirt, muscular legs . . .

Then he's lying next to me. The tent is suddenly so much smaller.

"Happy?" he says, sounding vaguely sullen.

I smile to myself. *Yes.* "That depends. Did you bring your hatchet?"

His sigh is epic. "I'll just have to choke the life out of the cave troll. Good enough?"

"Yes, that'll do, pig," I say in my best James Cromwell. "That'll do."

The hood of his sleeping bag looks fluffier than mine is, and he punches it around until it makes a pillow. Then he lies on his back, one arm over his head. Facing him, I curl on my side and stare in the murky light until my eyes adjust to him, my own gaze tracing over the sharp, straight line of his nose and the spiky fringe of hair over his brow.

"I'm sorry I wasn't there," I whisper in the dark.

"I needed you," he whispers back. "It was so terrible, and I needed you."

An image of his father fills my head, and then unexpectedly, I think of my birth mother. Her face. Her laugh. How empty I felt when she died. I know exactly how Lennon feels, and that makes it all so much worse. Because I'd never in a million years want him to hurt that badly.

A strange, stifled noise fills up the space in the tent, and it takes me a moment to realize he's crying. Lennon never cries. Never. Not as a kid, and not when we got older. The sound rips my heart to shreds.

On instinct, I reach out for him. When I lay my hand on his quaking chest, he seizes it with steely fingers. I can't tell if he's about to push me away, and for a brief moment, we're frozen midway between something.

A tense sort of twilight.

He turns toward me, and I'm pulling him closer, and he buries his head against my neck, sobbing quietly. I feel hot tears on my skin, and my arms are circling him. The scent of him fills my nostrils, shampoo and sunniness and wood smoke, the tang of sweat and fragrant pine needles. He's harder, stronger, and far more masculine than he was the last time I hugged him. It's like holding a brick wall.

Gradually, the quiet crying stops, and he goes completely limp in my arms.

We're in a strange cave, slightly lost. Off plan and definitely off trail.

But for the first time since we left home, I am not anxious.

19

We've been walking for several hours now, and we've only just made it past the valley below our cave. My back and legs hurt, despite the ibuprofen Lennon gave me at breakfast. He had it laid out for me on a bear canister when I woke up, along with one of the blue coffee cups. I'm not sure how he got out of the tent without me knowing. All I know is that every time I woke during the night, his arm was still wrapped around me. And then sometime around dawn, I was vaguely aware of being a lot colder. By the time I fully emerged from sleep, he'd already started a fire and was readying everything for our breakfast, last night's roller-coaster emotions exchanged for the promise of hot coffee and a new day.

Not a bad way to wake up. Except that my body feels as if I've been hit by a truck that's backed over me several times out of spite.

Hiking hurts.

It hurts even more when we crest over a steep hill. But it

doesn't matter, because I'm eager to see where we're going. Lennon made another map. He drew it inside his journal this morning and recalculated our route while I tried not to stare at the dark stubble growing over his jaw, because it gives me inappropriate feelings about him. After taking that wrong turn yesterday inside the cave, he said we're going to stick to a more established trail that I'll like better: It's marked on the official King's Forest map and leads to not only a ranger station but something scenic along the way—only, he insists on that scenic thing being a surprise.

He knows I hate surprises but talks me into accepting it. I tell myself that I'm relenting because of what he revealed last night, but it's probably the stubble. It's really good stubble.

We are at a crossroads where two trails diverge. A signpost tells us that the larger path in front of us is Emperor Trail. And through a break in the cedar trees, we are now staring at white-capped mountains that glitter in the bright sun.

"Oh, wow," I murmur.

"Right?" Lennon says. "The brown peak on the left is Mount Topaz and the gray jagged one on the right is Thunderbolt Mountain. So many climbers die up there."

It doesn't *look* deadly. In fact, it looks beautiful. Majestic. Yes, I definitely see why people say that about mountains. I stretch out my arms and fill my lungs with clean air. Something stings. I slap my arm.

"Oh, we're entering mosquito territory," Lennon says, turning around and pointing at his pack. "Dig around in the second pocket. There's a small bottle of insect repellent."

I unzip the pocket and slip my fingers inside, finding the bottle in question. We take turns anointing ourselves in citronella-scented oil that makes my eyes water. Once we're slathered up and mosquito-proof, we set out on the trail that cuts through a cedar grove. It doesn't take long for two things to happen: (1) we see other hikers ahead of us, and (2) we see them walking up a towering set of granite stairs that's been carved into the mountain.

"What the hell is that?" I say.

"Emperor's Staircase," Lennon says, waggling his brows. He's wearing a slouchy, black knit cap with a skull on it, and the spiky ends of his hair stick out from beneath it. I wish I had a hat to cover up the disaster that is my mass of frizzy curls. Nature is unforgiving.

"We're going up those rock stairs?" I ask.

"Not just rock stairs, Zorie. It's nature's noble staircase," he says in a grand voice. "More than eight hundred steps carved into the granite cliffs in the late eighteen hundreds. Three men died building them, and nearly every year since then, someone's died on these stairs. Fifteen in the last decade. This is the currently the deadliest trail in all the US national parks."

"*What?*" I say, alarmed.

He grins. "Don't worry. The people who die are generally just idiots who fall over the side trying to do stupid things. You'll understand why when we get farther up. If Brett were here, I'd give him a fifty–fifty chance of surviving, because he wouldn't be able to resist the call of death. Which almost makes me wish he were still with us."

"That's not nice," I complain, though I can't help but smile a little.

"*But*," he insists, "you and I will not be following in any daredevil footsteps."

"Um, I would hope not?"

"It's fine. Thousands of people with basic common sense hike these stairs every year and live to tell the tale. It's one of the park's most popular features. You are going to love it, I promise. There's a huge treat at the top."

"A hot tub and a pizza?"

He chuckles. "Not quite, but you're going to like it. We'll break for lunch halfway up. Let's do this, Everhart!" he says enthusiastically, an infectious smile splitting his face.

And so we begin the ascent.

We have to climb a normal uphill path for about a half hour before we hit the stairs. They're rough and wide, and pretty wildflowers and lacy grasses grow alongside them. They casually snake up the mountainside, and the top steps are hidden from view, around the back of the peak. The steps are steep in parts, and a little wonky, but apart from the strain on my calves, I can't really understand why they'd be dangerous. I hear water that gets louder as we ascend, so I assume there's a nearby river, just out of sight.

Climbing, I realize that I'm feeling better physically. Not

exactly 100 percent, but Lennon says it takes time for the body to get used to hiking. It's a slow and steady endurance, not a race. And the pristine scenery definitely helps to motivate me.

The problem with hiking is that it strips away everything. There's no distraction of checking your online feeds. No TV. No schedule to keep. It's just you and your thoughts and the steady pace of your feet moving over rocky ground. And even when I try to keep my head clear, it's busy working in the background, quietly trying to solve things that I don't want solved.

Like Lennon.

And me.

Us.

We haven't talked about last night. Not about sleeping in the same tent, and definitely not about his dad dying. I have questions upon questions, but I'm waiting for him to give me some sort of indication that he's ready to answer them.

Or maybe I'm not ready to hear those answers.

I hate quandaries.

After we've been hiking up the steps for twenty minutes or so, both my head and legs feel close to exploding. No amount of internal reflection or pretty scenery can distract me from the pain. "I can't go any farther," I tell him, breathless. "Worst StairMaster workout ever. I hate these dumb steps. I hate them, I hate them, I—"

"Take it easy. We're almost to the halfway point. Right up there," he tells me, and I spot a place where the steps break. There have been a few rest areas along the way up the mountain, but this one is a smooth granite plateau with several carved-rock benches. One is occupied by a family of tourists with day packs—two kids and a mom and dad. They're also loud, shouting to each other over the ever-present roar of that unseen river. This is startling after not hearing or seeing another soul all day yesterday.

Lennon dumps his backpack on a shady bench over near the mountainside of the plateau, and I collapse next to him, sitting for a moment perched on the edge of the bench before I unhook the straps on my pack. We're in a semiprivate, protected area, so the noise of the river isn't as bad here.

"I'm sweating," I tell him. "I don't remember the last time I sweated before this trip."

He opens up his bear canister and retrieves the same lunch we ate yesterday. "It's good for you."

"Is hiking how you went from skinny to jacked?"

Squinting eyes fix on mine. "I didn't realize I was."

"Oh, you are," I say as my neck warms. *Smooth, Everhart.* I'm veering too close to the subject of me spying on him in his room with my telescope and decide to quit while I'm ahead and drop it.

"You never got to look at the stars last night," he says after a moment.

Ugh. He was thinking about me spying too. Terrific.

"It's fine," I tell him.

"I promise that you'll get some quality stargazing time

tonight," he says, and after some reflection, clears his throat. "I haven't asked today if you want to keep going all the way to Condor Peak. The ranger station I told you about is on the other side of the mountain. We should get there this afternoon. I mean, I know I just assumed you'd be here tonight to stargaze, but if you want to call a car at the ranger station . . ."

Oh. I actually *hadn't* been thinking of that.

"You don't have to make a decision right now," he says. "Just think about it and let me know. So I can make contingency plans."

I nod, and the subject is dropped. We eat in silence, mostly because I'm too tired to do two things at once. Chewing is all I can handle. But by the time we're packing back up, the tourist family has left, and we're alone on the cliff. That's when I start to notice Lennon's leg bouncing like a jackhammer. He does that when he's concentrating too hard—when he takes tests—and also when he's antsy about something.

When he catches me staring at his leg, he immediately stops bouncing it and sighs. "This is stupid. We should just talk about it."

"Excuse me?"

"Last fall. Look, I told you about my dad. Now I want to know about yours."

"My dad?"

His eyes narrow and flick to mine. "I'd like to know what he told you about me after homecoming. I assume he told you something. I just want to know how much of it was true."

"Not following," I say, shaking my head.

"After homecoming. What he told you."

I stare at him. "Um, he just had a talk with me and told me I'd be better off staying away from you. That it would be best to make a clean break and move on, because it was causing me . . . stress."

"That's it?"

I don't know what he wants me to say. "Pretty much. I didn't tell him about . . . you know. The experiment."

Lennon squints at me. "And he didn't bring it up?"

"Why would he?"

He starts to answer, but then changes his mind. Twice. After biting his lower lip and another rapid leg bounce, he finally says, "I'm trying to figure out why you cut me out of your life and started seeing Andre."

"You ditched me at homecoming!"

"I texted you."

"Once. 'I'm sorry.' That's it. That's all you said. I texted you back a million times and you didn't answer."

"Well, excuse me if I was busy with my father attempting suicide."

My body stills. "That was . . . on homecoming?"

"It was one of many shitty things that happened that day."

"Umm . . . Do you want to share these things with the class?"

He stares at the mountains in the distance as if they might grow legs and walk away. "That's why I was asking about your dad. He didn't say anything about what happened that day? At the hotel?"

"What hotel?"

He closes his eyes and mumbles something to himself, slumping low on the park bench. "Never mind."

"Oh no, you don't," I say, getting irritated. "Absolutely not. You brought this up. You finish it. What hotel?"

He covers his eyes with one hand and groans.

Which totally cranks up my anxiety several notches. If Lennon thinks it's bad, it must be far worse than I ever imagined.

"Just tell me," I plead.

He slaps both hands on his knees, elbows bent, as if he's about to stand, but instead inhales sharply and blows out a hard breath. "Last fall, things had been, well, changing between us. The Great Experiment was undertaken."

"I was there," I remind him.

"I thought it was going well. Well enough that we agreed to tell our parents and go public," he says, leaning back against the bench and slouching lower, arms crossed over his chest. "And I guess I . . . was overenthusiastic about the importance of homecoming. I thought, well, you know. That we had the friend thing down. We were expert friends. And when we . . . I mean, my God. The things we did on that park bench."

"Not everything," I say, feeling my ears grow warm.

"No, but it was good. I mean, really, *really* good. Right?"

It was amazing. Awkward at times, especially at first. It's odd to kiss your best friend. But also not odd. Also very nice. So nice that I can't think about it right now, because it makes me flustered. This entire conversation is making me flustered. I think I'm sweating again.

He relaxes when I hesitantly nod to confirm. "So, yeah. Things were going well. We agreed to go public. It felt right. But then homecoming was approaching, and you were getting a little stressed out about telling your dad—"

My fingers are starting to go a little numb.

"—and I don't blame you. He's not friendly or approachable. And, you know, he's never liked me."

I don't correct him, because it's true. When we were kids, Dad didn't seem to have an opinion about Lennon—until he found out that Lennon had two mothers and a Muslim father. That's when he began to say snarky things about the Mackenzies.

Lennon continues. "I'm just saying that at the time, I understood you not wanting to tell him, but I especially understood after what happened the day of homecoming."

"Which was what, exactly?"

He sighs heavily. "I knew some seniors who were getting hotel rooms for homecoming night."

That happens every year, both at homecoming and prom. Sometimes the rooms are reserved by groups of kids who want to party, and sometimes it's just couples.

"I thought I'd get a hotel room for the two of us. Alone," Lennon says.

I make a strangled noise. This is . . . not what I expected to hear. At all.

"In retrospect," he says, "I'm aware that this sounds as if I was making some pretty big presumptions about where our relationship was headed. And I guess I was. But to be fair, I thought we were on the same page. Or at least, that's what I told myself."

I have no idea what I'm feeling right now. My skin feels like it's on fire and numb at the same time. "You couldn't have asked me about this?" Honestly, at the time, I probably would have been thrilled out of my mind, but it's weird to hear about it now. "Like, consulted me beforehand?"

"I thought I was being romantic by surprising you."

"By renting a room where we could have sex?"

He squints one eye shut. "Well, when you say it like *that*, yeah, it sounds pretty skanky. But I never would have pressured you. You know that. Right?"

"But that wasn't your intention?"

"Like I said, I thought we were simpatico on this subject. At the time."

Okay, maybe we were, that's true. There are only so many extreme, heavy-metal, *where did my bra go?* make-out sessions you can have before you start to lose your mind a little.

"Please do go on and tell me what happened next in your romantic hotel scheme," I say drily.

He sighs again. That's not good. When he sighs a lot, it's because he's about to say something he doesn't want to say. "So anyway, you may not remember this, but the day of homecoming, I wasn't at lunch."

I nod.

"I had sneaked off school grounds to reserve the hotel room. Only, I was worried the hotel wouldn't let me, because I was sixteen, and I knew that other kids getting rooms there were using their parents' credit cards, so . . . I sort of borrowed Mac's credit card."

"You . . ."

"Okay," he admits. "I guess I stole it."

"Oh, God."

"I know. It was stupid. I wasn't thinking straight. I thought I could charge the room, sneak the card back into Mac's purse, snag the bill when it came in, and pay for it before Mac noticed. And Ina Kipling's cousin was working the desk at the Edgemont Hotel—"

"Whoa. That's—"

"Fancy. I know. Ina told a few of us about it in drama class. She claimed her cousin would bend the hotel's minimum age policy, so I sneaked out of school and went to the Edgemont Hotel the day of homecoming. I was at the desk, and it was Ina's cousin, and she asked me what name to put on the reservation, and I didn't want to use our real names. So I panicked and used my dad's name. And as I'm spelling out 'Ahmed' for Ina's cousin, she's asking me if I'm Arabic—which sort of pisses me off, because first, I'm not a language, and second, she's acting like I'm a terrorist or something."

I roll my hand to move Lennon along. Get on with it, man!

"And as we're having this conversation, and I admit that

Ahmed is actually my father's name, she tells me that I have to give real names or she'll get in trouble. So I give her my name and your name, and then, out of nowhere, your dad shoves me."

Hold on. What?

"My dad?"

"Your dad," he repeats in a voice that's heavy with resentment.

"What in the world was he doing there?"

"He was apparently behind me in line and overheard the whole thing. Because he made a huge scene. We're in the middle of this luxury hotel, with bellhops and gold luggage carts, and he's screaming at me that if I so much as look at his daughter again, he will beat the shit out of me."

I cringe, covering my eyes in horror as Lennon continues.

"Then he threatens Ina, saying that she should be fired for giving a hotel room to a minor, and . . ." Lennon sighs loudly. "It was *horrible*. I wanted to die. And then your dad snatched Mac's credit card off the counter and demanded to know if my moms had sanctioned this. He called them 'dyke heathens.'"

"Oh, Jesus Christ."

"Yeah," he says. "That's when I lost it."

"What happened?"

"I slugged him."

WHAT? I stare at Lennon in disbelief.

"Yep," Lennon says, tapping his thigh repeatedly with his knuckles. "Punched him the jaw. Hurt like hell. My knuckles were bruised for days."

My mind flashes back to memories from last year. Dad had a swollen cheek and his jaw was bruised. He told us he'd been hit by falling scaffolding when he was walking past a construction site.

"After I landed the punch," Lennon continues, "he started to go after me, but one of the hotel employees stepped in. And then Ina ran to get the manager. And . . . to make a long story short, your dad hauled me outside the hotel and said he wouldn't call the cops and have me arrested for assault and battery if I stayed away from you. No homecoming dance. No visits at home. No talking at school. No phone calls or texts. He said he'd be monitoring your phone."

"Jesus," I say, shocked. Can he monitor my phone? Has he already? My parents have always given me a fair amount of freedom. I never thought in a million years that they would invade my privacy.

"So that was it, basically," Lennon says. "I planned on telling you anyway. At least, after I drove around town and stopped freaking out. That's when I texted Avani and told her to let you know that I'd meet you at the homecoming dance, because our plan for me to show up at your house and tell your parents we were dating was . . . not happening. So I thought I'd just tell you what happened with your dad at the dance and we could figure out what to do. But then Sunny called and said my dad had tried to commit suicide, and we rushed into the city to wait at the hospital, because they didn't know if he would live or not."

He swallows, and his throat bobs. "Dad made it through the

weekend. And my moms made sure his girlfriend was prepared to handle him at home—bought groceries for them, and stuff. And anyway, it was draining. And I didn't get back into town until Sunday night. I was going to try to talk to you at school the next day, to apologize for homecoming and explain what happened. But then my dad made his second suicide attempt, and that time, no one was there to stop him."

"Oh, Lennon."

"Yeah." He gives me a tight smile that fades. "That's when I texted you the last time."

I'm sorry.

I see the text in my mind as clearly as the day I received it. "I thought . . . you were saying that you didn't want to be in a relationship. That you were chickening out of telling me in person."

"I was afraid your dad was monitoring your texts, and I was in the middle of a nightmare. I couldn't think straight. I just told myself that when I got back after the funeral, we'd sort it out. The last thing I expected was to come back to school and see you with Andre."

Oh, Jesus.

Everything begins to slot together inside my head.

I remember that Monday with perfect clarity. I'd been crying all weekend, thinking he'd decided that being anything more than friends was too weird, and that he'd bailed on me. I didn't want to go back to school. Mom forced me to go after I confessed about the Great Experiment. She said I should talk to him and find out what happened. Give him the benefit of the doubt. And—

"My dad had a long talk with me," I say, too agitated to sit. I jump off the bench and pace around the plateau. "He said Mom told him I was upset and that I'd be better off not talking to you. To let it go, that all relationships change, and it was better to have pride than be the one begging. He . . ." I stop and put my hands on my hips to steady myself. I think I'm going to be sick. "I thought he was being a concerned father. Why would he care what we did or didn't do?"

Lennon throws his hands up. "Right? I never understood it. I mean, I know my parents are way less uptight about sex—"

Dear God. I feel myself flush.

"—but it was so weird to me that he blew up like that."

"Oh, he blows up, all right," I say, pacing again. "He's a keg of dynamite."

"He's petty, too. He kept Mac's credit card—for leverage, he told me. When she went into a tizzy, trying to find it after my dad's funeral, I couldn't stand lying to her. So I confessed to the whole thing. She was furious at me. You know how she is about stealing."

"I know."

"But afterward, she was more furious at your dad. All the shit he said about the sex shop . . . That was the first big screaming match between our families, you know. It was about you and me. Mac went over to your parents' clinic while we were in school and gave him a verbal ass-whipping."

It was about us? All of this mess is what started the bad blood between our families?

He nods his head. "I wanted to talk to you about everything, but after my dad's funeral, I walked into school, and there you were, kissing Andre in front of your locker."

"I thought we were over! I embarrassed myself, crying at home-coming, and he was nice to me. He was there, and you weren't, and I thought you didn't . . . I never would have, if I'd known the truth. I didn't know your dad died—you could have told me!"

"I thought you'd find out. It was on the news. But you didn't say anything, and I wasn't supposed to go near you, or your dad would kill me. The only time I could talk to you without him knowing was at school, but there you were, with Andre. Andre! And you wouldn't so much as look my way. I felt like a disease. You moved to the courtyard at lunch to sit with Reagan and Andre, and then I saw you guys on a date at Thai Palace. . . ."

"I thought you hated me. I thought we were finished."

He lifts his cap to run a hand through his hair and then settles it back down more tightly, tugging it low on his forehead. "I was messed up about my dad. . . . I didn't know what to do. Everything was completely screwed up, and I thought you didn't want anything to do with me anymore. I was shattered, Zorie. Shattered."

I hear the hurt in his voice, and it matches what I'm feeling in my heart.

Overwhelmed, I walk to the edge of the plateau and glance

down the twisting steps. They look otherworldly, like ancient steps of a Tibetan mountain temple. Only, it's just California, and there's nothing holy here. No monks. No shrine.

Just the mountain and the sun and the two of us with all this pain in the middle.

A group of hikers climbs the steps far below. They look like ants. I walk a few steps to the benches circling a short wooden rail and gaze out over the jagged scenery. I wonder if this is one of the spots at which people fall off the mountain. It certainly doesn't seem like a place people should die. It's far too beautiful.

I hear Lennon approaching, but I don't turn around. I don't know what to say. I can't process this. I'm trying, but I'm angry and utterly heartbroken, and everything feels raw.

Is all of this my fault, for crying on Andre's shoulder and assuming the worst about Lennon's motivations?

Is all of this Lennon's fault, for assuming the worst about me?

And then there's my father. . . .

"Everything that happened in the hotel . . . ," I finally manage, talking more to the mountains than to him. "I mean, it's almost blackmail, what my father did to you."

"Actually, it was. See, there was something niggling me. Why was he at that hotel checking in? It was the middle of the day. And who needs a hotel in town when they live twenty minutes away? I didn't really think about it much after everything went to hell. Not until that package was misdelivered to my parents' shop last week."

My body stills, heart racing erratically. "Why?" I ask, almost a whisper. I'm not even sure I want to know.

"Because the woman in those photos . . . I realized I'd seen her before. She was in the hotel lobby, standing near the registration desk. And then I saw her again, looking out the rotating doors when your dad dragged me outside." Lennon pauses, and then says, "When I thought about it later, I wondered if maybe he made such a big scene to distract me from seeing her."

This is the final blow. I want to hold my hands up in surrender. I'm dead now, so you can stop shooting, please and thank you. Nothing can hurt me anymore. I'm beyond pain. I'm just numb.

I stride toward our bench and slide into my pack, hoisting it onto my shoulders.

"What are you doing?" Lennon asks.

"I need to think," I tell him. "I just . . . need to think."

20

And that's exactly what I do. Alone with my thoughts, I ponder everything that's just happened all the way up the last hundred or so steps of the mountain staircase. Wondering if I'll ever stop being angry with my dad. Wondering if I'm angry with Lennon, too. And I'm so busy being lost in my own self-centered thoughts, it doesn't quite register that the water is getting louder. And louder. When the steps begin curving sharply to the right, I suddenly see why.

Waterfalls. Two of them. Not the small, tranquil cascade of Mackenzie Falls. If *that* was a roar, this is God herself speaking. And she is fierce.

Blue water plummets off a sharp-angled cliff many stories down into raging white foam. It's flowing so savagely, a good third of the falls are nothing but gauzy mist. I even can feel mist on my legs—and the base of the falls must be a good quarter mile or more away.

I hike the last few steps to a large lookout area on a plateau twice the size of the one below. No one's up here. How is that possible? I spy another set of stone steps at the end of the lookout leading to the topmost point. There appears to be a trail all the way around the falls, and at the top of the falls is where several tourists are taking photos and looking through viewfinders. If I'm not mistaken, there is a tram and a couple of toilets up there. Guess most people choose to ride up there instead of climbing the world's most dangerous steps.

I walk toward the edge of the lookout, dump my pack on a section of dry rock, and peer across the gap to watch the waterfalls.

"Emperor and Empress Falls," Lennon says loudly from my side, ditching his pack next to mine. "They're actually part of the same river, but that bumpy rock formation that sticks out between them is what splits the flow. Three hundred fifty feet tall."

They are beautiful. I'm truly stunned. By the view, and by the entire conversation we just had. I wonder if I can just keep looking at the falls, just pretend it never happened until I come up with a plan—

"Zorie," he pleads from behind me. "Say something. Please."

I have to speak louder than normal to be heard over the roar of the falls, and it sort of turns into yelling. "If you confessed everything to your parents, then my dad didn't have anything to hold over you as leverage." I swing around to face him, bitterness in my voice. "Why didn't you tell me then?"

"You weren't speaking to me."

"Because I was under the assumption that you hated me!"

"I never hated you. I was angry that you shut me out, and I damn sure was furious about Andre. Seeing you with him in front of your locker was one of the worst days of my life—and believe me, I had a *lot* of bad days last year."

"I was only with Andre because I was trying to get over you." I'm crying now—half in anger, half in grief—and I feel as if my chest is going to explode and I'm going to fall over the edge of the lookout and die in the waterfall mist. Because not only am I thinking about what I did with Andre, but I'm also thinking about Lennon doing the same thing with Jovana Ramirez. And I don't know which image is worse.

"And then," he yells, "I had to listen to Brett—fucking *Brett*, of all people—brag about how close he was to 'hitting that.'"

Ugh! What did I see in him?

"It was just a kiss!" I tell Lennon. "One kiss, and it wasn't even that good. It wasn't good with Andre, and it was less than nothing with Brett. Is that want you want to hear?"

"I don't mind hearing that, honestly," he says, cheeks dark with indignation.

"And what about Jovana? Andre and I had sex one time. Once! You probably screwed Jovana's brains out for months."

"I'm not going to dignify that. She's a nice person."

"Aha!" I say. "You avoided the question."

"There was a question? Because all I heard was an implication. And yeah, we had sex. But I wasn't in love with her."

"Does that make it better?"

"You're not hearing me. *I wasn't in love with her.*"

"I heard you."

"She left me because I was hung up on you."

"Then why didn't you talk to me?" I say.

"Because you made it clear that you didn't want me to. Because you were busy making out with Brett at parties. Because you made new friends and avoided me at school. Because your father was always watching me."

"You should have fought for me!" I shout. "Why didn't you fight for me?"

"You gave up on me!" he yells back. "How can I fight for someone who pretends I don't exist?"

"I was trying to protect myself. You hurt me. My entire world fell apart."

"So. Did. Mine."

I'm shaking now. At least the angry crying has stopped.

"It's not supposed to be like this!" I tell him.

"What isn't?"

I gesture angrily from him to me. "This! If this were meant to be, it would be easier. Maybe the universe is trying to tell us something."

"Oh?" He stalks closer, getting in my face. Towering above me. "Is that so?"

"Yes," I say, less sure.

"I really want to know, Zorie. What do *you* think the universe is trying to tell us?"

"That we . . ." My mouth hangs open, and I can't finish the thought. He's too close. Inches away. My head is empty; the words on my tongue have vanished. I don't know what I'm trying to say. What I'm feeling. I just have the sense that we've come to a decisive moment and something is about to snap. It's as if the energy between us has suddenly spiked and is now vibrating. Like the sign behind me warns: STAY CLEAR OF THE EDGE. ROCKS ARE SLIPPERY.

"You want to know what I think?" Lennon says, head dipping lower as he tries to get level with my eyes. "*I* think that if the universe were trying to keep us apart, it's doing a shitty job. Because otherwise, we wouldn't be out here together."

"I wish we weren't!"

"No, you don't," he says firmly.

"Yes, I do. I wish I'd never come on this trip. I wish I didn't know any of this, and I wish—"

Without warning, his mouth is on mine. He kisses me roughly. Completely unyielding. His hands are on the back of my head, holding me in place. And for a long, suspended moment, I'm frozen, unsure of whether I want to push him away. Then, all at once, heat spreads through me, and I thaw.

I kiss him back.

And, *oh*, it is good.

His hands relax, fingers tangling in my hair, soft tongue rolling against mine. And when I run out of air and have to pull back, he kisses the corner of my mouth. My cheek. My forehead. A trail of kisses on my jaw. All over my neck. My earlobe—and now I'm close to passing out with pleasure. He even tugs back the collar of my shirt to kiss the hidden skin beneath it. His mouth is hot, and his stubble is rough in the best way possible. The kisses are long and slow and deliberate, and they are very, *very* confident. And it feels as if he's drawing a map on my body, following a path of landmarks that he's plotted in his head.

He's relentless with all of his exploration, and I'm making weird groaning noises that are halfway embarrassing. But *I just can't stop.* And now I'm struggling to get my mouth back on his skin, any skin I can reach, and my arms are around him, pulling him closer, and I've found my way back to his mouth, and GOD, IT'S GOOD.

How could I have forgotten?

Did he get better at this? Did I?

Because *my God.*

Waterfall mist covers my legs, and my knees are giving out. My bones don't work anymore. It's as if he's pressed some sort of secret on switch, and I'm at the mercy of my body—which likes his body quite a lot and desperately wants to drop to the ground and let Lennon have his wicked way with me, right here in front of God's Voice. I absolutely would, too. In this moment, I'm a trollop. An unrepentant floozy. I'm a raging wildfire of feelings and sensations, and I can't put them out.

Oh, wow. I seriously can't breathe. I think I need to learn how to pace my trollop-y ways. Or at least learn how to breathe through my nostrils while kissing.

I try to steady myself, and that's when the voices in my head start whispering. *He abandoned you. He hurt you.*

The sound of approaching hikers intensifies my uneasy feelings.

I pull away from Lennon.

He pulls me back.

"People coming," I warn.

"Zorie," Lennon says, his hand roaming down my back. "I want to try again. I don't want to be enemies. Or friends. I want . . . everything. You and me. I don't care about your father anymore. I will fight for us, if that's what it takes. We'll figure something out together. Tell me you want that too."

And for a moment, I almost give in and agree, but then one of the hikers laughs—they are *way* closer than I expected—and it fractures the moment, a proverbial bucket of icy water over all our shared warmth. And with a jolt of clarity, I remember Lennon saying a lot of the same sentiments to me before homecoming, when we decided to take the Great Experiment public.

Can we be together again?

Do I want to?

Has what he's revealed changed how I feel about last fall?

Why can't I make an easy decision?

And finally: *What is wrong with me?*

"I need to think about things," I tell him.

The anguish on his face is unmistakable.

He closes his eyes and then blinks rapidly, gathering himself. Then he nods and steps back, putting distance between us.

"I'm sorry," I say. "I just . . . It's a lot at once, and . . ."

And I can't function like a normal human being.

He nods. "I know. I understand."

"Lennon—"

The approaching hikers surge onto our plateau. It's a group of college-aged boys. Their laughter scatters my thoughts and puts an invisible wall between Lennon and me.

"Come on. Let's get out of here," he says, gesturing toward our backpacks. All the emotion disappears from his voice and posture, and he's back to being unreadable.

I want to scream. I want to beg him to come back. I want to be alone so that I can think through every detail of what just happened. I want to stop thinking.

But I can't do any of those things, so we return to the trail in silence, both of us deep in thought . . . never closer, never further apart.

21

After leaving the falls, we hike Emerald Trail the rest of the afternoon, communicating only when necessary, and occasionally delving into safe subjects. The national park system. The weather. We maintain a polite distance from each other, as if we're just two acquaintances, sharing the trail. As if we didn't just kiss each other's faces off. As if my entire world hasn't flipped onto its back like some stranded, flailing turtle.

Though we pass quite a few hikers, when we get to the end of the trail in the early evening, I'm startled to see not only a ranger station, but also an entire campground bustling with people. A road. Cars. The scent of meat cooking on grills. Music playing in someone's RV.

"Camp Silver," Lennon informs me. "The trailhead is here. You need reservations to hike Silver Trail at this time of year. They try to keep the number of people on it at a certain level, so it's not elbow to elbow."

"It looks pretty elbow to elbow now," I say, scanning the campground.

"Everyone wants to walk where Ansel Adams took photos," he says. "The trail goes up to the Crown, which overlooks the whole park."

I think I've heard about that. It sounds familiar, so it must be a big tourist draw.

"There are campgrounds along the way for people who like a few modern conveniences, but this is probably the biggest one," Lennon says. "And here's the ranger station I told you about."

The station is a small, dark brown log cabin on the edge of the campground. Outside the door stands a board of printed notices—announcements about the weather, the status of each campsite, and which trails are closed. There's even a warning about a mountain lion in the area, several missing people, and another about a small, twin-engine plane that's crashed in the mountains. Hikers are to stay clear of the wreckage until the park can arrange to have it transported.

"What in the world?" I murmur, reading the flyers. I'm not sure which notice is worse.

Lennon doesn't seem worried about the mountain lion, because he taps on the plane-crash announcement and whistles softly. "I've heard about stuff like this. The entire Sierra Nevada mountain chain is a graveyard for lost planes. It's called the Nevada Triangle."

"Like the Bermuda Triangle?"

"Just like that. From Fresno to Las Vegas—basically, a big dead zone over the California-Nevada border where planes go down or disappear entirely." The drama in his voice increases. "Some say it's a combination of rapidly changing weather, strong winds, and hidden peaks. But the whole mountain chain has this spooky Area 51 mythos. More than two thousand planes have gone down here since 1960. Some just fell off the radar, never found."

"Whoa," I say, suitably impressed.

His lips pull into a gentle curve—just for a moment. Then he sobers up and goes quiet.

"So, this Silver Trail . . . ," I ask, trying to recall his map. "Is that where we'd be going to get to Condor Peak?"

He shakes his head. "We don't have hiking reservations, and it's headed south. We'd need to go west from here. There's a smaller trail through the backcountry. I've been on it before, so no surprises like the caves yesterday."

"I see."

He gestures toward the ranger station. "Unless you've decided to go home."

Have I? I've been thinking about that decision the entire afternoon. Along with everything that he told me about homecoming. And about the kiss.

Definitely thinking about the kiss.

I could continue on. (But what if we end up fighting?)

I could call for a ride home. (But what if I regret not staying?)

The energy between us feels heightened, strained, and slightly awkward. But Lennon is patient, not pushing me to decide, and for that, I'm grateful. He glances at his phone. "Still no service. There should be a phone inside the station."

"I should call my mom, at least," I say. "Just to let her know I'm alive."

His gaze intensifies. He's studying my face, trying to figure out what I'm going to do. If I knew that, I'd just tell him.

"Me too," he finally says. "And I need to report the abandoned gear Reagan and Brett left behind. Shall we?"

I nod and take a deep, steadying breath as we head to the door to the ranger station and step inside.

The single-room cabin is dim and cozy. Though the floor plan is small, the high ceiling is crossed with rough wooden beams, which makes it feel larger. There's a small desk at the front and a rack of local wilderness travel books for sale. In the middle of the room, a couple of chairs huddle around an old heating stove, and in the back, near a giant wall map of the park, there's an old pay phone.

"Evenin'," a ranger says with a quiet smile. "We're about to close for the day."

"We'll be quick," Lennon assures him before gesturing me toward the phone, eyes hooded. "You want to go first?"

I make my way past the chairs while Lennon begins telling the ranger about Reagan and Brett's abandoned gear. I'm worried that the national park might get judgmental about a couple of teens backpacking alone. But it seems fine, because Lennon sounds confident and knowledgeable, and the ranger is taking him seriously. They aren't paying attention to me, and that gives me to time to take a deep breath and focus.

Stay or go?

Go or stay?

If I stay, I don't think Lennon and I can just forget about everything that's happened and go back to being just friends. That much I know. There's too much history between us, and that kiss pretty much wiped out an entire year's worth of trying to bury old feelings. Now I'm right back where I was, ribs cracked open and heart exposed.

I wish I could ask Mom for advice, but if she knew I was out here alone with Lennon . . . Well, it's not so much her I worry about as my dad. But he'd find out eventually. I wish I had time to think out exactly what I need to say to her. Maybe write out a script. But the station is about to close, and if I'm going to call her, it's now or never.

It takes me a little while to figure out how to use the ancient pay phone, but after reading the posted instructions, I dig out some quarters and slip them inside. Then I dial my mom's cell phone.

"Joy Everhart," my mom's voice says, crackling over the line.

"Mom?"

"Zorie? Is that you? Are you okay?" She sounds frantic.

"I'm totally fine," I tell her, looking up at the giant map hanging on the wall. "I'm in King's Forest."

Her exhalation is loud. "Dammit, Zorie. I was so worried. You didn't answer my texts."

"No service out here," I say. "We talked about that, remember?"

"We did. You're right," she says. "But it's a relief to hear your voice. Wait, did you say you're in the national park? Why aren't you at the glamping compound?"

"Um . . ." Do I tell her what happened? I hate lying to her. But if I stay here with Lennon, I can't tell her that's what I'm doing. Now that I'm forced to make a decision, I close my eyes and just let whatever comes out of my mouth be my choice.

One, two, three—

"Remember how I told you we might go on that backcountry trail?" I say. "That's where I am. I'm hiking to the star party."

Oh my God, I'm doing this. I'm staying with Lennon?

I am.

Relief rushes through me, unknotting my shoulders and loosening my limbs.

"I can barely hear you. Did you say you're hiking to Condor Peak?" Mom asks, her voice going up an octave. "I thought you were taking the bus. Are you hiking alone?"

"It's not that far and I'm not alone," I assure her. "Dr. Viramontes and Avani will be at the star party to meet me when I get there."

"Okay, but who are you with now?"

Crap on toast. Why didn't I write a script? "We changed our

plans for the week. And I'm with a guide, so you don't have to worry."

"A guide?"

"Someone who really knows the wilderness. Right now we're in a campground at a ranger station."

"Zorie—"

"It's fine, I promise. There are families camping here and a park ranger. I'm completely safe. Please trust me. I need you to trust me, or I can't enjoy this. You told me to be careful, not cautious, remember?"

She sighs. "But you *are* being smart, right?"

"As smart as possible. I swear on my backpack."

"Oh, good. Okay. All right." I can hear the relief in her voice. "Hives?"

"Under control."

"Thank goodness. You have plenty of food?"

"Yep. Still have your emergency money too."

She pauses. "Are you having fun?"

I glance back at Lennon. He's several inches taller than the ranger is, and is now pointing out a location on a laminated map on the desk. He is insanely good-looking. I don't think I allowed myself to think about that too much over the last year, but I'm thinking it now, and it's making my stomach flutter. That voice, those lips, that—

"Zorie?"

Oh, crap. "What? Oh, um, yeah. I'm having fun." A snake

bite, a bear, and the greatest kiss of my life. "I'm sore from hiking, and I need a shower, but it's really pretty out here."

"I'm so glad. That's terrific," she says, sounding happy. I like it when she's happy. She deserves someone better than my shitty father. Lennon's story about the hotel pierces my thoughts, and the weight of this secret affair is becoming heavier and heavier. But I'm still too much of a coward to tell her about my dad. I can't do it on the phone, not like this. I'm scared of hurting her, but I'm even more terrified of losing her. So I just tell her what day I'll be at Condor Peak and assure her once more that everything's fine.

I'm a selfish, selfish person.

"Baby?" she says, her voice taking on a different tone. "Do you have anything else you need to tell me?"

My pulse increases. "What do you mean?"

"I mean, you know I don't like secrets."

"I know."

"And when people keep them, it's usually for a bad reason."

Oh, God. Does she know I'm here with Lennon? Or is she talking about my dad's affair? She couldn't be. I'm paranoid.

"I know that sometimes it seems like . . ." She pauses. "Zorie, I care about you more than you can fathom. But . . ."

"But what?" Why is there a *but*?

"I just want you to know that you can tell me anything," she says more firmly.

"I know that."

"Okay, that's all."

That's all? What is going on? Why is she being so cryptic? Maybe I should tell her about Lennon. But if I do, I'm worried she'll tell my dad, and they'll drive out here and make me come home. I made up my mind already. I know it took me forever, but now that I've decided, I really *don't* want to go back to Melita Hills.

I hate lying to her.

But I want to stay here with Lennon.

Why can't this be easier?

The phone is playing some prerecorded message in the background, telling me to deposit more money. "I don't have any more quarters, so I've got to go," I tell her. "But I just wanted to check in and tell you that I'm safe, and that . . . well, like I said, I have a really good trail guide out here. So you don't have to worry."

"Wait! When will you get to Condor Peak?"

"Day after tomorrow. Late."

"Promise me that you'll text when you get there."

"I promise. And I love you."

"I love you too, sweet thing." She sounds sad. Or disappointed? "And I miss you. Please stay safe."

Ugh. She's breaking my heart. And I don't even get to say anything else, because the pay phone finally realizes I'm not putting more money inside it and cuts me off. I hang up and lay my forehead against the receiver.

"Everything okay?" Lennon says in a low voice near my shoulder.

"I think so. Hope so."

"What did you decide?"

I turn around and absently scratch my arm. "I hope you haven't changed your mind about taking me to Condor Peak, because you're stuck with me now."

He sighs. Twice. On a third sigh, his hand tentatively reaches toward the side of my face, and he gently pushes an errant curl out of my eyes, fingers lingering. "I'm glad. Really glad."

"You are?"

"I am. No presumptions made. I'm not booking us a hotel room, or anything."

I groan softly, a little embarrassed.

"Too soon?" he says with the hint of a smile.

I shake my head and smile back.

His hand drops from my hair, and a moment of awkward silence passes before I speak again, attempting to move the focus away from the heavy topic of *us*. "I'm worried that I should have told Mom about the lady you saw last year at the hotel with my father. And about the photo book. I just couldn't."

"It's probably for the best. Some things you just don't want to say over the phone, believe me. Like, Hey, I'm an idiot who tried to get a hotel room because I have no clue about how to have a relationship, and, oh yeah, I punched your father, and we're not allowed to see each other. You know, things like that."

I chuckle a little.

"I still don't," he whispers.

"Don't what?" I whisper back.

"Know how to have a relationship."

"Oh good, because I don't either."

"We'll figure it out eventually. If you want to, that is."

"I think so," I whisper.

His smile is almost shy, but when he sighs one last time, exhaling sharply through his nostrils, he sounds content. And that makes me feel less anxious about everything.

He clears his throat. "So . . . I rented us a campsite," he says, holding up a small, perforated card with a number printed on it. "Not a presumption, by the way. If you were leaving, I needed a place to sleep tonight, and I really didn't—"

"Calm down. I believe you."

"Okay," he says, and we both smile at each other again.

Focus, Zorie. "Campsite. We're not camping in the wild?"

"The sites make things easier, so I thought why not take advantage of convenience for a night? And we're lucky to get it. They were completely booked until the mountain lion scare we saw posted on the board outside. Apparently one tried to attack a small child at another camp."

I'm suddenly alarmed, but Lennon holds up a calming hand.

"Mountain lions usually steer clear of populated areas, but if they try to attack, small children look like prey in their eyes. We aren't children. We'll be fine, especially with all the other campers around. And besides, that report was miles from here, and the little boy escaped unharmed."

Still not feeling better about this. . . .

"Now skootch," Lennon says, waving me aside. "Let me call the parental units before the ranger kicks us out."

I feel strange about listening in to his phone conversation, so I busy myself outside the station, picking up a free park map from a covered plastic box as the sun begins setting, shining warm orange light through the trees. When Lennon emerges, he's all smiles, poise, and swagger. Whatever was said between him and his moms lifted his mood considerably. But before I can ask about this, he waves the camping permit at me.

"Okay, Medusa. We're looking for an open site somewhere down there. Let's make camp. And bonus, there are toilets and hot showers."

(A) He hasn't called me that nickname in *forever*, and (B) showers. SHOWERS!

"You really know how to win a girl's heart," I say, grinning.

"I'm trying my best," he says, and I feel said heart skip a beat.

We wander down a trail through the camp, nodding at strangers who lift a hand in greeting. It must be a camping thing. I'm not accustomed to so much open friendliness among strangers. Don't these hippies know this is a good way to get mugged? Head down, eyes on the sidewalk—that's my motto. Then again, maybe they're so cheery because they all have cars, either pulled up right next to their tents or out in the nearby parking lot, and Car Camping seems to be a completely different ball game. These people have coolers of actual food—not freeze-dried meals—and portable chairs. Since when did I become jealous of a chair and a package of cheap hot dogs? But, gods above, it looks enticing.

"Bingo," Lennon says, pointing toward a deserted piece of dirt. "Ranger Bob said there were two sites open, and we can choose. I see another one open near the toilets, and I'm gonna suggest we pass on that, because I've camped near restrooms before. It's like sitting near the toilets on an airplane, but worse. So much worse."

"Say no more. This one smells and looks perfect." Well, that's a stretch. It's somewhat barren, and the sites on either side of it are a little closer than I'd like. But on the other hand, it's flat, there are no rocks or twigs to clear away, and it has a private picnic table, a bear locker, and a rusty fire pit ring with a grill. "Score. If only we had some hot dogs."

"We have freeze-dried macaroni and cheese, and if you're nice to me, I'll let you have some of my M&M stash."

"Deal," I say.

There's an awkward moment when we set our packs on the picnic table to fish out our tents. I don't know what he's thinking, but I'm remembering sleeping with him the night before. Only now . . .

Yeah. I look up and see the confirmation in his eyes. He's thinking it too.

Now it's different.

"Uh, should we set the tents up side by side, here?" he says after a few tense seconds.

"Sounds good."

It doesn't take us too long to get the tents in place, and Lennon eyes the forested area near the campsite. "I can probably collect wood out there, but it might take me a little while, especially if other campers regularly hunt for it. You want to take a shower while I'm looking?" He squints and holds up a finger. "That came out wrong. While I'm looking for wood. In the forest."

I snort a little laugh.

"Or the other thing," he says.

"Just get the firewood."

His smile is playful. "If you change your mind, holler."

"Aye, aye, Captain."

Before he heads out into the woods, Lennon informs me that now is a good time to wash out any clothes that need washing, and he digs out a minibottle of biodegradable castile soap. My snake-bitten, bloodied socks definitely need cleaning, as well as my underwear and a couple of tank tops. I gather them up, get my toiletries and a change of clothes, and head to the shower house, which is another rustic log cabin building that looks similar in design to the ranger station. After watching another camper parading through the campground in a bathrobe and flip-flops, I realize that this place truly is hippie-land, and no one's concerned about etiquette.

This is no glamping compound.

A slat-wood partition shields a door marked WOMEN. When I head inside, I find lockers for clothes and big, long sinks in front of mirrors. The water there is cold, and in order to get hot water in one of the three shower stalls, you have to feed money into a little machine. I have enough quarters for five minutes of hot water, and even though I rush to shampoo, wash, and shave, it still runs out when I'm peeling the bandages off my snake bite, making me yelp in surprise when the water turns icy cold. But I manage to endure it long enough to finish up, and after toweling off with a small microfiber camp towel—one of Reagan's purchases—I brush my teeth and wash out my clothes in the sink.

One problem with showering in the wild is the lack of hair dryers, and the temperature outside is starting to fall along with the setting sun. It's not chilly, but with a head full of wet curls, it's not exactly warm, either. Luckily, by the time I walk back to our site, Lennon has gotten a fire going. He's also set up a low-hanging rope between his tent and the picnic table for hanging up wet clothes to dry. I feel a little weird putting up my underwear for all the world to see, but other campers are doing it in their sites, so I guess this is one of those moments where I have to swallow my pride and say screw it. I quickly hang everything up before taking a seat on a bear canister in front of the fire, letting the heat dry my hair while Lennon takes his turn at the shower house.

The camp is really bustling, now that everyone's coming back from day hikes and getting ready for dinner. It's weird to be around so many people. It seems like a lifetime ago when Reagan abandoned us and I was freaking out about being alone with Lennon. I watch all the activity, wondering where all these people came from and why they decided to camp here. They're definitely different from the glampers. I don't know if that's good or bad, or if it just *is*. But at least I'm not on edge, wondering which fork to use at a four-course dinner. Plus, everyone here seems to be in a better mood. And despite a bit of lingering worry over that call to my mom, I think maybe I am too.

After a few minutes of combing my curls out upside down in front of the fire, I hear a soft whistle.

I jerk my head up to find Lennon's long legs walking up to our site. "My oh my. Look at all your unmentionables blowing in the wind. I mean, wow. I'm getting a real French-lingerie vibe here, and, to be honest, I expected plaid."

"Oh my God," I say, kicking his leg. "Stop looking, you perv."

He's hanging up his own underwear next to mine, a towel draped over his shoulders and his black hair damp and sticking up in the most adorable way. "I'll stop looking when you do."

"What's there to look at? Black boxers? I already saw those last night when you were getting in my tent."

"Mmm, that's right. And have you been thinking about me in my skivvies all day?"

"Please stop talking."

"Stop talking altogether, or . . . ?" He laughs and dances out of the way as I try to kick him again. I smell shaving cream and notice that he's gotten rid of his stubble. "Okay, okay. Try to control yourself, and I'll try to do the same. We have more important matters to take care of, like the fact that my stomach is trying to eat itself. Let's get to making with the macaroni and cheese, shall we?"

As he breaks out our cooking gear, I keep my eyes on the other campsites, watching the comings and goings of kids and adults. There's even a site filled with several teens, and one of the guys is unpacking an acoustic guitar. Lennon tells me there's a wannabe guitarist at every campground. It's practically required.

While the water for our dinner is heating up, Lennon checks my snake bite and fixes another bandage over the healing wound, proclaiming it "much better." Then we prepare and eat our not-so-fabulous macaroni meal, which along with a cloying cheese sauce, also has dried beef in it, so we do a whole comical bit together, wistfully pretending it's the same grilled hamburger we're smelling from the campsite next to ours. Halfway through eating, it's dark enough that Lennon needs to switch on our little camp lights—to see my underwear better, he jokes, and I throw my spork at him. When he pretends to be injured, the teen campsite with the guitar-playing dude starts group singing a hymn. Loudly.

"Noooo," I whisper. "Nightmare. They aren't even on key."

"And it's not even a good hymn. What about 'Holy, Holy,

Holy'? Now, *that* would be one you could really go nuts with."

"Aha!" I say. "I just realized why Mac has you going to church. It's not your diabolic ensemble of all-black clothes. It's because you stole her credit card to use for the hotel room."

He looks sheepish. "Busted. Though I *did* turn myself in, so that has to count for something. But yeah, she makes me sit through hymns as penance."

"It's all clear to me now."

"So basically, it's your fault."

"Mine?" I say.

"You're a tempting girl, Zorie. If you hadn't kissed me last year that first time, I would have never wanted to get the hotel room, and—"

"Me kiss you? That was an accident!"

"Kissing is never an accident. Never in the history of kissing has it been an accident."

"I slipped when I sat on the bench."

"And your mouth just happened to land on mine?"

"Andromeda was pulling against the leash, trying to chase a squirrel!"

"Keep lying to yourself. Meanwhile, I've made my peace with my part in it, which is that I was completely innocent."

"If it wasn't an accident, then it was both our faults."

"Not according to evangelicals." He switches to a street preacher voice. "And yea, though I was seduced by the sinful demon female in the garden—"

"Hey! You're the one with the dildo garden in the shop window."

"Dildo *forest*, Zorie. Get it right. I helped put that up, by the way. I took a photo of Ryuk walking around inside the display."

"I'm going to need to see that," I say, but my words are drowned under the hymn-a-thon at the tent across the path. "Ugh, all these people," I complain. "I wish we were camping in the backcountry. I mean, don't get me wrong, the shower is great, and it's much easier to get drinkable water out of a faucet than to scoop it out of a river and wait for it to filter. But jeez, civilization is noisy."

"Well, well, well. Look who's been bitten by the bug," Lennon says, pointing at me.

"What bug?" I frantically glance across my clothes and legs.

"No, the backpacking bug," he says, laughing. "You prefer the peace and quiet. That's how it started for me. I just wanted to get away from people and think."

"Well, I'm not ready to do this on a regular basis, but I'm starting to see the appeal."

He gestures toward the back of the camp. "You know what? When I was gathering firewood, I walked down that big hill there. It's just grassland and meadow, but I bet it has a decent view of the stars. At least it's away from the lights of the camp. Want to take your telescope there before they start singing 'Kumbaya'?"

Yes. Yes, I do. After we clean and put away everything, and

Lennon puts out the fire, we gather the rainfly from my tent and my telescope. After strapping on headlamps—and dumping Reagan's expensive broken headlamp in the trash—we haul all of our supplies out of camp and head toward the hill.

It doesn't take long to find a good spot where the lights from the camp are at our backs. We can still hear people, but it's not as loud. Lennon spreads out the rainfly, and we sit on it picnic-style. I flick off the light on my headlamp. The stars are amazing out here. I don't think I'll ever be used to seeing them this way, without light pollution from the city. Thousands upon thousands of them, glittering points of light. It's as if I'm looking at an entirely different sky.

"Look," I say, pointing up at a wispy white trail. "The Milky Way. You can't see that at home without a telescope. Not even at the observatory."

Lennon takes off his headlamp and leans back on his palms. "It looks unreal. I know it's not, but my mind doesn't want to accept that this isn't some fake, projected light show."

No projection could look like this. We both stare up at the sky for a long moment. "I don't even think I want to use the telescope," I say. "I think I just want to look at them. Is that weird?"

"Not at all. It's not every day you get to see all this."

My phone still has a little charge on it, and I quickly turn on the screen to use it as a flashlight in order to see where to move my telescope. That's when I notice something.

"We have service!"

"Well, what do you know?" Lennon says, taking out his phone. "Oh, look. I've got texts from the Brettster."

"You do?" My only texts are from Mom and Avani.

"He's apologizing for leaving us. Well, it's sort of a non-apology. Oh, wait. He's taking it back. No . . . He's apologizing again. Aren't Reagan's parents in Switzerland, or something?"

"Yeah, why?"

"Because he's not making any sense. Now he's blaming Reagan for ditching us. I think? He's an atrocious speller, by the way."

"How many texts did he send?" I say, glancing at his screen.

"One, two, three, four . . . eight. And the last one is asking if I can get him weed again."

"Again?"

"He's already asked once. He's laboring under the false presumption that because my dad was in a band, I somehow have unlimited access to drugs. I swear, Brett is the absolute worst. I'm not even responding."

Avani's message is just confirming that she's leaving for the star party tomorrow and will see me there. I quickly decide to tell her that I'm with Lennon, backpacking through the park—super casual, no details—and asking if it's okay that he rides home with us. After she confirms, and I tell her when we'll be arriving, I read my mom's message: I'm glad you called today. Please stay safe and text me when you get to Condor

Peak. If you ever want to talk about anything, you know I'm here, right?

Why does she keep saying this? I replay our phone conversation in my head and something starts to bother me. "I left that photo book in my desk at home."

"What?" Lennon says, switching his phone off.

"I'm worried that my mom might have found it. She keeps asking me if there's anything I want to tell her, like she's trying to get me to confess to something. And it's either that photo book, or she knows I'm here with you."

"How would she know?"

"Do your parents know that we're alone right now?"

He hesitates. "Yeah, actually. They're pretty happy about it."

They are?

"Look," he says, "they know your parents don't realize you're here with me, but they wouldn't go run and tell your mom that. They know we're safe, and that's all that matters."

"Then it must be the photo book," I say.

"Was Joy upset?"

"Not particularly. She sounded . . . disappointed."

He doesn't say anything for a while. "Look, if you want my opinion, I'm betting she already suspected something was up with your dad a long time ago. So if she found the photo book, then she found it. But there's nothing you can do about it now."

I know he's right. Worrying won't do me any good. It's just

hard to make myself stop. I don't like feeling unsettled.

But I try not to think about it, shutting off my phone and stuffing it in my pocket. Then I lie on my back and look up at the stars.

Lennon lies down next to me, shoulder to shoulder.

"We're under the same starry sky," I say.

"We always are."

"Not together," I argue.

"I think we've always been together, even when we were apart," he says, slipping his hand around mine.

"I know it's a cliché, but sometimes I would look up at the stars and wonder if you were ever looking at them at the same time," I admit.

"When I looked up at the stars, I saw us. You were the stars, and I was the dark sky behind you."

"Without dark sky, you couldn't see the stars."

"I knew I was useful," he says.

"You're essential."

He makes a happy sound and tucks his arm behind his head. "When we were apart, I would always try to find constellations and imagine you talking about them. Like the Great Cat."

"The Great Cat? You mean the Great Bear . . . or Leo?"

"Which one is Felis Major?"

"There is no Felis Major. There's Ursa Major, and that's the Great Bear. It's the one with the group of stars that make up the Big Dipper."

"I could have sworn there was a big cat constellation. The Great Tomcat."

"Tomcat?" I say, exasperated.

"Could have sworn there was a tomcat constellation with a long tail. Right there."

"Where?"

He points upward. "Standing on the fence."

"You mean Taurus?"

"Is Taurus a cat?" he asks.

"It's a bull!"

"I know," he says, rolling toward me. "I just wanted to hear you get riled up about stars."

"You're a jerk, you know that?" I say with a laugh, poking his ribs repeatedly.

He jumps and tries to grab my finger. "Such a jerk. If I were you, I wouldn't put up with this crap."

"Oh? What should I do about it? Leave you out here to find cat constellations while I go back to camp?"

I pretend to get up, but he grabs my arm and pulls me back down. "Noooo."

"You're going to make me squish my telescope."

He picks it up and moves it behind him. "There. Better?"

"Well, now I can't use it."

"You weren't using it anyway. Unless you had plans to spy on the Bible Camp kids up the hill. But I doubt you're going to see anything sordid, and we both know you like a little skin when you're spying on—Hey!" He shields himself with one arm, laughing. "Ouch! Stop hitting me! I didn't spy on *you* when you were naked. I'm the victim, here."

"You weren't naked."

"Five more seconds and I would've been. Would you have looked away if I hadn't caught you?"

I wait too long to answer.

He grabs me around the waist and pulls me closer. A lot closer. My boobs are pressing against his chest. "Or would you have taken photos?"

"You insult me, sir. I don't use my telescope like some peeping Tom." Usually.

"And I'm supposed to take your word on that? For all I know, you've already secretly photographed me with your spy lens," he says near my lips. "Should I be worried?"

"From what I saw, you don't have anything to worry about."

"You shock me, miss. Have you been watching me do bad things in my room?"

"You always shut the blinds. Spoilsport."

He chuckles in that deep voice of his, and the sound vibrates through his chest and into mine. "Zorie?"

"Yes?"

"God, I've missed you."

"I've missed you too."

"I'm going to accidentally kiss you now."

"Okay."

Softly, slowly, his lips graze over mine. His mouth is soft, and his hand is roaming up my back. I exhale a shaky breath, and he kisses me:

Once, briefly.

Warmth flickers in my chest.

A second time, longer.

Melting heat, uncurling low in my belly.

Three times, and . . .

I'm lost.

Drowning in him. Nothing but goose bumps and buzzing endorphins and pleasure rushing over my skin. Nothing but his mouth, connecting us, and my fingertips slipping up his shirt to dance over the hard planes of his back. Nothing but his arms wrapped around me like a warm blanket.

Nothing but us and the stars above.

It's perfect. As though we've been doing this for years. As if he knows exactly how to make me shiver, and I know exactly how to make him groan. We're brave explorers. The *best* explorers. Lewis and Clark. Ferdinand Magellan and Sir Francis Drake. Neil Armstrong and Sally Ride.

Zorie and Lennon.

We are *so* good at this.

And before I know it, we're rolling around, a tangle of arms and legs, half on the nylon rainfly, half in the night grass. Like we used to do, back during the Great Experiment. My glasses are somewhere, and his hand is up my shirt, and he's saying all these insanely shocking and intimate things he wants to do to me, which should be making my ears turn pink, but right now it all sounds like poetry. And my fingers are headed for his belt buckle, and—

A scream.

Not me. And not Lennon. It's in the woods.

It sounds like a woman. In trouble.

22

Another scream follows. It's from a different location. An answering scream.

Not a human scream. An animal?

"What the shit is that?" I whisper, hand stilling on the hard muscles of his bare stomach. Someone's lifted up his shirt in a completely indecent manner. Oh, that was me.

"It's fine. Just a little mountain lion. No danger," Lennon whispers, guiding my hand lower.

Oh.

Wow.

He's definitely excited about the mountain lion.

This makes me extra excited in return.

Wait. Mountain lion?

"*Mountain lion?*" I whisper hotly.

"Caterwauling. Probably trying to find a mate," Lennon confirms in a drugged voice. "God, your hand feels good."

"Are we about to get attacked?" My voice sounds drugged too. I know I should move my hand away from his jeans, but I'm having trouble relaying the message to my fingers, which *really* want to linger and continue with exploration. My body is saying: *Ahoy! I sailed on a deserted sea for months and have finally spotted land. Fertile land. Land better than I remembered. No way am I turning this ship around now.*

"What?" he whispers.

"Did I say that out loud?"

"Is this some dirty pirate routine? Because I've *really* got a thing for Anne Bonny."

Another scream rips through the night air.

"Jesus!" I say, heart racing, and not in the good way. "That sounds like a human being."

"It also sounds really, really close," he says, voice sobering up. "As much as I would like you to never, ever, ever, *ever* stop . . . I think we should—"

More screaming. Okay, talk about a bucket of ice water. I'm genuinely scared now, imagining something jumping out of the darkness and clawing my face to shreds. Nature is a horror movie. And we're out here in the middle of a field, being stalked by killer animals.

I panic, unable to find my glasses or my headlamp, but Lennon spots them. We can't gather up our stuff fast enough. Then we're jogging back up the hill as the horny wildcats scream behind our backs.

By the time we get up to the camp, several other campers are standing around in long underwear, warily listening to the caterwauling. All eyes turn to us, and—terrific—I'm flushing like a guilty person. Well, technically, I *am* guilty, but now I'm also the camp hussy, so yay?

Lennon, on the other hand, acts calm and collected, breezily talking to the other campers as he lugs the rainfly around, reporting that, yes, it's probably two mountain lions down in the tree line at the bottom of the hill, but no, they likely won't come up here. Someone else, a middle-aged man with a Jamaican accent who introduces himself as Gordon, says he's encountered several mountain lions in this park over the years, and agrees with Lennon. He's telling other campers to make sure their kids aren't wandering around alone, and to be cautious.

Since the camp ranger has left for the night, several people, including Lennon, volunteer to keep an eye out for a little while. And after we get our stuff put away, he digs out an extra camp light from his pack—another one of those palm-size ones—and puts that on our picnic table.

For a while, the camp is buzzing with murmured conversations, and a few campsites are lighting fires in their pits. We eat some of Lennon's M&M stash in a late-night anxiety binge, and when I'm on my second handful, his eyes go big.

"Oh, shit."

"What?" I say, frantically looking around for a wildcat.

"No, no," he says, turning me back around. "Hives."

I look down where he's gently tugging down the collar of my T-shirt. Pink welts all over my neck and chest. I pull up my shirt. They're on my stomach and arms, too.

My first thought is: I'm somehow now allergic to Lennon. And of *course* the universe would punish me for all that rolling around in the proverbial hay with him. Camp hussy, after all. I'm cursed. But Lennon's analysis is slightly less paranoid.

"All the long grass on the hill. Whatever kind it is, your hives don't like it." He inspects my body and asks me if I'm having trouble breathing. I'm not. No loss of vision. No throat swelling up. None of the urgent 911 symptoms.

"You have an EpiPen?" he asks.

"Yeah, but I don't think it's that bad. This has happened before, remember?"

"That day we were hunting for metal out by the abandoned warehouse," he murmurs.

We were fourteen, and someone had given his dad a used metal detector, which he'd passed along to Lennon. We were so positive we were going to get rich, finding hidden pirate gold. Our booty ended up being one vintage metal name tag that looked like it belonged to a waitress, an old quarter with a hole drilled in the middle, and a bent-up veterinarian syringe. All worthless. Lennon kept the name tag—the engraved name on it was "Dorothy"—and I kept the quarter.

Oh yeah, and I developed a superfast case of hives from overgrown dandelions.

"What about Benadryl?" he asks.

I nod. "Got plenty of that."

"Why don't you take the maximum dose," he suggests. "Like, now."

I do that, taking a couple extra pills just to be safe. The hives look ugly. I just had one of the best make-out sessions of my life, and now I'm a monster.

Screw you, universe. Screw you.

My sleeping bag is still rolled up, so I use it as a pillow, lying down on the floor of the tent. I try to concentrate on calming down, because stress will only make this worse. I'm vaguely cognizant of the "may cause drowsiness" effect of the antihistamines, which turns into "you bet your sweet ass these will cause drowsiness" when I double up on them, but the next thing I know, Lennon's waking me up, and I have a horrible neck cramp.

"Izzt morning?" I slur, utterly groggy.

"No, it's just past midnight. You've been snoring for about an hour."

"Good God."

He chuckles. "It was super cute. Not a loud snore. Your mouth was open."

I groan and stretch out my neck. "Stupid antihistamines."

Lennon lifts the hem of my shirt. "They're working, though. Hives are going down. Tired?"

"So tired," I whisper.

"The mountain lions are gone. Let's crash."

One step ahead of you, buddy.

But he doesn't let me fall back down on the tent floor. He gently urges me into the chilly night air, which makes me grumpy, until I see the magic he's working. He's managed to zip our sleeping bags together into one massive bag. They aren't quite the same size, so it's slightly askew and mismatched, but he rolls out his foam mat and arranges the merged super bag on top. He also makes a long pillow out of some of our clothes, covering them up with our now-dry camp towels.

He's a freaking camping genius.

And if I were more conscious and less addled, I'd like to show him how much I appreciate his skills by continuing where we left off before all the cougar screaming. But I can barely keep my eyes open. While he stows our packs in his tent, I climb into the double sleeping bag, shimmying out of my jeans once inside. And then he's slipping inside with me, warm and solid. We gravitate toward each other, and as I curl up against him, head on his chest, his arms around me, random thoughts pass through my head.

First: *This is heavenly.*

Second: *I don't want it to end.*

And the last thought, I say aloud. "The only way my dad will ever let me see you is if I confront him about his affair."

Lennon's response rumbles through my cheek after a long sigh. "I know."

"It's going to break up my parents."

"I would never wish that. Not in a million years. If my parents split up, I'm not sure I could handle it."

"What do we do, then?"

He runs his hand down my arm. "We'll figure something out. I promise. Stop worrying."

And I don't. I'm too tired. But somewhere in the back of my head, I know our time together is dwindling, and that once we get home, there's a chance everything will fall apart. I'll need to come up with a solid plan of action. Create some sort of mental safety bunker in case my world is destroyed.

All this time, I've thought my life would be easier if Lennon wasn't in it. I was half right. Now that he's back, things are a million times harder. I never realized "us" would be so complicated.

The next morning, we leave the camp sooner than expected.

I wake up to a cold sleeping bag and manage to track down Lennon outside, finding him dressed. He's also a ball of nervous energy. At first I fear that we still have a mountain lion problem, but he assures me they are long gone. There's something new to worry about.

A summer storm is coming. A big one. It's been brewing from the remnants of a tropical Pacific front off the coast of Southern California, and now it's gathered strength and is headed north.

If we're going to get to the star party, we need to make it

through Queen's Gap today—a narrow canyon passageway between two mountains. A river runs the length of it, and that river floods during storms. As in, floods the entire canyon.

"I talked to the ranger. He warned me that we can't get trapped in there," Lennon explains. "So we either need to hike through it before evening, or we need to stay here for another night. But there's a chance if we do that, it could be another day before the canyon is cleared for hiking."

"Are you sure we can get through it?"

"If the storm follows the track it's on, we should have no problem. But we need to leave soon. In the hour."

"Oh, wow."

"How are your hives?" He inspects my arms, pulling up my sleeves. "Not as scary, but still there."

"At least they're not itching all that bad at the moment." All I can do is keep an eye on them, manage them. Keep my stress level low and be proactive about medicating. I'm still groggy from the Benadryl, but I'll take a nondrowsy prescription antihistamine with breakfast. And there *is* breakfast, I see, because Lennon already has everything laid out, including the all-important coffee.

"I'm going to need that caffeine as soon as I get back from the restroom," I tell him. "As much as you can spare."

"I'll make it extra strong. It'll taste like burned sludge. Milkshake thick."

"I forgot how much I like you."

One side of his mouth twists up. "You'll like me better if I can get you to the star party without us being drowned in a storm, so hurry it up."

"Hurrying!"

We have to rush to eat and get our camp packed, which involves lining our backpacks with garbage bags in case of rain. Once we're ready, we head out of the campground with a few other wretched souls who are also up at the crack. It's not long before those hikers leave us for the Silver Trail. Our western path is much smaller. Smaller means no fellow hikers—good— but it also means that we're returning to the backcountry.

No posted signs, no bathrooms, no cell service.

We're on our own.

The morning fog wears off as we head toward a small chain of mountains covered in Ponderosa pines. And after a brisk uphill hike, the forest levels off and opens up to a river that snakes through a long canyon: Queen's Gap.

The canyon is fairly narrow and lush with ferns and moss. A slowly inclining trail on the right bank of the river is barely wide enough for two people to walk comfortably, and occasionally I fall behind to avoid running into overgrown brush. But it's worth all the hassle—the rough path, spiderwebs, and occasional low-hanging tree branches that nearly poke my eye out—because it's really spectacularly gorgeous here. The canyon river is babbling, creating a light mist where it dips down small hills of polished river rock, and unworldly ferns that cover the canyon floor seem to be growing larger and more luxuriant the farther we walk. It's an embarrassment of ferns. As if nature said, here, you deserve an extra helping.

We're making great time, and I'm glad to be away from guitar-playing campers and all their tempting grilled meats. I'm also glad to be alone with my thoughts. For once, instead of worrying about my parents or cataloging my plans for the day, I spend my hiking time in the canyon watching Lennon. Thinking about Lennon. In my head, I revisit our make-out session from the night before and throw some additional fantasies into the mix that are 50 percent dirtier. ·

But by midday, my energy wanes. Not even filthy thoughts can sustain me. I'm sore and tired, and I just want to drop on the ground and sleep. "I need to stop," I tell Lennon.

He glances at me, brows knitting together. "You all right?"

"Just tired."

"Me too, actually. Come here," he says, gesturing for me to come closer. "I want to check on your hives."

"You just want to gawk at my deformity," I tell him as he lifts the hem of my shirt to reveal a sliver of my stomach. The skin there is speckled with raised, pink bumps, but the bigger wheals are breaking up. "So sexy, right?"

"The sexiest," Lennon agrees, running the backs of his fingers over the puffy welts. "Itchy?"

"I'm not sure. It's hard to concentrate on feeling bad when you're feeling me up."

His lips curl at the corners. "Are you saying I've got magic hands, like Jesus?"

"Are you saying I'm a leper?"

He tugs the edge of my shirt back into place. "Totally. That's exactly what I'm saying. Please stay away from me and definitely don't kiss me."

"Got it."

"That was supposed to be reverse psychology."

"I know. I was just realizing something."

"Oh? What, pray tell?"

"You're the only person besides Joy who isn't afraid to touch my hives."

"They aren't contagious. And if you think a few splotches on your skin are going to stop me from touching you with my magic healing hands after what we did last night, think again."

"Good. I mean, uh . . ."

"It *was* pretty good, wasn't it?" he says.

Am I blushing? My ears feel hot. And a few other parts of my body.

We never did a lot of flirting last fall. It wasn't like this. We were friends in the daytime, make-out partners by night, and we managed both the secrecy of our relationship and this strange new world we were exploring together by keeping things separate.

Now there's a different energy. A thrilling kind of tension.

I know I'm not the only one feeling this new energy between

us. I've caught him sneaking glances at me out of the corner of his eyes, as if he's trying to measure me. Study me. It's exciting and maddening, and I feel as if I might have a heart attack if something doesn't give soon.

There's that smile again. "Anyhoo, your hives look a shit-ton better than last night, but you don't need to overtax your body."

"Is that your scientific opinion, Dr. Mackenzie?" Okay, maybe I have a *little* more energy for filthy thoughts. Definitely willing to overtax my body if he's going to help.

"Gordon told me they had to airlift a guy out of here with hives last summer."

"Gordon?" It takes my brain a second to crawl out of the gutter and realize it's the Jamaican man from the camp last night.

"We chatted this morning."

"Look at you, being all non-antisocial."

Lennon rolls his eyes humorously and continues. "Gordon said that apparently this hiker, he'd never even had hives before, or not in a big way. But he was mildly allergic to peanuts, and even though he could have them in small quantities from time to time, he ate a bunch of candy with nuts while climbing. And that, combined with exhaustion . . . His throat swelled up so much, he lost consciousness."

Angioedema. That's when your face swells up like a balloon. A lot of people with chronic hives have it. Luckily, I've managed to avoid it.

And I hear what Lennon's saying, but I'm more concerned

about the source of the airlift story. "You told Gordon about my hives?"

"He camps here a lot, and I was just trying to find out if he knew what kind of grass was on that hill. It's velvet grass and oxeye daisies, by the way."

"Ooh, *yeah*. That oxeye daisy weed is on my no-fly list. High-risk allergen."

He gives me a look that says *there you go*.

"And I'm sorry about that idiot hiker who decided to gorge on Snickers bars while climbing, but I'm not allergic to nuts," I say. "I mean, God. Can you imagine a world without peanuts?"

Lennon's mouth twists humorously. "The horror. You may not be allergic to peanuts, but look at all the other stuff that sets you off." He ticks off a list on his fingers. "Stress, daisies, shrimp that Sunny cooks—"

"Bad shrimp," I murmur cheerfully.

"Bad shrimp," he repeats in Sunny's voice. "Oh, and there was mean old Mr. McCrory's dog. Remember? He licked your hand and five minutes later . . ."

"That was just bizarre. I'm not allergic to Andromeda's kisses. How was I supposed to know his hellhound's saliva was poison?"

"Maybe it had been chomping on daisies."

"Or shrimp."

"You're an anomaly, Zorie Everhart."

"I am nothing if not an original."

"Well, OG, let's feed your hive-ridden body some lunch, so

we can get through this canyon before the storm hits."

After finding a good place to sit, we eat a quick meal out of our bear canisters, and when we hit the trail again, my body isn't hurting like it was earlier. Either the break helped, or the extra meds, or maybe I'm just getting used to hiking. Whatever the case, I'm able to get into a comfortable groove. Just one foot in front of the next, watching my surroundings, and breathing.

Clear head, steady steps. Moving forward.

We take a second break in the afternoon, and that's when I start to feel the change in the air. A different scent. Sweet, almost. It's sharp and fresh, and it's carried on winds that are picking up.

Lennon looks toward the sky. "See those? Cumulus clouds. They'll start stacking up to make cloud towers. That's when the rain's coming."

"Uh-oh."

He checks the GPS on his phone. "We're almost out of the—ah, crap. Phone died. Let me see yours."

I dig out my phone, but the battery's dead too. Crap. I can't text my mom. Surely she'll understand and chalk it up to no cell service.

He stares at the black screen for a long moment before handing it back. "Doesn't matter. I know where we are. We'll be out of the canyon in a half hour or less. Are you okay to keep walking?"

"If it means not getting wet, then hell yeah. Let's march."

We walk briskly for several minutes, but the winds are really whipping through the canyon now. Enough to blow my hair in my face. Lennon keeps looking up. I think it's getting darker. I'm sort of wishing I had asked him for more information about the storm. This isn't like me *at all,* but I'd been concentrating on the knowledge that we needed to get through the canyon without being eaten alive by mosquitoes. I didn't think about what would happen after. And this storm isn't going to give us a pass for winning. Like: *You guys made it through? Great job! I won't rain on you.*

What do we do when it rains?

"Am I good, or am I freaking fantastic?" he says, several paces ahead of me.

When I catch up to him, cresting a hill, I see what he's seeing.

A shady forest filled with giant trees.

23

The canyon's arms open up and deliver us straight into it, the river arrowing down the center.

"Majestic Grove," Lennon says, stopping to look up at the enormous trunks. "Giant sequoias. World's largest trees. Many of these beauties are a thousand years old. The redwoods on the coast can get taller, but these here in the Sierras are bigger."

I've seen coastal redwoods around the observatory at home, but I've never seen an entire forest of giant trees. Some of them here are as big around as a car and they nearly block out the sky. And the canyon ferns we've been walking through have nothing on these. They create a pale green carpet on the forest floor, and their fronds are so large, it's as if they're in competition with the sequoias to see who can grow bigger.

"It looks prehistoric," I murmur.

"Endor Forest scenes with the ewoks in *Return of the Jedi* were filmed in the Bay Area in a forest like this. So cool, right?"

"It's stunning," I say as we enter the ancient forest, craning my neck up at the gargantuan trunks. The ground is spongy, and it smells strange here, like an outdoor library—musty. A good kind of musty. And it's quiet. Which is odd, because the canyon was filled with the sounds of singing birds and the echo of the river off the rocky canyon walls. The water is still flowing here, but it's a softer babble, absorbed by the great trees.

I walk up to a sequoia and run my hand over soft, corrugated bark, marveling, and then stretch out my arms and try to hug it. "How many people would it take to reach all the way around?"

"Too many." Lennon stands near me and stretches his arms around the tree, too. We don't even make it a quarter of the way around together.

"I love this place," I say, and mean it.

"It's my favorite part of the park," he says, eyes sparkling. "My cathedral."

I understand why.

He points to our left. "There's a bigger trail that runs along the northern edge of the sequoias, several miles from here. No one comes down this way. It's secluded. From man and beast. The trees block out the sunlight, so there's less food for animals. Fewer insects for birds, so it's quieter."

"No mosquitoes."

"Fewer mosquitoes," he corrects.

"I'll take it. Any improvement is a good thing," I say, looking around. "This is surreal. I wish we could stay here."

"We can," he says. "This is where we're camping."

"Tonight?"

"Right now. We're stopping early."

"Really?"

"Truly. Reason one being that I love it here. I know it might sound weird, because it's so dark in here, but it's sort of my happy place. And when I first found it, one of the things I thought was that I wished you could be here to share it with me."

I look into his face and my heart melts.

"Now you can," he says, softer.

Thunder booms in the distance.

Lennon points upward. "And that right there is the second reason. That storm is going to be fierce, and we need to find a place to make camp. Let's get a little farther away from the canyon and find a good spot. Hurry."

There's not a trail here, so we have to pick our way around the trees and ferns as we follow the river and make our way deeper into the sequoias. The thunder's getting louder, which scares me, but every time I find a clear spot big enough to accommodate our tents, Lennon glances up and shakes his head.

"Why?" I finally say in frustration after the third rejection. "It's close to the river, but not too close. It's flat, it's—"

"There," he says, pointing to another spot. It looks the same as this one, basically. Maybe a little more room. I'm tired of looking, so I follow him and am relieved to stop and dump my pack on the ground.

He's looking up into the canopy. "Yes, this should be okay. We'll build the tents close to these two trees. They're half the height of the others around us." He's already unzipping his backpack, fishing out his tent as lightning flashes above the trees. He stills, listening.

Thunder booms in the distance.

"Fifteen seconds," he says. "Five seconds per mile. That storm is three miles away."

"Is that bad?"

"These trees will offer protection, but they're also tall, and tall attracts lightning. That's why I wanted to build under shorter ones"—he gestures between the two trees flanking our tents—"so that the taller surrounding trees would absorb any strikes. This isn't like a storm at home. People get hit by lightning out here and die."

"Everyone dies out here," I complain. "It's practically a tragedy."

His lips tilt upward. "I know, right?"

"But—"

"Build tent, talk later," he says, unsheathing his tent pieces.

I rush to get mine out, and by the time I do, he's already got his tent erected. I start to lay out my floor next to his, as we've been doing, but he shakes his head. "Let's build them door to door, facing each other."

I don't ask why, but just trust that he has a plan while he checks something on my tent and measures out space, showing me where to start. Wind is whipping through the forest pretty fast, and the sky is so dark, it's almost as if night's fallen beneath the tree canopy. I get the tent in place and fit all my poles together, but we have the extra step of securing rainflies on top. It seems to take forever, and I'm trying to rush to stake my tent down before it blows away. Lennon finishes his and helps me erect the small vestibule awning that extends over my front door. He's measured accurately, so apart from a tiny crack, it covers the space between the two tents, a tiny covered passageway.

He hauls our packs into his tent, minus our sleeping gear. "I'll get everything set up inside the big tent," he tells me. "You fill up our water bottles. Mine's almost empty, and we'll need it for cooking. Don't leave my line of sight, and hurry."

Thunder rumbles. I grab the water bottles and Lennon's water filter, which is faster than mine. There's a tiny path to the river that snakes between a pair of giant ferns. The water is running swiftly here, and though I could probably cross the river in a dozen steps, it looks deep. I bend by the water, careful that I have decent footing, and begin pumping water through the filter.

As the first Nalgene bottle fills, thunder rumbles. I mentally count the seconds and watch the trees. *One, two, three, four, five—*

Lightning flashes.

Five seconds. That strike was a mile away?

"Hurry!" Lennon's voice calls out from the campsite, making me jump.

"I can't make the water filter any faster," I mumble to myself.

Finally, the first bottle fills. I cap it and get the filter into the second one, then start pumping.

I feel something on my head. Is that a raindrop? I slant my face upward. Definitely a raindrop. Two. Four. Twenty. It seems silly to be so concerned with collecting water when it's about to fall all over us.

Thunder booms so loud, it's deafening. But almost immediately, the sky lights up. And just like that, the rain comes down. Hard. I hear Lennon calling my name, but I'm trying to concentrate. "Shit, shit, shit!" I say, pumping faster.

But not fast enough.

The entire forest lights up with the loudest bang I've ever heard.

I lunge away from the river. The second bottle falls into the rapids, along with the pump filter. I'm disoriented for a moment, unable to hear anything. The bottle bobs and disappears under the foam. I start to run after it, but a stony hand grabs my arm.

"Leave it!" Lennon shouts, dragging me away from the river.

He grabs my hand, and I can tell by how hard he jerks me down the path through the ferns that he's not fooling around. We're in trouble.

My heart hammers as I race after him in the rain, the green scent of sorrel and moss rising up from the soles of my shoes. And I smell something else, too: like Christmas on fire. The lightning. It singed the treetops.

That scent terrifies me.

I scramble across slick, springy ground, and our tents pop into view. Before we can make it there, lightning strikes again. For the first time in my life, I truly get the whole Zeus-throwing-bolts thing, because that's what it looks like. As though an angry god is zapping Earth with a giant laser gun. It sounds like a bomb, and shakes the entire ground. Shrubs, these enormous trees, us—everything.

I think I'm going to wet my pants in fear.

My mind has flipped off. I want to cry, but I'm too scared. I'm nothing but blind terror and am wholeheartedly convinced I'm going to die.

All these giant trees, and yet there's nothing here to protect us. No shelter. No door to close and hide behind. No car in which to outrun the storm. And it makes me feel small and helpless.

Right before we make it to the tents, Lennon pulls me down on the ground and crouches over me.

Boom!

My world goes white.

I'm squatting in something that's neither dirt nor mud, soaked to the bone, and the rain is driving down on us while burning wood fills my nostrils. It feels as if it will never end. *Just kill us*, I think. Go on, get it over with.

Lennon's muscles are steel when the next strike comes. But I feel him jump, too. It's as if we're in the middle of a war zone. Seconds later, another strike hits.

But.

This one isn't as loud. Or as close. The thunder and lightning are separating again. We wait—for seconds or minutes, I don't even know. But at some point, the world doesn't feel like it's falling apart around us, and Lennon's body loosens.

Is it over? I still hear thunder in the distance.

"We're all right," Lennon's voice is saying in my ear. "Told you it was a big storm, didn't I? And listen to that. It's moving more slowly now. I'm still counting thunder. Slow means a lot of rain, but we're out of the lighting zone for now. Come on, let's get up."

He pulls me to my feet, and I can't see. "My glasses," I say.

Lennon looks around. "You lost them somewhere."

"I lost the water bottles, too."

"One's on the riverbank. We'll get it later. And we have another filter. Worse comes to worst, we'll boil water."

And I can live without glasses for a couple of days. I'm too numb to worry.

He lifts up my chin. "It's all good. You okay?"

"Yeah," I say, nodding.

"That was intense."

"That was . . ." I laugh. I can't help it. I'm not sure if it's nervous laughter or just a release, but I'm pushing wet hair out of my face and laughing. "We just nearly got blown out of our shoes. We almost died."

"No, Zorie, we just *lived*." Lennon lifts up both arms and pumps victory fists, yowling. "We're alive! We won!"

He's right. We did live. Survival is a beautiful thing. I laugh again and hold up my dirty hands, letting them fill with rain until the mud washes away. Adrenaline is still coursing through my veins, and I feel invincible.

Lennon shoves dark hair out of his eyes. His clothes stick to him, clinging to his shape. Every sharp plane. Every muscle. It's practically X-rated. Or maybe that's *exactly* what it is, because I blink away rain and see his gaze roaming over me too. And there's nothing polite about the way he's looking at me.

Maybe the storm broke something in both of our brains.

I inhale sharply. He makes a low noise in the back of his throat. Our gazes lock.

We both pounce on each other at the same time.

He pulls me against him, one arm slung around my shoulders, his other hand cupping the back of my head. His rain-slick clothes are cold, but his mouth is hot on mine. He kisses me hard. It's an impatient, greedy kiss. Ravenous. And when thunder rumbles in the distance, I jump a little, but I don't let go.

My back hits the smooth, wet bark of a sequoia, and he presses himself against the length of me. He's taut and solid, a brick wall of lean muscle, lifting me up until my toes skim the tree's bumpy roots. And when he pushes his hips against mine, I push back, feeling unmistakable hardness between us. A thrill zips through me.

My legs wrap around his hips, and he's holding me in place against the tree, pinning me as he warms my neck with kisses. I smell his hair and the scent of sequoia bark, and the rain is coming down so hard, my grip around his shoulders is slipping. I throw both arms around his neck and cling.

"Tent," he says into my ear. I'm not sure if it's a question or a statement, but I'm telling him yes. And he tells me to hold on, but I think if I hold him any tighter, I'm going to break bones. My back leaves the tree, and he's carrying me several steps. We slide in the mud, and when he sloppily sets me down in front of the tents, I'm clutching so hard, I nearly pull us both down. His head bashes into mine.

"Oww!"

We're both laughing, and I feel a little delirious. "We're drenched," I say.

He pushes wet curls away from my face. "Yeah."

"The sleeping gear's going to get wet."

"Maybe we should just, I don't know"—he shrugs slowly—"get out of these clothes before we go in."

My pulse pounds in my ears.

Naked.

Lennon.

Me.

Us.

"That would be the practical thing to do," I agree, trying to sound casual.

But this is *so* not casual. And we both know it.

We lunge for each other, and he's stripping off my shirt. My arms are tangled, and he's laughing, trying to peel away the wet fabric. It gives, and his arm flies back. My shirt hits the tent with a loud slap.

Lennon pauses for a moment, looking me over, a slow smile lifting his cheeks. "Are we doing this?" He sounds dazed.

I'm a little embarrassed, but not enough to stop. "Oh, we're doing this."

Shoes and socks are dropped in the mud. And then I get his shirt off, and we're both attacking each other's jeans as if they'll self-destruct if we don't get them off fast enough. And oh, okay, wet boxer shorts are *definitely* pornographic. I CAN SEE EVERY-THING, and I can't stop looking—I don't even care that I'm shivering in my bra and panties in the middle of the woods.

"Wait, wait, wait." I put a hand on his chest. My mouth moves faster than my brain. "You can't get me pregnant," I tell him firmly.

Lennon's face contorts as several expressions flash. "That's something a guy never thinks he's going to hear."

"I mean, I'm sure you *could*, which is the problem. I just didn't plan for this. That's what I meant." *Ugh, idiot*, I think, suddenly self-conscious. I was thinking of what happened with Andre, and how stupid we were. And now I'm making assumptions, because we're getting naked. Should I not be making assumptions? I'm completely rattled now.

"Forget it," I say.

When he opens his mouth to respond, he pauses and then says, "Hold on."

He dives under the short canopy connecting the tents and unzips the door to his tent, disappearing. I don't know what to do. I'm standing in the rain, half-naked and humiliated, and—

Lennon emerges. He crawls under the canopy to the big tent, unzips the door, and throws our camp towels inside. Then he holds up a long line of shiny metallic condom packages to show me before tossing them inside the tent, too. "You may not have planned, but I did," he says, smiling. "Boy Scout motto. Be prepared."

"Good God." How many of those are there?

"Call it hopeful thinking. I guess I didn't learn anything after the hotel-room fiasco. And, you know, one good thing about Toys in the Attic is an endless supply of free condoms. Come here."

Heart racing, I duck beneath the canopy, taking his offered hand, and quickly crawl inside the double tent. It's dim inside, and it smells strongly of nylon and rain. I'm acutely aware of how cramped the space is, and how long Lennon's legs are. How much bare skin is on display, both his and mine. Those pornographic boxers—DO NOT LOOK.

Too late. Guess he's not anxious.

But all of the sudden I am. So, *so* anxious. Why?

I glance down at myself and see all my hives on display. That doesn't help. I hope it's dark enough that he can't see them, too, and quickly move my arm to cover my stomach.

"Hey," Lennon says in a soft voice, pulling my hand away from my stomach and threading his fingers through mine. "It's only me."

"*Only?*" I shake my head. "That's the problem. It's you. And me. And I just got you back. We don't even have a plan yet for what's going to happen when we go home. Everything could fall apart. My parents could divorce. I could be forced to move in with my dad—"

"Or things could work out just fine."

"That's the problem, though. Life is unpredictable, which is the worst part about it. I need dependable. I need something I can count on. And if this is terrible or weird, then—"

"Then what? How terrible could it be? I'm pretty sure I understand the basics."

"It's easier for you. You're a guy. Your body isn't a mystery."

He considers this for a moment. "I like mysteries. I'm very good at solving mysteries."

I hesitate. "How good?"

"Very, *very* good. I will not rest until a mystery is solved. I'm Nancy fucking Drew."

My chuckle is breathy. "Oh?"

"Remember Mr. Henry's missing tabby? Who figured out it had been catnapped by the white supremacist at the end of the cul-de-sac?"

"You did. Stop making me laugh."

Eyes merry, he opens a camp towel and crooks a finger. I lean forward and let him dry my hair. "And who discovered that the hair salon was siphoning electricity off of the Jitterbug after the manager kept complaining about her electricity bill?"

"You did," I murmur, head bowed. His hands feel good on my hair, and it's giving me a really good view of his chest and arms. "Wait, we both solved that mystery. I'm the one who first said someone could be stealing their electricity."

"But who looked up online how to do it and traced it back to the salon? Who made you sit in the alley and be my lookout while I checked the meters, and then you yelled at me because I wouldn't let you get coffee until we were finished?"

"I didn't yell at you."

"You totally did," he says, pulling the towel away and quickly rubbing it over his own wet hair until it stands up. "And it made me furious. And *that* was the first time I really wanted to kiss you."

"Wait, no. That couldn't be. We were . . ."

"Fourteen."

"You wanted to kiss me when we were fourteen?"

"I wanted to do lots of things to you when we were fourteen. Fifteen. Sixteen. By the time you kissed me, I'd built a Zorie vault of sexual fantasies bigger than Fort Knox. I thought you'd never catch up to me."

My voice fails. I'm stunned, trying to fit all of these confessions into my memories of what we were.

What we are now.

"And I know you hate my parents' shop, and sometimes I do too," he says, tossing the towel into the corner of the tent. "But other times, it has its advantages."

"Besides the free condoms?"

"Besides that," he says, a sly smile lifting his lips. "You'd be surprised what I've learned. Customers are surprisingly specific, and you would not believe the shit they tell you. Anything you can imagine that could go wrong—or right—someone else has probably had that happen to them, too."

"Um . . ."

"What I'm saying is, all bodies are weird. Throw whatever mystery you have at me. Let me help you solve it."

"It's not that I can't solve it by myself. I just want to make that clear."

"This is the best conversation we've ever had, by the way. And I'm definitely adding an image of you solving your own mysteries to the ol' vault for later—"

"Oh my God," I murmur, mildly horrified.

"But right now, wouldn't it be more fun to team up and solve crime together?"

"I'm worried it could be bad or awkward," I say in a small voice.

"I've worried about that too," he says, running the backs of his fingers along my shoulder, down my arm, following the path he's tracing with his eyes. "This isn't nothing. This isn't not serious. It's big. It's epic."

"It's you and me," I say.

He nods. "But after last night out on that hill, and then just now, out there?"

"We're so good together," I agree, opening my hand when he runs his finger over my knuckles. "Right?"

"We are goddamn amazing. We're a rocket ship filled with potential. Either we die in a fiery blaze before we leave the Earth's atmosphere, or we make it through and orbit the moon."

"If you're trying to seduce me with space stuff, it's totally working."

His smile is divine. "Yeah?"

"Yeah."

"Do you want to try?"

I nod slowly. "I think so."

"You sure?"

Yeah. I actually am. "Fly me to the moon."

Rain drums against the tent as he pulls me closer, and we sink into the sleeping bags. Mouth on mouth, hip on hip, heartbeat on heartbeat. We're less desperate than we were outside, more aware of each other. It's a fervent awareness, both nervous and thrilling, and when we remove the last layers of our clothes, he steadily talks to me in a calm, low voice, and I follow it like a lighthouse beacon.

He guides. Assures. Makes sure I don't veer off into dark waters and crash.

Then it's my turn to navigate. He listens. Follows directions. Uses my instructions to create a new path.

It's a brave new world.

And an all-consuming one. I'm ready to chuck everything

I've learned out the window, because he can't find the condoms, and I don't even care, and I definitely *should,* but I'm willing to give up my entire civilized existence and live in this tent like homeless hippies if he will just—

"They were right here!" He's about to have a panic attack.

"Wait, what's this?" I pull something out from under my back.

"Thank you, thank you, thank you," he murmurs.

"Hurry."

"No, don't say that. Believe me, I'm hanging on by a thread here."

"Please?" I whisper.

"You're killing me, Zorie."

Every time he says my name in that rumbling voice of his, I think I might die myself. I'm in pleasure overload, here, on the verge of something great, and I really, *really* don't want him to stop. But then . . . it's happening. It's actually happening. It's good, and a little awkward, and sometimes funny, because wow, human bodies *are* weird. But it's also more than I expected—than I even hoped.

It's all of him and all of me, and most of all, it's us, it's us, *it's us.*

24

"Told you I'd solve that mystery," Lennon says after we've been tangled up in each other's arms for a while, listening to the slowing rain outside. "Twice."

I smile against his chest. "I never doubted. You're Nancy goddamn Drew, after all."

"And you're Sherlock fucking Holmes."

"If we start our own detective agency, I want both of those names painted on the door, just like that."

"My parents should have named their shop 'The Detective Agency.'"

I chuckle and he pretends to bite my neck, and that makes me squeal. He just holds me tighter. Fine by me, because I can't stop touching him. The stubble on his jaw. His heavy eyebrows. The curving ridge of muscle above his hips. I've never been so close to him, and there's so much begging to be explored.

But when my stomach growls, we both realize how late it

is. Not *exactly* how late, because both our phones are dead, and Lennon's fancy compass—our only source of time—is currently sitting inside the pocket of his jeans, buried in mud outside the tent. But we've been at this detecting for a while now, and I'm in need of things that are stashed in the other tent. Like food. Wet wipes. Dry clothes. Okay, maybe I'm not in a hurry for those, but when Lennon volunteers to crawl beneath the canopy to the smaller tent, I add that to the list, and he bravely extricates himself from our sleeping bag.

The other tent is only a few feet away, and it's silly, but I hate for him to go that far. As I tie back the mesh flaps of our door to open it up, the sight of him crawling naked into the second tent's entrance has my complete attention. "That's an interesting view," I tell him from the open door of our tent.

"I aim to please," he calls back.

He has to make two trips, and between them, ducks outside into the rain for a couple of minutes. Naked Lennon in the woods. Now would be a good time for a photo. But when he comes back, he has one of our water bottles, which he hands to me through the door, shivering, and dives back into the other tent. This time, he emerges wearing boxers and tosses me a T-shirt. He's also raided our food stash, hallelujah!

Lying on our stomachs with our heads sticking outside the door flap, we set up the one-burner camping stove under the canopy. The stove is just a tiny bottle of fuel with four prongs that unfold above it to hold a pan. We heat up water for hot cocoa, which is inside two brown packs of military MREs that Lennon brought. There are also a million other things in each ration bag: a pastry bar, crackers, dried fruit, and holiest of holies, a packet of peanut butter.

"I thought you might like that," Lennon says with a smile as we look through the contents of the meal packs. There are spoons, napkins, matches, and even a tiny bottle of Tabasco and some candy. The entrée gets heated up inside a flameless heater bag that needs to be filled with a little water to activate the heating element. It doesn't taste quite as good as Reagan's gourmet freeze-dried camp meals, but I'm starving, and the peanut butter and crackers make up for everything.

After we've eaten and cleaned up, Lennon breaks out his journal and maps, and I lie on my side, watching him recalculate the last leg of our trip to Condor Peak. "Six hours of walking," he says. "Maybe seven with long breaks."

"That's not too bad."

"Nope."

"Huh. I thought it would be farther." We both look at the map that's unfolded atop his journal. "You sure you want to go to the star party with me?"

"Why wouldn't I?"

"It'll be a lot of people I don't know, and some people I see at club meetings every month."

"And Avani."

"I'll need to use her telescope to take decent photos, and setting them up takes a lot of time. It could be boring for you, just standing around while the rest of us star nerds look through lenses and try to get face time with Sandra Faber."

"I don't know who that is, but I'm assuming from that quiver in your voice that she's someone important."

"She only has an astronomical law named after her and figured out how to estimate the distance between galaxies. No big deal."

He grins. "Impressive."

"Anyway, I'm just saying that you might hate the star party."

"Don't worry, I won't be bored. I'll be with you. Besides, I'm interested in whatever you like."

"Yeah?"

"Meteor showers are cool. You can take lots of cool pictures and talk galaxies," he says. "And whenever you're ready to leave, we head back to civilization. Avani's not our only option for transportation."

"A regular bus runs up there several times a day," I confirm. "I know from my research."

"I've got a park bus schedule in here somewhere," he says, rummaging through a pile of papers stuck between the pages of his journal. "It's from last year, but I doubt much has changed."

As he's looking for it, something catches my eye in his journal, and I stick my fingers on the corner of the page to stop him from flipping. "What's this?"

"Ugh, don't look," he says, covering it with his hand.

"Why?"

"Because it's embarrassing."

"Well, *now* I'm going to just forget it," I tease, tugging his fingertips. "Show me."

He groans, but releases the page. I peer over his arm and see drawings of people. They look like anime characters, a bit stylized, with simple, clean lines and big eyes. It takes me a moment to realize they're all girls. The same girl. Repeated over and over, from different viewpoints. Sitting at a desk, bent over schoolwork. Eating at a picnic table. Reading on the stairs. Drinking coffee at a café. They're mostly drawn from behind her, so there's only a partial view of her face, but . . .

But . . .

She has dark, curly hair and glasses, and she's wearing plaid.

I slowly turn the page to find more drawings. The same girl, drawn dozens of times. Each one is dated in Lennon's careful, neat handwriting. They go back to last fall. Last spring. Early this summer.

The newest one is from last week. The girl is standing on a balcony, looking down with a telescope.

The drawings are flattering. The drawings are sad. The drawings are filled with longing. Lennon's heart on the page.

Tenderness and pain rise to my throat. It's a bittersweet pain, one that's tarnished by how awful this year has been for both of us. I tried so hard and for so long to push all my feelings for him away, to tamp them down into a tiny box and hide it somewhere dark in my mind. I did everything I could to forget.

And Lennon did all he could to remember.

Tears drop off my cheek onto the page, splattering. I try to wipe it away with my finger, but the ink bleeds.

"I'm sorry," I whisper. "They're beautiful and I ruined them."

He shuts the journal and tugs me closer to swipe tears from my cheek with his thumb. "It's okay," he murmurs, kissing my eyelids. "I don't need them anymore. I have you."

The next day, I beg him for one more day in our sequoia cathedral. We'll have plenty of time to get to the star party's final night, which is the best time to see the meteor shower anyway. Our phones are dead, so I can't tell Avani to expect us a day late, but what does it matter? She'll still be there. And likely she'll be so busy enjoying the star party, she won't even notice. The only thing I see as a potential problem is Mom, because I *did* promise I'd text when I arrived at the star party. But I also told her we'd be getting there late tonight, and what difference would one day make? Besides, I'm hiking, not taking a scheduled bus. Surely, she'll understand that this isn't an exact science. I can call her from Avani's phone the minute we get to Condor Peak tomorrow.

I argue all of this to Lennon, but frankly, I didn't need to convince him. He is completely agreeable, and we stay put.

The storm has passed, so we spend the day doing practical things. Washing mud out of our clothes in the river. Collecting firewood and putting it in the sun to dry. Finding my glasses.

We also spend it doing impractical things. Bathing in the river together. (Less bathing, more touching.) Reading the manga book Lennon brought in his backpack. (Less reading, more touching.) Taking a nap. (Less sleeping, more sex that nearly permanently blinds Lennon when a tent pole snaps.)

My hives are still there, but I'm not clawing at my arms as much. Partly because I'm keeping up with medicating, and partly because I caved and let Lennon slather me in Miss Angela's stinky sativa salve. I don't think I've ever been so relaxed—sexlaxation, Lennon dubs it, and says he'll make a fortune marketing it as a cure for allergies and stress.

But all good things must come to an end, and when we run out of condoms, we know it's time to go.

Goodbye, sex camp.

As we're packing everything up, I check to make sure my camera is still working, and it strikes me that I haven't taken one single photo on this trip. It's not just that. I haven't obsessively checked my messages or my social media feeds. I don't know what's trending, and I haven't posted anything. I can't check views or likes or favorites or reblogs. And I have no idea what's going on in the news.

"We disconnected," I tell Lennon.

"I know. Isn't it great?"

It actually is. Maybe I wouldn't want to do it forever, but I didn't die, either.

We've waited as long as we can, leaving well after lunch. My pack feels heavier, somehow, even though there's exactly the same amount of things inside. I think it's as reluctant to leave as I am.

But it's time to go.

We walk through a string of meadows all afternoon and have dinner near a lake that's one of the largest alpine bodies of water in the state. We're well above five thousand feet, so the water's too cold for swimming, but it's a calming view. Not as calming as sexlaxation, I point out. Lennon triple-checks: We're definitely out of condoms.

When we're back on the trail again, my mind starts wheeling. We haven't discussed what we're going to do about my father when we get back home. Or anything about the future. I don't want to think about it. I want to stay here. This is impossible, and I know it, but when I start thinking about what awaits us—parents, school, the so-called friends who abandoned us, the looming threat of my dad's affair . . . all of this creates doubt in my head. Doubt, worry, and a growing sense of dread.

The sun sets during the final stretch of the hike up the foothills. We've connected up to a major trail with official park signs informing distances to several nearby attractions. Condor Peak is outside King's Forest in a state-maintained area. There are several scenic points on and around the mountain, but the one we're headed to, the Northern Viewpoint, is right in front of us, point-five kilometers. The star party is gathered at a small campground below it, just across a road that borders the national park.

An actual road. With actual cars whizzing down it.

I never thought I'd be reluctant to return to civilization.

All my misgivings move to the back of my mind when we spy a big sign for the star party posted at the entrance to a parking lot connected to a small campground. The sign warns the public that they are approaching a protected Dark Sky area, and nothing but red lights are allowed past the campground, to avoid light pollution. The actual viewing area is a quarter mile up a short path that curves around the mountain. Even small amounts of white light are objectionable to astronomers, and many of the cars and RVs here have red tape adhered to their headlights. I'm prepared for this, and have brought along a small red penlight.

"Whoa," Lennon says. "Lots of people. This is a big viewing party, huh?"

Bigger than I expected. "Maybe we should see if Avani is down here before we go up to the viewing area. The meteors won't be fully visible for another half hour, at least, so we still have some time."

We walk through the parking lot, and it's jammed with cars. Overflow is parking on the side of the road. People are hauling telescope cases out of their cars—some professional, some not. Several families are here with small children. I try to spot anyone from my club, but it's dark, and the lot is chaotic.

A cedar split-rail fence divides the parking lot and campground. It's half the size of the one we stayed in three nights ago, and the individual campsites are all crammed together. It seems to be mostly RVs. A sign we pass as we enter says that it's at capacity.

We walk along the main road circling through the campground, and get only halfway around when someone comes barreling toward us, arms waving.

"Zorie!" It's Avani, and she slows just in time to throw her arms around my neck. "You're alive."

"Of course I'm alive," I say. "Sorry we're a day late."

Avani pulls away to blink at Lennon with wide eyes. "Whoa. You're really here. I mean, hey, Lennon. It's just weird to see you together again. But good!"

"It's good to see you too," Lennon says, mouth quirking up. He gives her a quick hug, and I'm reminded that they've spent more time interacting at school over the last year than I have with either one of them.

Avani is breathless, glancing back and forth between us. When she catches her breath, her brow furrows. "Look, I'm so, *so* sorry."

I squint at her. "About what?"

"I didn't have a choice. I never would have said anything, but he insisted."

What is she talking about?

"It's bad," she says, face twisting. "I feel like it's all my fault."

"Slow down and tell us what happened," Lennon says.

Avani glances over her shoulder. "From what I've been told, Reagan's mom called your mom, Zorie. And that's how it all started."

Oh, God. No, no, no . . .

"Reagan's dad got sick," she says, "and they couldn't fly to Switzerland, and then apparently Reagan came home with Brett, and she was supposed to be at that glamping thing with you. But you guys got kicked out?"

My stomach is turning to stone.

"It was Brett's fault," Lennon says.

"Oh," she says, distracted for a moment before shaking her head. "So, anyway, your dad called Dr. Viramontes yesterday, looking for you."

"What?" I say, alarmed.

She nods. "Your dad was really upset, and he said he and your mom had tried to get in touch with you, but you weren't answering texts—"

"Our phones died," I argue, but all I'm thinking about is that phone conversation with Mom at the ranger station three days ago. She knew!

"—and I guess the last time your mom had heard from you, you told her you'd be here at the star party yesterday, so he was freaking out. And Dr. Viramontes asked me if I knew anything, because your dad was going to call the police and file a missing persons report. And so . . ." She squeezes her eyes shut. "I told him what you texted me a couple days ago. That you were hiking here with Lennon. That you were supposed to arrive yesterday."

"Oh, God," I mumble.

"Dr. Viramontes called your dad back and told him. And he assured your dad that we would call when you guys got here. But you didn't show up last night—"

"We were just running late!" I say, exasperated.

She nods, glancing at Lennon, who is biting out filthy curses under his breath.

"What happened?" I ask.

"I just overheard a few things," she says. "Your dad is loud when he's angry. He was saying stuff about the Mackenzies, and how they allowed Lennon to kidnap you."

"What?" I say, pressing my hands against my temples.

"And I tried to butt in and defend you, Lennon," she says, glancing over her shoulder again. "But Mr. Everhart is . . . well, he yelled at me, and accused me of aiding and abetting—"

"Oh, for the love of Pete," I say. "Wait, wait, wait. You said you overheard . . . you said he yelled at you. On the phone?"

Avani bites her lip and shakes her head. "I'm so sorry, Zorie. I texted and called to warn you a couple hours ago, but you didn't answer."

And that's when I look in the direction she's been glancing. The door to an RV swings open, and three people file outside. Dr. Viramontes is the first. And behind him are my parents.

25

"Zorie!" my mom shouts from across the campsite, relief in her voice. She rushes ahead of the men and throws her arms around me. "You're all right."

"Mom . . . ," I say, hoping the right words will come out, but I'm stuck between her concern and the shit storm that's approaching.

She pulls back and holds my face. "You're fine."

"I'm fine."

She moves one of her hands to Lennon's face. "You're okay too?"

He nods. His expression is taut.

"What in God's name is going on?" my father roars over my mother's shoulder. He's not talking to me. He doesn't even give me anything but a cursory look. His eyes are on Lennon, and he pushes my mom aside to get in Lennon's face. "You snatch my daughter away and take her into the woods?"

"I didn't snatch anything," Lennon says, eyes narrowing.

"I asked him to take me," I tell my dad. "Reagan left us. She was our transportation home. And Lennon knows the park—"

"I don't give a damn," my dad says. "Reagan came home five days ago. Five days! You've been alone in the wilderness with my daughter—*my daughter*," he shouts at Lennon.

"Dan," my mom says, trying to pull him away from Lennon.

Dr. Viramontes clears his throat. "Zorie, I'm glad to see you and Mr. Mackenzie are well."

"There was never anything to worry about," I say, giving him a tight smile. "I'm sorry you were dragged into this."

He shakes his head. "I'm just glad you're all right. I invited you here, so I feel responsible."

"Damn right, you're responsible," my dad snaps. "These are underage kids."

"I find that most of our club members are smart, self-aware individuals who don't need a babysitter."

My dad snorts. "Then you're obviously not a parent, because these kids don't know their asses from their faces."

Dr. Viramontes holds up his hands in surrender. "I told you before, I'm not going to fight with you. Since my club member is seemingly unharmed and accounted for, I will leave you to sort this out among yourselves. I just ask that you don't upset the other campers. We're here to witness nature, not disturb it." Dr. Viramontes glances at me, a look of pity on his face, before he turns to walk away.

My mom gently inserts herself between Lennon and my dad. "Let's talk about this civilly."

"The time for being civil has passed," Dad says.

Something snaps inside my head. I glance back, making sure Dr. Viramontes in out of earshot, and then I turn to my father.

"It absolutely has," I tell him. "It passed when you threatened Lennon last fall in that hotel. Yeah, that's right. I know. I know *everything*."

"What hotel?" Mom says.

Something close to rage passes over my father's features. "Oh, really? Did he tell you that I caught him trying to use a stolen credit card and that he took a swing at me?"

"Yeah, and that's the bruise you told Mom and me that you'd gotten at a construction site," I shout. "You lied about that. You lied about Lennon. Instead of telling his parents, you took it upon yourself to administer justice that you had *no right* doing."

"What in the world are you talking about?" Mom says. "Dan, what's going on?"

"I caught him trying to get a hotel room for the two of them," Dad says.

Mom blinks rapidly. When she opens her mouth, a strangled noise comes out.

"That's right, he did. And my love life is my business alone," I tell my dad. "You took my best friend away from me. You ruined both of our lives just to keep your dirty little secret."

A tense silence follows. I can't believe I just said that. It just . . . came out, and now, as Mom's eyes narrow quizzically, I wish like anything I could take it back. I glance around to see if anyone at the campground can hear us arguing; no one seems to be paying attention but Avani, who looks as if she can't decide whether she should stay or go.

"Zorie," Mom says evenly. "What dirty little secret?"

"Nothing." I can't look at my dad. Why did I open my mouth?

"Zorie," Mom repeats, this time more firmly.

"Lennon was at the hotel because it was homecoming," I tell her, tears sliding down my cheeks. "Dad was at the hotel because . . . he was seeing another woman."

My mom stares at me and then calmly turns to my dad. "Was this Molly?"

He nods once, quickly.

"I see," my mom says.

What?

"That's it?" I look back and forth in disbelief, at her, then him.

"I know about her," she says. "We were going through a rough patch. We're past that now."

Now it's my turn to stare with an open mouth. When I finally speak, I sound like an idiot. "How . . . ? When? You knew? You didn't tell me. You knew?"

My mom glances at Avani, who is still standing nearby, pretending to look at the night sky. "It's not something I'd like to discuss in public. But yes, your father told me about . . . the other woman. He ended it. We worked through our issues."

"He cheated on you," I whisper.

"I'm not discussing this with you now," she says quietly.

"You didn't discuss it with me at all!"

"It wasn't your business," she says, now angry. Her dark eyes shine with intense emotion. "It was mine. Mine alone. And your father's."

"Am I not part of this family?" I ask. "Don't I deserve to know that my father is a piece of shit?"

"Hey!" my mom says.

"You're not going to talk to me like that," Dad says. "Joy's right. It wasn't your business."

Lennon crosses his arms over his chest. "You made it her business when you fucking lied to her."

My dad points a finger at Lennon and stalks toward him. "You listen to me—"

"No, I won't," Lennon says. "You want to punch me? Then do it, old man. I was too stupid to realize it then, but I know now that I didn't need to be afraid of your threats. We have a camp full of witnesses here. You want to hit a minor? My parents will see you in court."

"No one is hitting anyone," my mom shouts, angrily pushing my father back. "This is ridiculous. And everyone's emotions are out of control, so this is not the time or place to discuss this. The only thing I care about tonight is that Zorie and Lennon are safe. We will go home and talk about the rest of it later."

"I'm not taking that punk home," my father says, then peers

over my mom's head to address Lennon, pointing an angry finger in his direction. "You can find your own way. God knows you feel adult enough to trample through the woods with my daughter. Get a taxi, catch a bus, call your own parents. But you're not riding in my car."

"Dan," my mom argues.

"No, it's fine," Lennon says, mouth rigid. "I wouldn't dream of accepting a favor from him. I'll catch my own ride."

"We both can," I agree, clasping Lennon's hand. "Because I'm not getting in the car with you either, Dad. I'm staying here with Lennon."

"Like hell you are," Dad says. "You're going home with us."

New plan.

New plan.

New plan.

I can't think of a new plan! I'm crying, and vaguely aware that half of the campground is now staring at us—and probably some of them are people I know. People I wanted to meet. Sandra Faber! My God, a renowned astronomer could be witnessing all of the ugliness, right along with everyone else in the region who could help me potentially get into Stanford.

But none of it matters now, because my heart is shattering. My family is a sham, and I'm about to lose Lennon again.

"I've never hated you more than I do right now," I tell my father.

Hurt flashes behind his eyes, but instead of talking to me, he points at Lennon. "You did this. I blame you for corrupting my daughter. And guess what, hotshot? Nothing's changed. You're not allowed to see Zorie."

"I don't take orders from you," Lennon says.

"You may not, but she does," he says, nodding toward me. "And if you don't remember, I've got proof of what you did last fall."

Lennon shrugs. "My parents know about the credit card, and they know about the hotel room. They also know I'm here with Zorie, and you don't see them flipping out."

My dad is going to kill him. Straight-up murder. I seriously wonder if I should call for help, and then I see him physically force himself to calm down. Hard breaths. Crack of the jaw. Eyes on the ground. "Zorie, you're coming home with us. And that's final."

He's serious. This is all falling apart.

What am I going to do?

"I won't leave you," I tell Lennon through my tears, turning away from my parents. "I won't let him do this to us. I won't lose you. *I won't lose you*," I repeat, desperate, fisting my hands in his shirt.

Lennon's face is stony, and he's glancing over my shoulder at my father. His head dips low, and he speaks quickly in my ear. "Go home with them. I'll be okay here. And we'll figure something out."

How? How will we figure something out? I can't see how this

can work. But more than that, I can't see my life without him in it. I tried living like that over the last year, and it wasn't living. It was surviving.

Without thinking, I stand on my toes and kiss him. It's quick and hard, and I'm still crying. He kisses me back, and it feels like goodbye.

"Joy," my father says coldly, "talk sense into Zorie before I say something I regret. We're leaving in three minutes."

"I came here to take photos of the meteor shower," I protest weakly. It doesn't even matter anymore, and I'm fighting a battle I've already lost. "I was supposed to meet Sandra Faber."

My dad shakes his head. "You lost that privilege when you lied to us about who you were coming out here with."

"I came to the Sierras with Reagan! She didn't tell me Lennon was coming along, and she definitely didn't tell either one of us that she was going to abandon the glamping trip and take off with her friends. Lennon and I didn't know we were going to be stranded in the middle of the wilderness. We didn't plan this!"

"Life is hard," my dad says, turning away from me sharply, storm clouds behind his eyes. "None of us plan for any of it."

The atmosphere inside the car is silent and oppressive as my father drives out of the camp's parking lot. I turn around in the backseat and see all the red lights of the star party. Lennon is already lost among the masses, so I can't even see his face one last time. All I can see is my freedom slipping away as white meteoroids streak across the black sky. Dust and particles, some no bigger than a grain of sand, disintegrating as they pass through Earth's atmosphere. Something so small can create a brilliant flash of light. It looks like a miracle. Unearthly.

Shooting stars.

No wonder people wish upon them.

And though I know they aren't really stars, and that wishing is pointless, I watch the white streaks zipping over the mountains, and I wish. I wish so hard. *Don't let me lose him again.*

26

My father speeds the entire way home and heads straight for my parents' bedroom without saying a word. It's as if he can't get away from us fast enough. Fine by me. I don't have anything I want to say to him. I don't want to fight. I don't want to make up.

At this point, I never want to see his face again.

With Andromeda on my heels, I hike up the stairs and shut the door to my room so hard, one of my glow-in-the-dark stars falls off the ceiling. It's weird to be back here. This used to be a safe space, but now it feels tainted. Everything smells weird. Dusty and artificial. I think I was out in the wild for too long, because this feels like a prison, not a sanctuary. Andromeda is the only happy thing in this apartment. At least she seems to have missed me.

It's one in the morning, and I'm in that weird state of being exhausted but not tired. I can't even look at my wall calendars. Summer is a disaster, and right now, instead of helping me stay calm, they are a reminder of everything that's gone wrong. So I busy myself with what I can control, steadily unpacking my gear. And I'm in the process of making a pile of dirty clothes to take to the washer when I hear a soft knock on my door.

"It's open," I say flatly.

My mom's face appears in the doorway. "Can I come in for a second?"

"How am I going to stop you?"

She sighs, closes the door behind her, and sits on the bed next to my backpack. "I know you're angry with us right now."

"You have to admit, I have pretty good reasons to be."

Dark circles hang beneath her eyes. "And we've got reasons to be angry with you, too. You lied to me, Zorie. When we talked a couple of days ago, you could have told me you were with Lennon."

"Did you already know?"

She fiddles with a zipper on my backpack. "Reagan's mom called me. Apparently, Reagan came home early with Brett Seager, but she didn't tell her mother that they'd abandoned you and Lennon in the national park. The glamping compound got in touch with Mrs. Reid, and they're the ones who informed her what actually happened. Kicked out for stealing wine?"

"I wasn't a part of that plan," I argue. Mostly. "It was Brett's idea."

Mom sighs and shakes her head. "Regardless, the glamping compound's phone call poked holes in Reagan's story, and that's when Reagan admitted that they left you and Lennon. Mrs. Reid called me in a panic, a couple hours before I heard from you. Your dad wasn't here, so I went next door and talked to the Mackenzies."

I groan quietly.

"Yeaaahh," Mom drawls, and then gives me a tight smile. "It stung to find out that they knew you were on the trip. Lennon had told them, but you hadn't told *me*. It made me feel like a bad parent."

"I didn't know before I left, honestly. I knew . . ." I hesitate, but what's the point of lying anymore? "I knew Brett and the others would be there. But I didn't realize Lennon was coming until we were leaving."

"But you obviously made up with him. That wasn't a friendly kiss."

"No, it wasn't."

She sniffles. "I always knew it would be a matter of time before your friendship changed. The way he looked at you. The way you looked at him . . ."

"What's so wrong about that? You should be happy. You used to like Lennon."

"I still do. Quite a bit, actually."

"Then what's the problem?"

She doesn't answer, just pets Andromeda, who's jumped onto the bed and is trying to insert herself into the conversation.

Fine. She doesn't want to talk. I don't either. I lift my portable telescope out of the backpack and set it on the floor. Check all the pieces. So stupid to think that I lugged it up and down mountains for days and I didn't even use the damn thing.

"Lennon and you spent a lot of time alone," my mom finally says. "I hope you were safe."

"We were."

She makes a small noise and then blows out a hard breath.

I don't want to talk about that right now. I set my camera next to the telescope and steer the conversation in a different direction. "We had plenty of time to talk about all the secrets that everyone's been keeping from me."

"Zorie . . ."

"Did you know his father died last year?" I say angrily.

Mom blinks at me. "Adam . . . ?"

She didn't know either. I think this might be worse, somehow. Were we all so caught up in our own petty issues that we didn't realize our neighbors needed us? It makes me hurt all over again.

"Yes," I tell her. "Adam died. You can say it. He killed himself last October. None of us knew because Dad tore our families apart."

She covers her eyes and makes a low noise, and then pushes up from the bed to pace around the room. "I can't believe it."

"Believe it," I say. "Can you imagine what it must've felt like for Lennon? He was there for me when we first moved here and I was grieving. And all this time, he's been alone, trying to cope. How unfair is it that—" My voice warbles, and I have to stop for a moment. "None of us knew because Dad was too busy trying to cover up the fact that he was banging some side chick."

"Don't talk like that to me," she says sharply.

"Dad can do those things and get away with it, but I can't say it?"

"We went to counseling."

I stop unpacking. "Counseling? *Counseling?* Not only did you fail to mention that my dad was a cheating asshole, but you secretly went to counseling?"

"It was our issue, not yours."

"I thought we were friends."

Her face falls. "We *are* friends. Zorie, I care about you more than anyone else on this planet. More than . . ." She stops. Start again. "I only wanted to keep this family together. I didn't want to poison you against your father."

"Too late. He did that all on his own."

"Relationships are complicated," she says. "You will understand when you're older. Things aren't always black and white. People make mistakes because they're damaged inside, but that doesn't mean they don't deserve forgiveness. It doesn't mean they can't change."

"Dad is damaged all right," I mutter. "And I don't see how his forgiveness is elevated above the respect that you deserve. How is he worth more? He cheated on you with God knows how many women—"

"It was just one, and he was still mourning your mother."

"My mother? She's been dead for years! I never even saw him cry over her death. Never! Not once."

"That's how he coped. He tried to compartmentalize it—to box it away and forget about it. I don't know if he learned this from his jackass of a father, but it's something he does. He thinks if he ignores a problem, it will go away."

She's right. He does do this. All the time.

So do I.

Sighing, Joy looks out my balcony window. "Grief is sneaky. Sometimes you think you're over something, but you've just been lying to yourself. If you don't face up to it, grief will hang around until you do, whittling away small parts of your life. You don't even know it's happening."

This I understand.

My birth mother's death came unexpectedly. One day she was there, and the next, she was gone. It was the worst kind of surprise. My world was upended. I never even got to tell her goodbye. And that sudden loss triggered my anxiety problems . . . and altered how I dealt with change. If I have a plan for something that's stressful, if I've carefully considered all the angles and possibilities, then I'm controlling it. I'm in charge. Nothing can pop up and surprise me, because if I've planned very carefully, then I'm ready for any situation.

Except I'm not. Because you can't control everything. Sometimes, you can be minding your own business, but your father is busy having affairs. Sometimes, you can plan all the details of a trip with friends, but those people weren't really your friends at all. Sometimes, you can follow a well-planned route through the woods and still get stalked by mountain lions.

And sometimes, *sometimes*, you give up on your best friend, but he never gave up on you.

"I never knew Dad was struggling with my mother's death," I tell Joy. "But you know what? When I make bad choices, I have to pay for them. He's a grown man, so he gets a free pass? I think that's shitty. And I think you deserve better than him. We deserve better."

"Zorie," she pleads softly.

"I was so worried about what would happen if you and Dad got divorced, because I couldn't stand the thought of being forced to live with him. I imagined you deciding that you were done raising a kid who wasn't really yours, and then my life would fall apart all over again. I'd lose another mother."

"That will never happen," she says, grabbing my shoulders. "Do you hear me? You're the reason I agreed to make this marriage work. You, not him."

"What?" I say, confused.

"I stayed for you. Because you need me, and I need you." She cups my head in her hands. "I *am* raising my own kid. You are mine. I didn't need to give birth to you to love you, sweet thing."

I'm crying now, and I think she is too. We're apologizing in whispers, and she hugs me as she always does, hard enough to hurt.

And it's a good pain.

When the tears slow, she eases up on the hugging and strokes my back. "I'm sorry about tonight. About the meteor shower and the scene . . . about Lennon."

"I can't believe we left him there. He would never leave me."

"I called Sunny and apologized before I came up here to see you."

"Is she mad?"

"She's not happy. I didn't tell her much, but she sounded like she already knew more than I did about what's been going on." Her eyes catch mine. "Are you in love with Lennon?"

Am I?

Oh, God.

I am.

I'm in love with my best friend.

I blink at her through tear-stung eyes. "I think . . . I may have been for long time."

She nods and sniffles, smiling softly. "I'll talk to your father. He's emotional now, but maybe he'll realize that he's being stubborn. I can't promise he'll change his mind tomorrow, but eventually he'll have to see reason. Okay?"

That's actually not okay. I don't want to live with my hand out like a beggar, asking for my father's permission to see Lennon. But I don't say this. I know she's trying.

"It's late," she tells me. "And you've had an eventful night. Get some rest, and we'll talk tomorrow. Yes?"

I nod, and she gives me a tired smile before leaving my room.

Here I am, selfishly talking about being in love, as if she didn't have any problems of her own in that department. I can only fathom what she's gone through with my father. I think about how she matter-of-factly rattled off the name of Dad's mistress, as if it was just something she'd accepted.

Molly.

That's the name my mom used.

Only, that's not the name that was on the photo book's envelope.

Catherine Beatty.

One of many.

Was it the same woman? Maybe she was using a fake name to send the package. All I know is that Lennon recognized the woman from the photo book because he'd seen her in the hotel with my dad. And then there was Reagan's accusation that my dad tried to sleep with Michelle Johnson's mom after the Olympic fund-raiser. I don't know if that's true, but my mom said they went to counseling this past winter. The Olympic fund-raiser was this spring. Something doesn't add up.

What should I do?

I perch on the edge of my bed and begin analyzing my options. I could give her all this information and risk my parents getting into a fight—or worse. I could confront my dad privately and hope to what? Shame him into telling the truth? Then what? I could keep all of this to myself, and maybe things would go back to normal.

Isn't that the result I want? To avoid pain? To cling to some semblance of normality? Dueling images of my parents together and apart float in my head, and I try to sort them out and solve all the equations, but other things erode my thoughts. Things from the last week. The bear attacking Brett's tent. My snake bite. The mountain lion. Lightning in the sequoias. Falling asleep in Lennon's arms.

Unpredictable outcomes. Some of them bad, some good.

All at once, I realize that I need to let go. Of planning. Trying to control everything. It doesn't work. The best-laid plans of mice and men often turn to shit.

Could I have avoided some hives and a whole lot of nail biting if I'd just handed over the photo book to my mom? Because all that worry got me nowhere. Here I am, still knowing my father's a liar, but unsure what will happen. Still wondering about the fate of my family. Still unable to prevent a disaster.

I can't constantly be on guard, trying to avoid every single catastrophe, measuring and managing every expectation.

Besides, Lennon's right. Nobody expects the Spanish Inquisition.

From now on, no new plans. No trying to control every detail of my life. You can plot a course that will get you to your destination, but you can't predict what you'll find along the way. So I'm just going to let life happen, and whatever that brings, I'll face.

Starting now.

The photo book is still in the drawer where I left it. I take it out, along with the letter. It's not my secret to keep. It never was.

My purse is where I left it in the closet before the camping trip. I stuff clean clothes and my cell phone charger inside it. Then I head downstairs, calling Andromeda to follow and get in her dog bed at the foot of the stairs. All of the lights are off but the one over the kitchen sink, where Mom is drinking a glass of water. My dad is nowhere in sight.

"Here," I tell her in a quiet voice when she looks up at me. "This is the package you asked me to get from the Mackenzies the week before my camping trip. I told you they didn't have it, but they did. They opened it by accident, and when I was carrying it back to the office, I peeked. I hid it from you. I'm sorry."

Hesitantly, she takes it and opens the letter. Her hand shakes. She blinks several times. And then she closes the letter and slips it inside the photo book.

"Dad lied to you. It wasn't just Molly, or this Catherine person. Reagan knows about another incident. I saw Razan Abdullah at the glamping compound, and she asked me if you and Dad were still together."

She stares at me with a shocked look on her face.

"People are talking," I tell her. "That's probably why Dad's been losing clients and you haven't. Because everyone knows he's a scumbag."

We stand there, neither of us looking at each other for a long moment.

"I'm sorry," I tell her. "I love you, and I'm so sorry. For everything."

"I'll see you in the morning," she says quietly, and heads toward my parents' bedroom. A second later, she disappears, shutting the door.

I don't know what's going to happen now, but dread knots my stomach, and I feel the urge to run after her and snatch the photo book away.

But it's too late. Nothing I can do will turn back the clock. *Deep breath.* I scribble a quick note to my mother and leave it on the kitchen counter. And as the sound of my parents' voices arguing gets louder, I quietly head out the front door of the apartment.

It's cool outside. A soft breeze rustles through the fronds of the palm tree outside our house. I jog down the front steps, hiking my purse higher on my shoulder. It's so much lighter than the backpack. I almost miss its weight. Almost.

Half the stars have disappeared out of the sky. Like the universe just swiped a hand and erased them. But as I'm walking, a pale white streak appears, and I hope Lennon is watching it with Avani. Miles away, but the same starry sky.

I head toward the left apartment in the blue duplex across from our house. Lights are still on in the windows. The Mackenzies have always been night owls—another thing my dad points to as proof of their hedonism. But I'm not thinking about him now as I ring the doorbell and wait. In fact, I'm not thinking or planning anything past this moment, and when Sunny's oblong face appears, and she's blinking into the porch light, I say the first thing that comes to mind.

"I'm sorry to bother you so late. Can I spend the night here with you and Mac? My parents are having problems."

She stares at me, surprised, standing in a pair of pajama bottoms printed with tiny cartoon trolls. "Of course you can, baby. Come on inside before you freeze to death."

Then she pulls me over the threshold, past the photos of Lennon and his dad dressed in Halloween costumes. Their house smells just like it always has, like vanilla frosting and old books. And when I see Mac curled up on their worn living room sofa in front of the TV, looking up at me with welcoming eyes, I feel as if I'm finally home.

27

When I wake the next morning, I'm completely disoriented. It takes me several seconds to realize that I'm not in a tent with Lennon; I'm sleeping in his empty bed, and the sheets smell like him, freshly laundered and sunny. So good. For a moment, anyway. Then I spot his dastardly wall of reptiles, including Ryuk, who's staring at me through his lizard habitat.

"Sorry, buddy," I tell the bearded dragon. "Your dark master is not here."

And he won't be for several hours. Mac got a text from Avani last night before I showed up. Apparently, Lennon's phone is still dead, and she informed them that he was safe and would be riding home with her today.

I hope he's okay.

Sitting atop a pile of gruesome graphic novels, the clock on Lennon's beside table says it's half past nine. I smell bacon and coffee, and my stomach leaps with joy. Even though I showered here last night before I dropped dead in Lennon's bed, I didn't eat, and my body is more than aware that the last meal I had was freeze-dried stew yesterday afternoon when Lennon and I were hiking toward Condor Peak.

Part of me wants to hibernate in Lennon's room among the stacks of horror comics and DVDs, but I know I can't linger here forever. So after checking the state of my hives—not great, but not out of control—I dress in the clothes I stuffed in my purse last night and head down a short hall to the Mackenzies' main living area. Sunny and Mac are already dressed and sitting at the dining room table, browsing news headlines on a tablet with a cracked screen.

"Good morning," Sunny says brightly. "How'd you sleep?"

"Like the dead."

"Excellent," she says, getting up to head around the kitchen counter. "How about some sustenance?"

"Yes, please. I'm starving."

Mac squints at me. "You haven't developed any new allergies to eggs or pork, have you?"

"As long as no one's cooking shrimp scampi, I'm all good."

"Ugh," Mac says, pretending to be exasperated. "Will I ever live that down?"

"Bad shrimp," Sunny calls out cheerfully from behind the stove.

I exhale deeply and take a seat next to Mac. "I've missed you guys."

"We've missed you too," she assures me, bumping her shoulder against mine.

Sunny brings me a plate piled with eggs, bacon, and toast, and I help myself to the pot of coffee that's sitting on the table. "Any word from Lennon this morning?" I ask, hopeful. I charged my phone overnight, but there were no messages from him.

Mac lifts her coffee cup. "Avani said she'd text when they were leaving today. I told her to let him know you're here with us."

I'm glad, but I also feel left out and unconnected from him. It's weird to be on the other end of the no-phone-service problem. I liked it better when I was the one without reception.

I'm not sure what it is about civilization, but now that I'm here, the nagging urge to stay connected has returned. If I can't have him in front of me, I need him to be a text away.

Resisting the urge to double-triple-quadruple-check my phone, I instead answer Sunny and Mac's questions about the trip. They're curious, asking questions, and I tell them a lot of things . . . but not everything. I get the feeling they know exactly what Lennon and I have been doing in the woods; they're smiling a lot, and it's making me a little uncomfortable, so I just focus on the life-and-death parts of the trip, not the sexlaxation parts. The doorbell rings as I'm telling them about the lightning storm, and when Sunny answers it, she talks to someone for a moment and then calls me quietly into the hallway.

"It's for you," she whispers.

I glance down the front hall toward their cracked front door. "Is it my mom?"

She shakes her head. "Go on. It'll be fine. And we're steps away if you need us."

With trepidation, I shuffle to the door and open it. The face staring back at me is familiar, yet unexpected: a handsome Korean man in his fifties with short hair that's gray along the temples, black in the back.

"Grandpa Sam?" I say, utterly confused.

"Zorie," he says, enunciating carefully. Then he launches into a string of incomprehensible sentences that sound urgent and decisive.

"You know I don't understand Korean," I tell him. I can say hello (*Annyeong-haseyo*) and please (*juseyo*) and a few choice words that my mom uses when the man who owns Pizza Delight tries to overcharge us for extra toppings. Occasionally, I can figure out what the actors in my mom's favorite K-dramas are saying after we've binged several episodes in a row, but that's about it.

Grandpa Sam, on the other hand, understands most English. He just doesn't speak it well. He says "okay" and "yes" and "no," but he doesn't bother with much of anything else, which is why emojis are his preferred way of communicating with me.

Right now, he lifts his head and mutters to the sky. Then he sighs heavily and motions for me to come with him. "Okay?" he says.

"Okay, hold on." I run back into the house and get my stuff, and when Mac asks what's going on, I tell her, "I have no freaking idea."

They tell me everything will be fine, and I head outside where

Grandpa Sam is waiting. He silently guides me across the cul-de-sac, one gentle hand on my back. He's still talking to me in Korean, but now he sounds less upset. He's trying to assure me of something, but when I see my mom sitting in the backseat of his shiny Audi sedan, parked in front of our apartment, I have a horrible feeling.

"What's going on?" I ask. Mom is looking the other way. Is she avoiding me? What about her promises last night? She said she wouldn't leave.

Grandpa Sam points to our front door and gives me a command in Korean, then says, "Okay?"

"No, I don't want to stay here," I tell him, desperate. "Take me with you."

"Yes," he says, vexation in his voice.

"What do you mean, 'yes'? Yes, I can come? Yes *what*?"

Before he can give me another one of his exasperated rants, the front door of our apartment swings open to a torrent of swear words that I *do* understand. Only, they're coming from the mouth of my tiny Korean grandmother, which makes them sound so much worse—mostly creative combinations involving animals.

Esther Moon never swears. She never yells, either, so I know we're in uncharted territory now. She has Andromeda on her leash, and smoothly transitions from anger to murmuring baby talk at my dog in order to coax her down the front stairs. I'm not sure who's having more trouble navigating them: the old husky, or the woman in stiletto heels and a designer skirt that fits like a glove.

My grandfather calls out to her, and she lifts her head. "Zorie! Thank God. Pack a bag and say goodbye to your fly-covered dog turd of a father."

Like I said, unlike Grandpa Sam, she speaks English just fine.

"Grandma Esther," I say. "What's happening?"

"You and Joy are staying with us for a few days," she says brightly, scratching Andromeda's head while the dog tries to lick her skirt. Grandma Esther is the Korean dog whisperer. She has two Frenchies and a Boston terrier, and they adoringly follow her around the house like her posse. She coos at Andromeda, "And you're going to have so much fun with my girls, aren't you, sweetie?"

My head is trying to process everything. "We're going to Oakland?"

"No, to our vacation home in Bali," she says sarcastically. "Of course, to Oakland. Are you all right?" She tears herself away from the dog and gives me a thorough once-over, smoothing my curls with delicate fingers.

"I don't know," I say truthfully.

"You will be. I'll make you chicken and rice soup."

Admittedly, that's a strong motivator. Grandma Esther is an amazing cook. She does *that* in heels too.

Grandpa Sam pleads with me about . . . something. I can't tell. He talks too fast.

I look back and forth between them. "What?"

Grandma Esther sticks her tongue out my grandfather. "Don't

pay any attention to him. He's trying to rush back to watch the football game. Take your time. We'll be waiting in the car." She clucks at Andromeda, and as she heads toward the sedan, adds sweetly over her shoulder, "If your pig-shit father tries to talk you into staying, tell him he can sue for custody."

Oh, God.

Grandpa Sam chuckles to himself, pats me on the back, and follows her to the car. I'm left alone, and I really wish I weren't. It feels like I'm walking into a haunted house filled with ghouls waiting to jump out at me.

Steeling myself, I step inside our living room. My dad is there, red-eyed and bleary. He looks like he's just been told someone died. Shell-shocked. Blank. Unable to comprehend.

Confident, charming Diamond Dan has left the building.

"Hey," I say warily.

"Oh," he says, sitting down on our sofa. "Zorie."

"What's happening?"

He rubs his head. "That's an excellent question. I'm not quite sure, myself. What did Esther tell you?"

"That I'm staying with them for a few days."

"That's it?"

"That's it."

He nods while placing both hands on his knees as he gathers his thoughts. Then he gives me a reserved smile. "So, your mother and I may be separating. It's not decided yet. I won't go into the details, but you don't want to hear them anyway. Well, you already heard a few things last night, so I'm assuming this isn't a surprise—"

"Dad, the entire last two weeks have been nothing but surprises."

"Ah. Well."

That's it? That's all he's going to say? How about, *Hey, I've been sleeping around and this family is a sham. Oopsie!* I mean, come on. Give me something.

A silence hangs between us.

"Why?" I finally ask.

He shakes his head slowly. "You wouldn't understand."

"I understand more than you think."

After he looks away, I think about what Mom had told me—that my father was still having trouble getting over my birth mother's death after all these years. Last night, that sounded like a convenient excuse, but now I'm thinking about the photo book, and how that woman looked a little like my birth mother.

"You can't bring her back," I tell him. "She's dead, and there was only one of her, and you can't bring her back."

"I know," he says in a broken voice.

"You could have talked to me instead of shutting me out. I was mourning her too, you know? She was my mother."

"I know she was."

"Then why didn't you talk to me? Ever?"

One shoulder lifts slowly, and then falls. "I was unprepared to raise you on my own. I felt like a failure. And then I had to watch while Joy swept in and provided what I couldn't. She was a natural. How could she do better than I could, when I was your own flesh and blood? Her parents spoiled you—"

"Spoiled?" I hardly think so. It's not like Grandpa Sam showers me with gifts constantly. He just buys me practical stuff.

"Christ, even the Mackenzies do a better job raising you than I could," he says. "Your mother would roll over in her grave."

I don't remember my birth mother being homophobic, but maybe I blocked that out.

"You don't need me," my father says in a low voice, despondent.

"Dad—"

"It's true," he says. "I know it. Everyone knows it. You're better off without me."

I'm not sure if this pity party is genuine, or if he's trying to manipulate me into feeling sorry for him—or if he's trying to push me further away. But I give him the benefit of the doubt.

"It's going to take me a long time to forgive you for what you've done," I say. "To Mom, and to me. However . . . you're still my father. I'll always need you. At some point, I think you'll realize that you need *me*, too. And when that day comes, I'll be here."

He looks up at me, face pinched in pain.

"But today," I tell him, turning away, "my mom needs me more."

28

We spend the weekend at my grandparents' house in Oakland. They live in a small house in an upper-middle-class neighborhood, where everyone pays landscapers to maintain their lawns. Which may sound nice, but it's also boring, and it doesn't take long for me to feel unmoored and restless. As though my life is going backward instead of forward.

As though we've been fighting a war and lost.

Grandma Esther feeds us constantly, and that seems to help my mom. She's not completely falling apart like I worried she might, but she's crying a lot, and that makes *me* cry. And all the conversations in Korean between her and Grandpa Sam make me feel ineffectual.

Everything's chaos. I'm homeless. Our family's broken. My entire future is up in the air. And I'm missing Lennon desperately. Even though he made it home from Condor Peak just fine, and we text constantly and occasionally talk on the phone when I can get away from everyone, it's not the same.

I miss him in a way I never have.

I miss his deep voice and his dark sense of humor. I miss his face and the feeling of security I have when he's nearby. I miss the way he holds me, and the thrill of his fingers stroking down my back. I miss him so much, I feel physically ill.

I don't want more food or a nap or to watch a movie. I just want to go home and see Lennon. Only, I don't know where home is anymore. I think about how Lennon and I spent the last year avoiding each other, and what a waste that was. We didn't know how good we had it, living so close. We were both stupid. I wish I could erase the entire year and start all over. Stop him from getting that hotel room. Stop my father from cheating and ruining the business and our credit, because now Grandma Esther is saying that he's the reason my mom was having trouble with the bank before I left on the camping trip. He secretly spent all my parents' savings and credit on his affairs. Trips. Hotel rooms. Expensive restaurants. Gifts. He was living large while my mom was trying to keep the business afloat.

My grandparents say they're going to sue him for all the money they gave him to invest in the business. Grandma Esther is sure the judge will grant my mom full custody if my dad fights it. The good thing is that he won't; the *sad* thing is that he won't. I can't decide how I feel about him, and I'm tired of trying to figure it out and weary of my life being in limbo. Something has to give.

And on Tuesday morning, it does.

Everything changes.

I'm restless and a little depressed, watching Andromeda lounge listlessly in a dog bed that's too small for her while Grandma Esther's energetic dogs unsuccessfully try to coax her into playing. Mom appears in the doorway, and I think it's probably to check my hives again, because she's been monitoring me like a doctor.

But Mom is not interested in my allergies. She has a strange look on her face. It's like happiness, but a little angrier. Happy angry. Hapry.

"Get your stuff," she says. "We're going home."

"To Dad?"

"Your father has moved in with one of his mistresses in San Francisco. You and I are going home, changing the locks, and I'm going to figure out how to keep the clinic running without him."

It sounds too good to be true. "Can you do that?"

"Zorie, I can do anything I damn well want." she says, sounding unexpectedly confident and positive. "And what I want is to go back to Mission Street and be the East Bay's best acupuncturist while raising my future astrophysicist daughter. So that's what I'm going to do, goddammit."

"Maybe sound a little surer of yourself, while you're at it," I mumble, smiling.

And for the first time since all of this chaos exploded, she smiles too. Just for a second.

"I'm not sure," she admits. "Not yet. But I have to have faith that I will be one day. *We* will be. We'll make a plan and take action. And that's how we start."

Her words click into place inside my head, and I realize something.

Planning can't save you from everything. Change is inevitable and uncertainty is a given. And if you plan so much that you can't function without one, life's no fun. All the calendars, journals, and lists in the world won't save you when the sky falls. And maybe, just maybe, I've been using planning less as a coping mechanism and more as an excuse to avoid anything I couldn't control.

But that doesn't mean preparation is altogether bad. Planning can be useful when you've come out on the wrong side of a cave and need to figure out a new way to get back on route.

When all you can do is put one foot in front of the other and push forward.

"We'll be okay," Mom tells me, and I believe her.

"All right," I say. "Let's go make a plan."

All I wanted was to go home and see Lennon. So of *course* the Mackenzies would pick now of all times to leave their assistant manager in charge of Toys in the Attic while they go visit friends in the city—some old punk musicians who knew Lennon's father. I want to scream. I need to see Lennon. It's not optional. *Need.* And I know we spent an entire year apart, so a couple of days should be nothing. But it's not. It's painful.

Lennon briefly considers taking the BART train across the Oakland Bay Bridge to meet up with me. But we decide it's best to wait until he comes back on Thursday, when we can have an actual real, live date. Funny that we've never had one.

Meanwhile, he has tickets for a concert in San Francisco—some band that's dark and despairing—and I'm insanely busy. Grandma Esther is staying with us for a couple of days to help with something she's dubbed the Purge. It's not the horror movie by that name, but it might as well be, because it's endless hours of work that involves getting rid of everything that doesn't help us move forward.

It's as bad as it sounds. And as much as I love Grandma Esther, she's starting to drive me nuts. Apparently, my mom feels the same way.

"I'm going to kill her," she tells me privately.

"Please don't," I say. "Her body would be just one more thing we'd have to carry to the porch. She looks lightweight, but so did that box of shoes I just took downstairs."

"Right. Good thinking. We'll wait until she's outside. You trip her, and I'll push her into oncoming traffic."

"Who will cook for us?"

"Dammit, Zorie. I'm trying to plan a murder!"

"I don't think you can kill her. She has too much energy. It's unnatural."

"Imagine growing up with her," she says. "It's a wonder I'm not in jail."

By the time we're finished with the Purge, we're pretty sure Melita Hills is going to charge us extra for excess garbage pickup, because the curb outside the apartment is overflowing with black plastic bags—and that's not counting the stuff we gave away to a local charity. I never knew we had so much literal baggage. I even take down the old glow-in-the-dark stars from my ceiling, and Mom helps me paint my room a new color, a sunny yellow that contrasts nicely with all my night-sky photos.

All my homemade wall calendars? I threw them in the trash. But I'm not ready to give up on blueprints altogether. Instead of obsessively bulleting every detail of my schedule for every day of the year on multiple calendars, I use star-patterned *washi* tape to map out a single grid on a corkboard, and pin fun paper cutouts on major holidays and planetary events.

Baby steps.

Avani comes by on Wednesday with her mother. They bring hummus, homemade banana bread, and a tray filled with sandwiches. It feels like someone died, and when I point this out, my mom jokes that she should get divorced more often.

In her defense, it's *really* good banana bread.

While our moms chat, Avani tells me in detail what happened after we left Condor Peak—and everything that happened the two days before we arrived. Apparently, I missed both everything and not that much, all that the same time. It's only when she shows me some of her photos of the meteor shower that I feel a little envious. But there will be other meteor showers, other star parties. For the first time, it really hits me that if Lennon and I hadn't stayed in the sequoia grove that second night, no one would have worried that we were missing, and we may not have set off the chain of events that led to all of this.

The important thing is, I don't have any regrets.

When Thursday arrives, Grandma Esther leaves after buying massive amounts of toilet paper and laundry detergent as a house-warming gift "for good luck"—a Korean tradition, she says. I'm sad to see her go, because of all the home cooking, but also glad, because the murder fantasies were starting to get out of control. And I have better things to think about than bumping off nice old ladies.

Like Lennon.

I'm so eager about him coming back into town that I'm shifting into anxiety mode. It's been a week since we've seen each other—the longest, weirdest week of my life—and so much has changed. What if all of that alters the way we feel about each other? What if that week we spent in isolation was an anomaly? Sure, we reconnected in the wilderness, but what if we can't make it work in the real world? I worry that the delicate balance of our friendship and our more-than-friendship can't withstand the weight of everyday life.

My parents couldn't make it, and they were married.

How can the two of us fare any better?

The longer I'm away from him, the more a particular thought niggles: What if we were just seduced by nature? The magic of twinkling stars. The scent of redwood. Majestic mountains.

What if this is what influenced Lennon to kiss me that first time at the top of the granite staircase? If we were here at home without the alluring rush of waterfalls in the background, would he have still made that first move?

Would I have been as receptive to it?

Is there a nature-related equivalent to beer googles?

Making out on a blanket under starry skies certainly is more romantic than groping each other on a park bench while Andromeda watches.

The thing is, we had a chance to make this relationship work last year, but neither of us wanted it hard enough to try. I allowed my dad to talk me into shunning Lennon. Instead of wallowing in pain, I could have gotten off my ass and forced Lennon to tell me what happened at homecoming. And Lennon could have come told me what happened. If he was brave enough to confess stealing Mac's credit card for the hotel room to both his moms, he could have faced me.

But he wasn't.

And I wasn't.

And after all that time together in the woods, neither of us came up with a plan for what to do after we got back to civilization. No promises were made. No pacts. No *I love you*s were whispered in the dark. Does he still feel the same way about me, now that we're home?

Can we make it as real couple in the real world? Or are we better off staying friends?

It's easy to think you're falling in love out in the wilderness, where everything is beautiful and a tent full of condoms is just steps away. Did we just have one weeklong one-night stand?

How do I know for sure if what we shared together is fleeting or real?

It probably doesn't help that I haven't heard much from him over the last couple of days—only a few brief texts to make plans for our date when he gets back. I try not to let uncertainty get the best of me and do my best to ignore random thoughts of him meeting someone hipper than me in the city and deciding I'm not worth the trouble. I know that's just my monkey mind, chattering away, restless and distracted. But when he texts me that he needs to delay our date until after dinner, I have flashbacks about homecoming last year.

What if I'm being ditched again?

I know it's not logical, and my mom tells me to relax before I'm covered from head to toe in massive welts. But I'm dressed and ready, wearing my most flattering red-and-black plaid dress, and the sun is setting, and still no Lennon.

It's eight o'clock.

Eight thirty.

Eight forty-five.

The doorbell rings.

I nearly fall on my face, racing to answer it. And then he's there, standing in front of me. Black hair. Black jeans. Boyish smile.

Lennon.

My emotions go haywire, and I'm so happy to see him, my voice dries up and vanishes. We're both standing here stupidly, and I need one of us to say something—anything!

"You're late," I finally manage.

He looks dazed. "I had to arrange some stuff. God, you look beautiful."

Fireworks go off in my chest. I think I might faint if he doesn't touch me.

Just when I can't take it anymore, his arms are around me, and my arms are around him, and he's warm and solid, and he smells good, like freshly laundered clothes hanging in the sun. I'm overwhelmed with relief. Gratitude. Joy.

I know right at that moment that it wasn't just the twinkling stars. I don't want to be Just Friends. But what about him?

"Hi," he murmurs into my hair.

"I missed you," I say, tightening my arms around his back until I can hear his heart thudding inside his chest.

I want to tell him, *I missed you so much, it felt like I was dying.*
I want him to say that to me.

But we're both silent, and I feel his arms stiffen. He pulls back, looking over my shoulder. My mom is standing behind us, arms crossed.

"Hi, Lennon," she says. "It's good to see you."

"You too."

She hands him a bag with something in it. "Here you go."

"Thanks," he says, smiling.

I glance back and forth between them. "What's going on? Is this some sort of drug ring?"

Lennon's brows waggle. "You'll see."

My mom and Lennon in cahoots? That's definitely interesting.

He gives her a shy look. "Are you . . . ? I mean, is it okay that we leave?"

"It's fine. *I'm* fine." She makes a shooing gesture. "You guys go on out. I'm actually looking forward to some peace and quiet. Just come back at a semireasonable hour."

"We will," he tells her, lifting the bag she gave him in thanks.

As we head down the steps, she calls out, "And, Lennon? Keep her safe."

"Don't worry," he calls back. "I always do."

He leads me toward his car, which I haven't been inside since he got it last summer. The heavy door creaks—loudly—and the inside of the car smells like old leather and engine oil. It's not entirely unpleasant.

"No dead bodies in the back, right?" I ask when he slides into driver's seat next to me.

"Not this week." He smiles at me, and I feel like I'm melting into the seat.

For the love of God, get ahold of yourself, Everhart.

"Now, strap in," he instructs me, "so I can make good on my responsibility for your safety."

"Where are we going?"

"That's a secret, Medusa."

A tiny, electric thrill shoots through me when he uses my nickname. "I don't like secrets," I remind him.

"You'll like this one. I think. I hope. Let's find out."

He drives down Mission Street and won't give me any hints as we speed across town. I try to figure it out—a movie? A restaurant? Coffee at the Jitterbug?—but he just says, "Nope," after each guess. Honestly, I'm so happy just to be close enough to reach out and touch him that I genuinely don't care where we go. But when we pass familiar landmarks and the car's engine strains climbing a hill at the edge of town, I think I realize where we're headed.

The observatory.

He pulls into the parking lot, and we're the only car here. Not surprising, because it closed half an hour ago. But Lennon parks, and he pulls me across the parking lot toward a zigzagging cement pathway on the left side of the building, which heads to the public rooftop area. We head up inclines bordered with painted metal railings until we get to a locked gate. Lennon punches in a key code.

"How did you know that?" I ask.

"Guess I got lucky."

"*Lennon*," I say, serious.

"*Zorie*," he says, not serious. "I did not come by the code illegally, nor did I promise to do anything illegal in exchange for it. Now, please, if you would, Miss Everhart . . ." He holds the gate open and gestures.

I squint at him and step through.

Red lights border the low wall around the dark viewing plat-form. Below us, at the base of the mountain, the city unfurls to the Bay, a grid of white and yellow lights, sparkling like fallen stars on black ground. San Francisco's skyline glitters in the distance, and we can see both the Golden Gate and Bay bridges stretching over dark water. The wind blows, and I smell eucalyptus trees.

It's a beautiful view. A breathtaking view.

And it's our view; we are alone.

When the observatory is operational, a connecting oxidized green dome opens up to allow a large, high-powered professional telescope to scan the skies. That's closed right now, but the two smaller public telescopes that normally are rolled into a small metal shed every night are still sitting out.

"What is this?" I ask.

"I'm not positive," he says, scratching his chin, "but I think it's an observatory."

I slant a hard look at him.

He flashes me a smile. "Avani helped me arrange it with Dr. Viramontes. We talked a lot after you left the meteor shower. I thought he'd hate me after the big scene with your dad—"

I groan. It's still humiliating.

"But Dr. Viramontes was surprisingly cool about everything."

"He's a cool guy," I say.

"He likes you an awful lot," Lennon says. "Which makes two of us. Here. You'll need this."

I accept the bag that my mom gave him and look inside. It's my good camera. "My mom's in on this?"

"I wanted to make sure she was okay about where we were going. Things were weird between us in the past, and I didn't want her to hate me like your dad does."

I shake my head. "She always stood up for you."

"Are you okay? I mean, about your father moving out. I know it's not easy—for you or you mom."

"It's weird," I admit. "I'm not sure it's hit me fully yet."

"I wish things had been different. As much as I've fantasized about horrible things happening to him, I never wanted to see you or Joy hurting."

"I know," I tell him, crinkling the paper bag that holds my camera. "At least something good came out of it."

"What's that?"

"I'm not banned from seeing you," I say, feeling inexplicably shy.

"Not yet," Lennon says, eyes merry. "The night is young."

I set the bag with my camera on a stand next to one of the telescopes. "I can't believe you did all this."

"Pfft. I just got a key code," Lennon says. "Dr. Viramontes said you'd know how to use the camera mount or jig or tripod, or whatever the hell it is you use—it's supposed to be in the shed. We just have to lock everything up before we leave. And if we break anything, we're in huge trouble. I'm talking beheadings. Or lawsuits. I'm not sure which would be worse."

"Probably the lawsuit," I say, looking around. "I've never been up here alone."

"There's a lunar eclipse tonight," he says.

Huh. He's right. There is. I remember now.

He gives me a soft smile. "I know it's not as good as a meteor shower and the view isn't as good as Condor Peak, but I did promise you I'd take you to see the stars. I'm making good on that."

My breath hitches. I struggle for words, and after glancing around the rooftop dumbly, I blink up at Lennon. "I don't know what to say. It's one of the most thoughtful things anyone's ever done for me."

"I don't know . . . I'd argue that rescuing you from an angry bear should get me a few points."

I chuckle. "That's true. But I let you win at poker and gave you most of my M&M's stash. If that's not love, I don't know what is."

I suddenly realize what I've said.

He realizes it too.

Still holding my hand, he slings his other arm around my waist and pulls me closer. "I'm so glad to hear that."

"Are you?" I whisper.

"Yes, I am. Because I love you too."

Goose bumps rush over my arms. "You do?"

"I've always loved you," he murmurs. "And I probably always will. You're my best friend, and you're my family. The year I waited for you was the worst of my life, but it was worth every second. If I had to do it all over again just to hold you in my arms, I would."

"Well, I would not," I say, bleary-eyed. "Because I love you too, and I can't stand to be apart from you for another minute. So stop jinxing it."

"You love me," he says, grinning stupidly. He dips his head lower, until his nose brushes mine.

"Of course I love you. You're mine, and I can't go back to being just friends. So if we have to sleep in the woods or fight with our families, then that's just what we're going to do. I don't want to live a life that doesn't have you in it."

"Tell me again," he says as he kisses my neck right below my ear.

Warmth rushes across my skin. "I can't think straight when you do that."

"I'll stop, then."

"Don't you dare."

"Tell me again," he repeats, kissing my jaw.

"You're mine."

"The other thing."

"I love you."

He pulls back to look at me, pursing his lips as he blows out a hard breath. Then his smile is monumental. "That's the best thing I've ever heard. I'm going to need to hear it a lot. My ego is fragile."

I laugh, pushing away a tear. "Your ego has never been fragile."

"It is around you."

I kiss him under his chin, and he shivers with pleasure. "*I* can't think straight when you do that either."

"Good. Let's not think. It's overrated."

"I know we promised your mom that you'd be home at a decent hour, but that eclipse won't be happening until midnight—"

"You did say there were no bodies in the back of your hearse."

"It's *sooo* body-free back there," he assures me. "And it's no tent in the middle of the forest, but it's pretty private. There may even be a blanket and a pillow. You know I follow the Boy Scout motto. Be prepared."

"It's my favorite thing about you."

"When we were in the tent, you said it was something else," he murmurs, grinning as he pulls me closer.

"I was starving and scared and not in my right mind. I probably said a lot of things. You may have to remind me."

"Yeah? Well, I'm in the mood to solve a mystery. What do you say? Want to do some detectiving with the boy you love?"

I do. I absolutely do.

29

"I'm telling you, the members of KISS mixed their own blood into the red ink used to print the first KISS comic book," Sunny says. "Bet you a cupcake I'm right."

It's nearly dark outside, and I'm standing in Toys in the Attic next to Sunny, who is lording over a stack of boxes near the front window display. Her face is animated as she talks to us. "It was in the seventies, and one of the big publishers, Marvel or DC Comics, put out a KISS comic—you know, Gene Simmons and Paul Stanley in makeup, being superheroes, or whatever. And they used the band's blood in the ink. I swear it's true."

Mac rolls her eyes. "Who starts these demented rumors?" she says in her Scottish lilt. "That is *so* not true. And it's disgusting."

My mom crosses her arms, nodding at Mac. "Can you imagine how many STDs those guys had? Who would want their tainted blood in a comic book?"

"Plenty of people, apparently, because it's a fact," Sunny insists. "Ask Lennon."

I tug a belt loop on the back of his black jeans. He's bent over, half of his body inside the back of the shop's window display—a group of carved Halloween pumpkins and a black cauldron overflowing with condoms and bottles of massage gel instead of witch's brew. Halloween was last night, so we're swapping out the jack-o'-lanterns for a Thanksgiving cornucopia.

"Did you hear all that?" I ask.

He emerges from the window display, standing up to full height. "Sunny's right. A nurse drew their blood, and they flew to New York and had pictures taken at Marvel's printing plant, where they dumped vials of their blood into a vat of ink. A notary public witnessed and certified it."

"Eww," we all say in chorus.

Lennon shrugs. "KISS was always doing silly, shocking gimmicks like that to sell their merchandise. They were more interested in making money than music."

"And that's why *you* owe me a cupcake," Sunny tells Mac, her face lifting into a delighted grin.

Mac shakes her fists at the ceiling. "Curse you, Rock Star Urban Legend Game."

I'm not sure why she bothers siding against Sunny. She always loses. Or maybe that's the point. All I know is that a cupcake sounds pretty freaking good about right now, and I'm wishing this window display were filled with actual candy instead of condoms.

I think I've been eating too much junk food lately, which is something I didn't know could happen. But Mom and I have been too busy to go to the grocery store for real food. Our only home-cooked sustenance has been Sunday dinners at the Mackenzies'.

It's been a couple of months since my dad left. He's still in San Francisco, and he's already in full-on Diamond Dan pivot mode, doing something impulsive. He enrolled in a certification course for—I kid you not—equine massage therapy. That's right, he wants to move to Sonoma and give horses back rubs. Hey, it's his life, I suppose. I've talked to him on the phone a couple of times, but I haven't seen him. A good thing, probably. I'm not as angry as I once was, but I don't need any more disruptions in my life.

And Mom doesn't either. She's been busy too. Everhart Wellness Clinic is now Moon Wellness Spa. Yes, she's the one who decided to christen the spa with her maiden name, but I'm the one who suggested she use an actual moon in her new logo. Sunny and Mac found her a new masseuse—a friend of a friend who was moving out here to the East Bay, because she couldn't afford the rent in the city anymore. San Francisco got Dad and exchanged him for Anna, a young Latina who has purple hair and likes dogs. Win-win.

While Mom is busy rebuilding her business, my focus is on school. At first, I was hyperconcerned with college applications, but now Lennon and I are starting to think about taking a year off between high school and college—a so-called gap year. It would allow me to build my astrophotography portfolio and take a Korean language class at the local community college so I can communicate better with Grandpa Sam. Lennon wants to work full-time and save up some money. He wants us to go back-packing in Europe. I'm definitely amenable to this idea.

We're also talking seriously about trying to hike the Pacific Crest Trail. It's more than twenty-five hundred miles long, running through California, Oregon, and Washington—all the way from Mexico to Canada. It takes six months to hike the entire thing. I'm not sure if I'm up for that just yet—or ever, actually—but if we start next June, we can do part of the trail from the High Sierras up through the Cascade Mountains and stop at the Canadian border.

We'll see. Right now, we've been camping every other week-end. Just short two-night trips—nothing majorly off trail. This weekend, we're going up the coast to Redwood National Park in Humboldt County. I won't lie: Half the fun of camping is the potential for sexlaxation. But I'm actually enjoying being outside, away from the city. Lennon is using his mapping skills to get me to nearby areas with clear night skies; I finally started using my portable telescope to take photos, instead of hauling it around for no good reason.

"I hate to break it to you, but you'll have to get your own cupcakes," Lennon tells his moms. "I have a hot date with an astrophysicist at the Jitterbug."

"That's me," I say, waving my hand. "I'm the hot date."

"Isn't it too late for caffeine?" my mom warns.

"Is it ever?" I ask.

"Herbal tea, please," she says.

"I'll think about it."

"We're actually going there to do homework," Lennon admits. "Decent Wi-Fi and an employee discount are a potent combination."

I started working there part-time after school a couple weeks ago. I practically live there now, but that's okay because (1) I've always loved their coffee, and (2) now I get paid to drink it. I also need all the money I can get, because camping is expensive when you're broke.

"Back by ten," my mom says. "It's a school night."

Lennon salutes her as I tug Andromeda's leash. We tell everyone good night and head out of the shop into night air that's starting to get a little chilly. It feels pretty good, actually, and it's not so brisk that Andromeda minds. We've been walking her several nights a week, and she's perked up considerably, as if she has a new lease on life. And maybe she does. I think she missed walking with Lennon over the last year. My mom says pets can get depressed when their owners do. Or maybe it's just that we see a lot more of Grandma Esther's perky dogs, and Andromeda's had to learn to keep up.

Lennon takes her leash and she trots ahead of us, tail swinging as she scouts our trail. He slings an arm around my shoulder as we saunter to the corner and wait for the streetlight to turn green.

"Okay, milady," Lennon says. "We both know we're not doing homework at the coffee shop."

"I finished mine during fifth period," I confirm.

"Finished mine at work earlier while I cleaned out gecko cages. Multitasking to the rescue."

"We are so good," I say, holding up my hand for a fist bump.

"The best." He knocks knuckles with me, his arm still resting on my shoulder.

Juggling school and work and us hasn't been easy. It helps that we get to eat lunch together every day in the school courtyard. We sit with Avani and her boyfriend, and sometimes Brett, unfortunately. Once he begged Lennon for forgiveness in his part of what's now known as the Battle of Mackenzie Falls, we haven't been able to get rid of him. Reagan, on the other hand, transferred to private school. The official word is that she's no longer focused on the Olympics, so she doesn't need the support of our athletic department. Unofficially, Reagan's parents forced her to transfer after she was busted over the glamping incident.

I wish I could say we made up, but that hasn't happened yet. I'm ready to forgive her, but she has to meet me halfway. The days of me kowtowing are over.

"So where are we headed tonight?" Lennon says. "Mission and Western Avenue, or Mission and Euclid Street?"

We now have four different routes we walk. One is our old path, from when we were kids, and one goes through the farmers' market, which is so deserted at night, it's practically romantic— you'd be surprised what two people with dirty minds can do on bales of hay. Two of the routes go in different directions around the edge of the Bay, but my favorite one snakes through a park, where we can climb a hill and look at the city while sitting under a big old oak tree. It's not dark enough for ideal stargazing, but it's private enough for making out.

Oh, the make-out spots we've discovered. They're on all our routes.

"It's too brisk for the Bay routes," I say. "Andromeda will get fussy."

"We could take Wick Boulevard up through the edge of the warehouse district and cut through to the train tracks up on the hill."

"That sounds suspiciously like a fifth route."

"It does, doesn't it?"

For our one-month anniversary, he made me a picture map. It has all the milestones of our intersecting lives. Where we met. The night we played poker with his dad. Our first fight. Our first kiss. The homecoming debacle. The sequoia cathedral. The night we said *I love you* at the observatory.

A map of us.

It's years in the making, and it's messy and convoluted, some of it even tragic. But I wouldn't change the route, because we walked it together, even when we were apart. And the best part about it is that it's unfinished. Uncertainty isn't always a bad thing. Sometimes it can even be filled with extraordinary potential.

"So what will it be?" he asks when the light turns green. "Old route, or new route?"

"Surprise me," I say.

He smiles down at me, and I thread my fingers through his. We put one foot in front of the other. Clear head, steady steps. And we move forward.

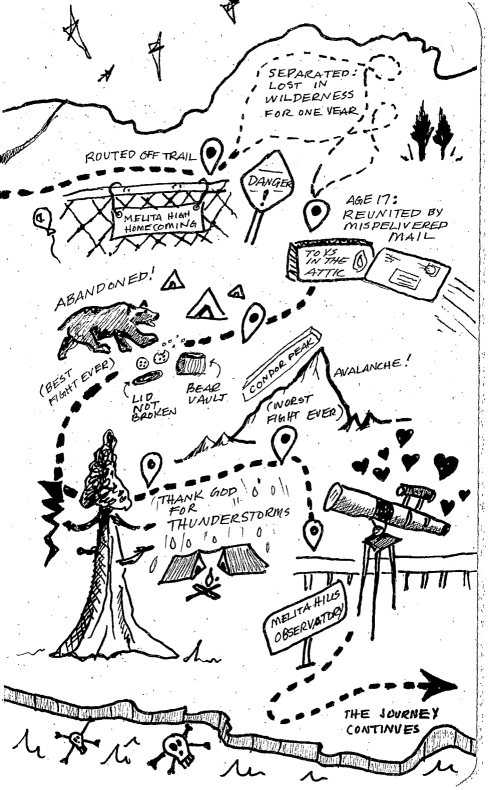

Acknowledgments and Thanks-a-Millions

For their hard work:
Laura Bradford, Taryn Fagerness
Nicole Ellul, Lucy Rogers, Sarah Creech
The entire Simon Pulse and Simon UK teams

For cheerleading:
Karen, Ron, Gregg, Heidi, Hank
Brian, Patsy, Don, Gina, Shane, Seph

For feedback:
Aya Sharif

For inspiration:
Yosemite, Sequoia, and Kings Canyon National Parks
City of Berkeley, California
Nancy Grace Roman, Neil DeGrasse Tyson, Carl Sagan
Tsugumi Ohba, Takeshi Obata
Kimberly Saul

For existing:
Every single librarian
Every single bookseller
And you

Shy and sheltered Birdie
never thought she'd fall in love . . .
but that was before Daniel came along.

Read on for a sneak peek into
Jenn Bennett's next charming romance,
Serious Moonlight.

I

He'd probably forgotten me already. It was a month ago. Practically forever.

He definitely wasn't here tonight. Just to be sure, I scanned the diner one more time, from the rain-speckled glass door to the PIE OF THE DAY chalkboard sign near the register, where the owner had carefully written: ANNE OF GREEN GRAPES, *featuring Yakima Valley chardonnay grapes and blueberries.*

All clear.

For the better part of May, I'd avoided coming to the diner, walking past the windows with my hood up, fearing he'd be here, and if we ever occupied the same space again it would rip open a hole in the universe and create the Most Awkward Moment in Modern History, and the diner—my haven in the city—would be tainted forever and ever.

But he wasn't here, and just because he worked somewhere nearby didn't mean he was a loyal patron of the Moonlight Diner.

And so what if he was? This was my home away from home. I'd spent most of my childhood living in a tiny two-bedroom apartment directly above it. This booth, with its tufted red leatherette seats? It was *my* booth. I'd learned the alphabet at this table. Read *Harriet the Spy* and every Nancy Drew mystery. Won dozens of games of Clue and Mystery Mansion with my mom and Aunt Mona. On the underside of the table I'd drawn crayon portraits of Ms. Patty and Mr. Frank, the diner's owners.

The Moonlight was my territory, and it wasn't cursed just because I'd met a boy here and done something stupid.

"I'd like to buy a vowel, Pat."

I glanced at the woman sitting across from me in the booth, drinking coffee, blinking at me through gold-tipped fake lashes. "Um, what?"

"I'm trying to solve this *Wheel of Fortune* puzzle in the illusive but always intriguing category of 'What is Birdie thinking about?' But I'm missing too many letters," Aunt Mona explained, gesturing like Vanna White at an imaginary game board with long fingernails that featured decals of bumblebees. They matched her 1960s yellow go-go dress (so much fringe), black lipstick, and towering golden beehive wig, complete with tiny winged bee pins.

Mona Rivera did *not* do anything halfway. Not when she was my mother's best friend in high school, and not now, at the ripe age of thirty-six. Most of her elaborate outfits were cobbled from vintage pieces, and she had an entire wall of wigs. She was somewhere between cosplayer and drag queen, and one of the best artists in the Seattle area. She was the bravest, most original person I knew and the most important person in my life.

It was *very* hard to keep secrets from her.

"You told me you weren't nervous about starting this job tonight, but if you are, it's totally normal," she said. "All your training has been during the day, and working at night is going to feel completely different. Graveyard shift is not for the faint of heart—trust me—and if you're worried about staying awake and worried about your sleep issues—"

"I'm not worried," I argued. Mostly not anyway. On one hand, I was a night person, so graveyard didn't bother me. On the other hand, it was my first real job. The first time since my grandmother died this past Christmas that I was allowed to take the ferry into the city alone. I would be spending the entire summer working in downtown Seattle, and I was excited. And a little nervous. And extraordinarily caffeinated—which, in hindsight, was probably a mistake. But on the Alertness Scale, which is a scale I just made up, I lean heavily toward the Always Sleepy side, as narcolepsy runs in my family, along with a slew of other weak genes. My mom used to joke that our Scandinavian ancestors must have gone through an inbreeding phase a couple of hundred years ago.

Aunt Mona frowned. "You haven't been listening to a word I've said over our celebratory Endless Hash Browns dinner, which is the finest of all the Moonlight's food groups."

"Agreed."

"So why are you watching everyone that comes through the door and making your Nancy Drew face?"

"I'm not making my Nancy Drew face."

"Squinty eyes, super alert. Ready to nab a criminal. Oh. I believe I know your Nancy Drew face, especially since I'm the one who coined it." Her gaze darted around the diner. "Who's the suspect? Are we talking robbery or murder?"

I'm a mystery fiend. Detectives, criminals, and clues are my catnip. When I was younger, Mona designed noir-style case files for me to fill out on my vintage Smith Corona typewriter, so that I could keep track of my ongoing neighborhood investigations. Case of Mr. Abernathy's missing garbage can? Solved. Case of the broken streetlights on Eagle Harbor Drive? Solved and reported to the city.

Case of why a sheltered, nerdy girl decided to flirt with a beautiful stranger who was *way* out of her league?

Completely unsolved.

If I had to profile myself, it would look something like this:

Suspect: Birdie Lindberg

Age: 18

Medical conditions: (1) Sleep problems, possibly inherited from grandfather. (2) Hospital phobia. (3) Bookworm disease. (4) Possible addiction to watching old *Columbo*, *Midsomer Murders*, and *Miss Fisher's Murder Mysteries* episodes.

Personality traits: Shy but curious.
Occasionally cowardly. Excellent with details.
Good observer.

Background: Mother got knocked up by an
unknown boy when she was a rebellious
seventeen-year-old, disappointing her small-
town parents. Mother dropped out of high
school, left her sleepy childhood home on
Bainbridge Island, and crossed Elliott Bay
into Seattle with her childhood best friend,
Mona Rivera. The two friends raised Birdie
together until the mother died unexpectedly
when the girl was ten. She was then taken in
by her grandparents on Bainbridge Island and
homeschooled, causing the suspect to develop
a profound sense of loneliness and rabid
curiosity about everything she was missing.
Her only refuge was Mona Rivera, who moved
back to the island to be closer to young
Birdie. When Birdie's strict grandmother
died six months ago of the same weak heart
condition that took her mother, Birdie was
sad but also relieved that her grandfather
realized she was eighteen and couldn't stay
trapped on the island forever and granted
her permission to get her first real job in

Seattle. Abusing her newly earned freedom,
the suspect promptly engaged in lewd and
lascivious acts with a boy she met in the
Moonlight after her first job interview.

"No suspects tonight," I told Aunt Mona, pushing away a plate of lacy hash browns indecently smeared with ketchup. "The Moonlight is free and clear of any ne'er-do-wells, hoodlums, and crooks. Which is good, because I probably should be heading to work soon."

She shook her head. "Not so fast. If there's no suspicious activity and you aren't worried about your first night on the job, then what in the world is going on with you?"

I groaned and laid my cheek on the cool linoleum tabletop, staring out a plate-glass window flecked with raindrops at the people beyond, who were dashing down the sidewalk in the twilight drizzle as streetlights came to life. Gray May would soon be turning to June Gloom, which meant more drizzle and overcast skies before summer truly arrived in Seattle.

"I did a stupid thing," I admitted. "And I can't stop thinking about it."

Bumblebee nails gently moved mousy-brown hair off my forehead, away from the ketchup-smeared rim of my unfinished plate, and tucked it behind a single lily I wore in my hair behind one ear. "Can't be that bad. Fess up."

After a couple of long sighs, I mumbled, "I met a boy."

"O-o-h," she murmured. "A *boy*, you say? A genuine member of the human race?"

"Possibly. He's really beautiful, so he may be a space alien or a clone or some kind of android."

"Mmm, sexy boy robot," she purred. "Tell me everything."

"There's not much to tell. He's a year older than me—nineteen. And a magician."

"Like, Las Vegas performer or Harry Potter?" she asked.

I huffed out a soft laugh. "Like card tricks and making a napkin with his phone number written on it appear inside the book I was reading."

"Wait. You met him here? At the diner?"

In answer, I held up a limp fist and mimicked a head nodding.

"Was this when you were interviewing last month?"

"For that part-time library job." That I *totally* thought was a sure thing . . . yet didn't get. Which was doubly depressing when I later realized that my misplaced confidence was one of the factors that led me to get carried away with "the boy" on that unfateful day.

"And you didn't tell me?" Aunt Mona said. "Birdie! You know I live for romantic drama. I've been waiting your entire life for one juicy story, one glorious piece of top-notch teen gossip that will make me swoon, and you don't tell me?"

"Maybe this is why."

She pretended to gasp. "Okay, fair point. But now the cat's out of the bag. Tell me more about this sexy, sexy cat—*meow*."

"First, he's a boy, not cat or a robot. And he was charming and sweet."

"Keep going," she said.

"He showed me some card tricks. I was feeling enthusiastic about the library job. It was raining pretty hard. He asked if I wanted to go see an indie movie at the Egyptian, and I told him I'd never been to the Egyptian, and he said it was in a Masonic Temple, which I didn't know. Did you? Apparently it was—"

"Birdie," Aunt Mona said, exasperated. *"What happened?"*

I sighed heavily. My cheek was sticking to the linoleum. "So we ran through the rain and went to his car, which was parked in the garage behind the diner, and it was pretty much deserted, and the next thing you know . . ."

"Oh. My. God. You didn't."

"We did."

"Tell me you used a condom."

I lifted my head and frantically glanced around the diner. "Can you please keep your voice down?"

"Condoms, Birdie. Did you use them?" she said, whispering entirely too loudly.

I checked to make sure Ms. Patty wasn't anywhere in sight. Or any of her nieces and nephews. There were almost a dozen of those, a couple of whom I'd gone to school with when I was a kid. "Do you really think that me, a product of unsafe teen sex, whose mother later *literally died* after getting pregnant a second time, someone who had to listen to a thousand and one safe-sex lectures from her former guardian—"

"Once a guardian, always a guardian. I will never be your former anything, Birdie."

"Her current guardian in spirit."

"That's better."

"I'm just saying. Yes. Of course. That wasn't the problem."

"There was a problem? Was he a jerk? Did you get caught?"

"Stop. It was none of that. It was me. I suddenly just got . . . weirded out."

One moment I was all caught up in feeling good. This beautiful, funny boy whom I'd just met was kissing me, and I was kissing him, and I think I may have just possibly suggested we get in the back seat instead of going to the movie theater. I don't know what I was thinking. I suppose I wasn't, and that was the problem. Because once we got back there and clothes started getting unbuttoned and unzipped, it all happened so fast. And in the middle of everything, I had a startling moment of clarity. He was a stranger. I mean, a *complete* stranger. I didn't know where he lived or anything about his family. I didn't know him at all. It got way too real, way too fast.

So when it was over, I bolted.

Ditched him like a guilty criminal fleeing a botched bank job.

Then I headed to the ferry terminal and never looked back.

"Oof," Mona said in sympathy, but I was pretty sure I heard some relief in her voice too. "Did he . . . ? I mean, was he upset about it?"

I shook my head and absently rearranged the salt and pepper shakers. "I heard him calling my name. I think he was confused. It all happened so fast. . . ."

"Maybe too fast?"

"He wasn't pushy or anything. He was nice, and I'm such a dud."

Mona made a chiding noise and quickly held up three fingers in a mock Scout salute. "On my honor—come on. Say it."

"Trying to be an adult here."

"Trying to help you be an adult. Say our pledge, Birdie."

I did the salute. "On my honor as a daring dame and gutsy gal, I will do my best to be true to myself, be kind to others, and never listen to any repressive poppycock."

When my grandmother was alive, she forbade swearing, cursing, and anything resembling rebellion under her roof. Adjusting to her rules after my mother died had often been draining. Aunt Mona had helped me cope by coming up with the Daring Dame pledge . . . and secretly teaching ten-year-old me a dozen words that contained the word "cock."

Aunt Mona and Grandma did *not* get along.

Satisfied with my Daring Dame pledge, she dropped her fingers. "I know it's hard for you to get close to people, and I know as much as you and Eleanor disagreed, she was still your grandmother and it hurts to lose someone. I know you must feel like everyone you love keeps leaving you, but it's not true. I'm here. And other people will be too. You just have to let them in."

"Aunt Mona—" I started, not wanting to talk about this right now.

"All I'm saying is that you didn't do anything wrong. And maybe if this boy is as awesome as you say he is, he could be understanding about how things ended if you gave it another chance. You said he gave you his phone number. Maybe you should call him."

"Must have fallen out of my book when I was running," I lied, shaking my head. I actually tossed if off the side of the ferry on my way home that afternoon when I was still freaking out about what I'd done. "But maybe it's for the best. What would I say? Sorry I bailed on you like a weirdo?"

"*Aren't* you sorry you bailed on him, though?"

I wasn't sure. But it didn't matter. I'd probably never see him again. And that was a good thing. It was one thing to say the Daring Dame pledge and a whole other to live it. Maybe I needed to build up some real-world experience before I braved dating. Perhaps I needed to put on my detective glasses and figure out where I went wrong.

But after all the mystery shows I'd binged, I should've known that detectives never investigate their own crimes.

2

The Cascadia was a five-story historic brick building on the corner of First Avenue in downtown Seattle near the waterfront. It was a luxury landmark hotel built in 1920 and was recently restored to showcase its Pacific Northwest roots while offering thoroughly modern amenities—at least, according to the website.

And I was going to work here.

Its unassuming entrance sat beneath an awning that sheltered the sidewalk. And beneath that awning, leaning against a hotel van parked at the curb, stood a Native American porter in a green uniform, perhaps a couple of years older than me. When I approached, he mistook me for a hotel guest, straightened, and opened one of two gold-trimmed doors. "Good evening, miss."

"I work here," I told him. "Tonight's my first shift. Birdie Lindberg."

"Oh." He allowed the door to swing shut. "I'm Joseph," he said, quickly looking me over until his gaze briefly lit on the pink-and-white stargazer lily pinned over my ear. "You're a Bat, right?"

"I'm the new night auditor?"

"You're a Bat, then," he said with a smile.

Right. I remembered now. Melinda was the night manager, and "Bats" made up the graveyard crew. My position was basically just a glorified front desk clerk who worked graveyard shift at the hotel and, after midnight, ran the software program that tabulated all the room bills and settled accounts. I was being paid a dime over minimum wage.

"Been through training?" Joseph asked.

"Last week," I said. "With Roxanne, during the day. I was hoping for midday shifts, but this was all that was open."

"It's almost always open. The only people who want to work graveyard are college students and nighthawks. Or people with no alternatives."

"This is my first job," I admitted.

"Well, welcome to the night crew, Birdie," he said with a smile, opening the hotel's gold entrance door for me. "Try not to fall asleep. There's free coffee in the break room."

More caffeine was the last thing my nerves needed right now, and I wasn't a coffee fan. I thanked him, blew out a quick breath, and stepped inside.

The Cascadia's Pacific Northwest style and vintage glamour was as dazzling as it had been the first time I'd stepped into the grand lobby. So dazzling, in fact, that it took me a moment to realize how different it was at night. No constant click of heels on the madrone wood floor. No dueling *dings* of the two gold elevators near the entrance, with their tribal salmon design covering the doors. And no tourists pressing their noses to the lobby's giant aquarium, which housed a giant Pacific octopus named Octavia—maybe the best thing in the entire hotel.

As I walked past the softly glowing tank beneath a row of painted canoes hanging from the mezzanine, jazz floated over the lobby's speakers. A well-dressed couple headed up to their room for the night, and a single businessman sat on one of the soft leather sofas, staring into the screen of his laptop.

Amazing to think that any one of these guests could be famous or important. Agatha Christie stayed here when she was touring the world with her husband. President Franklin Roosevelt gave a secret fundraising speech in the ballroom. Rock stars. Presidents. Mobsters. The Cascadia had hosted them all.

The hotel even had its own murder mystery: beloved Hollywood starlet Tippie Talbot had died on the fifth floor in 1938. Foul play was suspected but never proven, and her unsolved death had made headlines around the country. Who knows. Maybe I'd uncover some new clues on one of my shifts.

Anything could happen!